Taming the Rebel Tycoon

LEE WILKINSON
ALLY BLAKE
CRYSTAL GREEN

Published in Great Britain 2014
by Mills & Boon, an imprint of Harlequin (UK) Limited,
Eton House, 18-24 Paradise Road, Richmond, Surrey, TW9 1SR

TAMING THE REBEL TYCOON © 2014 Harlequin Books S.A.

Wife by Approval, *Dating the Rebel Tycoon* and *The Playboy Takes a Wife* were first published in Great Britain by Harlequin (UK) Limited.

Wife by Approval © 2007 Lee Wilkinson
Dating the Rebel Tycoon © 2009 Ally Blake
The Playboy Takes a Wife © 2007 Chris Marie Green

ISBN: 978-0-263-91192-3
eBook ISBN: 978-1-472-04487-7

05-0714

Harlequin (UK) Limited's policy is to use papers that are natural, renewable and recyclable products and made from wood grown in sustainable forests. The logging and manufacturing processes conform to the legal environmental regulations of the country of origin.

Printed and bound in Spain
by Blackprint CPI, Barcelona

WIFE BY APPROVAL

BY
LEE WILKINSON

Lee Wilkinson lives with her husband in a three-hundred-year-old stone cottage in a Derbyshire village, which most winters gets cut off by snow. They both enjoy travelling, and recently, joining forces with their daughter and son-in-law, spent a year going round the world 'on a shoestring' while their son looked after Kelly, their much loved German shepherd dog. Her hobbies are reading and gardening, and holding impromptu barbecues for her long-suffering family and friends.

CHAPTER ONE

SEATED at her desk in her first-floor office, Valentina Dunbar was gazing absently through the rain-spattered window which overlooked Cartel Wines's long, narrow car park and, beyond the high wall, the River Thames.

Dusk had begun to creep stealthily out of hiding and lights were coming on, gleaming on the dark water and glowing orange against the cloudy purple sky.

Most of the day staff tried to get away early on a Friday night and a steady stream of vehicles were already leaving the car park to join the London evening rush hour.

Responsible for organising the social gatherings and the informative literature that invariably accompanied Cartel Wines's latest sales push, Tina was endeavouring to put the finishing touches to the pre-Christmas campaign. But for once she wasn't giving the job her full attention.

It was Friday the thirteenth. A day that, for her at least, had lived up to its unlucky reputation.

First thing that morning she had slipped and hurt her ankle getting out of the shower. Gritting her teeth, she had been forced to stand on one leg while she had dried and dressed and taken her thick, silky hair, naturally blonde on top but with darker undertones, into a neat chignon.

By the time she'd finished, the pain had eased quite a bit

and she was able to hobble into the living-room to get her toast and coffee.

Ruth, her friend and temporary flatmate, who was breakfasting in her dressing gown, looked up to ask, 'Why are you limping?'

As Tina finished telling her, the phone rang.

'I hope this is Jules,' Ruth exclaimed eagerly, grabbing the receiver.

It was.

Her fiancé's firm had transferred him to Paris for six months and she was missing him badly.

'He's coming to London for the weekend,' she said after a minute or so, her elfin face full of excitement, her black hair standing up in spikes. 'He'll be arriving this afternoon and going back Monday morning.'

Then, apologetically, 'By the way, he's expecting to stay at the flat with me…'

The 'flat' was nothing more than a large bedsitter, which meant that Tina would have to make other arrangements for the three nights.

Her own flat was in a run-down Victorian house that the new owner had decided to have refurbished and modernized, and Ruth had offered her a put-you-up for the ten weeks or so that would elapse before she could move back in again.

'Perhaps you could ask Lexi or Jo to give you a bed for the weekend?' Ruth suggested.

'I'll think about it,' Tina said non-committally. Then, seeing Ruth's concerned expression and knowing she owed it to her friend, she added cheerfully, 'Don't worry, I'll get something fixed up. You just make sure you have a great time.'

'I will,' Ruth assured her as she went to shower and dress.

Both Lexi and Jo had resident boyfriends and, with no intention of playing gooseberry, Tina had already made up her mind to book into a hotel.

As soon as she had pushed a handful of underwear, a few changes of clothing and some necessities into a small case, she collected her shoulder bag and mac and, calling, 'Have a good weekend…see you Monday,' let herself out.

When she had descended the stairs with care, she crossed the foyer to check for mail. In Ruth's pigeon-hole was a single redirected letter addressed to her, which she thrust unopened into her bag.

Until now the autumn weather had proved to be glorious, an Indian Summer of warm golden days and balmy nights. But today it was grey and chilly, a thin curtain of drizzle being blown along by a strong blustery wind.

She turned up the collar of her mac and, her ankle still a little painful, made her way to where her car was parked in the *residents only* space that belonged to the building.

Her offside front tyre was flat.

By the time the local garage had checked the tyre, repaired the damage and re-inflated it, she was late for work.

The morning had passed in something of a whirl and it had been practically twelve o'clock before she'd realised that, owing to the earlier upheaval, she had forgotten to pack her usual sandwiches or her small flask of coffee.

But there was a delicatessen just around the corner that made up rolls and sandwiches to order. If she could get there before the rush…

As she reached in her bag for her purse she came across the forgotten letter. Glancing at it, she noticed that in red, on the left-hand side of the envelope, was stamped what appeared to be the name of some firm.

Dropping it on her desk to read when she got back, she pulled on her mac and made her way out of the rear entrance.

In a few minutes she returned, carrying a ham and salad roll and a fruit yogurt in a paper bag. She was crossing the deserted car park, her head down against the now driving rain when, glancing up, she saw a man watching her.

Tall, dark-haired and arresting, he was standing quite still beneath the roofed loading bay, his eyes fixed on her.

Since Kevin's defection, shattered and wholly disillusioned, she had steered well clear of all men. Especially handsome ones.

Though this man couldn't be called handsome in the film star sense. He was very good-looking but in a tough, wholly masculine way.

Her pulse rate quickening, she found herself wondering who he could be.

As she drew nearer, their eyes met.

Some glances were like collisions. The impact of those dark eyes stopped her in her tracks and made her heart start to throw itself against her ribs.

She was still standing rooted to the spot, staring at him as though mesmerized, when the bottom of the wet paper bag gave way, allowing her lunch to fall through.

The roll, though soggy, was fairly easy to pick up, but the plastic yogurt carton had split and its contents were oozing out.

Making use of one of the paper napkins that had been included, she managed to scoop up the mess and deposit the remains of her lunch in the nearest litter bin.

As she wiped her hands on the remaining napkin, her gaze was drawn once more to where the dark-haired stranger had been standing.

With a strange sinking feeling in the pit of her stomach, as though she had dropped too fast in an express lift, she found herself staring at the now empty space.

He had vanished.

She was certain he hadn't passed her and she had neither seen nor heard a car start, which meant he must have gone inside.

So who was he?

She knew all the admin and general office staff by sight and this man didn't belong to either. Nor, she was quite sure, was he one of the warehouse staff. Apart from an unmistakable air of assurance and authority, he had been far too well-dressed to be doing manual work.

However, to have been here at all, he must have some connection with Cartel Wines.

Perhaps he was a visitor.

But visitors always used the visitors' car park and the main entrance. They didn't come in the back way and go through the warehouse, as he must have done...

A trickle of icy-cold water ran down the back of her neck, making her shiver. Belatedly aware that she was standing like a fool getting saturated, she hurried into the building.

As she walked through the warehouse she glanced about her. But there was no sign of him amongst the men at work and she knew she couldn't mistake him.

When she reached the top of the stairs she found that her office door was a little ajar and realised that in her haste to beat the rush she couldn't have latched it properly.

While she fetched a towel from the small adjoining cloak-room to pat dry her hair and face, her thoughts winged their way back to the dark-haired stranger like homing pigeons.

In spite of the fact that she had seen him only briefly, his height and the width of his shoulders, the image of his lean, attractive face was clear in her mind. And, though she had tried her hardest to dismiss it, it had haunted her for the rest of the afternoon, displacing any thoughts of hunger.

Now, gazing through the window, her blue-violet eyes abstracted, she was still wondering about him... Who was he? Why had he been here? If he *had* been a visitor, would she see him again...?

But she must stop this fruitless speculation, she told herself

sternly, and concentrate on practicalities. At almost five
o'clock on a wet Friday afternoon, with darkness hovering in
the wings, she still hadn't decided where to stay.

But after urging Didi, her stepsister, to accept the place at
the prestigious Ramon Bonaventure School of Drama that she
had been offered, and promising to pay her fees, it would have
to be somewhere not too expensive.

Still, she would manage somehow. It might mean stringent
economies for a couple of years, but to have Didi—who had
been christened Valerie, but had always been Val to her friends
and acquaintances and Didi to her family—on course again
it would be well worth it…

The bleep of the internal phone cut through her thoughts.
Pushing aside the lists of dates and tasting notes that littered
her desk, Tina picked up the receiver.

'Miss Dunbar,' Sandra Langton's somewhat nasal voice
said, 'Mr De Vere would like to see you before you leave.'

'I'll be straight down.'

Wondering at the unexpected summons, she left her office,
a slim figure in a smart grey suit, and, still limping slightly,
descended the flight of bare stone steps that led down to a
wide corridor.

On the right, the heavy double doors into the warehouse—
where the wines for the domestic customers were stored
before being put into stout cartons to be despatched nation-
wide—were closed.

To the left were the main offices. In the outer office, Sandra
Langton, the boss's middle-aged PA, gave her an odd look
before saying, 'If you'd like to go straight through?'

Frowning a little, Tina tapped at the door of the inner
sanctum and waited for the curt, 'Come in.'

She thought, not for the first time, that if Frenchmen were
noted for their charm, Maurice De Vere had to be the excep-
tion to the rule.

A short, dry man with grey hair, thin features and an irascible manner, he was due to retire at the end of the month.

He hadn't really been a bad boss, she reflected, but, a diehard who disliked modern technology, he had refused to install computers or any equipment that would have made office life easier.

Added to that, he had always believed in the stick rather than the carrot, so whoever took his place would almost certainly be an improvement.

Ensconced behind a large, imposing desk, with a motion of one claw-like hand he waved her to a chair.

She was barely seated when, looking down at a sheaf of papers, he began, 'I'm afraid I have some bad news for you, Miss Dunbar...'

He hesitated, then, looking at her over his rimless glasses, went on abruptly, 'When I decided to retire and I sold out to the Matterhorn group, they promised very few changes. On the whole they've kept their word. But this afternoon I learnt that John Marsden, the man who'll be coming in on Monday to start running Cartel Wines, has his own very definite ideas about how the sales campaigns should be staged.'

'I don't see that as a problem,' Tina said quietly. 'The suggestions I've already made can easily be changed or adapted to suit—'

The words died on her lips as De Vere began to shake his head. 'I'm afraid Marsden's insisting on bringing in his own team of organisers, which means you're redundant.'

As she stared at him in stunned silence, he added, 'I'm more sorry than I can say. Your work has always been excellent...'

Coming from a man who had never been known to compliment his staff, that was praise indeed. But what use was it when she was now out of a job?

'Bearing that in mind, I'll make sure you have very good references.'

'When…?' Her voice wobbled dangerously and she stopped speaking.

Looking uncomfortable, he said, 'As Marsden will need your office for his own team, it would be best if you left immediately. I've authorized six months' salary in lieu of notice, which will be paid directly into your bank…'

That was very generous. Her contract had only specified one month.

'A reference and any other appropriate papers will be sent to your temporary address in due course.'

Rising to his feet, he held out his hand. 'May I wish you well.'

Her voice under control now, she said, 'Thank you,' then shook the cold, papery hand and walked out of the room with her head held high.

In the outer office, Sandra Langton, who was just putting on her coat, said with obvious sympathy, 'Tough luck.'

Then, dropping her voice, 'I must admit I was surprised by how hard old Sourpuss took it… When will you be leaving?'

'Now… As soon as I've cleared my desk.'

'Well, all the best.'

'Thank you.'

Shock setting in, Tina climbed the stairs on legs that felt as wadded and useless as a rag doll's and, sinking down at her desk, gazed blindly into space.

She had been with Cartel Wines since she left college two years ago. It was a job she had loved and been good at. Even old Sourpuss—as the staff called De Vere behind his back—had admitted it.

But that made no difference whatsoever. Due to circumstances, she was now unemployed.

A kind of futile panic gripped her. Six months' salary was a buffer, but when the alterations to the house had been completed and she moved back into her flat, her rent would be considerably higher. That, added to Didi's expenses, meant losing her job couldn't have come at a worse time.

Over the past year, life had been a series of downs with scarcely any ups. Now, with this final blow, she seemed to have hit rock-bottom.

Well, if that *was* the case, the only way was up.

Allowing herself no more time for regrets, she rose, squared her shoulders and started to tidy her desk top.

Only when it was clear, did she suddenly recall the letter she had been going to read. Seeing the handsome dark-haired stranger had put it right out of her mind.

But where was the letter?

A quick search through the papers she was taking failed to bring it to light.

Oh, well, it must be there somewhere. She would look more thoroughly later.

Finding an almost empty box in the cupboard, she transferred the few remaining items in it to one of the shelves, then, taking her personal belongings from the desk drawers, stacked them in the box.

The plants she had brought to brighten the somewhat spartan office, she would leave.

She pulled on her coat, put the strap of her bag over her shoulder, tucked the box under one arm and, switching off the light, closed and locked the door behind her for the last time. There was nothing of value in the office, so she left the key in the lock.

Just the night security lights were burning, which meant that the rest of the staff had already gone and she was probably the only person still left in this part of the building.

The main entrance doors at the front would have been locked and bolted some time ago. But her car was in the rear car park, so it was just as quick to go through the warehouse.

As, without looking back, she began to descend the stairs

to the dimly lit passage, a movement she *heard* rather than *saw* made her realise that she had been wrong. There *was* someone else still here.

At the bottom of the stairs she turned right and in the gloom saw that the double doors at the end of the passageway were swinging slightly.

Whoever was still here was obviously only a little way in front of her and heading for the car park, as she was.

When she went through the doors, however, the long warehouse appeared to be deserted.

More than a little puzzled, she frowned and, her footsteps echoing in the vast space, began to walk past the various bays, with their rows of pallets stacked with crates and boxes of château bottled imported wine.

Last autumn and winter, on the nights she had worked late, she had walked through the warehouse without a qualm. But tonight, for no good reason, she felt on edge, uneasy.

The night security lighting was high up in the roof of the building and left areas of deep shadow that suddenly seemed sinister, providing as they did an opportunity for someone to lie in wait…

She was doing her utmost to ignore the far from comfortable thought, when some sixth sense insisted that she wasn't alone, that someone was watching her from the shadows.

The fine hairs on the back of her neck rose and her skin goose-fleshed. Instinctively, she paused and glanced behind her.

Not a soul was in sight.

Gritting her teeth, she was about to walk on when in the silence she heard a faint noise like the brush of a furtive footfall.

The echoing vastness of the warehouse made it impossible to tell where the whisper of sound had come from.

She was standing rooted to the spot when she realised that it would be George Tomlinson, the night security man.

Feeling foolish, she took a deep breath and called out, 'George, is that you?'

Only the echo of her own voice answered.

She tried again, louder.

Still no answer, apart from the mocking echoes.

It occurred to her that he was probably doing his early evening rounds of the offices, checking that all the lights were out and the doors locked.

But if it *wasn't* George she'd heard, who was it?

Perhaps someone had slipped in through the small door the employees used and had been heading for the wages office when they had heard her coming and decided to hide?

Reason soon put paid to that theory. It was Friday night and, as any would-be thief would undoubtedly know, Friday was pay day and the safe would be empty.

After a moment she recalled that there were a couple of cats who lived on the premises.

But cats moved silently and they didn't go through heavy doors and leave them swinging.

A shiver ran down her spine at the memory.

Don't be a fool, she chided herself sharply; it was time she used her common sense rather than letting her imagination run away with her.

Instead of someone going out ahead of her, it must have been George, coming the opposite way to check the offices, who had left the doors swinging.

It was a perfectly logical explanation.

Yet, illogically, she didn't believe it.

Well, whether she believed it or not, it was high time she made a move.

If George had already locked up and completed all his checks—he wouldn't have worried about a light in her office; he was used to her working late—he could well be ensconced in his little cabin on the far side of the annex, having his tea.

Which meant that he might not emerge until it was time to do his rounds again and she couldn't stand here much longer. Her ankle hurt and the box under her arm was getting heavy.

Glancing round her, she could see no sign of life or movement. Still the feeling of being watched persisted, as though the watcher was patiently waiting to see which way she would jump.

She pushed the thought away and, summoning all her will-power, decided that as she had already walked more than half the length of the warehouse it made sense to go on, rather than turn back.

Fighting down a panicky impulse to run, she forced herself to walk steadily towards the huge sliding doors at the end of the hangar-like building.

Her legs felt curiously stiff and alien, her breathing was rapid and shallow and every muscle in her body had grown tense. Try as she might, she was unable to stop herself from glancing repeatedly over her shoulder.

When she reached the small staff door to the left of the big main doors and found it securely closed, she breathed a sigh of relief. It boasted a Yale lock so, unless someone had a key, it could only be opened from the inside.

So much for some thief slipping in and hiding! With an overactive imagination like that, she should be writing stories…

Her tension relaxing, she let herself out into the dark, wet night and closed the door carefully behind her. Everywhere appeared to be deserted, though a dozen or so cars remained and, outside despatch, a couple of Cartel's vans were waiting to be loaded.

The pre-harvest sales push had been phenomenally successful and extra orders for hotels and restaurants were being dealt with by a special evening shift working over in the annex.

Beyond the range of the annex's lights, however, the car

park, poorly lit apart from the entrance, had areas that looked pitch-black.

Having come in almost an hour late that morning, she had been forced to park in one of the old, narrow, brick-walled bays that sloped steeply down towards the river. None of the employees used the bays if they could help it because of the difficult manoeuvring that was entailed, and the fact that they were at the far end of the car park.

There wasn't a soul in sight as she began to limp to where she'd left her car, but once again she felt that uncomfortable *awareness*, that disturbing sensation of unseen eyes watching her, and a tingle of fear ran down her spine.

She felt a cowardly urge to head for the annex where there were lights and people...

But then what would she do? Admit that she was scared to walk through the car park alone? They would think she was mad.

And they wouldn't be far wrong, she thought crossly as, resolutely ignoring her fear, she carried on. Perhaps all the stress of the last year had caught up with her and was making her paranoid? If so, the sooner she got a grip the better.

Unable to see more than a few yards ahead, it took her a moment or two to locate her small navy-blue Ford. When she did, it was a relief to put her carton on the back seat alongside her case and slide behind the wheel.

There! Safe! So much for these stupid fancies.

As she started the engine and began to back out, it occurred to her that she still had no idea where she was heading.

For someone who was...*had been*...paid to organise things, she wasn't doing too well on her own account, she told herself wryly. But, for once in her life, she hadn't been thinking straight, otherwise she would have looked for somewhere inexpensive and booked before she'd left the office.

Her left ankle had stiffened up and she was finding it

painful to use the clutch, so it would be as well if she could find somewhere comparatively close.

As she started to turn, it occurred to her that there used to be a smallish hotel a couple of streets away. Now, what was it called…? Fairfax? Fairhaven? Fairbourn? Yes, that was it. She couldn't remember noticing it lately, which might mean that it had closed down, but—'

From behind there was a sudden dazzling blaze of headlights and a glancing rear impact sent the front of her car swerving into the wall with a grinding of metal and a tinkling of broken glass.

Momentarily paralysed by shock, she was sitting motionless when the driver's door was jerked open and a male voice demanded urgently, 'Are you all right?'

'Yes… Yes. Quite all right…' Her own voice seemed to come from a long way away.

The car had stalled when her foot slipped off the clutch but, even so, he reached inside and felt for the ignition key to turn everything off.

'Then I suggest you stay where you are for a minute while I assess the damage.' He closed the door against the rain.

Though she felt dazed, part of her mind registered that his voice was low-pitched and pleasant, a cultured voice and not one she recognised.

But that attractive voice had said, '*while I assess the damage*'… She groaned inwardly. From what little she could see, his car appeared to be a big expensive one. And, though he had hit her, she was to blame. If she had been concentrating, instead of thinking about where she was to stay, it might not have happened.

She had just managed to gather herself and was about to unfasten her safety belt and climb out, when the door opened and he was back.

'How bad is it?' she asked fearfully.

'The original impact was only a glancing blow, so there's hardly a mark on my car…'

She could only be thankful for that.

'But I'm very much afraid that the damage caused when your nearside front wing hit the wall will make your car undriveable.'

After the kind of day she'd had, it was the last straw and she gave way to a crazy impulse to laugh.

His face was in deep shadow and she couldn't see his expression but, sounding concerned and obviously wondering if she was about to become hysterical, he asked, '*Sure* you're all right?'

'Quite sure…'

A shade apologetically, she explained, 'I was just seeing the funny side. It's been an awful day and I'm afraid I'd reached the stage where I either had to laugh or cry.'

'Then you made the right decision.'

As he held the door against the wind, a scattering of rain blew in.

Suddenly realising that he was standing getting wet when, but for her, he would no doubt be on his way home to his wife, she made to clamber out, favouring her bad ankle.

He stepped back and put a steadying hand beneath her elbow.

Startled by his touch, she said jerkily, 'I'm really very sorry about all this…'

'As my car hit yours, I'm the one who should be apologizing,' he told her.

Honesty made her insist, 'No, it was my fault. My mind was on other things and when I started to back out I hadn't realised there was anyone else about.'

'Rather than stand in the rain arguing,' he said dryly, 'I suggest that, for the moment at least, you allow me to accept the blame. Later, if necessary, we can always agree on six of one and half a dozen of the other.'

Opening the door of what, at close quarters, she could see was a top-of-the-range Porsche, he added briskly, 'Now, before you get wet through, suppose you jump in and I'll take you home.'

'That's very good of you, but I…' Her words tailed off as, in the glow of his headlights, she recognised the dark, powerful face she had thought never to see again.

When, her wits scattered, her heart starting to race, she stood rooted to the spot, he said, 'Is there a problem?'

When she didn't immediately answer, he suggested, 'Perhaps you don't trust me?'

'No… No, it's not that.'

'Then what is it?'

She blurted out the first thing that came into her head. 'I—I was just wondering if I should try and move my car.'

'Leave it where it is,' he told her decidedly. 'It shouldn't be in anyone's way and first thing tomorrow morning I'll get my garage to tow it in and do the necessary repairs.

'Now, is there anything you need out of it?'

'A small case on the back seat.'

'Jump in and I'll get it.'

He had left the engine running and in a moment she was installed in the warmth and comfort of the most luxurious car she had ever been in.

Not even Maurice De Vere had a car in that class.

She found herself wondering what a visitor—and, as she had never seen either him or his car before, the dark-haired stranger *must* be a visitor—was doing in Cartel's car park so late in the evening…

Her case deposited in the boot, he slid in beside her and reached to fasten both their seat belts. That done, he turned to her and, in the light from the dashboard, studied her face.

Embarrassed by his close scrutiny and only too aware that with wet, bedraggled hair and a shiny nose she must look an absolute fright, she felt her cheeks grow warm.

As though sensing her discomfort, he moved away a little and asked, 'Where to?'

'I—I don't know,' she stammered.

He raised a dark brow. 'Amnesia?'

Knowing he was making fun of her and vexed with herself for losing her usual calm composure and acting like a fool, she took a deep breath and said crisply, 'Certainly not.'

Pulling a mournful face, he observed, 'Oh, dear... now you're mad with me.'

For an instant she wavered between annoyance and amusement. Amusement won and she smiled.

Smiling back, he observed, 'That's better.'

His smile increased his charm a thousandfold and she found herself thinking that a lot of women would find him irresistible...

Suddenly becoming aware that he'd asked a question she hadn't caught, she pulled herself together and said, 'I'm sorry?'

'I asked *why* don't you know?'

Trying to be brief and succinct, she explained, 'Well, the house I live in is being refurbished, which means my flat is uninhabitable, and I'm staying with a friend...'

He listened, his dark eyes fixed on her face.

Thrown by the intentness of his gaze, she momentarily lost the thread.

Then, realising he was waiting, she carried on a shade distractedly, 'Her boyfriend is in London and expecting to stay with her. But her flat is really only a bedsit, so you see I have to find a hotel.'

It seemed like a heaven-sent opportunity and, his thoughts racing, he said, 'That shouldn't be a problem. There are plenty of hotels in London. You don't have any particular preference?'

'No, anywhere will do... So long as it's not too expensive,' she added hurriedly.

But, judging by his clothes and his car, he wouldn't have to consider expense, so he was hardly likely to know any of the cheaper places. And she couldn't expect him to go touring London on her behalf when he'd already been held up and inconvenienced.

Recalling her earlier thought, she said, 'I'm not sure if it's still there, but there used to be a small hotel quite close to here, on Mather Street... I think it was called the Fairbourn...'

His well-marked brows drew together over a straight nose. 'If it's the place I'm thinking of, I wouldn't say it was particularly prepossessing.'

So long as it was clean and respectable, she wasn't in a position to be over-fussy. 'As it's only for three nights, I can manage.'

Three nights suited his purpose even better, he thought jubilantly.

Things had been going smoothly, but the business trip he'd been forced to take had cost him precious time and they had managed to trace her much faster than he'd anticipated.

Hence the sudden need for drastic action.

Which had worked so far, he reminded himself. But with so much at stake, he simply couldn't afford to mess things up.

'As the Fairbourn may well have closed down,' he said smoothly, 'and it's hardly the sort of night to be touring the town in search of accommodation, I suggest you come home with me.'

CHAPTER TWO

WHEN, staggered, wondering what he had in mind, Tina simply stared at him, he repeated evenly, 'Come home with me.'

Knowing what kind of woman she was, he hadn't expected much in the way of opposition and was shaken when she said, as if she meant it, 'I couldn't possibly do that.'

'Why not? There's a perfectly good guest room standing empty.'

Though she was reassured by the mention of a guest room, there were other considerations. A mature man in his late twenties or early thirties, he might well be married. 'Thank you,' she began, 'but I—'

'It makes sense to come for tonight at least,' he broke in decidedly. 'Then tomorrow, if you want to move into a hotel, you'd have all day to find somewhere suitable.'

Rather than ask if he was married, she said, 'What on earth would your wife say?'

'As I don't have a wife, not a lot.'

He hadn't a wife. Her spirits rose with a bound.

Then common sense took over. If he hadn't a wife, he would almost certainly have a live-in lover.

'But you must have... I mean there must be...'

'A woman around?' he supplied quizzically.

'Well...yes.'

'Oh, there is.'

Though she had half expected it, her heart sank.

'Thank you,' she said carefully. 'It's very kind of you to suggest it, but—'

He sighed. 'Now I've put you off and I thought you'd feel easier, knowing there was another woman around the place.'

She shook her head. 'I really think I should go to a hotel. It'll be far less trouble for—'

'Oh, Gwen won't mind,' he said easily.

If *she* was living with him she wouldn't be too happy if he brought a woman home he didn't even know. Decidedly, she began, 'I'm quite sure your girlfriend would—'

'Oh, Gwen's not my girlfriend. She's my housekeeper. A very upright woman,' he added solemnly. 'A pillar of the church and so forth.'

Feeling as though she was on a roller coaster and with the disturbing impression that he was enjoying teasing her, Tina frowned.

'Is that a problem?' he asked, straight faced. 'Do you have anything against religious women?'

'Of course not,' she began. Then, seeing the wicked gleam in his eye, she stopped speaking and gritted her teeth.

'In that case it's all settled,' he announced calmly and let in the clutch.

He had managed it so smoothly that they had pulled out of the car park and joined the evening stream of traffic that flowed down Lansdale Road before she could gather her wits enough to assess the situation.

Though she was very attracted to him and *wanted* to be with him, the voice of caution warned that to meekly go off with a man she knew nothing about was reckless in the extreme.

Just because he was well-dressed and well-spoken and had a big expensive car, it didn't necessarily mean that he was trustworthy.

As her mother would have phrased it, he might have designs on her.

Though why should he?

She was tall and slim with good skin and neatish features, but she was nothing to write home about, certainly not the sort to drive men wild.

And a man with his looks and charisma wouldn't be short of lady friends. In fact, with so much going for him he wouldn't need to lift a finger to have eager females queuing up.

But, apart from that, there was something about him, she felt, a kind of basic integrity that was oddly reassuring. And this might well be her one and only chance to get to know him. If she insisted on being dropped off at a hotel, in all probability she would never see him again.

The thought was like a hand squeezing her heart.

It didn't seem possible for a quiet, self-contained woman like herself to feel so strongly about a man she had only just met and didn't know.

Yet she did.

Throwing caution to the wind, she asked, 'Where do you live?'

His build-up of tension relaxing, he smiled. 'I've a house in Pemberley Square, close to St James's Park.'

'Oh…' A far cry from Mather Street and the Fairbourn Hotel.

'As we'll be spending the night…' He paused. 'I was about to say *together*…but, as that might be misconstrued, I'll say *under the same roof*, I think we should introduce ourselves, don't you? My name's Richard Anders.'

'Mine's Tina Dunbar.'

'Tina?' He sounded surprised.

'Short for Valentina,' she explained reluctantly.

He gave her a sideways glance and, his voice casual, asked, 'Is Valentina a family name?'

'No.'

'Born on February the fourteenth?'

She nodded. 'That's right. Though these days Valentine is used for either sex, unfortunately my mother preferred to stick with the feminine form.'

'Unfortunately?'

'Valentina is a bit of a mouthful.'

'I like it.'

'Oh…' She felt a little warm glow.

As they headed for the West End, the wipers rhythmically swishing, the wet, almost deserted pavements reflecting back the brightly lit shop windows, he said, 'So you're with Cartel Wines… What do you do, Valentina…?'

Very conscious of him, of the handsome, clear-cut profile, the closeness of his muscular thigh to hers, the faint male scent of his cologne, she tried to drag her mind away from the man himself and focus on the question.

'Are you a buyer?'

'No. I'm responsible for public relations and sales promotions.' Then, with a sinking feeling, 'Or, rather, I *was*.'

'You're leaving?'

'I've no choice. I learnt this afternoon that Matterhorn, the group who have taken over Cartel's, have their own promotional team coming in next week, which makes me redundant.'

'So you won't be going back?' he pursued.

'No. I've cleared my desk.'

'Have you been working for Cartel Wines long?'

'Ever since I left college,' she answered without thinking.

He gave her a quick sideways smile. 'As you look about sixteen…'

Wishing fruitlessly that she looked her usual cool, composed self, she said quickly, 'I'm twenty-three,' and was aware that she had sounded indignant.

'That old!'

Now he was laughing at her openly. But it was in a nice way, a way that invited her to join in.

With a smile, she said, 'I suppose in a few more years being told I look about sixteen will seem like a compliment.'

Then, keen to remove the spotlight from herself and wondering what he'd been doing at Cartel Wines, she changed the subject by remarking, *'You're* not employed by Cartel?'

'No.'

'I didn't think so. But I wouldn't have put you down as a visitor. Or certainly not an ordinary one.'

'Is that a complaint or a compliment?'

'A comment. Ordinary visitors use the front car park and the main entrance and always leave before the staff.'

'Well, as I did none of those things, I plead guilty to being out of the ordinary...'

It occurred to her that she still didn't know why he'd been at Cartel Wines, but, before she could pursue the matter, he remarked, 'Incidentally, I caught sight of you earlier in the day...'

So he'd recognised her.

'Yes, I'd slipped out to buy some lunch.'

To give her no chance to ask the question that he wasn't yet ready to answer, he went on, 'I fear it came to a sad end. Did you manage to replace it?'

'No.'

'You must be ravenous. But we'll soon be home and Gwen's sure to have dinner waiting.'

Wondering how the housekeeper would cope when he turned up with an unexpected guest, Tina began, 'I'm afraid it—'

'Don't worry,' he broke in, 'there'll be no problem.' Then, deciding to stick with a safe topic, at least for the moment, he went on, 'As a young woman, Gwen had a family of six boys to feed, so she's always been used to cooking for what seems like an army. She still does.

'Her church runs a centre for the homeless and each evening she fills her car boot with food and takes it round there.'

He had just finished telling her about his housekeeper's charitable activities when they reached Pemberley Square and drew up outside a handsome porticoed town house.

It was still raining hard and he retrieved Tina's case before escorting her across the leaf-strewn pavement and into a chandelier-hung hall.

As he closed the door behind them, a small, thin, neatly dressed woman appeared.

'Ah, Gwen,' he said, 'we have an unexpected guest.' He introduced the two women, adding, 'Miss Dunbar was with Cartel Wines.'

The housekeeper smiled and said, 'I'm pleased to meet you, Miss Dunbar.'

Smiling back, Tina said a little anxiously, 'I hope I'm not causing you a lot of trouble, Mrs Baxter?'

'Not at all. The guest room is always kept ready. Now, if you'd like to freshen up before dinner…?'

'If there's time?'

'Plenty of time,' the housekeeper announced comfortably. 'Luckily I'd decided on a casserole, which will keep hot without spoiling.'

'In that case,' Richard said, 'I'll check my emails and when Miss Dunbar comes down we'll have a quick pre-dinner drink in the study.'

With a glance at his watch, he added, 'But, so your regulars won't have to wait too long for their supper, I suggest you leave ours on the hotplate and we'll serve ourselves…'

Mrs Baxter nodded gratefully, then said, 'Oh, there's one more thing… Miss O'Connell has been trying to get hold of you. She said your mobile has been switched off all day. She seemed extremely upset about it…'

Reading his housekeeper's tight-lipped expression correctly, Richard hazarded, 'So Helen's been giving you a hard time? Sorry about that.'

Her face softening, Mrs Baxter said, 'The young lady would like you to give her a ring.'

'I'll do that. Thanks, Gwen.'

Taking Tina's case, the housekeeper led the way up a long, curved staircase and across a balustraded landing, remarking as they went, 'Mr Anders is always kind and thoughtful. They don't come any better.'

Doing her best not to hobble, though her ankle was, if anything, worse, Tina asked, 'How long have you worked for him?'

'Just over six years and in all that time I've never known him be anything other than even-tempered and pleasant.'

'That's praise indeed.'

'And well earned. He's one of the most generous people I know.

'In the two years that it's been in existence the centre that I help to run must have saved quite a few lives, especially in the winter.

'They have him to thank. Not only did he buy a big warehouse and have it converted into comfortable living quarters, but he pays all the running expenses out of his own pocket and provides money for food and other necessities.

'He's even managed to save a few of the poor souls who come there... Oh, not by preaching to them, but by trusting them and giving them a decent job...'

Tina was about to ask what kind of business he was in when she was ushered into a large pastel-walled bedroom that overlooked the rain-lashed lamplit square, with its central garden and mature trees.

Having deposited the case on a low chest, the housekeeper closed the curtains, remarking, 'It looks like a nasty wet, chilly night, so I'd best get off and make sure that everyone's taken care of.'

Her hand was on the latch when she turned to say, 'Oh, when you come down again, the study is straight across the hall.'

The guest room was pleasant and airy, with a pale deep-pile carpet, modern furniture, a large, comfortable-looking bed and walk-in wardrobes, while the *en suite* bathroom was frankly luxurious.

Feeling grubby and dishevelled, Tina decided to take a quick shower.

While she enjoyed the flow of hot water over her bare skin she thought about Richard Anders.

Any remaining doubts about what kind of man he was had been set at rest by Mrs Baxter's unstinting praise and she could only be thankful that she had accepted his hospitality rather than turning it down.

Refreshed, she towelled herself dry, quickly found some clean underwear and swopped her suit for a fine wool button-through dress in oatmeal.

Her ankle was distinctly swollen now so, instead of changing into high-heeled sandals, she stayed with her flat shoes.

When she had put on a discreet touch of make-up and brushed and re-coiled her dark blonde hair, she made her way carefully down the stairs.

She felt eager and excited, if a touch nervous, at the prospect of spending the evening alone with Richard Anders and getting to know him better.

For perhaps the first time in her life she found herself wishing that she was clever, beautiful, exciting, alluring—whatever it took to arouse and hold his interest.

But of course she wasn't. She was just an ordinary girl, unable even to keep the interest of a man like Kevin who, though undeniably tall and handsome, hadn't been in the same class as Richard Anders for looks and presence.

But perhaps it was wealth that had given him his presence, his force of personality?

No, she was oddly convinced that it wasn't so. If he'd been a poor man he would still have had those assets and, with them, he wouldn't have remained a poor man for long.

Arriving at the study door, after a momentary hesitation, she tapped and walked in.

It was a pleasant book-lined room with a rich burgundy carpet and matching velvet curtains. An Adam fireplace and an ornate plaster ceiling with flowers and cherubs added to its beauty.

The lighting was low and intimate and a log fire blazed cheerfully in the grate. A small table and a couple of soft leather armchairs had been placed in front of the fire.

Richard, who had been standing by the hearth, advanced to meet her. He looked coolly elegant and just the sight of him made her heart lurch wildly.

He too had made time to shower and change. Instead of the business suit and tie he'd been wearing, he was dressed in smart casuals. His thick dark hair was brushed back from his high forehead and his jaw was clean-shaven.

'So there you are. Come and make yourself at home.'

A hand at her waist—just that impersonal touch made her go all of a dither—he ushered her to the nearest chair.

Trying to look cool and composed, she sank into it.

His glance taking in the touch of make-up, he smiled at her and said teasingly, 'My, now you look all of eighteen.'

That white smile, with its unstudied charm, rocked her afresh and made her feel as though her very bones were as pliable as warm candle wax.

'I'd just started to wonder if you knew which was the study,' he went on, 'or if you were wandering around, lost.'

'No, I knew. Mrs Baxter told me.' She was aware that she sounded more than a little breathless.

Indicating a drinks trolley, he queried, 'What's it to be?'

Bearing in mind that she'd had nothing to eat since breakfast, she plumped for orange juice.

While he added crushed ice to the glass and poured the freshly squeezed juice, she watched him from beneath long lashes.

In dark well-cut trousers and a black polo-neck sweater, he looked even more handsome and attractive and, in spite of all her efforts, her heart began to pick up speed.

He glanced up and, unwilling to be caught staring, she looked hastily away.

A moment or two later he was by her side. Handing her a tall, narrow, frosted glass, he said, 'Here you are.'

While she sipped, he leaned against the mantel, a whisky and soda in his hand, firelight flickering on his face, and studied her appraisingly.

He would have expected the sort of life she'd been leading to have left its mark, but at close quarters she looked clear-eyed and healthy and altogether too *untouched* to be the kind of woman he knew her to be.

He'd known from the start that she was blonde and blue-eyed, had even seen photographs of her, which had convinced him that she was attractive.

But the first time he had seen her in the flesh coming out of De Vere's office he had realised that the photographs didn't do her justice.

She was beautiful.

Now, taking in the long-lashed blue-violet eyes that slanted slightly upwards at the outer corners, the lovely silky hair the colour of corn-syrup—and natural too, he'd bet—winged brows and high cheekbones, the straight nose and the mouth that his own suddenly felt the urge to kiss, he revised his earlier opinion.

She was more than merely beautiful.

Much more.

She was bewitching, haunting, a fascinating contradiction. Despite that passionate mouth, she had an air of innocence, of vulnerability that, however false, had got under his skin the instant he saw her. And that could be dangerous.

He shrugged off the thought.

Being attracted to her was all very well so long as he kept in mind what his goal was and didn't allow that attraction to affect his judgement.

Over the past few weeks he had considered several courses of action. But, thinking it would be easier to judge when he knew her better, he had been waiting to decide exactly how to play it, which would be his best option.

In the end, however, things had moved so fast that he'd had no time for a leisurely appraisal.

Still, most of his plans were in place, even his final contingency plan. Which, because of the time element, he was now going to have to go with.

If he could bring it off.

There was no *if* about it. He *had* to bring it off.

But, having seen her at close quarters, he knew that taking her to bed would be no hardship. In fact the mere prospect made his blood quicken.

Of course, if he could get her *emotionally* involved, make her fall in love with him, it would ease his task enormously.

Experience told him that she was already attracted to him, though oddly enough she wasn't giving out the kind of overt signals he would have expected from a woman like her.

He knew from the reports he'd received that she was, to put it mildly, a child of her times and, despite her air of naivety, he found it almost impossible to believe that she had any scruples or inhibitions.

But, as time was short and he was unwilling to take any chances, it would do no harm to make certain that *if* she had, they were well and truly banished...

Tina glanced up and, thrown by the expression of almost savage intensity and purpose on his face, asked jerkily, 'Is something wrong?'

'Wrong? Of course not.'

His voice sounded quite normal and the expression that had startled her was gone as if it had never been. Realising it must have been a trick of the firelight, she breathed a sigh of relief.

Straightening, he asked easily, 'Another drink?'

'Please.'

Taking her glass and moving over to the drinks table, he said, 'I suggest this time you try it with a secret ingredient.'

Curiously, she asked, 'What *is* the secret ingredient?'

He gave her a lopsided smile. 'I have to confess that it's nothing out of the ordinary. Merely a dash of Cointreau.'

She laughed and took a sip of the drink he handed her. As he stood looking down at her, she saw for the first time that his eyes weren't simply brown, as she'd thought, but a dark green flecked with gold. Handsome tawny eyes, with long heavy lids and thick curly lashes.

As she gazed up at him, he took the glass from her hand and set in down on the low table. Then, stooping unhurriedly and as if—rather than obeying a sudden impulse—he knew exactly what he was doing and could take all the time in the world to do it, he kissed her mouth.

She had been held closely and kissed many times. But never like that. Without holding her in any way, with only their lips touching, his kiss held everything she had ever wanted—warmth, tenderness, passion, sweetness. It both gave and took, coaxed and effortlessly mastered.

When finally he lifted his head and drew away, she felt radiant, enchanted.

Satisfaction in his voice, he remarked, 'I've been wanting to kiss you since the first moment I caught sight of you standing there in the rain.'

Though—now she had seen his house—common sense told her he was right out of her league as far as any serious relationship went, she was filled with pleasure and excitement. He'd felt the same kind of instant attraction that she'd felt and, for the moment at least, that was enough.

Though it could lead nowhere.

And it was dangerous.

Especially if Richard had seduction on his mind. And, after the way he had kissed her, she could no longer rule that out.

But she wasn't one to have affairs or indulge in casual sex, so if he *did* intend to try and seduce her, she would just have to stay cool and uninterested.

Cool and uninterested! Who was she trying to kid?

So she would have to *appear* to be cool and uninterested. In the past she had always been good at quietly freezing men off, she reminded herself. But then she had been *genuinely* uninterested or, for one reason or another, unwilling to take that particular relationship any further.

Though it was old-fashioned, almost ludicrous in this modern age, she had been brought up to believe that love and commitment went hand in hand and that sex should belong within the framework of marriage.

It hadn't made her narrow-minded or critical of other people's behaviour. It was simply a standard that had been set for her and that she had so far adhered to.

While some of her friends laughed and said she was mad and others admired her, Ruth had suggested it was because she had never been seriously tempted. 'No, I haven't forgotten Kevin,' she had said, 'but while he was tall, dark and handsome, he obviously hadn't got what it takes to turn you on.

'It's a jolly good thing you didn't marry him,' she had added seriously, 'otherwise you might have ended up just going through the motions and missing out on one of life's most wonderful experiences…'

'Penny for them…'

Richard's voice brought Tina back to the present.

Her cheeks growing warm, she stammered, 'I—I was just thinking about something my friend said.'

'You're not angry that I kissed you?'

She shook her head.

Sounding confident, he added, 'And I take it there's no current boyfriend to object?'

A little piqued by that assumption, she said, 'What if there is?'

With a kind of wry self-mockery, he told her, 'If there is I'll have to wrest you from him…'

She had the strangest feeling that he would be prepared to wrest her from the archangel Gabriel himself should it prove necessary.

'Is there?'

She shook her head.

'But you didn't like me assuming that?' he queried shrewdly.

'As it happens, my fiancé and I split up earlier in the year.'

He raised a brow, not expecting her to have had such a serious past relationship. 'How long were you engaged?'

'About three months.'

'Officially?' he queried.

'You mean did I have a ring?'

He looked casually down at her left hand. 'Did you?'

'Yes.'

'Who broke things off?' Richard queried.

'I did,' Tina answered.

'Why?'

She paused, then looked up at him. 'I caught him playing around with another woman.'

'Do you still love him?'

'No, I don't,' she said, and knew it was the truth.

'But you still feel upset about it?'

She *had* until now. Though it wasn't so much that it had happened as the *way* it had happened.

Realising he was waiting for an answer, she said, 'I did at first, but now it no longer matters.'

Suddenly wondering if her words had been too revealing and feeling uncomfortable, she began to sip her drink once more.

Nursing his whisky and soda, Richard sat down on the other side of the hearth and changed the subject with smooth aplomb. 'I understand the sunny summer and autumn they've had on the Continent has helped to produce an excellent grape harvest...'

While they talked about the good weather they'd been enjoying and the climate in general, though he barely touched his own drink, an attentive host, he refilled her glass once more.

At length he rose and, having put some fresh logs on the fire, remarked, 'We'd better get something to eat before you starve to death.'

As they walked to the door, he told her, 'The dining-room is at the other end of the hall.' Adding, as she favoured her injured ankle, 'Can you manage?'

A little flustered, she said, 'Oh, yes, thank you.'

'Sure? I can see your left ankle's swollen and I've noticed you limping from time to time.'

'I'm sure I can manage, thank you.'

The gold and ivory dining-room was elegant, the table laid with cut glass and porcelain, while a bottle of wine encased in a silver cool-jacket waited to be poured.

Dinner, though simple, proved to be most enjoyable. Richard played the part of host with panache, filling Tina's plate and helping her to some of the excellent white wine.

Somewhat to her relief, he chose impersonal topics of conversation and as they ate they discussed books, music, art and the theatre. It didn't take long to discover that their tastes matched in most things and they both much preferred reading to watching television.

'I sometimes think television is the bane of modern living,' he observed, 'especially when the set takes over the room and becomes the focus of it.'

She agreed entirely and said so.

By the time the leisurely meal came to an end and Tina had finished her second glass of wine, starting to feel distinctly light-headed, she elected to take her coffee black and refused a liqueur.

It was getting late by the time their cups were empty but, knowing it made sense not to rush this part, he led the way back to the study.

Having stirred the glowing fire into life and settled her in front of it, he suggested, 'Let's have a small nightcap before we turn in.'

As, hazily happy just to be here with him, she was gazing into the flames, he handed her a balloon glass containing a swirl of golden cognac. Then, taking a seat opposite, he raised his own glass in a kind of toast and took a sip.

When she followed suit, he asked conversationally, 'How did you hurt your ankle?'

'I slipped when I was getting out of the shower.'

'Hardly a good start to Friday the thirteenth,' he commented dryly, 'and I gather things didn't improve very much?'

'Not a lot,' she said and, when he waited expectantly, went on to tell him about having a flat tyre and being late for work.

'Then at lunch time I discovered I'd forgotten to pack any sandwiches...'

He shook his head sympathetically. 'And, after losing your lunch, you end the day with a badly damaged car and no job.'

Though having no job still had to be a major worry, it didn't seem half so bad now she was sitting opposite Richard, sleepily watching the flickering firelight turn his face into a changing mask of highlights and shadows.

Hoping she hadn't sounded sorry for herself, she said hardily,

'But it could be worse. Mr De Vere has promised me a good reference, so it shouldn't take too long to find another position.'

'I presume you know a lot about wine?'

'Quite a lot,' she said simply. 'Otherwise I couldn't have done my job.'

Studying her reflectively, he queried, 'Any idea where tonight's wine came from?'

'France,' she answered without hesitation. 'I'd say the Loire Valley.'

'Can you put a name to it?'

Recognising that she was a bit squiffy, she said cautiously, 'Yes, I believe so.'

When he waited, one eyebrow slightly raised, she correctly named both the wine and the year.

Looking surprised, he remarked, 'Surely you weren't able to learn how to identify the area and the vintage merely from tutorials and course work?'

Sensing faint disparagement, she said, 'No, of course not.' Then, realising that she was starting to slur her words, she made an effort to enunciate more clearly. 'That has to come from the hands-on side, the bouquet and tasting...'

She stopped speaking, feeling dazed, overcome by tiredness. All she wanted to do at that moment was lie down and go to sleep.

Watching her trying to keep her eyes open, he said, 'You look more than ready for bed.'

He rose and in one lithe movement put the fireguard in place.

'I'm sorry...' she began.

'There's nothing to be sorry about. It's been a long, eventful day...'

He was right about that, she thought as she struggled to her feet.

'Need any help?' he queried.

'No, no...I'm fine,' she lied as, limping, she wove her way

somewhat unsteadily to the door. Oh, why had she accepted that cognac? She should have had more sense.

Having bided his time until she reached the hall, he said firmly, 'I think I'd better carry you.'

Not at all sure that she'd heard him aright, she echoed, 'Carry me?'

'Carry you,' he repeated firmly.

Going hot all over at the thought of being held in his arms and cradled against that broad chest, she stammered, 'R-really there's no need. I can manage quite well.'

Her normally low, slightly husky voice sounded agitated and squeaky.

Ignoring the assurance, he stooped and effortlessly lifted her high in his arms.

With a little gasp, she begged, 'Please put me down.' Adding distractedly, 'What on earth will your housekeeper think if she sees us?'

Looking unperturbed, he said, 'No one will see us.'

'How can you be so sure?'

'Because Jervis, the chauffeur and handyman, lives at the rear above the garages, and Gwen, who used to be a nurse, is staying at the centre overnight. Old Tom, one of her "regulars", is just recovering from a bad bout of flu, so she's remaining on hand in case he needs her.'

'Oh,' Tina said in a small voice.

As he crossed the hall and began to climb the stairs, Richard smiled down at her and added with soft emphasis, 'So you see, we're all alone.'

CHAPTER THREE

ALL alone.

Just for a second Tina had the absurd feeling that she'd walked into a trap.

There had been something in his voice, his choice of words—satisfaction? a touch of menace?—that made her heart start to thump against her ribs and a shiver run through her.

Noticing that betraying movement, Richard glanced down at her. 'There's no need to look so scared—' now his tone was reassuringly normal '—I haven't lured you here to imprison you in the cellar or lock you in the attic…'

Suddenly feeling foolish, she denied, 'I never thought you had.'

'Though I do have plans for you.'

The rider, though added jokingly, brought a touch of alarm.

'Plans?' she said thickly. 'What kind of plans?'

He laughed. 'Don't worry; I'm sure you'll like what I have in mind.'

Realising that he was teasing her, her head spinning, she let it go.

He carried her easily and when they reached the top of the stairs there was still no sign of him being out of breath.

As well as strong, he must be very fit.

Virile was the word that sprang to mind. It was a word that immediately produced some erotic images...

Shocked by her own thoughts, she told herself hazily that this wasn't like her. It must be alcohol swamping her inhibitions. Normally she drank very little and the amount she'd had tonight, some of it on an empty stomach, had gone straight to her head. As he crossed the landing and fumbled briefly to open her bedroom door, everything began to whirl gently round her and she closed her eyes.

Crossing to the bed, he pulled back the duvet and laid her down, supporting her head while he unfastened the clip that held her heavy coil of hair in place.

As the silken mass tumbled around her shoulders, he settled her head on the pillows and, sitting down beside her, slipped off her shoes.

She lay like a beautiful doll, her eyes closed, the long lashes making dark gold fans on her cheeks, her soft lips a little parted, the lovely creamy column of her throat exposed, vulnerable.

It was obvious that the alcohol had done its work too well and she was almost out for the count.

Frowning, he realised that she couldn't be as used to drinking as he'd been led to believe. It had been his intention to get rid of any possible inhibitions, not to make her practically incapable and he felt like a heel.

However, he couldn't afford too many scruples. Everything he held dear was at stake. If he'd been certain she would be reasonable...

But he *couldn't* be certain. It would depend entirely on what kind of woman she really was, and he wouldn't know that until he knew her better.

By that time it would be too late.

So he needed to go through with it.

As he made the decision, she opened her eyes.

Smiling down at her, he started to undo the buttons of her dress.

He had reached her waist when, pushing herself up groggily and brushing his hands away, she said hoarsely, 'It's all right… I can manage.'

'Sure?'

'Quite sure.'

'But you would like me to stay.' He made it sound as if it had all been decided.

The true answer was yes.

But even in her tipsy state she knew that all he wanted was a one-night stand and, making an effort to stick with her long-held principles, she started to shake her head.

It was a mistake and, as the world began to spin once more, she closed her eyes and mumbled, 'I'd like you to go.'

'Then I'll say goodnight.' He leaned forward and kissed her.

The light pressure of his lips against hers was enough to make her sink back against the pillows.

His mouth still keeping contact, he followed her down and, when her lips parted helplessly, he deepened the kiss until her head was whirling even more and her whole being melted.

Without conscious volition, her arms went round his neck and she was holding on to him as if he were the only stable object worth anything in her world…

Her brain came to life slowly, consciousness ebbing and flowing. As she lay with closed eyes, she became aware that she was unusually warm and comfortable on the rather uncomfortable put-you-up.

And, what was even more unusual, her hair was loose around her shoulders—normally she braided it—and she was naked. Why wasn't she wearing her nightdress? Unable to think, she let the thought go and drifted off again.

It was the sound of a shower running that eventually began to penetrate her stupefied state.

Ruth must be up early this morning. Usually she was last in the bathroom, preferring to breakfast in her dressing gown even on a weekday.

But surely this was the weekend? Hadn't it been Friday yesterday?

Friday the thirteenth and everything had gone wrong...

Like a tide carrying flotsam, the events of the day washed into her mind and for a moment or two she sorted dazedly through them until she found the one thing that mattered above all else.

She had met Richard Anders.

The recollection banished sleep and focused her attention. A moment later, memory filled in the details with a rush.

The car accident, the invitation to go home with him, the drive to Pemberley Square, his kiss in the study, dinner together, brandy in front of the fire... Then him carrying her upstairs after saying with a strange intonation in his voice, 'So you see we're all alone.'

He had taken her into her room, laid her on the bed and kissed her goodnight...

But she had a vague memory of wanting him to stay, of kissing him back and putting her arms around his neck... Her eyes flew open and she sat bolt upright.

She was briefly aware that the room was light, sunshine slanting in through a gap in the curtains, then, the sudden movement making her head spin, she groaned and, squeezing her eyes tightly shut, pressed her fingertips to her temples.

'Headache?' a male voice asked sympathetically.

She opened her eyes again to find Richard just emerging from the bathroom. His dark, attractively rumpled hair was still damp from the shower and he hadn't a stitch on.

The sight of that beautifully toned male body with its

muscular chest and lean hips, its trim waist and taut belly, made her heart lurch wildly and her stomach tighten.

Oh, but he was gorgeous. A superb male animal.

As she gaped at him speechlessly, he strolled over and, bending, kissed her lightly on the lips as if he had every right.

As if they were lovers.

Which, no doubt, they were, otherwise what was he doing in her room stark naked?

Transfixed by the thought, she froze.

When, sitting still as a statue, she failed to respond to his kiss, he looked at her appraisingly, trying to sum her up.

He knew what kind of woman she was and, though he was sure that she wanted him, she wasn't acting as he would have expected. Most of the women he had known would have twined their arms around his neck and done their best to coax him back to bed.

But, instead of trying to look seductive, she looked positively embarrassed, as if she wasn't used to sleeping around.

Had she reacted like those other women, he would have accepted the invitation. Even first thing in the morning and with a hangover, she was the most beautiful woman he had ever seen.

Her neck was long and slender, her breasts small and firm, with dusky-pink velvety nipples that he felt the urge to stroke with his tongue…

Realising that his eyes were fixed appreciatively on her breasts, in a panicky reflex action she jerked up the duvet to cover her nakedness.

A gleam of amusement in his eyes, he said, 'I'll get you something for that headache.'

As he turned and walked to the door, she caught her breath at the seductive back view of his tall, well-built figure.

His skin, with its golden all-over tan, was clear and glowed with health, his shoulders were broad, his buttocks firm, his long legs strong and straight. The line of his spine was elegant. Even the back of his neck, with the damp hair trying to curl a little into his nape, was sexy.

The thought of the housekeeper catching sight of him leaving her room naked made Tina exclaim, 'But what will Mrs Baxter think if she—'

Further amused by this show of propriety, he turned and said, 'I'm not expecting her home for a while. I told her I'd rustle up some breakfast and she could take as much time as she needed. So no doubt she'll stay and feed her flock.'

Grinning, he added, 'By the time she gets back, rather than shock her, I'll be dressed and my bed will look suitably slept in.'

A second later the latch clicked and he was gone.

With a strange hollow sensation in the pit of her stomach that she identified as shame, Tina sat and stared at the closed door.

Last night she had obviously waved goodbye to her principles and enjoyed what Ruth had called 'one of life's most wonderful experiences' *and she couldn't remember a thing.*

Now, as well as feeling ashamed, she felt cheated.

If she hadn't had too much to drink…

But if she hadn't had too much to drink, she reminded herself grimly, she wouldn't have slept with him in the first place.

She knew from the way her contemporaries talked that that kind of thing wasn't uncommon, but she had never expected it to happen to *her*.

Well, now it had and it was too late. What was done couldn't be undone. She would just have to live with the shame.

She bit her lip.

If they had known and loved one another it would have been different… Or if there'd been any promise of a serious relationship…

But neither of those things applied.

It had been purely and simply a one-night stand. On his part, at least.

From a kaleidoscope of emotions, anger and dismay and regret at her own behaviour stood out.

She almost wished she could say he'd taken advantage of her but, recalling the way she had put her arms round his neck and clung to him, in all honesty she couldn't.

He must think she was easy, that this was her usual behaviour. Cringing, she wondered how she was going to face him.

And he would be back before too long.

The mere thought turned her insides into a quivering mass of jelly.

Trying to get a grip, she told herself bracingly that she was bound to feel better, more confident, when she had showered and got dressed.

Averting her gaze from the chair that held last night's discarded clothes, she stumbled out of bed. The movement made her temples pound so violently that for a moment she was forced to stand with her eyes shut, too dizzy to move.

When the world stopped spinning, she located her clip on the bedside cabinet and fastened her hair on top of her head.

Then, moving more carefully now, both for the sake of her head and her ankle which, though a great deal better, still wasn't quite right, went into the bathroom to clean her teeth and shower.

While the hot water and lavender-scented gel flowed slickly over her bare flesh, it occurred to her that, in the circumstances, she would have expected her body to look and feel different—a faint redness here and there, a little stiffness, some tenderness perhaps? '*Fulfilled, more like a real woman,*' would have been Ruth's poetic way of putting it.

But, apart from a headache and feeling slightly nauseous, which were obviously the effects of too much alcohol, there wasn't a mark on her and physically she felt just the same.

Only nothing *was* the same.

It never would be again.

As she dried herself and cleaned her teeth, trying to ignore the fact that in a single day her whole world had somehow been turned topsy-turvy, she made what plans she could.

Richard Anders had promised to get her car fixed so, hopefully, if she gave him Ruth's address, the garage would let her know when it was done.

In the meantime she would leave Pemberley Square as soon as possible and book into a hotel.

Though her heart plummeted at the thought of walking away from Richard, it was something she *had* to do. If she looked as if she was making any attempt to cling or prolong things he would only secretly despise her...

She had just returned to the bedroom to find some fresh clothes when a tap at the door sent her scurrying back into bed.

A moment later Richard strode in carrying a loaded breakfast tray. He was wearing a short navy-blue silk robe and, apart from one dark lock that had escaped to fall over his forehead, his hair had been tamed into submission.

He looked clear-eyed and incredibly handsome and, though she tried her hardest to appear cool and composed, her heart picked up speed.

Studying her shiny nose and the damp strands of hair escaping from the clip, he commented gravely, 'You've had your shower, I see.'

Feeling a disturbing mixture of embarrassment and powerful attraction and knowing her hair must look ridiculous bundled on top of her head like this, she wished she'd had time to brush it.

'How's the ankle this morning?'

Somehow she found her voice and said huskily, 'Much better, thank you.'

Having set the tray on the bedside cabinet, he crossed to the window to draw back the curtains. 'We seem to have our good weather back,' he observed as the sunshine flooded in. 'Which should be a relief after yesterday.'

Almost to himself and with a little reminiscent smile, he added, 'However, rain like that can create some lasting memories…'

She was wondering what kind of memories he had in mind when, returning to the bedside, he stooped to touch his lips to hers before asking, 'Now, about ready for some breakfast?'

Quivering from that casual little caress, she trapped the duvet under her arms and looked anywhere but at him as he set the tray across her knees.

It held freshly squeezed grapefruit juice and a full English breakfast, including toast and marmalade and a pot of coffee.

'As I'm aiming for a black belt in cooking and I don't get a chance to practise while Gwen's here, I thought I might as well go the whole hog.

'But, first of all, drink this.' He handed her a glass containing a small amount of cloudy liquid.

Though the actual taste wasn't too bad, the concoction had an unpleasant slimy texture and she shuddered as she swallowed it.

'Pretty revolting, isn't it?' he commented cheerfully. 'But it's extremely effective; the best cure for a hangover I know. By the time you've had something to eat, your headache will be gone.'

He poured the coffee, which was hot and fragrant, and, having divided the sausages, bacon, button mushrooms and grilled tomatoes between two plates, paused to ask, 'Now, then, how brave do you feel?'

'Brave?'

He grinned. 'While everything else is usually eatable, my scrambled eggs have been known to resemble foam rubber, so it's up to you.'

Raising a well-marked brow, he added quizzically, 'Are you brave enough to try a spoonful?'

Suddenly *liking* him a lot, she smiled and nodded.

'Your courage is only exceeded by your personal beauty,'

he told her and, having added the eggs, put a plate in front of her. 'There you are, tuck in. You'll feel a lot better when you've eaten.'

He took a napkin and his own plate and sat down companionably on the edge of the bed.

It was all so intimate they could have been lovers for years, she found herself thinking, or an old married couple.

But familiarity brought, if not contempt, a kind of serenity, and serenity was absent. His close proximity, her keen awareness of him, alerted all her senses and made her heart race and her temperature rise like a rocket.

Distracted, her appetite suddenly non-existent, she sipped her coffee and considered telling him that she wasn't hungry after all.

But, unwilling to hurt his feelings, she finally picked up her knife and fork and began to eat. After the first mouthful or two she found, unexpectedly, that her appetite had returned.

Somewhat to her surprise—most of the men she had known in the past could scarcely boil water—everything was cooked to perfection and the eggs proved to be deliciously light and fluffy.

But then he was the kind of man who would excel at anything he set his hand to.

Glancing up, she met his tawny eyes.

'Well?' he queried.

'You're awarded a black belt.'

'That's good.' With a small secret smile he added, 'It's my aim to please you in every way.'

That smile and the gleam in his eyes made her wonder if the innocent words had a double meaning and, feeling the colour rise in her cheeks, she hastily returned her attention to her meal.

He had put their empty plates on one side and offered her the toast rack before he broke the silence to ask, 'Feeling any better?'

Starting to butter her toast, she answered, 'Much better, thank you,' and was surprised to find it was the truth. Her headache had lifted and the feeling of nausea had vanished.

Smiling at her, he said, 'That's good.'

He had leaned forward to help himself to a piece of toast when, glancing up, she saw that a stray shaft of sunshine had fallen across his handsome face, lighting it up.

Fascinated, she stared into his eyes. The irises, dark green and ringed with gold, had flecks of hazel and gold swimming in their tawny depths.

It seemed an age before she could tear her gaze away and return to her toast.

As, somewhat distractedly, she finished spreading it, she got a smear of marmalade on the index finger of her left hand. She was about to lick if off when he lifted her hand and, putting her finger in his mouth, sucked.

Feeling the warmth and wetness, the slight roughness of his tongue, she caught her breath and her stomach tied itself in knots.

A moment later he released her hand and, as if nothing had happened, as if he hadn't shaken her to the very core, remarked, 'By the way, while breakfast was cooking I phoned the garage. I've made arrangements to have your car picked up and repaired as soon as possible.'

Her voice impeded, she said, 'Thank you. That's very kind of you.'

'It's the least I can do.'

'Perhaps if I give you my friend's address, you'll ask the garage to let me have the bill?'

Flatly, he said, 'I shall do no such thing. As I ran into you, the responsibility is mine... Now, then, more coffee?'

'Please.'

As he reached to replenish their coffee cups, his tone careless, he enquired, 'I take it you have no plans for the weekend?'

'I've trespassed long enough on your hospitality, so the first thing I must do is find a hotel…'

His mouth tightened. Once again she wasn't reacting as he might have expected and he couldn't afford to let her move into a hotel. While she was under his roof, he wanted to keep her there.

'Then I intend to visit some employment agencies,' she went on, determinedly, 'and see what kind of jobs are currently available…'

That was another thing he couldn't let her do.

'Surely there's no need to look for work immediately? Won't you be receiving some kind of redundancy payment?'

'I was given six months' salary, which is really very generous. But when my flat is finished the rent will go up considerably. And, apart from that, I have financial commitments that make it necessary to find another job without too much delay.'

That could well be to his advantage, he thought. And then, though he already knew, he asked, 'What exactly did your previous job entail?'

'Tying up with the buyer to gather data and taste as many of the new vintages as possible; describing and cataloguing the wines; sending out promotional leaflets; organising the various social occasions and parties that are part of a sales push and making sure we received maximum press coverage.'

'Sounds like a job and a half. But I gather you enjoyed it?'

She sighed. 'Yes, I did, very much. Losing it came as a blow.'

'It must have done.'

'What are the chances of joining another vintner?'

'Unfortunately, not very high, unless I was prepared to work abroad.'

'And you don't want to do that?'

'Not really.' She needed to be on hand to try and make sure that Didi didn't go off the rails again.

'But you'd prefer to be in the wine trade?'

'It's what I spent over three years studying for.'

'Three years?' He seemed surprised.

'I did one year at college and another two on the practical side.'

'Where did you get your hands-on experience?'

'I spent two years working at the Château de Renard, learning about soil composition, planting methods, culture and yields, what factors need to be present to produce a good vintage, how to most successfully blend the various grape types—'

She stopped speaking abruptly, wondering if she was boring him.

But, looking anything but bored, he exclaimed, 'Then you're just the woman I need!'

As she stared at him, he explained, 'You have exactly the kind of knowledge and experience that I've been hoping to find.

'Our family home is at Castle Anders…'

'Is Castle Anders the name of a place or is it a…?' She hesitated and broke off in confusion.

'A real castle?' he finished for her.

'Well, yes…' she said, flushing a little.

Looking amused, he told her, 'It's a real castle.'

So his family home was a castle!

Her heart sank. If, hating the thought of never seeing him again, she had harboured any faint hope of staying in his life, that killed it stone dead. With money and a privileged background like that, he was right out of her class.

'Though the estate is still extensive,' he went on, 'the castle itself is quite small as castles go. No larger, in fact, than, say, a reasonably sized hall, but with more turrets.

'But, to get back to the point, although Anders is only just over an hour's drive from London, we've a small vineyard on the estate.

'The winery hasn't been in production for quite a number

of years but I've always had it in mind that if and when the opportunity arose I'd try and give it a new lease of life.'

Finding her voice, Tina hazarded, 'So you'd like some advice?'

'I was thinking of rather more than that. As your needs and my needs seem to coincide, I was offering you a job.'

'A job?'

By rights she should have been ecstatic, but now a miracle had happened she simply felt numb.

'You said you needed one,' he pointed out.

With no chance of any other relationship developing, working for him would be one way of staying in his life.

But wouldn't it be awkward and embarrassing, put her in an untenable position, to work for a man she had been to bed with?

'I do, but I…I really don't think…'

He had hoped for a more positive, a more favourable, response. But, wary of exerting too much pressure, he said easily, 'Well, you don't have to decide right this minute…

'Tell you what, I'll ask Jervis to bring the car round and as soon as you're up and dressed we'll go over to Anders. After you've seen the castle and the vineyard we can talk about it further.'

She had opened her mouth to refuse, when she hesitated. Though nothing could come of it, she found she badly wanted to spend a little more time with him, see his family home.

Watching her face, trying to gauge her reaction, he wondered how to play it. Would it be best to turn on the heat or allow her a breathing space?

But what if she decided against going to Anders? He couldn't afford to let her take the initiative and walk away. Somehow he had to make her *want* to stay with him.

His mind made up, he rose to his feet in a leisurely manner and, removing the tray, set it down on the Elizabethan blanket chest.

When he didn't immediately leave, unwilling to let him see her get out of bed naked, she stayed where she was until, with an innocent look, he queried, 'Something wrong?'

'My dressing gown's still in my case,' she explained awkwardly.

He crossed to where her case was and returned a moment later with her lightweight dressing gown over his arm. Instead of handing it to her, however, he stood by the bed and held it for her.

When still she hesitated, he said quizzically, 'Don't tell me you're shy, after last night?'

Watching her bite her lip, he laughed softly. 'Why, I do believe you are. But then if you remember how—'

'I'm afraid I don't remember much about it,' she broke in desperately.

'Much?'

'Anything,' she admitted.

'Ah,' he murmured softly. 'Well, if you'd like me to refresh your memory…?'

Thoroughly hot and bothered, her equilibrium gone, she exclaimed, 'No!' Then, less vehemently, 'No, I wouldn't…I mean I…I just want to get dressed.'

He frowned. Though she had been wrong-footed from the start, it was already clear that she had much more strength of character than he'd envisaged and he couldn't make up his mind whether, in the long run, that was a good thing or not.

But one thing he did know. While she was off balance it would pay him to *keep* her off balance…

With a sigh he said, 'Then perhaps I'd better stop teasing you.'

The mock contrition on his face and the devilish gleam in his eyes made him totally irresistible.

Realising that he had no real intention of stopping and knowing she would have to make a move or endure even more, she slid out of bed and, her back turned to him, slipped into the silky gown.

Wrapping it round her and holding it in place with his arms, he touched his lips to the warmth of her nape, planting soft little baby kisses until he reached the warm hollow behind her ear.

As, shivers running up and down her spine, she stood perfectly still, not daring to move, his mouth travelled down the side of her neck, nibbling and sucking, making her want to squirm.

At the same time his hands slid up to cup her breasts. Through the thin material of her gown, she could feel the warmth of his palms and her heart began to race madly. When his thumbs brushed over her sensitive nipples she gasped.

Part of her mind was aware that she ought to pull free, put a stop to this madness before she reached the point of no return.

But still she continued to stand rooted to the spot while his hands caressed her breasts, sending needle-sharp darts of pleasure running through her.

Just when she thought she could stand no more of such exquisite torment, he stopped and, turning her into his arms, lifted her chin and began to kiss her.

While she tried to hold on to the coat tails of her fast disappearing self-control and call a halt, he plundered her mouth with a masterful expertise that soon, caught in the spell of the black magic he was weaving, left her limp and quivering all over.

She had never known it could be like this. Had never imagined anyone being able to make her feel such longing, such naked need.

When finally he slipped the dressing gown from her shoulders and laid her down on the bed, mindless with desire, she made no demur.

For a brief moment he stood looking down at her, half regretting what he intended to do, wishing that circumstances were other than what they were.

Her flawless skin, her long slender limbs, her beautifully shaped breasts, her slim waist and flat stomach, the seductive curve of her hips, would have tempted the most dedicated of monks.

Tossing aside his own robe, he stretched out naked beside her and, murmuring how beautiful she was, began to kiss her again, expertly and thoroughly.

CHAPTER FOUR

WHILE he kissed her his skilful hands travelled caressingly over her body, filling her with a singing delight. A sensation that intensified almost unbearably as, his finger and thumb teasing one pink nipple, he took the other into his mouth and stroked it with the tip of his tongue.

While he continued to ravish her, his free hand began to explore the silky honey-gold triangle of curls and the satiny skin of her inner thighs.

She began to make soft little sounds deep in her throat, wordless pleas that he heard with a wholly masculine satisfaction.

But now was the time to make his move while he was still in control. If he left it any longer...

When, in response to her urging, he moved over her, after a lifetime of discipline and self-restraint it seemed the most natural thing in the world to welcome him and, feeling his weight, she gave a little murmur of pleasure.

A murmur that died in her throat as, all at once, muttering something she didn't catch, he drew away.

Her eyes flew open.

He got to his feet, pulled the duvet over her and shrugged into his robe while she lay there, bereft and bewildered.

Deplorably innocent she might be, but there wasn't the

faintest doubt that he'd wanted her, so what had made him change his mind so suddenly?

Bending down, he kissed her and said quietly, 'Gwen's back early…'

She hadn't heard a thing, Tina thought dazedly, but in the circumstances that wasn't surprising.

'There's no guarantee that she won't come upstairs,' he went on, 'and the guest room doesn't have a key, so to save everyone's blushes I'll take the evidence and make myself scarce.'

Picking up the tray, he headed for the door.

Watching it close behind him, it struck her that, far from being seriously annoyed, he seemed to be taking the whole thing in his stride.

Almost as if he had planned to walk away at that point…

But why on earth should he? It didn't make sense. She dismissed the ridiculous thought. It would simply be that what would have been new and earth-shaking for her wouldn't mean the same to him.

Though, judging by the care he had taken to avoid upsetting his housekeeper, he didn't bring his women here, he must be used to having his every need met. Which meant he could regard the interruption as just a slight annoyance.

Whereas she felt empty and desolate, like someone who had been torn from the gates of paradise just as they were about to open…

But, unless she wanted to risk Mrs Baxter finding her like this, she mustn't lie here repining.

The thought galvanizing her into action, she got out of bed and pulled on her gown while she found fresh underwear and a clean blouse.

While she had been drifting along, sexually unawakened, it had been comparatively easy to deny her body's needs. But being awakened, feeling really alive for the first time, though wonderful, was a two-edged sword.

Trying to ignore the way her body still cried out for fulfil-
ment, the demons of frustration that clamoured for release,
she put on her suit, coiled her hair and made-up lightly.

Then she repacked her case, gathered up her coat and
handbag and, allowing herself no more time for regrets or
thoughts of what might have been, made her way downstairs.

There was no sign of either the housekeeper or Richard and
everything was quiet as she descended the stairs.

In the hall she hesitated, suddenly embarrassed at the thought
of having to face him after everything that had happened.

It would be so much easier if she was free to just slip
away, as self-sufficient, as *uninvolved* as she had been before
she had first seen him standing in Cartel's car park.

But she wasn't.

No longer mistress of her own destiny, at this precise
moment she could no more make herself walk away and leave
him than she could fly to the moon. As though caught in a
spell, she was held by invisible bonds, ties she didn't begin
to understand but couldn't escape.

It was both a frightening and strangely exhilarating thought.

She couldn't be in love. It couldn't have happened this fast.
But from being a woman very much alone, trapped in an
emotional vacuum, overnight everything had changed. She
had finally been awakened and was alive in a way that she
had never known before.

Even when she and Kevin had been newly engaged and she
had thought she loved him, she had never felt like this.

But, no matter how she felt, when they got back from
Castle Anders, for the sake of her self-respect, she must move
into a hotel.

Leaving her case in the hall, she headed for the study. As
she reached the door she heard Richard's voice and hesitated.

'Yes, I'm sorry about that, but as things are...' he was

saying. Then, after a pause, 'I have to act now…I simply can't afford to risk waiting…'

She had started to turn away as, his voice brisk and determined, he went on, 'I certainly hope so… Straight away, all being well… Now, I'd better get moving… Yes, I'll do that… Bye.'

The door opened abruptly and he came striding out. His dark face more than a little tense, he said, 'I was just coming to look for you. About ready to go?'

'Yes.' Whatever the trip to Castle Anders brought, it was something she felt impelled to do.

His face relaxing into a smile, he said, 'That's good,' and put a hand at her waist.

Just that light touch seemed to brand her through her clothing.

'As it's a Saturday morning and the traffic's often bad,' he went on, 'it might take us longer than usual to get there. But we can always have lunch on the way—' Seeing her case, he stopped speaking abruptly.

Quickly, before she could weaken, she explained, 'I've brought my belongings in the hope that when we get back to London you'll be kind enough to drop me at a hotel.'

'Of course,' he agreed smoothly, 'if you're sure that's what you want.'

Outside, the sky was a Mediterranean blue and it was warm and sunny, with a return to the Indian summer they had been enjoying. A balmy breeze carried the scent of late roses and somewhere close at hand a bird sang, turning town into country.

The sleek silver Porsche was standing by the kerb with a dark blue limousine drawn up behind it and Jervis—stocky and middle-aged—standing by.

Handing the chauffeur Tina's case, Richard said, 'I've decided to drive myself, so you can put that in the Porsche, garage the limo and take the rest of the day off.'

'Very good, sir.' There was gladness and relief in the man's voice. 'Thank you, sir.'

'I suppose you know your favourite team's on the box this afternoon?' Richard queried with a grin.

Jervis returned the grin. 'Don't I just! And they stand a good chance of winning.

'There's a special preview before the run-up to the match,' he went on, 'so as soon as Mrs Baxter gets back—they're her favourite team too—we'll have an early lunch and get settled.'

So the housekeeper *wasn't* back. Richard must have been mistaken. *Or lying deliberately.*

Oh, don't start that again! Tina scolded herself and wondered what had got into her. Usually she was well-balanced, not one to harbour foolish thoughts, but somehow, since yesterday lunch time, she had lost her common sense along with her equilibrium.

As soon as her case was in the boot and she was installed in the passenger seat, with a word of thanks and a nod to the chauffeur, Richard slid in beside her. A moment later they had left the quiet square and joined the busy Saturday morning mêlée.

As they headed out of town, the traffic proved to be very heavy and it was stop-start for most of the way. Once the suburbs had been left behind them, however, and they reached the quieter country roads, things improved enormously.

When it was obvious that the most stressful part of the journey was over, she asked, 'Where exactly is Castle Anders?'

'Some five miles from the picturesque market town of Anders Cross and a couple of miles from the village of West Anders.'

It seemed that Anders was a name to be reckoned with, Tina thought a shade dazedly and asked, 'How long have the Anders family lived there?'

'Our branch of the family have lived at the castle for well over six hundred years.'

She was still marvelling at that when he went on, 'My

mother, who lost both her parents in a plane crash when she was just a toddler, was brought up there by her grandparents.

'When she met and fell in love with my father, Richard Cavendish, and wanted to marry him, they gave the couple their blessing on condition that he changed his name from Cavendish to Anders and made his home at the castle. Which he did.

'When my great-grandfather passed away at ninety-three, he left me his business empire and bequeathed Castle Anders to my mother on the understanding that after her death it should come to me...'

'So your parents still live there?'

He shook his head. 'They're both dead.' Heavily, he added, 'My mother died earlier this year.'

'I'm sorry,' she said. 'You must miss her.'

He acknowledged her condolence with a glance from those tawny eyes and a little nod.

'Have you any brothers or sisters?'

'No. I'm the last of this particular branch of the family—at least until I marry and have children of my own.

'Then, as great-grandfather knew, it's always been my intention to take my wife and family and live at Anders on a permanent basis.'

Tina felt a queer tug at her heartstrings to think that some lucky woman was destined to be everything to him—his friend and confidante, his lover and his wife, the mother of his children.

Trying to push the poignant thought aside, she relapsed into silence and stared out at the scenery. Without being particularly dramatic, the countryside was pleasantly picturesque and rolling.

The woods were decked in bronze and gold and russet, the newly washed meadows were green and lush and the silver flash of water told of quiet streams and rivers.

As they breasted a rise to see a pleasing panorama spread

out below them, Richard broke the silence to say, 'A mile or so ahead, there's a nice old coaching inn called the Posthorn. I thought we might stop there. The place has character and the food's good.'

She nodded agreement. 'That sounds lovely.'

The Posthorn was a black and white half-timbered place with tubs of trailing scarlet geraniums adding a vivid splash of colour.

Richard drove through an archway into a cobbled yard and parked outside what had obviously once been stabling and now appeared to be a small brewery.

'As you can see, they brew their own ale here,' he remarked, 'and it's excellent.'

They went in through a back door and into a panelled lounge, where the windows were open to the balmy air and sunshine streamed in.

In the huge fireplace the grate was screened by a large jar filled with beech and autumn foliage and the polished furniture smelt of apples and honey.

Having settled her in a seat by a window, he handed her a menu and asked, 'What do you fancy to eat?'

'I'm not particularly hungry after such a good breakfast...' she began and, recalling the intimacy of that breakfast, felt her cheeks grow hot.

Seeing the gleam of amusement in his eyes and knowing he'd guessed the cause of her confusion, she found herself blushing even harder.

His face straight, he suggested, 'Then perhaps just a sandwich?'

Not knowing where to look, she bent her head over the menu and studied it with unnecessary care.

Oh, why was she acting like an overgrown schoolgirl? she wondered crossly. Where had yesterday's cool, self-contained young woman gone?

But, after all that had happened last night and this

morning… She pushed away the uncomfortable thought, determined not to go along *that* route, and dragged her mind back to the present.

There was an extensive range of light snacks and, by the time a cheerful buxom woman came to take their order, Tina had decided on home-cooked ham in a piece of French stick and a side salad.

Richard followed suit.

'And to drink?' he queried. Adding, 'They have a good wine cellar here.'

'I was thinking of trying half a pint of ale.'

Looking surprised, he said, 'A good choice. I'll have the same.'

Their ale came almost at once and, when she had sampled it and agreed that it was some of the best she'd ever tasted, he said, 'Tell me a bit about yourself. Are you London born and bred?'

'No. I was born and brought up in a small village. I only went to live in London when I started to work for Cartel Wines.'

'So which do you prefer? Town or country?'

She smiled wistfully. 'I quite like London but I'd much sooner live in the country.'

'Have you any brothers or sisters?'

'I've a stepsister, Didi. My mother died when I was seven and a year later my father married a widow with a daughter of almost the same age.'

'Did you get on well?'

'Not too well,' Tina admitted. 'Despite the fact that we were born in the same month and within three days of each other, we were completely different both in character and temperament.'

'Does your stepsister still live in the country?'

Tina shook her head. 'No. Didi left home and got a job in London when she was seventeen.'

'What about your parents?'

'A couple of years ago a relative left my father a hotel in Melbourne and they decided to give up their house and go to live in Australia.

'Before they went, they asked me to keep an eye on Didi— she'd been ill and was having problems.

'By that time I was working for Cartel Wines and renting a two-bedroomed flat, so when I found she couldn't pay the rent for her crummy bedsit and was about to be thrown out, I persuaded her to move in with me.'

Frowning, he asked, 'But she doesn't still live with you?'

'Oh, no. She moved out when she was offered a place at the Ramon Bonaventure School of Drama.'

'She wants to be an actress?'

'Yes. Though her mother had been very much against it, it was something Didi had always hoped to do...'

Tina stopped speaking as their lunch arrived, accompanied by various jars of homemade chutney, all with frilled muslin covers.

'I can thoroughly recommend the mango,' Richard told her.

'Mmm,' Tina agreed when she'd tried some. 'It's absolutely delicious.'

'I thought you'd like it. It's almost as good as Hannah makes.'

'Hannah?'

'Our old cook/housekeeper at the castle. Her family have been retainers there for donkey's years. Though Hannah's semi-retired, she still rules the staff with a rod of iron.

'She was born there and stayed on when she married one of the estate workers. Mullins, her son, is a general manservant who takes care of just about everything, including the cars, and her youngest granddaughter, Milly, is a maid.'

For a while they ate without speaking and, though Tina strove to appear relaxed and easy, she was *aware* of him—of his presence, his nearness, his every slight movement.

From beneath her thick lashes she watched him as he

helped himself to more chutney and lifted his glass to drink. He had strong, well-shaped hands with lean fingers and neatly trimmed nails.

Masculine hands.

Exciting hands.

A half-remembered line from Donne started to run through her mind: *'Licence my roving hands, and let them go—'*

She snapped off the thought like snapping a dry twig and, feeling the sexual tension tightening, hurried into speech. 'How did the castle come to have a vineyard?'

'While my great-grandfather, who was a merchant banker, was staying in a French château in the Loire Valley, he became very interested in wine-making. When he got back to Anders, he planted vines on some south-facing slopes on the edge of the estate and set up a small winery.

'By the time he passed away he had quite a successful little business which eventually my father took over. But when *he* became ill it was neglected and after his death I regret to say that it was closed down altogether.

'I was at Oxford at the time and after I graduated, though my mother begged me to go back to live at Anders, I decided, in the end, not to.'

'So you prefer to live in London?'

'No, not at all. Though I've lived in London since I left university, it isn't really from choice.'

'Oh.'

'My father died when I was eighteen and two years later my mother married again. She and my father had been very close and it was when she was alone and grief-stricken that she met Bradley Sanderson, a childless widower fifteen years older than herself.'

Seeing Tina's slightly puzzled frown, Richard explained, 'My mother decided that she would keep her own name. It seemed like the simplest solution—there is always meant to be an Anders in the castle. Though they had the same surname, he wasn't a blood relation. When he was five or six he'd been adopted by Jonathan Anders, a member of the Wiltshire branch of the family, whose wife was unable to have children.

'Unfortunately Bradley and I didn't get along. I disliked and distrusted him and he hated my guts for opposing the marriage.

'That's why, after leaving university, I decided it would be better all round if I lived in London. So I bought the house in Pemberley Square and just paid periodic visits to the castle, where I had my own suite of rooms.'

It must have been hard to visit a place he'd always regarded as home and confine himself to a suite of rooms, while a man he disliked intensely was, nominally at least, master there.

Impulsively, she said, 'It couldn't have been easy for you.'

For a moment he looked surprised, then he admitted, 'It wasn't. Especially when I realised Mother wasn't very happy...

'To give Bradley his due, he did a good job of running the estate and she was grateful. But he turned out to be a difficult man to live with and, though she never admitted as much, I think she regretted marrying him, and felt guilty that she *did* regret it.

'Shortly after she had been diagnosed with a terminal illness, Bradley was found to have a heart disease which cut his life expectancy to a year or two at the most.

'I promised Mother that if she predeceased him, I wouldn't turn him out. But he wasn't happy with that assurance. He wanted her to put a codicil in her will to the effect that he could continue to live at Anders until his death, and I agreed.'

'Then your stepfather's still living there?'

'He was until he died of a heart attack a little while ago.'

'So now the castle's all yours and you intend to keep it?'

Richard's handsome face looked oddly grim and his voice was steely as he answered, 'Oh, yes, I intend to keep it.'

The casement clock in the corner struck a sonorous two-thirty and, his voice and manner back to normal, Richard asked, 'About ready to move?'

Realising that at the rate they were going it would be quite late by the time they got back to London, she said, 'Yes, I'm ready,' and rose to her feet.

Apart from some brief embarrassment, it had been a very pleasant interlude and she had learned quite a lot about him and his family.

None of it had given her any hope that she might be lucky enough to fit into his life, but even so, knowing more about him, getting to understand him, was oddly precious to her.

While they continued their journey she mulled over what she had learned and was still thinking about it when Richard said with satisfaction, 'Almost there.'

A minute or so later they left a quiet country road for an even quieter lane, with open countryside on their right and a high mellow-brick wall on their left. In a few hundred yards they came to an imposing entrance guarded by two huge stone lions crouched on stone plinths.

As they swung between them, the tall electronically operated wrought iron gates slid aside and a moment later the Porsche was purring up a well-kept serpentine drive. On either hand, rolling, lightly wooded parkland studded with sheep stretched away into the distance.

'Time's getting on, so I suggest that before I show you the castle we take a quick look at the vineyard,' Richard said.

She nodded. 'Whatever suits you best.'

Having agreed to come with him, she could hardly refuse to look at the vineyard. Besides, rather against her will, she was interested. If things had been different, the job would have been ideal.

After about three quarters of a mile they turned down a side road and eventually came to a collection of purpose-built sheds and buildings that housed the wine-making plant. On the nearby south-facing slopes stretched row upon row of vines.

Having stopped the car, he asked, 'Ankle up to a little walking?'

'Yes, certainly.'

He came round to help her out and, with an intimate little gesture that made her catch her breath, reached for her hand and tucked it under his arm.

Though the sun was still shining, the air seemed appreciably cooler and a slight breeze had sprung up as they strolled through what had once been a thriving little vineyard.

Now the vines were overgrown and neglected and, through the grass and weeds that partially obscured them, Tina could see purple grapes hanging in great heavy clusters.

'I presume that a lot of these vines will have to come out?' Richard enquired.

'Not necessarily if they're healthy stock. Though some re-planting might be advisable, depending on what kind of wine you're hoping to produce.'

'I see… Well, I suggest that we discuss the whole thing later when you've had time to consider exactly what's involved.'

'I really don't think there's any point in—'

He pre-empted her refusal. 'Unless, having seen how badly neglected everything's been, you don't feel you want to take it on?'

She shook her head. 'No, it isn't that.' It was exactly the kind of challenge she would enjoy. Or *would have* enjoyed had the circumstances been other than they were.

'Then what is it?'

'I would have liked the job, but…'

'But?'

'In the circumstances, it w-would be awkward,' she stammered.

'You mean after last night?'

Her silence was answer enough.

Once again she wasn't acting as he might have expected but, as he'd only used the job offer as a ploy to get her to the castle, it didn't much matter if she did refuse it.

She was here, out of harm's way, so to speak, and here he intended her to stay just in case they tried to make contact by phone.

Following that train of thought, he frowned. They wouldn't be able to reach her at Cartel Wines—he'd seen to that but if they tried to contact her at home, the friend she was staying with would no doubt be able to give them her mobile number...

Which, come Monday, could pose a problem if he didn't do something about it...

As the silence lengthened uncomfortably, she glanced at him and, seeing the grim look on his face, said unhappily, 'I'm sorry...'

Collecting himself, he smiled down at her reassuringly. 'Don't worry about it... Let's go on up to the castle, shall we?'

They had returned to the main drive and followed it for perhaps half a mile when, at the end of a narrow track to the left, she saw part of a ruined tower built on a mound.

'That's Daland Tower,' Richard told her. 'All that's still standing of the original eleventh-century castle. Anders is a few hundred yards to the east. There, it's just coming into view...'

She caught a brief glimpse of grey walls and battlements but, before she could take any of it in, it had vanished from view behind a stand of tall trees decked in their autumn livery.

It wasn't until after they had climbed a little more and rounded the next bend that Richard stopped the car and she saw it clearly.

She caught her breath.

Small it might be, a castle in miniature, but it was a perfect little gem. Serene and enchanted, its grey towers and turrets etched against the deep blue of the sky, it was like something out of a fairy tale.

When, wholly entranced, she had gazed her fill, she turned shining eyes on her companion, who had been sitting quietly watching her reaction, and breathed, 'I'm not surprised you love it. It's wonderful.'

Her enthusiasm was so genuine, so spontaneous, that he found himself with very mixed feelings.

'Of course an old pile like this has its drawbacks,' he said carefully, 'and, though over the years parts of it have been modernized to make it more liveable in, structurally it's the same…'

'Which means it needs a great deal of maintenance and takes almost every penny the estate makes to keep it in good order.'

Turning her head to smile at him, she said dreamily, 'But it must be well worth it to have a place like this.'

Throwing in his hand, he admitted, 'I think so.'

Her eyes turned once more to the castle and, watching her glowing face, he thought she looked like a child gazing at something rare and magical.

He felt a strange pang. If only she hadn't been who she was; if only she had been as sweet and innocent as she appeared. But she was, and she wasn't.

After a few moments, as she continued to gaze, enraptured, he started the car and drove on.

As they passed a track to the right, he told her, 'Down there, beyond the back entrance, is the old stabling and coach house, the orangery, the herb garden and the kitchen gardens…'

Half hidden behind the towering grey walls of the castle, Tina could make out a sizable area of outbuildings and glasshouses.

'Apart from a couple of stalls that are in use,' Richard went on, 'the stabling has been converted into garages.'

'So you still have horses?'

'Two. Jupiter and Juno. Though Bradley disliked horses

and wanted Mother to get rid of them both, she refused to part with them.

'Until she got too ill to ride, on my visits home I used to go out with her. Do you ride?'

'I used to love to. Though it's been years since I was on a horse.'

They were nearing the castle now and, craning her neck, she cried excitedly, 'Oh, there's a moat...'

'Yes and quite a deep one. But where, in the past, it was one of the castle's main defences, these days it's simply home to a variety of ducks and carp.

'It's fed by an underground stream. The same stream supplied the household wells and, because of its pureness, kept the inhabitants free from the diseases caused by contaminated water.'

As they drew nearer she exclaimed, 'And what a lovely old bridge...'

In truth it was a picture, its lichen-covered stones draped with delicate trails of small-leafed creeper spangled with tiny mauve and white flowers.

'This bridge wasn't built until about a hundred and fifty years ago,' he told her as they drove across it and through an archway into a cobbled courtyard. 'Before that there was a wooden drawbridge and a portcullis.'

His voice holding a hint of derision, he added, 'Now it's your turn to cry, "How romantic!"'

Flushing a little, she said quietly, 'I'm sorry. Did I go over the top?'

Feeling ashamed, he brought the car to a halt in front of an imposing oak door and, taking her hand, raised it to his lips. 'No, I'm the one who should be sorry. I'm just being a bear. As a matter of fact it's nice to find someone genuinely enthusiastic about the old place.'

Despite his apology she still looked uncomfortable and,

watching her half-averted face, he cursed himself for the way he had lashed out at her simply because she liked it.

For one thing, none of this mess was her fault and, for another, if he lost ground it could easily wreck all his plans.

Bearing that in mind, he released the hand he was still holding, then turned to unfasten both their seat belts.

He was so close she could feel his breath on her cheek and she sat still as any statue.

When she continued to look straight ahead, using a single finger he turned her face to his.

'Forgive me?'

'There's nothing to forgive.'

'Kind and generous as well as beautiful,' he murmured softly.

His mouth was only inches from hers and she froze.

Afraid he was going to kiss her.

Afraid he wasn't.

His kiss, when it came, was as light as thistledown, but it scattered her wits, brought every nerve-ending in her body zinging into life and effortlessly rekindled that morning's burning desire. As her lips quivered beneath his, he ran the tip of his tongue between them, finding the silky, sensitive inner skin, teasing and tantalizing, coaxing them to part.

When they did, he deepened the kiss until her head reeled and, caught in a spell of sensual delight, she lost all sense of time and place.

Slipping his hand inside her jacket, he brushed his finger-tips lightly over her breasts and, feeling the nipples firm beneath his touch, smiled to himself. She was obviously a passionate woman and quick to respond, as he'd discovered that morning.

The only problem was that in deliberately arousing her he'd been hoist with his own petard and had felt as frustrated as hell ever since.

But now wasn't the time to take her to bed, he reminded himself, there were still things to do, things to be settled. There would be time for pleasure when everything was going smoothly.

CHAPTER FIVE

DRAWING away with reluctance, Richard said, 'We'd better go
in before Hannah, who never misses a thing though she's
nearly eighty, comes out to see what could be keeping us.'

As he spoke, one leaf of the heavy studded door opened
and a small woman, hardly bigger than a child, with a silver
bun and a very straight back, appeared.

'What did I tell you?' he murmured, and left the car to
come round and help Tina out.

In something of a daze, she picked up her shoulder bag and
allowed herself to be led across the cobbles to where the old
woman waited.

As they approached, the housekeeper, who was neatly
dressed in old-fashioned black and wore a jet necklace and
earrings, came forward to meet them.

'Mr Richard...' Her wizened face creased into a beam of
pleasure. 'Welcome home! Everything's ready for you.

'It seems to have turned a shade cooler and, as I know how
much you like a good fire, I've had one lit in the living-room.'
Then, with genuine emotion, 'It's nice to have you back.'

'It's nice to be back, Hannah.' His arm around Tina's shoulders, he added, 'This is the lady I told you about when I rang.'

Shrewd dark eyes, bright as a bird's, acknowledged Tina's
smile and weighed her up. Then, apparently satisfied with

what she saw, the housekeeper's face relaxed into a smile. 'It's a pleasure to meet you, Miss Dunbar. If you need a ladies' maid, please let me know.'

Hannah appeared to think they were staying and, before Richard could put her right, she went on, 'I've ordered roast pheasant for dinner, which cook's timing for seven-thirty if that suits you? But the kettle's just boiled if you'd like a cup of tea in the meantime?'

'We'd love one,' he told her. 'But get young Milly to do the running about.'

'I must admit that these days I'm glad to,' Hannah confessed. 'Though I keep very well, thank the good Lord, I'm not as nimble on my feet as I used to be.'

But, as though to disprove those words, she led the way into the hall in a sprightly fashion and disappeared through a small door at the rear.

The panelled hall, with its black oak floorboards and huge stone fireplace, was furnished with lovingly polished antiques and lit by long, intricately leaded windows that bore the maker's name and the date. On the right, an elegant oak staircase with a lion's head on the newel post climbed to a small minstrels' gallery.

Tina thought it was absolutely beautiful, but hesitated to say so. Even when Richard gave her an interrogative glance, she refrained from comment.

He turned to face her and, putting a hand against her cheek in an oddly remorseful gesture, remarked quietly, 'I'm sorry. It wasn't my intention to spoil it for you.'

Finding her voice, she said, 'You haven't. I'm enjoying it all very much.'

'But afraid to say so?'

'A little wary,' she admitted.

'Please don't be.' He bent his head and kissed her lightly on the lips, making her pulses leap, before going on, 'These rooms off the hall form the main living area. The breakfast room, the morning room, the formal dining-room…' As he spoke he led her round the hall, opening doors to show glimpses of beautiful old rooms with wood-panelled walls and period furniture.

'The library-cum-study,' he went on, 'is the only room where the twenty-first century has been allowed to hold unreserved sway…'

Glancing in, Tina saw a pleasant room with book-lined walls and an oak-panelled ceiling. Ranged on an impressive leather-topped desk was a businesslike computer and an array of up-to-date communication equipment.

'And next door is the living-room…' A hand at her waist, he led her into a beautifully proportioned room with panelled walls and a white ceiling. Once again the leaded windows that looked across the courtyard were a work of art executed and signed by a master craftsman.

Most of the furniture was antique and bore the glorious patina of age, but the soft natural leather suite grouped around the inglenook fireplace was up-to-date and comfortable-looking.

A log fire blazed cheerfully in the grate, a grandfather clock tick-tocked in the corner and flowers and photographs made the room feel lived-in and homely.

This time Tina said without hesitation, 'What a lovely room.'

He gave her the kind of smile that made her heart turn over. 'I'm glad you like it.'

'And not a television in sight,' she added quizzically, remembering the comments he'd made the previous evening.

His smile widened into a grin. 'It wasn't easy to bring in modern technology without spoiling the atmosphere. But *voilà*!'

Sliding aside the doors of a large and handsome oak cabinet, he revealed a state-of-the-art television, a video, a DVD player and a comprehensive music centre.

'All the trappings of modern-day entertainment,' he said a

shade wryly, 'though blessedly not on view unless they're in use.'

They had just settled themselves by the fireside when there was a tap at the door and a young maid brought in a tray of tea and cake.

'Thanks, Milly,' Richard said. Adding, 'We'll pour our own.'

While Tina sat in front of the fire, he helped her to tea in a delicate china cup and a slice of homemade fruit cake, before sitting down opposite.

Though the setting seemed relaxed and homely, the silence companionable, there was still an undercurrent of sexual tension that rasped along her nerves like rough silk and, as she sipped her tea, she watched him surreptitiously.

Leaning back, his long legs stretched towards the hearth, he looked completely at his ease and she envied his cool detachment.

Glancing up, he caught her eye.

Her colour rising, she looked hastily away.

Hiding a smile, he said conversationally, 'Tell me something; if you had no intention of taking the job, why did you agree to come?'

Her flush deepening, she confessed, 'I wanted to see the castle.'

'Ah,' he murmured softly.

'I'm sorry. I suppose it was a waste of your time.'

'Not at all,' he denied. 'I've enjoyed the day.'

'So have I,' she admitted. Then, reminding herself that it was something she *had* to do, she added, 'But I really ought to be getting back before too long. I've still got to find a hotel.'

Softly he said, 'After last night I was rather hoping you'd change your mind and stay with me.'

'Last night was a mistake,' she told him jerkily. 'If I hadn't had too much to drink…'

'And this morning?'

'That was a mistake too,' she insisted. 'I should never have let it happen.'

She sounded as if she meant it and he sighed inwardly. So much for trying to make sure she stayed. He could swear she still wanted him, but for some reason she was now playing hard to get.

He wondered why she was bothering. Was it possible that she was hoping for more than just an affair? Hoping to make him keen enough to get seriously involved?

In the past he'd frequently been the target for gold-diggers and women who were trying to land a rich husband, though usually they had gone about it in a different way.

However, if that *was* her aim and he moved with care, it could fit in nicely with his own plans.

The only thing he couldn't allow her was time…

When he remained silent, angry with herself for being weak enough to come, she said, 'If you were intending to stay here, as your housekeeper seems to think, I can always get a taxi back.'

It would cost a fortune but, having got herself into this mess…

'My dear Valentina,' he drawled, 'I haven't the slightest intention of allowing you to get a taxi. If you insist on going back, I'll take you myself.'

Uncomfortably, she said, 'Well, if you're sure you don't mind?'

'Of course I don't mind. I'm at your disposal. But, as you came to see the castle, it would be a shame to start back without taking a look at it, so I suggest a guided tour of the place and then dinner before we think of leaving. What do you say?'

There was only one thing she could say, and she said it. 'Thank you very much—that sounds lovely.'

'Sure your ankle will stand it?'

'Quite sure.'

'Then let's go.'

Leaving her bag where it was, she accompanied him across the hall and along a wide stone corridor.

'It's beginning to get dusk,' he remarked, 'so I suggest that, before we start the tour proper, we go up to the gatehouse, where there's a nice view across the park to the oval lake.'

As they began to climb the spiralling stone stairway, lit by candle bulbs in metal sconces, the air coming through the embrasures felt distinctly fresh and she half wished she had her coat, which she'd left in the car along with her case.

She found the gatehouse, with its huge stone fireplace and garderobe, fascinating, and lingered there for a while imagining what it must have been like when it was occupied. Only the realisation that time was flying and there was lots more to see made her move on.

Another flight of stone steps brought them to a small, thick, studded door, from which they emerged on to the roof of the gatehouse.

Tina glanced down into the courtyard, with its huge central well, now covered with a latticework of heavy metal, and, noticing that the Porsche was no longer there, remarked, 'Your car's gone.'

His voice casual, Richard said, 'Mullins must have presumed we were staying and put it away.'

Then, seeing she looked uneasy, 'Don't let it worry you; it's no major problem. After dinner, when we're ready to go, I can ask for it to be brought round. Now, come and look at the view.'

Hung with blue veils of twilight, the view across the rolling park to the faintly shimmering oval of the lake, the darkening woods and, closer at hand, Daland Tower, was beautiful.

One arm lightly around her shoulders, he pointed a steady finger. 'Over there, through a gap in the trees, you can just catch a glimpse of the lights of Farrington Hall. The O'Connells, who live there, are our nearest neighbours.'

The name *O'Connell* seemed oddly familiar, but it was a

moment or two before Tina recalled that it had been a Helen O'Connell who had been trying to phone Richard the previous day.

It was a lovely evening and above the western horizon, where a pinky-gold afterglow was fading into greeny-blue, a single bright star shone.

Half under her breath, she murmured the jingle she remembered from childhood, 'Starlight, star bright, first star I've seen tonight…'

'The evening star,' Richard said. 'Are you going to wish on it?'

'Why not?' she agreed lightly. 'Though I fear my wish might be unattainable.'

'So might mine. But nothing ventured nothing gained, so let's give it a try.'

Folding his arms around her, he drew her back against his hard, muscular body and held her there. Then, bending his head so that his cheek touched hers, he urged, 'Wish away.'

Knees turned to water by his nearness, and only too aware that she might as well wish for the moon, she looked up at the glittering star and silently wished that one day Richard might come to care for her.

After a little while when, rooted to the spot by the feel of his slightly roughened cheek against hers, she continued to stand quite still, he debated whether to make his move now.

Deciding the time wasn't right, he straightened and said prosaically, 'We'd better get on with the tour, otherwise we'll be late for dinner.'

Like someone in a dream, she turned to walk back the way they had come.

'Careful on the stairs,' he warned and, an arm at her waist, guided her somewhat uncertain steps back down the stone stairway and thence to the passageway, to begin their tour proper.

Her first impression on seeing Anders had been that it was

a gem of a place and that was amply confirmed as he showed her over it.

A picturesque castle with towers and turrets, secret passages and deep cellars, its own serenely beautiful little chapel with a resident priest, it was something very special. The fact that it was also a home made it rare indeed.

As they returned to the hall, glancing at his watch, Richard suggested, 'If you'd like to freshen up before dinner…?'

'Oh, yes, please.'

Having escorted her up the main staircase and past the minstrels' gallery, he opened a door on the right and ushered her inside a spacious suite, with a bedroom and bathroom either side of a central sitting-room.

'This suite was used by my parents when my father was alive,' he told her. 'My mother had this room as a den, to "sit and cogitate" as she put it, and deal with her correspondence.

'That's her escritoire.' He pointed to a small, exquisitely proportioned writing desk. 'It was made in the reign of Queen Anne.'

'It's absolutely beautiful,' Tina said, coming to take a closer look.

'My mother loved it. Apparently as a child she was fascinated by the fact that it has a secret drawer.

'When she came of age, her grandmother gave it to her as a twenty-first birthday present and she used it for the rest of her life.

'After my father died, and Mother remarried, these rooms were kept for my use when I visited the castle. Though Mother continued to use the sitting-room…

'This is the master bedroom…'

The master bedroom—simple yet grand, with its panelled walls and polished oak floorboards—had fine furniture and a handsomely carved four-poster bed with a scarlet and gold canopy.

'And this is the guest room...'

The guest room was equally spacious and beautiful, with period furniture and a four-poster bed with a dark blue tester.

One of the first things Tina noticed was that her coat and case had been brought up and placed on a low blanket chest.

Though Richard must have noticed it too, he made no comment. He merely went on, 'At one time this room was used as a dressing room. It was Mother's idea to make it into a guest bedroom, in case I wanted to bring a friend. Though I never did,' he added wryly.

Indicating the guest bathroom, he asked, 'How long do you need? Will fifteen minutes be enough?'

'Ample, thank you.'

'Then I'll have a quick shower and shave and wait for you in the hall.' He turned away.

Remembering the intimacy of that morning, she felt a queer sense of loss and disappointment. But she recognised that it was *her* attitude that was responsible for the change in him. *She* had altered things by her refusal to get involved any further.

Biting her lip, she went into an ivory and peach tiled bathroom which was not only well-equipped but sumptuous in the extreme, with a shelf full of luxurious toiletries, a couple of towelling robes and a pile of big soft towels.

It was in marked contrast to the bathroom in Ruth's bedsit, which was small and dingy, with a rusty boiler, a cracked sink and a shower stall that leaked.

When Tina had finished showering and dried herself, she wondered whether or not to change. Perhaps Richard wouldn't bother as they were going straight back to London after they'd eaten?

But a suit and flat-heeled shoes seemed all wrong for dining in a castle, and as her case was handy...

After a quick sort through what few clothes she had

brought, she decided on a silky dress the purply-blue of heliotrope and, her ankle having so far stood the strain, a pair of high-heeled court shoes.

As she stood in front of an elegant cheval-glass to brush and re-coil her hair, she saw the four-poster reflected in it and imagined her friend's reaction to a bedroom like this.

Thinking about Ruth, it struck Tina what a lot she would have to tell her on Monday.

Only there were some things she couldn't even tell Ruth. Things that were far too intimate, far too precious, to talk about to anyone.

Sighing, she gazed into the mirror. Her eyes looked big and dark with secrets, her cheeks and lips a little pale.

With eyebrows and lashes that were naturally several shades darker than her hair, she didn't need mascara, but some blusher and a touch of lip gloss would improve things enormously.

Her small cosmetic case was in her bag and she toyed with the idea of slipping downstairs to fetch it, before deciding there wasn't really time.

Ready to go down, she debated whether or not to take her coat and case with her. But in the end she put her coat over her arm and left her case where it was. No doubt Richard would ask whoever had taken it up to fetch it down again.

Though she was in good time, as she descended the stairs she saw that he was waiting for her in the hall. He had not only showered and shaved but had changed into a well-cut dinner jacket.

He looked heart-stoppingly virile and handsome and she felt all quivery inside to think what might have happened if, rather than going back to London, she'd been staying here.

But she *wasn't* staying, she reminded herself sharply. As soon as dinner was over they were leaving for town.

Stepping forward, he took her hand. 'You look delightful. That colour exactly matches your eyes.'

A shade awkwardly, she said, 'I wasn't sure whether you'd bother changing.'

Relieving her of her coat, he put it over a dark oak settle and tucked her hand through his arm. 'Given the circumstances, I wouldn't, only Mullins had laid everything out ready for me and I didn't want to hurt his feelings.

'Now, how about a pre-dinner drink in the study?'

'A drink?' She sounded as horrified as she felt.

Glancing at her, he burst out laughing.

He had a nice laugh, deep and infectious. 'If you could see your face!' Still smiling, he went on, 'I don't blame you for being wary, but I promise I was going to suggest something innocuous. A small sherry at the most. Nothing that would induce a hangover.'

'Thank heaven for that,' she said with feeling. And thought that with his tawny eyes still gleaming with amusement and his lean cheeks creased with laughter lines, he was totally irresistible.

He led her to the library-cum-study, where a cheerful log fire burnt in the grate and a drinks trolley waited.

'So what's it to be?'

Taking a seat by the fire, she said, 'I'll have that small sherry, please.'

'Cream or dry?'

'Dry.'

When he'd handed her a glass he sat down opposite and smiled at her.

'Aren't you having a drink?'

'As I'll be driving shortly, I'd better stick to a glass of wine with the meal.'

'I'm sorry,' she said. 'I feel guilty.'

'There's really no need. You made it clear from the start that you intended to go back to town and book into a hotel. I was just hoping that when you saw Anders you might change your mind.

'If you don't like the idea of sharing my bed,' he went on, 'you could always sleep in solitary state in the guest room.'

She was sorely tempted. But if she agreed to stay and he turned on the heat, could she trust herself to hold out against him?

As he waited for her answer, he decided that if this gamble didn't come off he would have to use delaying tactics until he found some other way to keep her here. *Without rousing her suspicions.*

When still she hesitated he asked, 'Have you ever slept in a four-poster bed in a castle?'

Silently she shook her head.

'Then why don't you try it?' he said persuasively. 'It would be a new experience.'

Through lips that felt oddly stiff, she said, 'No, I'd rather stick to my original plan,' and braced herself to withstand an onslaught.

But, to her surprise, he gave in immediately and with good grace. 'Very well. If that's really what you want...'

Seeing that surprise and knowing he needed to disarm her, he added in a businesslike tone, 'With regard to a hotel, I suggest the Rochester on Crombie Street. It's far from luxurious, but it's pleasant and central and not too expensive.'

'That sounds fine,' she agreed. 'As we'll be late back, it might be as well if I fetch my bag and give them a ring now.'

Damn! he thought. So much for trying to disarm her.

As she started to rise, he pressed her gently back. 'Don't worry, I'll talk to reception while you drink your sherry.'

He crossed to his desk and, picking up the phone, queried, 'Shall I make it tonight *and* tomorrow?'

Already regretting her decision, but knowing it was the right one, she said huskily, 'Please.'

Depressing the receiver rest, he pretended to make the booking.

While she listened, and watched his broad back, she wondered what had made him give in so easily.

The answer came swiftly. Though it would no doubt have suited him if she *had* stayed, it was obviously of no great importance. If *she* wasn't willing, there must be plenty of women who were.

But *she* wasn't cut out for affairs. She couldn't treat sex lightly, or as just another appetite to be indulged, as most men and a lot of today's women seemed able to do.

If Richard had been an ordinary man and she and he had been in love with each other and intending to stay together, it would have been different.

But he wasn't, and they weren't.

And, no matter how much she wanted him, her pride, her self-respect, insisted that she shouldn't let herself be swept up and then discarded at a rich man's whim...

'All settled,' he said, replacing the receiver and returning to his chair by the fire.

'Thank you.' In the end he'd been very civilized about it and she was grateful.

Though she couldn't regret coming to Anders—it would always shine in her memory—she was guiltily aware that, despite his earlier polite denial, he would no doubt regard it as a wasted day.

As though reading her mind, he said, 'I hope you're not sorry you came to the castle?'

'No, I'm not. I've loved being here and seeing over it. The only thing I *am* sorry about is that I've wasted your day.'

'I can assure you I don't regard it as a wasted day. Apart from enjoying your company, which I do very much, it's a pleasure to have someone here who genuinely likes the old place...'

When her sherry was finished, he led the way to a long white-walled dining-room where a refectory table was beautifully set with fine linen, crystal glasses and fresh flowers.

Throughout an excellent meal, as though to put her at her ease, he played the suave host, talking easily about the history of the castle and the Anders family. 'At one time the estate supported a lot of tenant farmers and labourers who owed their allegiance to the family…'

With a little crooked smile that made her heart start to beat faster, he went on, 'It all sounds a bit feudal, doesn't it?'

'It does rather.'

'But, from what I've read in the archives, most of the Anders were good overlords and their serfs and vassals—some of the descendants of whom still live on the estate—were well-treated.'

'How big is the present-day estate?'

He told her, adding, 'It used to be considerably larger. But, before my great-grandfather went into banking, the need to raise money for taxes and death duties had meant selling off certain of the more lucrative areas.

'Luckily there was plenty to go at. The family, who were staunch Royalists, had been given huge tracts of land for their loyalty to the Crown.'

'What happened when Cromwell came to power?'

'It could well have been the end of them all. But when, after the battle of Worcester, a lot of Royalist strongholds were laid waste, because one of Cromwell's closest friends and allies had married Lady Eleanor Anders, the castle and its occupants were mercifully spared…'

As soon as their coffee was finished, Tina—who had been psyching herself up to mention leaving—was about to speak when Richard forestalled her by asking, 'About ready to go?'

'I'll just get my coat and bag.'

'While you do that I'll ring for Mullins to bring your case down and fetch the car round.'

She had just collected her belongings when Richard

appeared and said, 'I'm afraid Mullins is out at the moment, but his wife is expecting him back in half an hour or so...'

'Oh,' Tina said a little blankly. 'But can't we—'

'It seems,' Richard added smoothly, 'that he has the car keys in his pocket and unfortunately I've left the spare set in town.'

Before she could think of anything to say, he went on, 'As it's a beautiful moonlit night, I suggest that, rather than just sitting indoors waiting for him, we take a stroll along the battlements.'

Helping her into her coat, he added, 'We may be lucky enough to see our resident ghost.'

Distracted, she exclaimed, 'A ghost?'

'Have you ever seen a ghost?'

She shook her head. 'Have you?'

'No,' he admitted.

'I'm not sure I believe in them.'

'But are you sure you *don't?* There are quite a few sightings of Mag mentioned in the archives.'

'Mag?'

'Today we'd say Maggie, but apparently in the Middle Ages the short form Mag was common.'

Opening the top drawer of a walnut bureau, he took out a pencil torch and slipped it into his pocket. 'Come along then, and I'll tell you all about her as we go.'

Wondering why he needed a torch on a moonlit night, she allowed herself to be escorted to the east tower. There, they climbed the spiralling stone steps and at the top emerged on to the battlements.

The sky was a deep velvety blue with a huge silver disk of moon hanging above the eastern rim of trees. Though it looked shimmering and insubstantial as any mirage, its pale ethereal light was almost as bright as day, yet strangely eerie.

In this kind of setting, she could almost imagine seeing a ghost.

As they started to stroll along the walls, the scented air cool and silky against her face, she shivered a little with nervous excitement.

'Cold?' he asked.

'No, not really.'

He put an arm around her all the same and she found herself glad of it.

'You were going to tell me about your ghost,' she prompted as they walked on.

'According to the legend, Mag was the beautiful and chaste young daughter of Lord Anders's household steward. She fell madly in love with Sir Gerwain, the son of a neighbouring nobleman.

'He told her he loved her and promised that when his elderly father died and he was his own master, he would marry her. They used to meet in Daland Tower, away from prying eyes, and on moonlit nights he would ride over to keep their trysts.

'Mag used to climb up to the battlements to watch for him and when she saw him coming she would slip down a hidden stairway to the cellars and take a secret passage that comes out inside the tower.'

Frowning, Tina asked, 'But what about the moat?'

'The passage runs beneath the moat. It's quite a clever bit of construction.'

With a grin, he added, 'As a boy, it used to be my escape route if I wanted to leave the castle without anyone knowing.'

'Is it still there?'

'Certainly. I could take you through it now if—'

'Oh, yes, please,' she broke in eagerly. It would be another unique memory.

He frowned. 'What about those heels?'

'Is it very rough?'

'A bit tricky in parts, but not a great deal worse than the climb up here.'

'In that case I can manage perfectly well.'

'You don't suffer from claustrophobia?'

'No.'

'Then let's go.' He shepherded her to the west tower, where a low door at the head of the stairway gave on to what appeared to be a short dead-end passage, until his torch showed up a small opening on the left.

'It isn't lit, so I'd better lead the way.'

Stooping a little, the torch lighting up the rough stone, they descended a small stairway hidden in the thickness of the wall until the steps gave way to a low tunnel.

'Go carefully through here,' he warned.

Cramped and narrow, built of old brick with an arched roof, the tunnel sloped downwards for a while before levelling out.

The air was unpleasantly dank, the walls black in parts and slimy to the touch, the hard-packed earth floor decidedly damp and slippery.

Tina was just thinking that she wouldn't be sorry when they reached the end, when the torch flickered and went out, leaving them in total darkness.

She gave an involuntary gasp and stood quite still. After a second or two she heard a movement and, needing reassurance, reached out to touch him.

But her searching hand found nothing and, in the silence, the terrifying thought popped into her head that he had walked away and abandoned her in this Stygian blackness.

CHAPTER SIX

BITING back the surge of panic, Tina told herself not to be ridiculous and said, 'Richard?' To her everlasting credit, her voice was steady.

'I'm here.' A hand reached out of the pitch-blackness and took hers. 'All right?'

'Yes.'

'I was just checking the torch. I'm afraid the bulb's gone.'

'What do we do now?'

'As we're about halfway, we may as well go on.'

'Very well,' she agreed.

His fingers tightened on hers. 'All you have to do is move slowly and carefully and keep your head down. For a while it's relatively straight and level, then it starts to gradually climb again.'

For what seemed an age, they moved forward at a snail's pace and eventually the ground began to slope upwards. Hampered by her high heels, it became more difficult to keep her footing and her ankle started to throb painfully.

She was accordingly grateful when Richard announced, 'Not far now.'

After a few more yards he released her hand. 'Wait here a moment.'

Once again she experienced that scary feeling of being abandoned in the smothering darkness and was forced to bite her lip.

Then she heard the brush of feet on stone, the scrape of metal on metal and the protesting creak of old hinges. A moment later moonlight came flooding coldly in to illuminate a flight of crumbling steps.

Richard returned to take her hand and they climbed them together, emerging through a small iron-banded door into a roofless half-ruined tower full of bright moonlight and deep shadow.

'So this is where they used to meet,' she said wonderingly.

'Yes. But of course in those days it was merely deserted, not ruined. However, despite the state it's in, it's steeped in history and well worth seeing.'

Closing the door behind them, he turned to look at her and, taking a spotless handkerchief from his pocket, cleaned a smear of black from her cheek. Then, wiping the hand he had used to follow the tunnel wall, he continued, 'However, given the ordeal you've just gone through, you must be sorry you ever agreed to come.'

'No, not at all. It was quite an experience.'

From the picture he'd built up in his mind after reading Grimshaw's reports, he wouldn't have thought her capable of exercising such self-control and the fact that she'd taken things so calmly had both surprised and intrigued him.

Raising her hand to his lips, he said quietly, 'I thought you might go to pieces, but obviously I'd underestimated your courage.'

As he had underestimated her beauty.

Still holding her hand, he looked into her face, made both fascinating and mysterious by the moonlight, his eyes lingering on her mouth.

Flustered by his praise and afraid that if he kissed her she would weaken, she half turned away. 'At least I wasn't alone, as Mag must have been. And presumably she had only a taper or a candle.'

'Which was, I daresay, somewhat more reliable than our torch,' he commented dryly.

Tina had started to smile when, taking her completely by surprise, he turned her into his arms and lifted her face to his. For an instant he looked down at her with queer darkened eyes, then his mouth covered hers.

Her lips parted helplessly beneath the masterful pressure of his and he deepened the kiss, reawakening all the clamouring demons of that morning and sending pleasure coursing through her like red-hot lava.

Lost in a world of sensual delight, she was limp and quivering, almost mindless with desire, when a warning bell began to ring and she stiffened.

His blood heated with anticipation of the night ahead, Richard found it far from easy to play a waiting game, but, feeling that tacit resistance, he ended the kiss and lifted his head.

Drawing a deep, ragged breath, she told herself that she was thankful he'd called a halt. She had virtually no defences against him and if he *hadn't* drawn away when he did, if he'd laid her down there and then on the moonlit grass, she would have been his for the taking.

And he would have thought her easy.

For a moment or two she struggled to pull herself together. When she had, to some extent, succeeded, she found her voice and said a little breathlessly, 'The tower's bigger than I first thought. How many rooms did it have?'

He told her and began to point out where the different floors had once been, where the fireplaces had been situated and where the old stone stairs had spiralled upwards.

When she had seen all there was to see, he turned away and reached to take her hand. Afraid of his touch, afraid of weakening, she pulled it free.

Without comment, he led the way through a gap in the crumbling walls, where long grass and weeds were thrusting up between the fallen stones.

Favouring her bad ankle and trying her best not to hobble, she followed him as best she could.

He made no further attempt to hold her hand; indeed he appeared to be deep in thought as they headed back towards the castle.

They were skirting the beechwood—the glorious blaze of colour bleached to a pale bluey-purple by the moonlight—when, wanting to break the silence, she reminded him, 'You didn't finish telling me what happened to Mag.'

He roused himself and said, 'I'm afraid it's a sad tale. One night, it seems, she waited for Sir Gerwain in vain and the next day she learnt—'

Tina was looking up at him, concentrating on what he was telling her, when her injured ankle turned painfully.

At her little gasp, he stopped speaking abruptly and threw an arm around her to steady her as she wobbled on one leg.

His voice grim, he said, 'I should have had more sense than to take you walking in those heels.'

'I should have had more sense than wear them,' she admitted ruefully.

He took off his jacket and, spreading it on the grass, lowered her on to it. Then, squatting down, he examined her ankle, which was already showing signs of swelling.

'Well, that settles it,' he announced firmly. 'You can't possibly go back to town in this state. The best place for you is bed.'

'Oh, but I—'

Rising to his feet, he said, 'There's no way you can walk on that. A cold compress, a good night's sleep and we'll see how it is in the morning…'

He'd had two objectives and his first had been achieved

more or less by chance. Now, with a bit of luck, he could make use of that same chance to achieve his second.

'However,' he went on, 'at the moment our priority is to get you back.'

Gathering herself, she made a valiant attempt to struggle up.

'Stay where you are,' he ordered. 'No doubt we *could* make it back under our own steam, but it's a fair distance, so it would make more sense to have some transport.'

She was waiting for him to say he would walk back and fetch the car, when he asked, 'Do you have your mobile handy? I'm afraid I left mine in my jacket pocket when I changed.'

'Yes.' She fished in her shoulder bag and produced her phone.

'Thanks… I'll ask Mullins to drive round and fetch us…

'Ah, Mullins,' he said after a moment, 'Miss Dunbar has hurt her ankle walking back from Daland Tower. We're by the beechwood, if you could pick us up…'

Then, to Tina, 'He'll be here directly.' Switching off the phone, he slipped it casually into his trousers pocket and sat down beside her, his muscular thigh brushing hers. 'Now, I was telling you about Mag. Where had I got to exactly?'

'One night Sir Gerwain didn't turn up…' she prompted somewhat distractedly.

'Right… Well, the next day, Mag learnt that he was about to marry a lady of rank. A lady he'd been betrothed to since they were both children.

'Left pregnant and alone, Mag threw herself off the battlements into the moat.

'But, if the ghostly legend is to be believed, on moonlit nights she still walks there, waiting for her faithless lover.'

Hearing Tina's sigh, he said, 'I told you it was a sad story.'

'To be honest, I hadn't expected anything else. I've never heard of any ghost who haunted a place because he or she had been happy there.'

His teeth gleamed as he laughed. 'And I always thought it was men who were practical and women who were romantic.'

'Perhaps it is as a rule.'

Looking into her eyes, he said, 'But you're a fascinating mixture of both.' Then, sounding almost surprised, 'I've never met a woman who intrigued me as much as you do.'

The intensity of his gaze was as intimate as a touch. It made her senses reel.

Still gazing into her eyes, he leaned forward and, while she sat there as though mesmerized, touched his lips lightly to hers.

Then, a hand on her nape, he deepened the kiss until there was nothing in the whole world but him and what he was making her feel.

Eyes closed, heart pounding, she had just accepted that she was lost, when he drew away and said, 'Mullins will be here at any moment.'

As he spoke she heard an engine and a second or two later an estate car came bumping over the rough grass towards them.

Richard helped her up and into the car before pulling on his jacket and climbing in beside her.

'If I'm not going back to town tonight—' she spoke the thought aloud '—I ought to let the hotel know.'

'Don't worry,' he said easily. 'I'll take care of that as soon as we get back.'

When they reached the castle, Mullins drove carefully over the cobbled courtyard and, stopping by the impressive door, got out to open it, while Richard came round to Tina's side and, stooping, instructed, 'Put your arms round my neck.'

When she obeyed, he lifted her out effortlessly and carried her inside, saying to Mullins on the way, 'Thanks and goodnight.'

'Goodnight, sir, madam.'

'Goodnight,' Tina said huskily.

Though she tried to stay calm, being held in Richard's arms

and cradled against his broad chest made her heart start to throw itself against her ribcage and her breathing quicken and grow ragged.

Since she had first seen him standing in Cartel's loading bay she had been drawn to him, fascinated by him, beguiled and bewitched.

And that dark enchantment and the sexual tension that accompanied it had never slackened. In fact it had increased, so that she no longer trusted her ability to be strong, to follow the course she had set herself…

But somehow she had to hide that growing weakness, otherwise he would take advantage of it and then she would lose what little was left of her pride…

As he carried her up the stairs and into his suite she realised that, like the previous night, though *her* breathing had quickened, his hadn't altered in the slightest.

Carrying her through to the guest room, he said, 'I presume, from all you said earlier, that you'd prefer to sleep here.'

It was a statement rather than a question and it made it easier to answer, 'Yes, thank you. I would,' and sound as if she meant it.

When she had dropped her bag on the nearest chair he carried her into the bathroom and, setting her down carefully, helped her off with her coat before asking, 'Shall I ring for one of the maids?'

'Oh, no. There's no need to disturb anyone so late. I can manage perfectly well.'

'In that case I'll fetch your bag.'

Returning with them almost immediately, he queried, 'Sure you're all right for the moment?'

'Quite sure, thank you.'

'Then I'll ring the hotel and find some strapping for that ankle.'

Handicapped as she was, it took her longer than usual to

shower, clean her teeth and put on her nightdress and gown. Finally, warm and dry and scented, she brushed out her long corn-gold hair. Normally, for bed, she braided it, but, fearing a plait might look childish, she returned to the bedroom with it loose around her shoulders.

He was sitting in one of the low chairs, his long legs stretched out, his ankles crossed negligently.

Rising to his feet at her approach, he said lightly, 'All ready with the first aid kit.'

'I'm sorry to have been so long,' she apologized.

'Considering the difficulties, I think you've been re-remarkably quick...'

He turned the quilt back. 'Now, then, if you'd like to get into bed, I'll take a look at that ankle.'

Her calf-length nightdress was relatively modest and, slipping off her gown, she got into bed, praying he would do what he needed to do and go quickly.

When she was settled against the pillows, he examined her ankle once more, his strong fingers gently probing the slight swelling.

Seeing her wince, he said, 'It should be a lot less painful once it's strapped up.'

Taking a pad soaked in something cold and a stretch bandage, he sat down on the edge of the bed and proceeded to deftly apply them.

'There—' he tucked the end in neatly '—how does that feel?'

'Much better already, thank you.'

'With a bit of luck it will be as good as new by morning.' He rose to his feet and pulled the quilt up in preparation for going.

She was just breathing a sigh of relief when he sat down again and studied her face. 'You look a bit pale and tense; would you like a hot drink and a couple of painkillers before I leave you?'

Very conscious of him, she shook her head. 'Thank you, but I don't really need them. My ankle's fine while I'm lying down.

It only hurts when I try to put any weight on it…' Realising that nervousness was making her babble, she stopped abruptly.

'Then if there's nothing else I can do for you, I'll say goodnight.'

Leaning over, he kissed her, his mouth brushing hers lightly, seductively. Then, his lips tracing the soft underside of her chin and travelling down the creamy column of her throat, he whispered, 'Unless you've changed your mind about sharing my bed?'

Feeling as though she was drowning in honey, she struggled against the temptation to say she had. Though she couldn't remember anything about it, she was no longer a virgin, so what had she got to lose?

Her self-respect, that was what! And it was important to her. Last night she had been drunk and unable to help herself, but tonight she was stone cold sober and responsible for her actions.

'I want to make love to you,' he murmured softly, while his hands found the soft curves of her breasts and the firming nipples beneath the thin satin of her nightdress, 'I want to sleep with you in my arms, to wake to find you beside me and make love to you all over again… Tell me you want it, too…'

Her lips moved, but no sound came.

'Tell me,' he insisted.

'I can't!' It was almost a sob. 'I can't…'

'Why can't you? I know you want me. Your whole body's telling me so.'

'I've never…' She swallowed hard, then went on desperately, 'I've never gone in for one-night stands or casual sex and I don't want to start now.'

He frowned a little. 'Who said anything about a one-night stand or casual sex? Neither the way I feel about you, nor my intentions are in any way casual.'

His words held a ring of truth and her heart leapt. If it really *was* true, it altered everything.

Then common sense told her not to be foolish. How could he feel anything for her when they'd only known each other for twenty-four hours?

But why couldn't he?

What she felt for him, whether she called it infatuation or falling in love, was anything but casual. In fact it was so strong, so overwhelming, it made anything she had felt for Kevin fade into insignificance.

Shaken and confused, she stared down at the old patchwork quilt, its colours faded and mellowed by time, while a part of her mind, standing detached, aloof, thought how pretty it was.

After a moment or two when, head bent, she remained silent, he rose to his feet and said evenly, 'Sleep well. I'll see you in the morning.'

She watched him head for the door, her thoughts racing. Just for the sake of her pride or the fear of what the future might hold, was she going to let him walk away? Turn her back on this chance to be with him? If it all ended in tears, at least she would have known some happiness…

His hand was on the latch when she spoke his name.

Though her voice was barely above a whisper, he turned and looked at her.

'Please don't go.'

He came to the side of the bed and, his handsome face alight with satisfaction and triumph, asked, 'You've never slept in a centuries-old four-poster on a goosefeather bed?'

'No.' Nor did she know what it was like to sleep in a man's arms.

Pulling back the quilt, he scooped her up. 'Then this will be a first.'

In the master bedroom, which was unlit save for a log fire that blazed cheerfully in the wide stone hearth, the air smelt pleasantly of pine-resin, beeswax and lavender. The pillows on the splendid four-poster had been plumped up and the bedclothes turned down invitingly.

He carried her over to the bed, which was so high that on either side there was a wooden step up to it, and laid her down. Saying, 'We won't need this,' he eased her night-dress over her head and tossed it aside, before pulling up the covers.

When he had quickly stripped off his own clothes and hung them over a chair, he disappeared into the bathroom, promising softly, 'I won't be long.'

As the door closed behind him, some lines from an anony-mous poem began to run through her head:

> The day had faded fast and gone,
> and in that shining night,
> he offered me a precious gift,
> a promise of delight...

A thrill of excitement and anticipation ran through her, making her breath catch in her throat and her heart beat er-ratically.

Moonlight gleamed on the casements and somewhere close at hand an owl hooted with melancholy mirth, while in the grate a log slipped and settled, sending up a shower of bright sparks and making long shadows dance across the ceiling.

The bathroom door opened and he came out, his dark hair still damp from the shower and without a stitch on, as she had seen him that morning.

Was it only that morning? It seemed so long ago.

She had thought then what a magnificent male animal he was. Now, she couldn't take her eyes off him. Every bone in her body seemed to melt with longing and her entire being cried out for his possession.

Her face must have registered what she was thinking and

feeling, because he said in a voice shaken between passion and laughter, 'When you look at me like that you make me feel like Suleiman.'

He slid beneath the covers and joined her.

The moment he touched her she began to tremble.

Running his hands down her slender body and feeling her response, he said softly, 'You're all fizz and sparkle, like champagne.

'But though champagne is heady and exhilarating, it's light, surface stuff.'

Taking first one pink nipple in his mouth and then the other, he suckled sweetly while his long fingers found the silken warmth of her inner thighs.

Not wanting it to be over almost before it had begun, she tried to push his hand away, to hold back. But he would have none of it.

A few seconds later she gave a little cry as sensation followed sensation, like surface ripples on a pool that spread in ever-widening circles round a flung stone.

When the sensations had died away, unconsciously she sighed. Though he had given her a great deal of pleasure, she had wanted the experience to be a *shared* one…

As she lay with closed eyes, he kissed her and said, 'Now the fizz has been disposed of we can go on to enjoy something altogether deeper and more rewarding, like a rich, satisfying Burgundy.'

His hands began to move lightly over her, stroking and caressing, making each nerve-ending spring into life and effortlessly reviving the desire she had thought sated.

By the time he fitted himself into the cradle of her hips, eager for his possession, she welcomed his weight. Even so, his first strong thrust made her gasp and, as though taken by surprise, he paused and asked, 'Did I hurt you?'

'Yes… No… It doesn't matter.' With an instinct as old as

Eve, she lifted her hips enticingly and he began to move again, but a little more cautiously.

'All right?' he queried after a moment or two.

Caught up now in a spiralling pleasure, she was past answering, but her flung back head and soft gasping cries were answer enough.

Reassured, he carried them both to a shattering climax that sent them tumbling and spinning through time and space.

Wrapped in black velvet, the sensations so deep and intense that she was shaken to the very core of her being, she lay beneath him, shuddering helplessly.

At the same time she felt exalted, omnipotent, the feel of his flesh against hers and the weight of his dark head on her breast a priceless gift.

She knew a sudden poignant happiness. He was her man. Her mate. Her *love*.

So this was what love was really like, what all the love songs and poetry added up to. Two people coming together and meeting on every level, a meeting as much spiritual as physical.

She could only feel glad that, instead of giving herself lightly for a moment's gratification, she had waited for this one man.

When their breathing and heart rate returned to something like normal, he lifted himself away and turned on his back. Then, gathering her close, he settled her head comfortably at the juncture between chest and shoulder and, his arm holding her securely, bent his head to kiss her.

His kiss seemed gentle and caring and she found herself hoping against hope that he shared at least some of her feelings.

After a little while she became aware of a quiet but persistent thought tugging at the sleeve of her consciousness, trying to gain her attention. Still euphoric, unwilling to think, she mentally waved it away. But refusing to be banished, it became even more insistent.

It was another moment or two before she identified it, then

surprise made her blurt out what she was now certain of. 'You *didn't* make love to me… Last night, I mean…'

'No,' he agreed.

'But I thought… Though I couldn't remember, I was sure we'd slept together…'

'So we had. That is to say, we slept in the same bed. That's all.'

'I don't understand why…'

She felt the movement as he glanced down at her. 'You went out like a light so, apart from taking off your clothes, I never laid a finger on you. I cursed myself for getting you in that state, but by then it was too late.'

'But you said we'd…'

Realising he'd never actually *said* anything, she changed it to, 'You deliberately made me think we'd slept together.'

'When you jumped to that conclusion, I just didn't correct you.'

And she could guess why not. With her believing they were already lovers, tonight's seduction had been so much easier. Had she known the truth, would she have behaved differently?

But it was too late to ask herself that.

'Mad with me?' he queried.

She ought to be.

But she wasn't really.

How could she be mad with a man who had given her so much, and with such tenderness?

'No,' she whispered.

His arm tightened round her.

Beneath her cheek she could feel the strong, steady beat of his heart, hear the quiet evenness of his breathing, smell the scent of his skin, with its heady combination of fresh perspiration and shower gel.

It was so sweet, so intimate, that she gave thanks as she

lay blissfully savouring the warmth and happiness, the feeling of belonging, of having finally come home.

She was still marvelling at the peace and beauty of it when sleep crept up and wrapped her in a soft, dark blanket.

Next morning she awoke to full remembrance and a singing happiness. A smile on her lips, she turned her head to look at Richard, but she was alone in the big four-poster.

Sunshine was streaming in through the leaded glass of the windows and a glance at her watch showed it was almost a quarter to nine.

Some time during the night he had wakened her with a kiss and made long, delectable love to her once more and, though a little tender in parts, her body felt as sleek and well-satisfied as a pampered pedigree cat.

She stretched luxuriously, while her mind drifted on a cloud of euphoria. She had found her one and only love. He filled her heart and banished her loneliness, satisfied a gnawing hunger that had never been fed.

He was so right for her. He had strength and humour, warmth and understanding, a willingness to reach out, to meet her on her own ground.

Yet, like herself, he had a certain reserve, so there would always be thoughts and dreams to surprise. An element of spice to keep their relationship fresh.

Their relationship...

Like a train hitting the buffers, her rhapsodizing came to an abrupt halt. Could she call what they had a *relationship*?

Why not? she thought boldly. Though it was still in its early stages, it *was* a relationship. Hadn't he made it clear that his feelings and his intentions weren't merely casual?

It was a start and if, in spite of their vastly different backgrounds and lifestyles, he could come to care for her, she could ask no more of life.

And if he couldn't?

She pushed the intrusive thought away.

At least she knew what it was like to really be in love, and it was a marvellous feeling! No wonder people said that love made the world go round.

All at once she wanted to say it out loud, to shout it from the rooftops.

Bubbling over with excitement, she decided that as soon as she had showered and dressed she would ring her flatmate.

Normally, she wouldn't have made contact until Jules had gone back to Paris, but her news was so exciting she just couldn't wait to tell somebody.

Ruth, who knew nothing of the weekend's events and still thought Tina was staying in London with one of their friends, would be surprised, to say the least. But when she had heard everything, she would understand and be pleased…

Climbing out of the high bed, Tina cautiously tested her ankle. Finding it supported her without pain, she gathered up her discarded nightdress and, her bare feet squeaking a little on the polished oak floorboards, made her way back to the guest room.

Fresh and glowing from the shower, she brushed her blonde hair and, leaving it loose around her shoulders, pulled on clean underwear, a pair of cream trousers and a silky shirt the colour of burnt toffee.

Her ankle had returned to virtually normal, so she left the strapping off and donned flat slip-ons, all the time anticipating Ruth's reaction to her wonderful news.

She had located her bag and started to fish around for her phone before she recalled that Richard had borrowed it the previous evening and must have absent-mindedly pocketed it.

Well, she would have to find him and ask him for it. Unless… On an impulse she returned to the master bedroom, where the suit he had worn had been hung over a chair.

Locating his jacket, after a momentary hesitation, she felt in the nearest pocket.

There was no sign of her phone, but her fingers closed around his pencil torch which lit as she inadvertently pressed the button.

So the bulb hadn't gone after all. If Richard had paused long enough to double-check, it would have saved that long, slow, nightmare journey through the Stygian passageway.

The second pocket yielded nothing more than the handkerchief he had wiped her cheek with, and only then did she recall that she had been *sitting* on his jacket. Which meant he must have slipped the phone into his trousers pocket.

Feeling uncomfortable, but *committed* now, she gritted her teeth and searched both pockets, but once again she drew a blank.

Oh, well, she would just have to go down and ask him what he'd done with it.

Her step light, a smile on her lips as she imagined how he'd lift her face to his and kiss her, she left the suite and descended the elegant oak staircase.

As she paused to stroke the lion's head on the newel post, Hannah appeared in the hall, neat and Sundayish in a sober black hat, a prayer book in her gloved hand.

'Good morning, Miss Dunbar. I hope you slept well?'

Feeling her cheeks grow warm at the innocent enquiry, Tina answered, 'Very well, thank you, Hannah. You're off to church?'

Her manner prim, Hannah said, 'It's customary for all the staff to attend the Sunday morning service at our own chapel.'

Flustered by her previous lack of thought, Tina hastened to say, 'Of course. It must be a great blessing to have a resident priest.'

'Indeed it is,' Hannah told her. Adding proudly, 'The Reverend Peter has been in the family's service and lived in the rooms adjoining the chapel ever since he was ordained nearly fifty years ago.'

'What a wonderful record.'

'Apart from the mistress's second marriage, which took place in a register office, he's officiated at every wedding, christening and funeral of both the family and the staff.

'It's his dearest wish, before he's called to his maker, to officiate at the master's wedding.

'When Miss O'Connell's family first moved into Farrington Hall and the young couple became friendly, we began to wonder if she might be the one. But after the mistress's death, Mr Richard no longer came home and Miss O'Connell stopped calling…'

Beaming, as if Tina should be pleased too, she went on, 'But now—though Mr Richard has made it clear that it's still unofficial—we're delighted by the news that at long last the Reverend Peter is going to have his wish…'

So Richard was going to be married.

'Well, I must get along. The master was in the study earlier, if you're looking for him…' Her back ramrod straight, Hannah hurried away.

CHAPTER SEVEN

COLD and sick and shattered, Tina stood stricken, unable to move, knowing how Mag must have felt.

In her ears was his voice saying, 'Who said anything about a one-night stand or casual sex? Neither the way I feel about you, nor my intentions are in any way casual'... And, fool that she was, she had believed his lies.

Unless he was planning on having an ongoing affair *after* he was married?

Well, if he was, she thought bitterly, he could count her out.

When she had recovered enough to move, her first impulse was to run and hide. To leave his home and never see him again. But she had no way of leaving unless she could find a phone and call for a taxi.

There must be phones at the castle but, apart from the one in the library-cum-study that Richard had used the previous night, she hadn't noticed any. Perhaps, like the television, they were hidden away.

But all that was beside the point; she needed her own mobile. So somehow she had to face him, to tell him she was leaving. But if she wanted to go with some shred of pride intact, she had, somehow, to hide just how shattered she felt.

On legs that trembled so much they would scarcely carry her, she made her way across the hall to the study. As she was passing the living-room door, which was a little ajar, she heard Richard's voice and, pausing, once again found herself eavesdropping on a phone conversation.

'As the time factor is of overriding importance,' he was saying, 'there isn't a moment to lose—'

Only it *wasn't* a phone conversation, she realised a second later, as a woman's voice broke in, 'But surely it's already too late. It just can't be done in the time.'

'It *can* be done,' Richard insisted quietly. 'In fact the arrangements are already in place.'

Feeling like death, lacking the will to walk away, Tina listened dully to the argument.

'There must be some other way,' the woman insisted shrilly. 'You're not short of money; couldn't you—?'

'That was my first thought, but money isn't necessarily the answer. I don't know for sure what I'm up against, and by the time I *do* know it'll be too late.'

'But Richard—' It was a wail.

'It's no use, Helen, I simply can't afford to chance doing it any other way…'

Helen… Helen O'Connell. So it was his future wife he was talking to.

'It's only too easy to be held to ransom and drained dry. But once I'm in a position of strength, my money can be used to greater effect.'

'But it's so…so *drastic*.'

'I've given it a lot of thought and I'm satisfied that it's by far the safest option.'

'What do you suppose will happen when—?'

'There's bound to be a backlash of course,' he broke in a trifle curtly, 'but I'll deal with that as and when it happens.'

'Well, I think you're making a dreadful mistake.' Then, with a flare of hope, 'You could always fight it through the courts.'

'I considered that, of course, but it might take years and, as things stand at present, there's no guarantee I'd win.'

'But have you considered the ethics of it?'

'You mean two wrongs don't make a right?' he suggested a shade grimly. 'Oh, yes, I've considered all that. But I'll do whatever it takes. As far as I'm concerned, the end jus tifies the means. I've far too much to lose to think of playing Sir Galahad...'

Standing, shivering and miserable, outside the living-room door, Tina was chilled anew by the icy ruthlessness in his voice.

This was a side of him that she hadn't yet seen. But perhaps, as a successful businessman, he needed to have a ruthless streak.

Though his future wife didn't seem to care for it. Sounding close to breaking-point, she cried, 'Well, I still think you're wrong. There has to be a better way...' Then, with a touch of venom, 'Unless, of course, it's really what you want...'

As she heard the doorknob rattle beneath fumbling fingers, terrified of being caught eavesdropping, Tina turned to run.

Knowing she would never make it across the hall and up the stairs without being seen, she fled into the neighbouring study just as the living-room door opened and closed.

Through the window, which overlooked the courtyard, she could see a bright red open-topped sports car standing by the main entrance, sun ricocheting from its polished bonnet.

A few seconds later the front door opened and a tall, slim, dark-haired woman came hurrying out with Richard at her heels.

While he had remained calm and implacable, the argument—whatever it had been about—had clearly upset Helen O'Connell and she was in tears.

His face showing concern now, he made an obvious attempt to reason with her.

When, beside herself, she refused to listen, he took her arm. She pulled it free. He tried again to detain her but, with sudden unbridled fury, she turned and slapped his face.

Then, jumping into the car, she started the ignition, stamped her foot down and, with a reckless burst of acceleration, roared across the cobbles, through the archway and over the bridge.

Richard stood for a moment, his hand to his cheek, staring after her.

When he turned to make his way back inside, afraid that he might see her watching, Tina hurriedly moved away from the window.

She was heading for the door when, unwilling to chance running into him in the hall in case he guessed what she had seen and heard, she hesitated. It might be safest to stay where she was until the coast was clear.

The next second found her wondering if that was the right decision. He'd obviously been working in here when his visitor had arrived and a file had been tossed down and left on his desk.

Suppose he came straight back to the study?

Knowing she was trapped, she waited in an agony of suspense, listening for his approaching footsteps, wondering how best to explain her presence there.

When several minutes had dragged past without her hearing a sound, realising that he *wasn't* coming straight back, she heaved a sigh of relief.

If she used the phone on the desk to ring for a taxi and arranged to meet it at the top of the drive rather than let it come through into the courtyard, she might be able to leave without anyone knowing.

It would mean going without her mobile, but that was a small price to pay.

She was just reaching for the receiver when, without warning, the door opened, making her gasp.

A second later Richard walked in, looking coolly elegant in well-cut fawn trousers and a short-sleeved olive-green silk shirt open at the neck.

'So there you are,' he said, his taut expression clearing. 'When you weren't upstairs I started to wonder where you'd got to. How's the ankle this morning? It looks as if the swelling's gone down…'

Appearing relaxed and easy now, he came over and, tilting her chin, kissed her mouth.

A lover's kiss.

For a split second she stood as though turned to stone, then, on a reflex action, she jerked her head sharply away.

His dark level brows drawing together in a frown, he queried, 'What's the matter?'

Momentarily unable to speak, she shook her head.

'Something must be.'

'I couldn't find my phone,' she said in a rush, 'and I wanted to call a taxi.'

'Why do you want a taxi?' he asked evenly.

'Because I'm leaving.'

His tawny eyes narrowed. 'What's happened to make you want to leave?'

'Nothing,' she lied desperately. 'I just think it's time I went. So, if you don't mind—'

'Oh, but I do.' Suddenly he was looming over her. 'After all we've shared, I mind very much that you want to walk out without any explanation.'

Gritting her teeth, she said boldly, 'I don't have to give an explanation. Surely the fact that I want to leave is enough. Now, if you'll please let me have my mobile back.'

When he merely looked at her, she reminded him, 'You kept it last night after you'd called Mullins—'

'In that case it must be in my pocket…'

Shaking her head, she began, 'It isn't—'

He raised a dark brow. 'How do you know?'

Seeing her flush guiltily, he observed, 'So you've been going through my pockets?'

'I'm sorry,' she said jerkily. 'I should have asked you, I know, but I'm afraid I acted on impulse…' The explanation petered out.

'And did you find anything interesting?' he queried with smooth mockery.

Nettled by his tone, she flashed back, 'Only a torch that lit.'

'Really?' he drawled. 'Then there must have been a loose connection.'

When he said nothing further, deciding to let it go, she gritted her teeth and returned to the point. 'So please can I have my mobile?'

'If it isn't in my pocket, I'm afraid…' With an elegant gesture of apology, he spread his hands, palms upward.

'I don't believe you don't know where it is.'

'And I don't believe that you suddenly want to leave Anders for no good reason.'

Realising that she was fighting a losing battle, she said shortly, 'Whatever you believe, you can't prevent me from going.'

'Don't be too sure about that.'

Suddenly scared, she brushed past him, catching the edge of the file that was lying on his desk, knocking it to the floor and spreading the contents.

Even as she stepped over the papers and headed for the door, part of her mind registered the fact that several of them bore a stylized logo.

Her hand was on the knob when Richard caught her arm and swung her round. Then, turning the big key in the lock, he dropped it into his trousers pocket and stooped to gather together the contents of the file.

As he dropped it back on his desk, she faced him defiantly. 'You can't keep me here against my will.'

'Maybe not for any length of time,' he admitted. 'But certainly for the moment.'

'I insist that you let me go.'

'Even if I did, it would be extremely difficult for you to leave without some kind of transport... So suppose you tell me the truth.'

Biting her lip, she said nothing.

'I can only presume it's something to do with Helen's visit,' he hazarded. 'Something you overheard, perhaps?'

When she remained stubbornly silent, he sighed.

'What a shame the thumbscrews aren't handy,' she taunted with sudden recklessness.

Between thick dark lashes his eyes gleamed green as a cat's. 'There are other ways.'

Though he spoke lightly, she felt her blood run cold. Still she braved it out. 'Such as?'

He smiled mirthlessly. 'Judging by the way you shied away when I kissed you, I gather you'd prefer me not to touch you?'

She lifted her chin defiantly. 'You're quite right, I would.'

'You didn't seem to feel that way last night.'

'I do now.'

A little smile playing around his chiselled mouth, with slow deliberation he began to unbutton his shirt before pulling it from the waistband of his trousers.

'What are you doing?' she cried, aghast.

'Taking off my clothes. Perhaps you'd like to do the same?'

'No, I wouldn't.'

'Well, I could take them off for you,' he suggested. 'On the other hand, I haven't made love fully clothed since I was an impetuous teenager, so it might be something of a novelty.'

'I don't want you to make love to me,' she cried in a strangled voice. 'I don't want you to touch me.'

'So you said. But if you really don't want that, then you'll tell me why you're so intent on leaving.' When she stayed mute, with a suddenness that took her completely by surprise, he pulled her close and, neatly hooking her feet from beneath her, followed her down, his arms breaking her fall.

Flat on her back on the thick-pile carpet, she made an attempt to struggle free but, catching her wrists, he pinned them over her head.

His shirt was open and, looking up at his broad chest, the strong column of his neck, the tender hollow at the base, she felt her stomach clench.

As calmly as possible, she said, 'Let me go.'

By way of answer, he put his lips to the pulse fluttering wildly in her throat.

Thickly, she insisted, 'If you don't let me go this instant I'll scream.'

His smile maddeningly cool, he said, 'Do you think I'd allow you to? In any case, there's no one to hear you. All the household servants are at chapel.'

He brought her wrists together and, holding them in one hand, used the other to unfasten the buttons of her blouse.

Then, flicking it open, he ran a fingertip beneath the edge of her low-cut bra and heard her breathing quicken even more. His finger delved a little deeper and he watched with satisfaction as her nipples firmed visibly beneath the delicate material.

Still she held out and he bent his head.

Feeling the heat and dampness of his mouth through the satin and lace, she began to shudder. 'Don't,' she whispered in desperation. 'Don't…'

'Why not? You liked it last night.'

'That was before…'

'Before what?'

She threw in the towel. 'Before I knew you were planning to get married.'

'Ah,' he said softly, 'so that's it.' Then, quick as a rattlesnake striking, 'How do you know I'm planning to get married?'

'Hannah mentioned it.'

He relaxed a little. 'When did you see Hannah?'

'I met her as I was coming downstairs. She was on her way to the chapel.'

'I see. So that's what all the fuss is about.'

'If you're going to try and tell me it isn't true—'

'I've no intention of telling you any such thing.'

'Oh…' Perhaps even now she had been treasuring some faint hope that Hannah had got it wrong.

Irony in his voice, he asked, 'As you know I'm getting married, perhaps you also know who my bride-to-be is?'

'Yes, I do. It's Helen O'Connell.'

He raised a dark brow. 'What makes you presume that? It's not just because she came here, surely?'

'It's what I understood from Hannah.'

Frowning, he suggested, 'Perhaps you'd better tell me word for word exactly what Hannah said.'

As near as she could remember, Tina repeated what the housekeeper had told her, adding with unconscious bitterness, 'I gather she's delighted.'

'But you're not?'

'As far as I'm concerned, Miss O'Connell is more than welcome to you.'

'Jealous?'

'No, I'm not.'

'Tell me,' he said, his face sardonic, 'if you're not jealous, why are you so angry about it?'

Made furious by his cavalier attitude, she cried, 'Because you're a brute and a beast and an unfeeling devil! How *could* you bring me here like this? What would your fiancée think if she found out?'

'Do I take it you're planning to tell her?' he asked mockingly.

'No, I'm not. The only thing I'm planning is to go and never get within a mile of you again.'

He shook his head regretfully. 'In that case I'm afraid our schedules don't match. You see I have no intention of letting you go and every intention of keeping you close by my side.'

Bending his head, he kissed her.

The casual arrogance of that kiss was the last straw and she began to struggle furiously, writhing and kicking, fighting to free her hands.

She was young and fit and, despite her slender build, strong.

But he was so much stronger.

Holding her down with the weight of his body, he ordered, 'Lie still or you'll hurt yourself.'

When, from sheer exhaustion, she was forced to obey, he said quietly, 'That's better.'

'Oh, please, Richard,' she begged raggedly, 'let me get up.'

Perhaps he realised how close to tears she was, because without further ado he released her wrists and his weight lifted from her.

Having helped her up, he rebuttoned her blouse before pushing her gently into the nearest chair. Then, having fastened his own shirt and tucked it into the waistband of his trousers, he stood looking down at her.

All trace of mockery gone now, he said, 'I want you to listen to me. You're right in thinking that I'm hoping to be married...'

Fool that she was, she had still half hoped that he might deny it.

'However, you're quite wrong in believing that the lady in question is Helen O'Connell...'

'Oh...' Tina said in a small voice.

'At one time Hannah may have had hopes in that direction but, when she mentioned the Reverend Peter getting his wish, you were mistaken in thinking she was referring to Helen.'

Feeling foolish, Tina stared blindly down at her hands clasped together in her lap.

When she said nothing, he went on evenly, 'Because

Hannah's been part of the family for so long, I told her my plans… Though I must admit I hadn't expected her to say anything until I'd had a chance to discuss those plans with the woman I'm hoping to marry.'

When Tina continued to sit in silence, head bent, the mockery back in his voice, he suggested, 'Now aren't you going to ask me who that woman is?'

She shook her head. It didn't really matter who it was. The mere fact that he had found a woman he wanted to marry had turned her own short-lived happiness into dust and ashes.

'Does that mean you're not interested, or you feel reluctant to ask?'

Apart from saying that his intentions were in no way casual, he'd made no commitment, had promised her nothing, so what right had she to ask?

'Well?' he pressed.

'I feel I've no right to ask,' she admitted dully.

A hand beneath her chin, he lifted her face and said firmly, 'After the way I've treated you, you've *every* right to ask.'

Her breath taken away, she gazed up at him mutely as he went on, 'I got you to come here by offering you a job. A job you turned down on the grounds that, because we'd been to bed together, you would find it awkward to work for me.

'That shows a rare sensitivity in this day and age, when a lot of women wouldn't have given it a second thought or would have regarded a sexual interest as a plus.

'Well, now I'm offering you a different kind of job, a job where a sexual interest is not only a plus but absolutely vital…'

When, her blue-violet eyes wide, she continued to stare up at him, he said, 'I want *you* to be my wife.'

'What?' she whispered, unable to believe her ears.

'I want *you* to be my wife,' he repeated. 'Or, as Marlowe put it, "Come live with me and be my love…"'

'It's sudden, I admit,' he added quizzically, 'but there's no need to look quite so taken aback. After all, I did make it plain that my interest was far from casual…'

'Yes, I know, but I… I never thought… I never dreamt…' Wanting to believe it, but afraid to, needing desperately to be reassured that this wasn't some kind of cruel joke, she asked huskily, 'Do you really want to marry me?'

'Yes,' he answered, a touch of amusement in his voice, 'I really do.'

When, still struggling to take it in, she said nothing, he offered teasingly, 'Would you like me to say it again?'

'I—I'm sorry, but I just find it hard to believe,' she admitted.

'But my proposal isn't unwelcome, I hope?' A finger tracing the curve of her cheek, he asked with apparent irrelevance, 'When we saw the evening star and both made a wish, what did you wish for?'

Seeing her colour rise, he smiled, as if that was answer enough, and told her softly, '*You* are what *I* wished for.' Bending his head, he kissed her lips. A light coaxing kiss. 'All you have to do is marry me to make my wish come true.

'I would have waited a little and proposed to you in a more romantic setting,' he added seriously, 'if Hannah hadn't let the cat out of the bag.

'However,' he went on after a moment, 'I hope the setting won't make any difference to your answer?'

The setting wasn't important, Tina thought, winging her way up to cloud nine—Richard loved her and wanted to marry her; that was all that mattered.

She would have been content with his love—more than content, deliriously happy. The fact that he wanted to make her his wife was more than she had ever dared to hope for and her heart swelled with joy and gratitude.

Watching her glowing face, he was almost sure that he'd pulled it off. But he needed to hear her say it out loud.

When she continued to sit as though in a trance, her eyes

soft and full of dreams, growing impatient, he took her shoulders and, lifting her to her feet, urged, 'I'm still waiting for an answer. Will you marry me?'

She gave him the most glorious smile and answered simply, 'Yes.'

That smile made him feel despicable and, for a split second, in spite of everything, he wondered if he was doing the right thing.

But he couldn't afford to weaken now.

Shrugging off the feeling, he hardened his heart.

Though it was over in an instant, she picked up that fleeting doubt. 'But perhaps we should have time to think it over?'

He frowned. 'Do you need time?'

She shook her head. 'No, not really. But I thought *you* might.'

'*I* don't need time to think it over. I know exactly what I'm doing.'

'But you don't really know enough about me.'

'I know everything I need to know.'

Though he sounded certain, a lingering unease made her ask, 'On the drive here you talked about your wife and children living at Anders... Suppose I dislike children and don't want any...?'

'*Do* you dislike children?'

'No, of course I don't. I don't think a marriage is complete without children, but—'

His mouth covered hers, stopping the words, before he said, 'Then I know everything I need to know.'

'How can you be so sure when we only met a couple of days ago?'

'The first time I saw you I knew you were all I'd ever dreamed of or wanted in a woman.'

Though his answer was sweet and romantic, something impelled her to say, 'It just seems so sudden...'

He brushed her lips lightly with his. 'Have you never heard of love at first sight?'

'Of course, but—'

'I had hoped the feeling might have been mutual.'

After a moment she admitted softly, 'It was.'

Making no attempt to hide his elation, he pulled her into his arms and began to kiss her in earnest.

For a while they stood embracing, lost to the world, like Donne's ecstatic lovers.

Eventually, the intrusive thought that there were still things to be done, one final hurdle to surmount, disturbed the blissful mood.

Lifting his head reluctantly and opting for a change of scene, Richard suggested, 'It's a lovely morning—shall we get some fresh air?'

A fountain of happiness welling inside her, she nodded. 'Let's.'

'Sure the ankle's up to it?'

'It's as good as new this morning.'

'Oh, wait a minute, you won't have had anything to eat yet…'

'I haven't, but—'

'There'll be bacon and eggs and coffee keeping hot in the breakfast room.'

'I'm not hungry, but I'd like a cup of coffee before we go.'

When they'd each had a coffee, wondering how best to play it without appearing to rush things, he suggested casually, 'Would you like to stroll down and see the horses?'

'I'd love to.'

'You said you used to ride.'

'Oh, yes. Though I haven't been on a horse for some time now, I rode a lot when I was younger.'

'Then perhaps we could take them out.'

He captured her hand and laced his fingers through hers

as they left the breakfast room and made their way along the length of the hall.

Beyond the servants' quarters, the kitchens and a flagged outer hall—all of which appeared to be deserted—a huge studded-oak door opened on to a wide area of decking and a sturdy wooden bridge.

'The tradesmen's entrance,' Richard told her with a grin as they crossed the bridge hand in hand.

It was a beautiful morning, calm and sunny, the balmy air full of the oddly poignant scents of autumn: freshly sawn pine logs, late wallflowers, decaying leaves and woodsmoke.

On the far side of the bridge was a paved carriageway, one fork of which served the garden area, while the other, running between smooth lawns, sloped gently down to an old-fashioned stone-built stable block and coach house.

The large central archway was surmounted by a cupola, on top of which a black wrought iron weathervane—a horse taking the place of the traditional cock—stood motionless in the still air.

On all four sides of the cupola was a large clock with a blue face and golden hands that declared it was almost ten-thirty.

In the stable yard a short bow-legged man wearing a flat cap, a flannel shirt and riding breeches was grooming a large black stallion, whose coat gleamed with good health and care.

'Morning, Josh,' Richard said cheerfully. 'I'd like you to meet Miss Dunbar.'

'Good morning, miss... Morning, Mr Richard.' The groom touched his forelock in a gesture Tina had thought obsolete.

Indicating a chestnut mare with pricked ears and gentle eyes who was regarding them quietly over one of the stable doors, Richard told her, 'This is Juno.'

'Well, hello...' Tina stroked the waiting head and was nuzzled in return. 'You're beautiful...'

'And, as you've no doubt guessed, this is Jupiter.' Richard clapped the black horse on the shoulder.

Taking a liking to the big placid-looking animal, she stroked his velvety muzzle and told him, 'My, but you're a handsome fellow…'

Lifting his head, he snuffled her cheek appreciatively.

'If you were thinking of taking un out,' Josh said, 'I can have un saddled up in no time at all.'

'What about Juno?' Richard asked.

'Yesterday when 'er was out, 'er cast a near hind shoe. I'm waiting on Tom Ferris. Said 'e'd fetch 'er some time this morning, so if you were wanting to take 'er out later…'

As if sensing Tina's disappointment, Richard glanced at her and suggested, 'If you fancy a ride now, Jupiter will easily take both of us.'

At her eager acceptance, he nodded to the groom. 'Saddle him up, Josh.'

As soon as the horse was ready, the groom disappeared, to return almost immediately with two riding hats.

'There be yours, Mr Richard, and I fancy the mistress's old un'll do fine for Miss Dunbar.'

The protective headgear buckled into place, Tina climbed the two steps to the mounting block and in a trice was astride Jupiter's broad back, taking care to leave the stirrups free for Richard.

He swung himself lightly into the saddle behind her and a moment later, with a wave to Josh, they were off.

Holding the reins in his left hand, his right arm securely around Tina, for a while they ambled along, heading south through pleasant undulating parkland.

After they had gone some half a mile, in response to Jupiter's urging, Richard gave the beast his head and, making light of his load, the big horse broke into an easy canter.

It was exhilarating and Tina laughed aloud with the sheer

joy of it. In response to such spontaneous gladness, Richard's arm tightened around her.

When a shallow stream came into view, unwilling to overtax the horse, he reined him in and they ambled down to the water's edge.

There, where the grass was still green and lush and the trees made a dappled shade, he slid to the ground and, having lifted Tina down, looped the reins over a low branch.

Then, leaving the horse to graze peacefully, they took off their riding hats and went to sit on a fallen tree trunk by the fast-flowing stream.

Held in the crook of Richard's arm, Tina watched the glittering water as it ran leaping and chuckling over its stony bed and knew what perfect happiness and contentment felt like.

After a while he broke the silence to say, 'I'd like us to be married as soon as possible.'

When something in his tone, a kind of tension, made her glance up at him, he added almost roughly, 'I sound impatient, I know, but I just can't wait to make you mine.'

Her heart fluttered and swelled with gratitude that he should feel so strongly about her.

'If you were hoping for a big wedding with dozens of guests and all the trimmings,' he went on, 'we can always have a second ceremony later.'

Nestling against him, she said simply, 'I don't need a big wedding and all the trimmings,' and heard his quick sigh of relief.

'That's my girl.' His arm tightened round her. 'So shall we say tomorrow morning?'

Thinking he was joking, she laughed and said, 'Why not? Except that it can't be done so quickly.'

'As we have our own priest and our own chapel, all we need to do is warn the Reverend Peter and arrange for two witnesses.'

Realising he wasn't joking after all, she said breathlessly, 'B-but surely we need a…a licence of some kind?'

'I have a special licence lined up.'

Through lips gone suddenly stiff, she said, 'Then you must have intended it for someone else.'

'You are the only woman I've ever wanted to marry.' His green-gold eyes on her face, he added, 'I told you earlier that the first time I saw you I knew you were the one I'd been waiting for.'

She half shook her head. 'I realise that being who you are, you must have quite a pull. But, even with your own chapel and your own family priest, I don't believe you could have got a licence in the time. You hadn't set eyes on me until Friday…'

'That's where you're wrong,' he told her quietly.

CHAPTER EIGHT

'I DON'T understand,' Tina protested, puzzled.

Richard brushed a strand of silky blonde hair away from her cheek with his free hand and said, 'It's over three weeks since I first saw you.'

'Three weeks?'

'I was visiting Cartel Wines when I caught sight of you coming out of De Vere's office. I thought you were the most beautiful woman I'd ever seen and I knew I had to have you...'

She was still endeavouring to catch her breath when he went on, 'Unfortunately, the following day I was forced to travel to the Far East on an extremely important business trip, so I couldn't follow things through myself.

'However, I had some checks made and, finding you were free, I discussed getting married with the Reverend Peter, who made all the necessary arrangements—'

Completely flabbergasted, she protested, 'But you hadn't even spoken to me. How could you be so sure I'd marry you?'

'I couldn't be *sure*, of course...' With a trace of arrogance, he added, 'But I usually get what I want.'

She could easily believe it. Especially when it came to women.

'The trip dragged on until the middle of last week,' he continued, 'but for the first time in my life I found I couldn't keep my mind on business matters. I kept thinking about you, planning how to meet you when I got back.'

'And then we met by accident...' But, even as she said the words, some sixth sense made her wonder—*had* running into her been an accident?

Oh, don't be a fool, she chided herself. What man in his right mind would do such a thing deliberately when there were plenty of other ways he could have met her?

For instance, if he'd wanted to get to know her so badly, why hadn't he spoken to her in the car park at midday, while she had been disposing of her ruined lunch? It would have been a perfect opportunity.

Or, failing that, surely the next time he visited Cartel Wines he could have made some excuse to—

No, she wouldn't have been there.

Though he couldn't have known that she was leaving.

Or could he?

Somewhere at the back of her mind, a memory, an impression, tried to struggle to the surface and she knew that if she could only recall what it was she would have the answer to her question.

She was still cudgelling her brains when Richard glanced at his watch and said briskly, 'We ought to be starting for home. You must be famished and, as we're being married tomorrow, we have a lot to do.'

Though she wanted to marry him more than anything in the world, a vague uneasiness still nagging at her, a feeling that something wasn't quite right, she began, 'I don't understand why we have to rush into it like this... Couldn't we wait until—?'

Just for an instant his beautiful mouth tightened. Then he said coaxingly, 'You've agreed to marry me, we have a priest, a chapel and a marriage licence, so why wait?'

'I've nothing to wear,' she pointed out. 'I need to go back to the flat and fetch some clothes—'

He bent his dark head and kissed her mouth, nipping delicately at her bottom lip, distracting her, as he whispered, 'I'd rather have you without any clothes.'

Trying to collect herself and sound severe, she began, 'That's all very well, but I must have *something* to get married in—'

'Failing anything else, you could always wear the dress you wore to dinner last night.'

'But it got marked when we walked though the tunnel,' she pleaded.

'I'll ask Hannah to see that all your things are laundered and we'll make time to buy you a whole new wardrobe before we go on our honeymoon.'

Diverted, she asked, 'Are we going on honeymoon?'

He looked surprised. 'Of course. I thought we'd stick with the old tradition of spending our wedding night at Anders, in the nuptial bed…'

The nuptial bed… A little shiver of excitement ran down her spine.

'Then go on to our chosen honeymoon destination the following day.'

It all sounded so *solid*, so conventional, that, her uneasiness taking flight, she teased, 'I dare say you've already got it all arranged?'

He grinned appreciatively. ''Fraid not. I decided to find out where you wanted to go before I made any definite plans.'

'How long will we be going for?'

'A month. Longer if you wish…'

There was no harm in delaying the showdown; in fact it might be all to the good to allow a breathing space while they really got to know one other.

'So, if you'd like to give it some thought and let me know,' he added, 'I'll have Murray standing by.'

'Murray?'

'Captain Murray Tyler. I have a small private jet.'

That casual mention of owning his own plane made Tina realise afresh what a wealthy man she was marrying. But it wasn't his money or his lifestyle that had attracted her. She would still have married him if he hadn't had a penny.

'We'd best be moving.' He stood up and, taking her hands, pulled her to her feet. 'Matthew Caradine, my solicitor, is coming at two o'clock.'

Surprised, she said, 'On a Sunday?'

'There are one or two things that need to be settled before tomorrow,' he told her casually.

When they had both donned their riding hats, he lifted her into the saddle, swung himself up behind her and a moment later they were heading for home at a canter.

Admittedly it hadn't been quite as easy as he might have hoped, but he had achieved what he'd set out to achieve. Tomorrow he would be her husband; he would be in a much stronger position once she'd signed the marriage contract that Matthew Caradine had drawn up.

When lunch was over Richard asked for coffee to be served in their suite and, an arm around Tina's waist, escorted her up the stairs.

Once their coffee cups were empty, he said seriously, 'When we get married I shall use the wedding ring my mother bought my father…'

Knowing that some men preferred to hide the fact that they were married, Tina was only too pleased that Richard wasn't one of them.

'Until we have time to go and choose *your* rings,' he was going on, 'I'd like you to use my mother's. If you're quite happy with that?'

'Are you sure she wouldn't have minded?'

'I'm certain. It was her stated intention to give her rings to my future wife—should she want them, that is.'

A warm feeling spreading inside, Tina assured him, 'Then, if they fit, I'd love to wear them.'

'Of course I'm talking about the rings my father bought her. Bradley, who apparently was very jealous, hated to see her wearing them, so when they were married she took them off and kept them in her secret drawer along with my father's wedding ring…'

He went over to the writing desk where, placed centrally above several small drawers faced with oyster shell and inlaid with box, their handles made of mother-of-pearl, was a shallow recess.

Tina watched with undisguised interest as, a hand at either end, he reached into the space and a moment later what had appeared to be a solid back slid forward to reveal a drawer some thirty centimetres long, twenty wide and ten deep.

From it he took a small box covered in dark blue velvet and flicked open the lid to show a heavy gold signet ring, a delicate chased gold wedding band and an exquisite matching diamond solitaire.

'Her fingers were very slim, like yours, so I think they'll fit.'

He took out the solitaire and, lifting Tina's strong but slender left hand with its pearly oval nails, slid it on to the fourth finger.

It fitted perfectly and she caught her breath as the huge stone flashed with internal fire.

Nodding his approval, Richard replaced the box containing both the wedding rings and sent the secret drawer sliding back into the recess. It seemed to catch slightly before finally settling into place.

The long-case clock in the corner was just striking two o'clock and at that instant Milly tapped at the door to announce that the solicitor had arrived.

'Coming?' Richard cocked an eyebrow at Tina.

'I thought I'd stay here while you—'

He shook his head firmly. 'There's one thing that concerns you.'

'What kind of thing?' she asked as they made their way back downstairs.

'We need to agree on a suitable settlement in the event of a divorce.'

A cold chill ran down her spine. 'Oh, but I—'

Seeing that involuntary shiver, he said reassuringly, 'Don't worry, it's just a formality. But it's something that has to be gone through.'

The solicitor was waiting in the study. Almost as tall as Richard but a good deal heavier, he was a pleasant-looking middle-aged man with greying hair and jowls.

'Good of you to come at such short notice,' Richard said as the two men shook hands.

He turned to Tina and, drawing her forward, went on, 'Darling, this is Matthew Caradine... Matthew, my fiancée, Valentina Dunbar.'

The solicitor took Tina's proffered hand with a friendly smile and said, 'It's nice to meet you, Miss Dunbar...'

Then, to Richard, 'I've drawn up the necessary documents to cover all the points you mentioned.'

'Good.'

'There's really only the one pertaining to your marriage that concerns Miss Dunbar and, as you requested, I've kept it simple. So, if you'd like to get that out of the way first?'

At Richard's nod he opened his black briefcase and, taking out a single sheet of paper, handed it to Tina. 'Perhaps you'd be good enough to read that and, if you're satisfied with the contents, sign it?'

She took the document and, sitting down in one of the armchairs, proceeded to read it while the two men stood and watched her in silence.

It was, as the solicitor had said, short and simple. It stated that if, for whatever reason, they were divorced, while Richard would be happy to buy her a house and pay her maintenance—the amount was so generous it made her blink—she had to relinquish any claim to the castle.

It further stated that if there were children from the marriage, in the event of a separation, their father would be responsible for their upbringing and they would remain in his care.

Having read it through twice, she put it down on the coffee table and said flatly, 'I'm sorry, but I can't sign this.'

She saw Richard's jaw tighten and a white line appear round his mouth.

It was a moment before he asked evenly, 'Why not?'

'With regard to the castle...' she began.

For a split second he looked so angry that she cringed inwardly and the words died on her lips.

Then that look was gone and, his voice quiet and controlled, he queried, 'What about the castle?'

'I—I was just going to say that there's no question that it belongs to you. I would never dream of—'

She glimpsed what might have been relief, before he broke in, 'So what exactly is the problem?'

Well aware that he might not marry her if she refused to toe the line, she took a deep breath and told him, 'There's no way I would be prepared to give up my children...'

A flicker of some emotion she was unable to decipher crossed his face before he said, 'Then perhaps we could agree on joint custody?'

'How do you mean, exactly?'

'I mean that if we separated, they could live with you but I would have unlimited access and an equal right to a say in their upbringing. Would you be happy with that arrangement?'

'Yes,' she said simply. 'Though I hope it will never come to that.'

He took her hand and raised it to his lips. 'With you as my wife, I'm sure it won't.'

Caradine came forward and, picking up the document, sat down at the desk. 'As you're both in agreement, I'll amend it immediately.'

The amendment completed, he suggested, 'If you'd both be good enough to read it and put your signatures at the bottom?'

That done to his satisfaction, he replaced the paper in his briefcase and took out several more. 'Now, for the remainder of the business…'

Tina got to her feet. 'If you don't need me any longer, I'll go and leave you to it.'

A detaining hand on her arm, Richard asked, 'What were you thinking of doing?'

A little surprised by the barely concealed urgency of his manner, she said, 'It's such a lovely day I thought I might go for a stroll along the battlements and enjoy the view.'

His fingers relaxed their grip and, dropping a light kiss on her lips, he said, 'What a good idea… While you're up there, give some thought to our honeymoon. Try and decide where you'd like to go and what you'd like to see…

'By the time you've gone full circle,' he added, 'I should be finished here. Then, after I've seen Matthew off, we can go and talk to the Reverend Peter and make some precise arrangements for tomorrow.'

She smiled and nodded, then thanked the solicitor and shook hands with him, before going out and closing the door quietly behind her.

Having crossed the deserted hall, where the sun threw elaborate patterns of the leaded windows on to the polished oak floorboards, she made her way to the tower they had ascended the previous evening and climbed the stone stairway.

Emerging on to the castle walls, she paused to look down into the courtyard, which was asymmetrically painted with deep shadows and bright sunshine. A sleek blue Jaguar, no doubt Matthew Caradine's, was drawn up by the main entrance.

Though Richard had tried hard to get her to focus on their wedding day and honeymoon, as she began to walk slowly along the sunny battlements, her mind went back over the past half hour and the little scene that had taken place in his study.

Why had he deemed it necessary to insist that she should relinquish any claim to the castle?

And why had he been so angry when he'd thought that she was refusing to? Because, clearly, that was what he *had* thought.

Which was absurd.

Even if she'd wanted to, which she never would, how could she possibly lay claim to something that had belonged to his family for generations?

Giving up the puzzle for the time being, she moved at a leisurely pace, simply enjoying the view and the fresh air, the warmth of the sunshine,

She had almost completed the circuit when she became aware of something hovering on the edge of her consciousness. Something nebulous and insubstantial, yet oddly persistent.

Instinctively she knew that it was the same thing that had troubled her that morning as she'd sat by the river with Richard.

After struggling, and once again failing, to identify it, she realised that it was useless to rack her brains and gave up trying.

No doubt it would crystallize eventually.

A glance down into the courtyard below showed that the solicitor's Jaguar had disappeared, but there was no sign of Richard.

Thinking he might have returned to his study, she made her way there and put her head round the door. Though there were still papers spread on the desk, the room was empty.

As she turned to leave, she noticed the file she had knocked off the desk that morning and paused as a fleeting picture, an image she couldn't pin down, came into her mind, convincing her that *that* held the answer to whatever had been troubling her.

She went in, leaving the door ajar, and opened the file.

It contained various emails and papers that Richard had roughly gathered together, along with a brown envelope from which some photographs were protruding.

The top one showed part of a woman's face, which looked oddly familiar. Curiosity having prompted Tina to pull it out and take a better look, she found she was staring down at a very good likeness of herself.

There were several more, all taken—judging by the background—at Cartel Wines, and all taken without her knowledge.

She felt uncomfortable, exposed, spied on.

But, even as she stared at them, she knew that the photographs weren't the solution to what had been niggling at her.

A second or two later, catching sight of a logo on one of the papers, she had her answer. *That* was what she had glimpsed earlier in the morning and subconsciously registered.

It was a stylized representation of a mountain that she recognised as the distinctive shape of the Matterhorn.

She was still gazing down at it, her mind racing, when the door was pushed open and Richard walked in.

'I'm sorry if I've kept you waiting. I was just seeing Caradine off when Hannah told me that the new Estate Manager wanted a word—'

Noticing the open file, he stopped speaking abruptly and his eyes caught and held hers.

Knowing she couldn't really justify her prying, Tina's eyes were the first to drop.

'Find what you were looking for?' he enquired sardonically.

'As a matter of fact, I did.' Then, taking the bull by the horns, she asked bluntly, 'What exactly is your connection with the Matterhorn group?'

Just as bluntly he answered, 'I own it.'

So that explained his presence at Cartel Wines.

Gathering herself, she challenged, 'When I talked about Cartel Wines being taken over by Matterhorn, you didn't tell me you owned it.'

'No,' he agreed calmly.

'Why didn't you?' she persisted.

'After you'd just lost your job because of the takeover, it didn't seem to be quite the right time,' he answered quizzically.

'Well, I still think you should have told me.'

'What difference would it have made?'

None really, she admitted silently. It wasn't as if he'd been *trying* to hide the fact that he owned the Matterhorn group. Once she had asked him, he'd answered without a moment's hesitation.

So why did she feel as if she'd been bamboozled, as if he'd been deliberately keeping it from her?

But what possible reason could he have had for not telling her?

After a moment she recalled the doubts that had entered her mind that morning as they'd sat by the river bank.

Suppose the accident *hadn't* been an accident? Suppose, on returning from his business trip and visiting Cartel Wines, he'd discovered that she was leaving that evening for good. Could he have thought it urgent enough to stage an 'accident' so he could get to know her?

No, surely not.

For one thing, in the pitch-dark he couldn't have known who he was running into.

Unless he'd been following her. Keeping an eye on her. Recalling that disturbing sensation of being watched, she shivered.

No, she was just being ridiculous. If he *had* discovered at the last minute that she was leaving, all he would have needed to do was make himself known and offer her a place on the new team. That way he would have had all the time in the world to get to know her.

So why on earth should he need to take such drastic action? It didn't make sense.

All the same, she found herself saying accusingly, 'You knew I was leaving Cartel Wines that night.'

'You told me,' he pointed out.

'You must have known before that.'

He lifted a dark brow. 'Why must I have known?'

'As Matterhorn's boss you must have been aware that having your own promotional team would make the job I do redundant.'

Patiently, as though speaking to a not-very-bright child, he pointed out, 'As Matterhorn's boss, I only keep hold of the reins and make the executive decisions. I just don't have time to get involved with the ins and outs of company policy, or the day-to-day running of things. That's what I employ managers for.'

Feeling silly, she said, 'Of course... I'm sorry.'

What on earth had she been thinking of? she berated herself. Naturally the big boss wouldn't be au fait with minor details.

It was high time she pulled herself together and stopped letting her imagination run away with her.

But she hadn't imagined the photographs.

As though he'd read that searing thought, he remarked casually, 'I see you've come across your photographs.'

Taken aback by his cool nonchalance, she asked unsteadily, 'Why did you take them?'

'I didn't.'

'Then who did, and why?'

'If you remember, I mentioned earlier that just after I'd first seen you, and while I was still reeling from finding the woman I'd been waiting for, I had to go away on a business trip...

'At that point, all I knew about you was your name and the

fact that you were working for Cartel Wines. Two things De Vere had grudgingly admitted when I'd asked him who you were.

'I wanted to know a whole lot more so, before I went away, I hired a detective to find out as much as he could about you. *He* took the photographs.'

The thought of being kept under surveillance and photographed without her knowledge was far from pleasant, and she said so.

'Yes, I'm sorry I had to resort to that. But I needed to know, and in the circumstances…'

Honestly puzzled, she protested, 'I don't understand why you were in such a hurry, why you couldn't have waited. Even if I'd left Cartel Wines, the personnel department had my address; you could have—'

'Call me impetuous.' Pulling her into his arms, he began to kiss her deeply, his ardour sweeping her away, swamping any further attempt at logical thought or protest.

She was limp and quivering all over by the time he released her lips and, putting his cheek to hers, whispered in her ear, 'Shall we go upstairs…?'

Though she was sorely tempted, a sense of what was fitting made her say a little breathlessly, 'But suppose someone wants you?'

He kissed the warm hollow behind her ear before nibbling the lobe. 'I rather hoped *you* would.'

Feeling her resolve beginning to slip away, she said hastily, 'What about the Reverend Peter? Don't we need to talk to him?'

'You're quite right, we do… What a very practical woman you are… Ah, well, once all the arrangements have been finalized we can give each other our undivided attention.'

Rubbing his cheek against hers, he asked seductively, 'Have you ever made love in the open air with the sun pouring down and a gentle breeze caressing your skin?'

'No,' she whispered.

'Then it's high time you did. It adds a whole new dimension. After we've talked to the Reverend Peter, I propose that we go for a stroll.'

His voice deepening, he added, 'On the far side of the beechwood there's a sunny and secluded little clearing that's ideal…'

The words tailed off as his lips moved down the side of her neck, making her shiver deliciously, and his fingers undid the top two buttons of her silk shirt and slipped inside to fondle her breast.

Though it took all her willpower, disliking the thought of facing the priest looking all hot and bothered, she made a muffled protest.

With a sigh, Richard reluctantly removed his hand and, pulling the front of her shirt together, refastened the buttons.

'No wonder newly married couples go away on honeymoon,' he said wryly. 'For that length of time, at least, they can forget everything and lose themselves in each other.

'And, speaking of honeymoons, have you decided where you'd like to go on yours?'

'I don't mind in the slightest,' she said happily. 'I'll leave it to you.' Anywhere on earth would be heaven so long as he was there.

'Come along then, my love.'

So she really was his love… Her heart soared like a bird.

As, hand in hand, they made their way to the priest's quarters, which adjoined the little chapel, Richard said, 'I'd prefer the ceremony to take place in the morning. Unless you have any objections?'

She shook her head. 'If that's what you want.'

'Then shall we say ten o'clock? That way, when we've had lunch we can go into Anders Cross and shop for a trousseau…'

If they shopped in the morning and got married in the afternoon, she could have a new dress to be married in.

She had opened her mouth to point that out when something…pride? Pique?…made her bite back the words.

He was the one who was calling the tune and perhaps, manlike, he simply wasn't interested in clothes.

So if it didn't matter to him that she had nothing to wear, perhaps he was just plain insensitive and didn't realise that it *did* matter to her.

But he was going on, 'There are several good little boutiques and a branch of Bertolli's Fashion House if you like his designs?'

Taking a deep breath, she said evenly, 'Yes, I do.'

And it was true. She had always admired Bertolli's classical collections, though until now they had been way out of her price range. It would seem strange to be able to choose a new wardrobe without having to worry about the cost.

As they approached the priest's quarters he emerged from the door and came to greet them.

He was a short, tubby man with a jolly face and a fringe of pure white hair surrounding a large bald spot that reminded Tina of a monk's tonsure.

She was forced to stifle a chuckle when Richard leaned closer and said, *sotto voce*, 'Put him in a habit and you've got Friar Tuck.'

After the introductions had been made, beaming, he shepherded them into the chapel, which appeared dim after the brightness of the sunshine.

When her eyes adjusted to the gloom, Tina glanced around her. To one side of a simple altar, with a plain gold cross and twin candles, a short flight of wooden steps with a curving handrail led up to a small, intricately carved pulpit.

A lectern in the form of a brass eagle with spread wings held a large black Bible and either side of the chancel steps a tall flower arrangement added colour and scented the air.

At the rear was a screened organ and a stone font, while a

dozen well-polished pews that smelled of beeswax and lavender took up most of the floor space. Shafts of sunshine slanting through the stained glass windows threw jewelled patterns across the backs of the pews and the red carpet that ran down the central aisle.

Tina sighed. It was beautiful and tranquil, a lovely place to be married in.

As though in response to that thought, Richard's fingers tightened on hers and, her pique forgotten, her heart swelled with love and gratitude.

When the arrangements had been discussed and settled on, the Reverend Peter turned to Richard and remarked, 'I'm delighted you've decided to use your parents' rings. I know it would have made your mother very happy.

'Oh, and speaking of your mother, I've been thinking about the second will that Hannah and I witnessed…'

Apparently not noticing the warning look that Richard gave him, the cleric went on, 'It occurred to me that it might have got mixed up with some of the ecclesiastical papers that she was going through at the time, so if you could spare a few minutes to—'

'I'd prefer to make it later,' Richard broke in. Putting an arm around Tina's waist, he explained, 'We were just about to take a walk.'

'If you've something to deal with, I can always start walking and you can follow on when you're ready,' she suggested practically.

His face clearing, he asked, 'Sure you don't mind?'

'Of course not.'

'Then if you take the path round the moat and head for the beechwood, I'll catch you up.'

He bent his dark head and kissed her, the promise explicit in that kiss taking her breath away and making her heart beat faster.

A little flushed, she thanked the cleric and said goodbye, before leaving the chapel.

When she got outside, the engagement ring she wore caught the sun and sparkled brilliantly. Imagining Ruth's face when she saw it, Tina smiled to herself.

Which reminded her, Ruth would be expecting her back on Monday, so she must ring the flat later and let the other girl know what was happening.

When she reached the bridge she leaned her arms on the old creeper-covered parapet and dawdled for a while, looking at the pleasant scene.

Fluffy white clouds hung in the deep blue sky and, along with tall feathery reeds and grey stone walls, were reflected in the still waters of the moat. Then a paddle of ducks came swimming busily along, breaking the smooth picture into a series of ripples.

Beneath the surface, she could see huge golden carp moving idly and a water rat, sleek and streamlined, surfaced briefly before disappearing into a hole in the bank.

When some fifteen minutes had passed and there was no sign of Richard, she set off to stroll round the moat. After she had gone a little way it occurred to her that she was walking widdershins and she hoped it wasn't unlucky.

After a while she glanced back and, finding Richard was still nowhere in sight, she decided to sit down and wait.

All the cottonwool clouds had vanished now and the sun, low in a sky the colour of forget-me-nots, was bathing the parkland and the individual trees in a low golden light that cast long blue-black shadows across the turf.

Lack of sleep the previous night and the warmth of the dying sun on her face combined to make her feel soporific and, stretching out on the grass, her head pillowed on a handy tussock, she closed her eyes.

She was drifting, half asleep and half awake, when she heard the sound of a horse's hooves.

Sitting up, she looked around, half expecting to see Richard had changed his mind about walking and had brought Jupiter.

But the rider who was approaching was a woman on a bay mare. A woman she recognised as Helen O'Connell.

CHAPTER NINE

THE newcomer dismounted and, leaving the mare, which began to graze quietly, crossed to where Tina was sitting and sat down beside her.

She was dressed in jodhpurs and a well-tailored riding jacket. Pulling off her riding hat, she put it on the grass beside her and said without preamble, 'My name's Helen O'Connell…'

At close quarters Tina could see that the newcomer was somewhere in her early thirties, with glossy dark hair, big blue eyes and a smooth, creamy skin.

Her eyes fixed on the sparkling solitaire that Tina wore, she said, 'You must be Valentina Dunbar, the woman Richard's planning to marry. When I caught sight of you I decided to take the chance to talk to you. When is this wedding supposed to take place?'

Trying not to let the other woman's abrupt manner throw her, Tina answered, 'Tomorrow morning.'

Helen laughed bitterly. 'I have to hand it to him. He said there was no time to lose, but I didn't think he could bring it off so soon.

'And when you're safely married he's planning to take you away on a nice little honeymoon, I imagine?'

'Well, yes, but I really don't see—'

'Let me give you a word of warning. Don't go ahead with

the wedding whatever you do. If you marry him you'll find you've made a serious mistake.'

Before Tina could speak, she hurried on, 'I know he's a very wealthy man, but—'

'I'm not marrying him for his money.'

Helen glanced at her sharply. 'Well, all I can say is if you've fallen for him you have my sympathy. He doesn't care a jot about you.

'I don't suppose he's told you—it wouldn't pay him to—but he and I have been lovers for years and if all this trouble hadn't blown up he would have married me.'

'I'm sorry,' Tina began helplessly, 'but I—'

'Oh, I don't blame *you*,' Helen broke in. 'As far as I'm concerned, *you're* the innocent party. It's Richard who, for once in his life, is behaving like a fool. He seems to think that marrying you is the only way.

'But don't let yourself be conned; as soon as he's got what he wants and the honeymoon's over, he'll divorce you—' She broke off abruptly as, in the distance, a tall figure came into view.

Springing to her feet, she pulled on her riding hat and re-mounted the mare.

'Believe me, you'll be a lot better off if you don't listen to a word Richard says. Just pack your bags and go.' Clapping her heels to the animal's flanks, she galloped away.

Thrown totally off balance, her mind in a whirl, Tina was still sitting staring after her when Richard came striding up, his good-looking face tense.

Dropping down beside her on the grass, he asked, 'What's wrong? You look like a ghost.'

'Nothing's wrong. I—'

'Don't lie to me,' he broke in curtly. 'I saw Helen ride off. What's she been saying to you?'

Struggling to keep her voice steady, Tina admitted, 'She warned me not to marry you.'

Mentally cursing Helen and her meddling, he demanded, 'Did she give you any reason for saying such a thing?'

Tina shook her head. 'She just said I'd be making a serious mistake.'

'What else did she say?'

'That you didn't care a jot about me. That you and she have been lovers for years…'

'Go on,' he ordered tersely.

'There's not a great deal more.'

His voice inexorable, he repeated, 'Go on.'

Tina looked down at her hands shyly. 'She said, "He seems to think that marrying you is the only way. But don't let yourself be conned; as soon as he's got what he wants…he'll divorce you".'

'I see,' he said grimly. 'Well, I hope you don't believe any of that nonsense.'

When she stayed silent, he sighed. 'I see you do.'

'I don't know what to believe,' Tina admitted helplessly. 'It doesn't make any sense, but why should she say something like that if it isn't—?'

He smirked. 'Try jealousy.'

'Then it's true that you and she are lovers?'

'It's true that we have been,' he admitted. 'But that's all in the past. Though we're still good friends, as far as I'm concerned anything more ended a long time ago.'

'Then you're not still in love with her?'

'I was never in love with her. Nor she with me. It was just a light-hearted affair that suited us both. A temporary thing with no serious future.'

'*She* doesn't seem to think so,' Tina said flatly. 'She said that if all this trouble hadn't blown up you would have married her.'

'But she didn't say what "all this trouble" was?' he asked quickly.

Tina shook her head again. 'No, she didn't.'

A flicker of emotion crossed his face but was quickly hidden before he went on, 'Probably something she invented. I'm sorry to say that she's prone to fancies.

'And, as for marrying her, that's another thing she must have dreamt up. At no time have I ever considered making her my wife.'

Seeing Tina's quick glance, he added firmly, 'Nor have I ever given her the slightest reason to think that I would. Now stop worrying over Helen's jealous nonsense. It's *you* I love. *You* I want to marry.'

Putting an arm around her shoulders, he drew her close and turned her face up to his. 'I hope that sets your mind at rest.'

But her mind, buzzing with doubts and questions, was anything but at rest and when he leaned forward to kiss her she tensed.

After a moment or two, however, as his mouth worked its magic, she relaxed and let all the doubts and unanswered questions slip away. Richard was here by her side. He loved her and he wanted to marry her. Why let another woman's jealousy spoil her happiness?

By the time he had seduced her with his kisses, though the sun was now slipping below the horizon and a little breeze had sprung up, she would still have gone with him to the beechwood, had he asked.

But when, released from the shelter of his arms, she shivered, he noticed at once and said, 'Straight home, I think.'

With a rueful sigh, he added, 'Due to my tardiness it'll soon be dusk and it can turn cool quickly at this time of the year.'

Rising to his feet and holding out a strong right hand to pull her up, he added, 'I admit that a bed lacks that alfresco touch, but being comfortable and warm does have its advantages.'

Wanting to keep her mind off Helen's unforeseen—and potentially disastrous—intervention, he went on, 'And of course our bed is centuries old, which makes it somewhat special…'

Thrilled at the *our bed*, she said, 'You called it the nuptial bed…'

'Yes, apart from Mother and Bradley—who went straight away on honeymoon—for generations the master and his bride have spent their wedding night in it. If it were able to talk, I imagine it could tell some tales…'

As they started to walk back, his fingers entwined in hers, he said, 'Part of a piece of poetry by the Scottish poet, James Thomson sums it up nicely:

> *"And while the black night nothing saw,*
> *And till the cold morn came at last,*
> *That old bed held the room in awe*
> *With tales of its experience vast.*
> *It thrilled the gloom; it told such tales*
> *Of human sorrows and delights,*
> *Of fever moans and infant wails,*
> *Of births and deaths and bridal nights".'*

He had an attractive voice and she listened, enthralled. When he'd finished, she said, 'I see what you mean.' Then, 'Do you like poetry?'

Picking up the surprise she had failed to hide, he laughed. 'You sound as if you think liking poetry is in some way effeminate.'

'No, of course I don't. I just hadn't put you down as someone who would…' The words tailed off.

As though afraid of spoiling his macho image, Kevin had frequently decried poetry as being only for women or sissies.

'But in answer to your question,' Richard went on, 'yes, I like poetry. Mainly the classical stuff. People like Marvell and Donne. How about you?'

For the rest of the way back they discussed poetry.

When they reached the castle, the housekeeper appeared in the hall and beamed at them both, before addressing Richard. 'The Reverend Peter mentioned that the wedding ceremony will be taking place tomorrow morning.'

'That's right.'

'Cook and I will be pleased to organise a wedding breakfast, if you can give me some idea of numbers?'

'As I intend to keep things quiet and private, only ourselves, the indoor staff and the estate workers.

'Later, when we return from our honeymoon, I hope to have another ceremony, with guests, a reception and all the trimmings.'

Hannah smiled and nodded, before saying, 'All the things you asked for have been delivered and are waiting in your suite.

'Signora Diomede, who brought them over personally, asked me to say that should there be the slightest problem, if you give her a ring she'll sort it out.'

Turning to Tina, she went on, 'If you would like some help dressing tomorrow, please let me know.'

Visualizing her simple blue sheath, Tina said, 'Thank you, Hannah, but I really don't think I'll need any help.'

Hannah nodded. 'As you wish. Now, would you like tea served in the downstairs sitting-room, Mr Richard, or in your suite? As it seems to have turned appreciably cooler, I've had all the fires lit.'

'Then we'll have tea upstairs, please, Hannah.'

When they reached the suite, a blue dusk was pressing against the leaded panes while a log fire blazed cheerfully in the grate.

They had just settled themselves on the couch in front of it, when Milly arrived with the tea tray and put it down on a low table before giving a little bob and departing.

Along with the tea were some muffins, a large pat of butter and a bowl of clear golden honey and a long-handled toasting fork.

'Shall I toast the muffins?' Richard asked, 'or would you like to join in the fun?'

'I'd like to join in,' Tina answered without hesitation. 'I haven't toasted a muffin since I was a child and though, to be honest, I nearly always burnt them, I used to love it.'

Amused by her enthusiasm, he handed her the toasting fork and said, 'Right, you can do the first two, I'll do the second.'

Spearing a muffin, she knelt down in front of the blaze and, a little frown of concentration furrowing her forehead, set to work.

He watched the flames flickering on her lovely profile and her cheeks growing pink from the heat when she turned her head to smile at him. He was filled with a sudden fierce, all-consuming anger that made him want to smash his fist against something and rage against fate.

Although he was well aware that she wasn't the sweet innocent she seemed, he knew without a shadow of a doubt that she was the woman he'd been waiting for. The only woman who had ever got under his skin and into his blood.

In addition, he was starting to appreciate that, as well as outward beauty, she had an inner strength, a mind of a curiously tough quality that stimulated his own. And, perhaps most important of all, an *integrity* that made him wonder if he shouldn't have chosen one of the other options.

But, despite the fact that so much hung in the balance, he could only go forward. It was far too late to alter his plans...

'There!' she said triumphantly. 'Two perfectly toasted muffins...'

Having admired the golden buns, he said quizzically, 'I can see that when it's my turn I've got a lot to live up to.'

When the tea had been drunk and the last of the muffins

eaten, Tina sighed contentedly and with the end of a pink tongue licked a dribble of honey from her index finger. 'I won't need anything else to eat for a week.'

His white teeth gleamed as he laughed. 'At the moment I feel much the same, so it's just as well we settled on an eight o'clock dinner. I dare say by then we'll both have changed our minds.'

Having moved the tea things out of the way, he crossed to one of the occasional tables and, picking up a small pile of midnight-blue boxes, dropped them on to the couch beside her.

'In the meantime, suppose you open your things?'

'My things?' she exclaimed. 'But I thought you said we'd shop for a trousseau tomorrow afternoon.'

'And so we will. However, you need something to be married in.'

Taking a seat in one of the armchairs, he watched her face and heard her catch her breath as she untied the silver ribbon and lifted the first lid.

Inside, enfolded in the finest tissue paper, was a beautiful ivory silk wedding gown, with a medieval-style neckline and sleeves. A discreet label stated that it was designed by Bertolli.

Accompanying it was a rhinestone coronet, a gossamer veil, matching shoes, sheer silk stockings and delicate underwear.

Everything a bride could need, and all things she would have chosen herself.

How could she have suspected him of being insensitive?

She looked up, her eyes swimming with tears, and said simply, 'Thank you.'

'I hope you like the dress.'

'Oh, I do.' As, impulsively, she went over to him and stooped to kiss him, a single bright tear escaped and rolled down her cheek.

He made an inarticulate sound and, pulling her on to his knee, kissed it away before finding her mouth once more.

When finally he reluctantly freed her lips, she said huskily, 'I don't understand how you managed to get it on a Sunday.'

'Apart from the fact that I have a financial interest in Bertolli's, Signora Diomede, the head of that particular branch, is a friend of mine, so it was easy. All I needed to do was phone and tell her your size and what I wanted.

'Unfortunately, because it was such short notice, it had to be a dress that was already in stock, but—'

Tina put a slim finger to his lips. 'Don't say *unfortunately*. I couldn't have wished for anything lovelier, truly.'

He looked pleased, then, his hands at her waist, he lifted her to her feet and rose with her. 'Though I was fairly confident about your size, it might be as well to make sure it fits.'

Then, briskly, 'While you're trying things on I've a spot of business to catch up with. As soon as that's sorted I'll talk to Murray Tyler and start making the arrangements for our honeymoon.'

Dropping a light kiss on her lips, he turned to go. As he reached the door he paused to say, 'When I get back, we can give each other our undivided attention for the rest of the evening.'

But the mention of a honeymoon had broken the spell he had so successfully woven and once again she could hear Helen O'Connell's voice saying derisively, '...he's planning to take you away on a nice little honeymoon, I imagine?'

Doing her utmost to push the unpleasant memory away, Tina carried the packages through to her bedroom—where a neat pile of freshly laundered clothes awaited her—and, having unpacked the contents, tried them on.

But her heart was no longer in it and, though everything fitted perfectly and in a detached kind of way she knew she had never looked so beautiful, her happiness had dispersed like morning mist.

Remembering that disturbing little scene by the moat, she

felt tense and anxious and, as she took off her wedding dress and hung it up, she marvelled at how skilfully Richard had managed to take, and keep, her mind off it.

Until that fatal mention of a honeymoon.

Now all the doubts and questions were back, buzzing through her head, distracting and dangerous as a swarm of hornets.

What had Helen meant when she'd said, 'He seems to think that marrying you is the only way…'?

The only way to achieve *what*?

And then the even more disturbing, '…don't let yourself be conned; as soon as he's got what he wants and the honeymoon's over, he'll divorce you—'

Conned…that was a very emotive word…and *as soon as he's got what he wants*…

But what could he possibly want?

She was already sharing his bed and, compared to him, she was a mere nobody, with no money, no job and no background, so it just didn't add up.

If he *didn't* love her, but for some obscure reason he needed a wife, surely he could have married Helen?

Confused and agitated, trapped in a maze of doubts and conjectures, Tina was sitting by the fire still brooding over it when Richard returned.

It was nearly eight o'clock and as he came in he said apologetically, 'I'm sorry to have been so long, but my business took a lot more time than I'd anticipated.

'I take it you've tried your things—?' Catching sight of her face, he broke off to ask, 'What's the matter? Did I get the size wrong?'

A little jerkily, she assured him, 'No, no… everything's fine. The dress fits perfectly…'

'But you don't like it on?'

'Yes, I do. It looks lovely.'

'So what's the problem?'

For a moment she considered telling him and asking for answers to her questions, but almost instantly she dismissed the thought. Instinctively she knew he wouldn't give her any. He would dismiss the whole thing as nothing more than a jealous woman trying to make trouble.

Which perhaps it was.

Summoning a smile, she said, 'There is no problem.'

He came over and, tilting her face up to his, insisted, 'Sure?'

'Quite sure.'

But her blue-violet eyes were clouded and, guessing what was bothering her, he cursed Helen's interference afresh.

The moment he removed his hand and stepped back, she rose to her feet and said hurriedly, 'I'd better see about getting showered and changed, otherwise I'll hold you up.'

She saw his mouth tighten, but he let her go without comment.

Dinner that night was a strained meal. Tina tried hard to appear her usual self and even managed to keep up a desultory conversation. But, uneasy and preoccupied, her head aching dully, she could scarcely eat a thing.

Watching her push her food round and round her plate, he remarked carefully, 'You don't appear to be eating much.'

A shade defensively, she said, 'It was a mistake to have two muffins.'

He said nothing further and she was relieved when, a little later, coffee was served.

When their cups were empty, he asked, 'What would you like to do for the rest of the evening?'

Feeling the need to be alone, she said, 'I'm rather tired. I'd like to have an early night.'

When she got to her feet, he rose with her. 'Not a bad idea.' Taking her hand, he studied her through long thick lashes. 'We could provide our bed with another tale to tell.'

She half shook her head.

He sighed. 'It's Helen, isn't it? I've told you not to take any notice of all that nonsense, but you're still worrying about it, aren't you?'

Knowing it was useless to discuss it, she denied, 'Not really.'

'Don't lie to me.'

Her throat desert-dry, her voice ragged, she said, 'I've got a headache.' Then, sensing his angry impatience, she stammered, 'I—I'm sorry, but I…'

'Don't worry, I subscribe to every woman's right to say no when she wants to.'

'I really do have a headache.'

'In that case I'll just hold you in my arms while you sleep.'

'I'd rather sleep alone,' she blurted out.

His jaw tightened before he said, 'Very well, if that's what you want, I'll say goodnight.'

He lifted her hand to his lips.

Chilled by that frigid courtesy, she mumbled, 'Goodnight,' and hurried upstairs.

Though it was true that she was tired, both physically and mentally, once in bed she was unable to sleep.

For what seemed an age she tossed and turned restlessly, plagued by unanswerable questions, her thoughts circling endlessly and always coming back to the same thing.

She had nothing to give Richard, apart from her love and a lifetime's commitment, so if he didn't love her, why was he so eager to marry her?

Surely he *must* love her, otherwise it didn't make any sense.

So why was she here alone? Why—she thought as she'd thought earlier—was she allowing another woman's jealousy to spoil her happiness?

Taking a deep breath, she got out of bed and, making her way to the master bedroom, opened the door quietly and slipped inside.

There were no lights burning, but in the glow from the dying fire she could see that Richard was lying flat on his back, his chest and shoulders bare, his hands clasped behind his dark head.

He was awake, she could see the gleam of his eyes in the semi-darkness as he turned his head to look at her, but he said nothing.

She quailed inwardly. Perhaps he was still angry at the way she had rejected him? Perhaps she was no longer welcome?

As she stood shivering, uncertain whether to go or stay, he reached out a hand.

When she slipped hers into it, he lifted the quilt and, still without a word, drew her into the bed and against the warmth of his naked body.

With a little sigh, she nestled against him, her head at the comfortable juncture between breastbone and shoulder, her hand flat on his chest.

The brush of fine body hair against her palm was both exciting and erotic and, feeling desire stir, she waited for him to make a move.

When he continued to lie there quite still, she realised he wasn't going to. She had pleaded a headache and he had taken her at her word. If she wanted to alter the scenario, *she* would have to make the running.

After a momentary hesitation she snuggled closer and, her fingers stroking over his smooth pectoral muscles, ran the sole of her foot up and down his hair-roughened leg.

When he continued to lie motionless, she let her hand slide over his ribcage and trim waist and down his flat stomach until it reached the crisp silkiness of hair.

All at once, his hand closed over hers and held it stationary. 'Be careful,' he warned softly. 'Don't tease unless you're prepared for the consequences.'

'Consequences?' she asked innocently.

'Yes, consequences.' He took his hand away.

Reminding herself that tomorrow he would be her husband, she did what she'd been longing to do and boldly let her fingers close around the warm firmness of his flesh.

She heard the breath hiss through his teeth before he remarked evenly, 'I thought you had a headache?'

'I did.'

'Does that mean it's gone?'

'Yes.'

'How convenient,' he said sarcastically.

She bit her lip and started to move away, but his arm tightened, pinning her there.

'Sorry, but it's too late to change your mind. I did warn you not to tease.'

'I wasn't teasing. At least not exactly… I—I wanted you to make love to me.'

'Wanted? Past tense?'

'I still do.'

'In that case…' With a sudden movement she was unprepared for, he turned and flipped her on to her back. 'Let me see what I can do to oblige.'

Suddenly scared of him in this mood, scared of what she had provoked, she whispered, 'Please, Richard.'

'Don't worry, I intend to.' With ruthless hands he stripped off her nightdress and tossed it aside.

A moment later she was quivering helplessly as, starting at her feet, his mouth began to move up her slim legs, planting soft baby kisses, lingering on the smooth skin on the insides of her knees and inner thighs as it moved inexorably towards its goal.

His lovemaking was prolonged and inventive and he wrung sensation after sensation from her, so piercingly sweet, so exquisite, that she was limp and shattered before he finally allowed her to sleep.

* * *

When she awoke in the morning, though it was quite early, she was alone in the big bed, the space beside her cold and empty.

Sitting up against the pillows, she sighed.

In spite of last night's attempt to put things right, the doubts and uncertainties Helen O'Connell's words had caused had driven a wedge between Richard and herself.

Though his lovemaking had been both skilful and passionate, she recognised unhappily that it had been fuelled by anger rather than love.

She sighed once more.

Today she was getting married. It should have been the most wonderful day of her life. *Would* have been the most wonderful day of her life if… But what earthly use was there in going over it all again?

She made an effort to focus on happier things.

In just a few hours she would be Richard's wife and tomorrow they would be going on their honeymoon. It seemed incredible. Everything had happened so quickly that not another soul knew.

Apart from Helen O'Connell…

She could hear the other woman's bitter laugh on being told, and her comment, 'I have to hand it to him. He said there was no time to lose, but I didn't think he could bring it off so soon.'

As the words echoed and re-echoed in her mind, Tina had a sudden vivid recollection of standing outside the living-room door yesterday morning, listening to the exchange between Richard and Helen.

Agitation making her heart beat faster, she went over in her mind everything she had overheard.

At the time she hadn't known what the argument was about. Now she did. Or at least to some extent.

Though she couldn't make heads nor tails of a lot of what had been said, it was clear that Helen had being trying to dissuade Richard from rushing into this marriage.

The quarrel had ended with her asking desperately, 'But have you considered the ethics of it?'

Richard had answered, 'You mean two wrongs don't make a right? Oh, yes, I've considered all that. But I'll do whatever it takes. As far as I'm concerned, the end justifies the means. I've far too much to lose to think of playing Sir Galahad...'

As Tina recalled the icy ruthlessness in his voice, shivers ran down her spine.

'I've far too much to lose...'

Though she still had no idea what it was he wanted from her, one thing was suddenly clear in her mind, until she knew the truth she couldn't marry him.

But obviously it was no use asking him; he wouldn't tell her. *Though Helen O'Connell might.* If she could find a way of getting to talk to the other woman without Richard knowing.

After some thought, Tina dismissed the idea of trying to phone. This was something that needed to be tackled face to face. But it must be three or four miles to Farrington Hall where the O'Connells lived and there wasn't much time...

How long would it take her to walk?

Too long.

Then it came to her in a flash. If she could sneak out of the house and get to the stables—rather than chance running into any of the servants, she would have to leave by the main entrance—she could say she wanted to ride and borrow Juno.

Scrambling out of bed, she picked up her discarded night-dress and hurried through to the guest room.

When she had showered and dressed in the trousers and silky shirt she had worn the previous morning, she went quietly down the stairs. She had just reached the hall when she heard the sound of a door opening and closing somewhere near at hand.

She froze, her heart beating fast.

After a moment or two when there was no sound of approaching footsteps, feeling like a criminal, she crept across the hall and out of the house.

Already the morning was warm and sunny and by the time she had hurried to the stables she was hot and out of breath.

Josh was in the yard moving some bales of hay while the two horses looked out of their stalls.

'Morning, miss.' He touched his forelock.

'Morning, Josh.'

'You'll be wanting a ride?'

'If it's no trouble?'

'Why, bless my soul, none at all. Juno's raring to go. I'll 'ave 'er saddled up in a trice.'

Passing Tina the riding hat she'd worn the previous day, he queried, 'Is Mr Richard following on?'

'No, he's… he's busy just at the moment.'

While the groom was saddling the mare, Tina pulled on the hat and, in an absolute fever of impatience, hovered by the mounting block. What would she do if Richard suddenly appeared?

But, to her great relief, he didn't and, a minute or so later, with a word of thanks to Josh, she was in the saddle and heading for Farrington Hall.

CHAPTER TEN

KNOWING roughly where the Hall lay but unsure of the exact route, Tina set off across the park until she reached a pleasant track that appeared to lead in the right general direction.

The going was smooth and easy and, after a hundred yards or so, she urged the mare to a canter for a while before dropping to a trot.

They had almost reached the perimeter of the park when she caught sight of a house in the distance surrounded by a stone wall and fronted by sloping green lawns. An oblong built of mellow stone with symmetrical rows of windows and chimneys and a porticoed entrance, it was solid-looking and stately rather than beautiful.

This had to be Farrington Hall.

Skirting a cattle grid, she opened a weighted gate to the right without dismounting and left the park to follow a quiet lane.

After a while she came to a grand gateway, but the gate-house appeared to be unoccupied and the black wrought iron gates, flanked by stone pillars surmounted by huge stone balls, stood wide.

Subduing her qualms, she rode in and followed a carefully tended drive up to a paved apron and the front entrance. There she dismounted and, still holding the reins, rang a large old-fashioned bell. When the door was answered by a neatly dressed elderly housekeeper, Tina gave her name and asked to speak to Miss O'Connell.

'If you'll be good enough to wait there a moment, Miss Dunbar, I'll tell Miss Helen you're here and get young Tom to take care of your horse.'

She had been gone a minute or so when a young man in shirt sleeves appeared round the side of the house. As he said a civil, 'Good morning,' to Tina and took Juno's reins, Helen O'Connell appeared in the hall.

Looking as if Tina's unexpected visit had flustered her, she said shortly, 'I was just finishing breakfast. You'd better come through.'

Having led the way into a sunny morning room, she waved Tina to a chair and asked, 'Would you like some coffee?'

'No, thanks. I don't want to take up a lot of your time, but I need to know what you meant by, "…don't let yourself be conned; as soon as he's got what he wants…he'll divorce you".'

Helen's lips tightened. 'Try asking Richard.'

'Do you think he'd tell me?'

'I very much doubt it,' Helen admitted.

'You said, "…if all this trouble hadn't blown up he would have married me…" If you really believe that, and you don't want me to marry him, you'd better tell me what you meant by "all this trouble" and what it is he wants from me.'

'And if I don't?'

'Then I'll go ahead with the wedding. If you're so confident he'll divorce me, perhaps you—'

Her face contorted as though in pain, Helen cried, 'I don't believe in divorce.'

Tina felt sorry for the other woman but, reminding herself firmly that she *needed* to know, she said, 'Then it might pay you to tell me.'

'If I do, Richard will never forgive me.'

'He will if he cares at all for you.'

The other woman stayed silent and, realising she was beaten, Tina rose and was turning away when Helen said, 'Very well, I'll chance it. If he marries you, I've lost him anyway…

'It started when Bradley Sanderson died. He'd made a will leaving the castle to his daughter…'

'But I understood he hadn't got any children… And surely the castle wasn't his to—'

'That's just it—it *was*. He'd double-crossed Richard and left Anders to an illegitimate daughter no one knew he had.

'Apparently he'd had no contact with her and he didn't know where she was currently living. All he knew about her was her name, roughly how old she was and where she'd lived after being adopted, so it was left to his solicitors to trace her. Which they did, surprisingly quickly—'

'But I don't see what this has to—'

'*You're* Bradley Sanderson's daughter.'

As Tina gaped at her, deprived of speech, Helen went on, 'Richard realised that, once the solicitors had been in touch with you, it would be too late.

'He dreaded the thought of losing Anders and he decided that his best chance of keeping it under his control was to marry you before you learnt about your inheritance. That was the reason for all the haste.'

It made a terrible kind of sense, apart from one thing. Finding her voice, Tina said flatly, 'There's no way I can be Bradley Sanderson's daughter.'

For a moment Helen looked shaken. Then she said, 'The solicitors believe you are. They've already written to you…'

As Tina began to shake her head, Helen added, 'Richard told me he'd intercepted their letter.'

Recalling the unopened letter that had so mysteriously vanished, Tina felt shock hit her like a blow over the heart.

But she couldn't be Bradley Sanderson's daughter.

Though clearly Richard believed she was, and that was

why he'd tried to rush her into this marriage. Why he had wanted her to sign the paper saying that, if they were divorced, she relinquished any claim to the castle.

All the talk of love at first sight had only been a lie, a sham. He cared nothing for her. His only concern had been to safeguard his inheritance.

She was filled with pain, an agony so intense that it gripped her like an iron maiden, paralysing her heart and her lungs and making cold perspiration break out on her forehead.

After a moment or two the worst of the pain passed, leaving her cold and numb and empty, as though some vital life force had been extinguished.

Through stiff lips, she said, 'Thank you for telling me,' and made her way blindly across the hall and out to where Tom was waiting with Juno.

Having thanked him, she mounted and, thoughts tumbling through her mind, chaotic as clowns, set off back to the castle.

When she had returned Juno and the borrowed riding hat and assured Josh she'd had an enjoyable ride, she crossed the wooden bridge and went in through the rear entrance.

As she was crossing the servants' hall, Hannah appeared and, a look of relief on her face, said, 'Good morning, Miss Dunbar.'

'Good morning, Hannah.' Tina was pleased to find that her voice sounded relatively normal.

'Mr Richard will be glad to see you,' Hannah went on. 'He couldn't imagine where you'd got to.'

'Where is he now?'

'He's out looking for you. I'll send Mullins to tell him you're back…'

The grandfather clock in the corner wheezed asthmatically and struck nine-thirty.

'If you've changed your mind about needing any help with your wedding dress—' the housekeeper began.

'Thank you, Hannah, but I haven't. Perhaps you'll be kind enough to ask Mullins to tell Mr Richard that I'll wait for him in his study?'

Leaving the housekeeper looking perplexed and uneasy, Tina squared her shoulders in preparation for the forthcoming confrontation and made her way to the study.

She had been there only a short time when the latch clicked and Richard came striding in.

He was smartly dressed in a grey suit and a matching silk shirt and tie, but for once his calm self-control was absent. He looked rattled, his face pale, his dark hair untidy, as though he'd been raking agitated fingers through it.

'Where the devil have you been?' he demanded urgently. 'I've looked everywhere for you.'

Steadily, she said, 'I took Juno and rode over to see Helen O'Connell. There were some questions I needed answers to.'

A shutter came down. 'And?'

'I got them.'

With a glance at his watch, he suggested, 'Perhaps we can discuss what Helen told you later? The Reverend Peter will be waiting.'

'Now I know *why* you want to marry me I've no intention of going through with the wedding,' she informed him quietly and held her breath, waiting for the storm.

It never came.

Just as quietly, he said, 'Then, if you'll excuse me for a few minutes, I'll let the Reverend Peter know that the ceremony is postponed.'

'*Cancelled.*'

His mouth twisted. 'It seems that Helen's done a good job.'

'As it's the truth, it isn't fair to blame *her*.'

'Are you quite satisfied that what she told you *is* the truth?'

Tina swallowed hard. 'Yes.'

He turned on his heel and left without a word.

Suddenly feeling limp and slightly sick, she sank down in the nearest chair.

She was still sitting staring unseeingly into space when he came back a few minutes later.

Glancing up at his entrance, she saw that he had regained his self-control and was now the cool, assured man she was used to.

Dropping into a chair opposite, he suggested levelly, 'Perhaps you'd better tell me exactly what Helen said.'

'At first she didn't want to say anything, but when I pushed her she told me that Bradley Sanderson had double-crossed you and left the castle to his illegitimate daughter.

'She said you thought that *I* was that daughter and you were trying to rush me into marriage before I discovered that I'd inherited the castle.'

His tawny eyes on her face, he asked, 'And do you believe that?'

'It's the truth, isn't it?'

'Yes,' he admitted.

'What did you intend to do when I discovered *why* you'd married me? Presumably you couldn't have hidden the reason for too long.'

'At first I wasn't sure,' he admitted. 'I told myself I would deal with that when it happened.

'Then, when I started to get to know you, I decided that as soon as we got back from our honeymoon I'd tell you everything. I hoped very much that when you knew the truth you'd stay with me.'

'Helen O'Connell was sure that you intended to divorce me and, as you'd got me to sign a paper giving up all rights to the castle—'

'That wasn't because I intended to divorce you,' he broke in. 'It was a precaution in case you wanted to divorce me.'

'If I had, you'd got everything sewn up quite nicely,' she said with some bitterness. 'And if I'd tried to take it to court, you had the necessary money and clout to make sure you'd win.'

Quietly, he said, 'Believe me, I'm not proud of the way I've acted. Everything I've done was done out of sheer desperation.'

All the pain she felt evident in her voice, she cried, 'I just don't see why you felt you had to marry me. There must have been some other way. It isn't as if you haven't got money—'

'Oh, yes, I've got money. But I couldn't be sure you'd be willing to sell the castle. And even if you *had* been willing, not knowing what kind of woman you were, I didn't want to find myself over a barrel and bled dry.'

'I would never have done such a thing.'

Leaning forward, he took her hand. 'Now I know you better, I'm sure you wouldn't. But there was no time to find out what kind of woman I was dealing with.

'I had to take drastic action in order to keep Anders. Apart from the fact that I love the old place, it's my heritage, my birthright.

'Please try to understand…'

'I do, in a way.'

Unsettled by his touch, she pulled her hand free before going on, 'What I *don't* understand is how Bradley was able to will it away from you.'

Richard sighed. 'As I told you, I'd agreed to my mother putting a codicil in her will giving him the right to live at the castle until his death.

'At the time he seemed satisfied with that, but when she became really ill he began to put pressure on her to change it. He told her it was his dearest wish to actually be master of the castle for the short time he had left. He added that he thought she owed it to him.

'Finally, when she couldn't hold out against him any longer, she agreed to do as he asked on condition that he then bequeathed it to me.

'Both those wills were formally drawn up by Alexander Fry, the family's solicitor.

'A few weeks later, Fry rang up and spoke to my mother. He asked if she knew that Bradley had been in and made another will.

'When she admitted that she hadn't known, he said, "I rather thought not".

'He added that he was unable to disclose the contents of the second will, but he thought she should be aware that it invalidated the first.

'Though she knew of no one Bradley would want to leave anything to, she was seriously concerned.

'She talked the whole thing over with Hannah and the Reverend Peter—that's how I came to learn about it—and, afraid that Bradley was planning something underhand, she decided to make a second will herself.

'By now she was far too ill to go out and she didn't want to arouse Bradley's suspicions by having Fry come to the house, so on a single sheet of parchment she wrote that she bequeathed everything she owned to me and got the Reverend Peter and Hannah to witness it—'

Tina gave a sigh of relief. 'Then I don't see what the problem is.'

'The problem is that second will can't be found. I would have expected her to have put it in her secret drawer, but it wasn't there. And, after an intensive search, it still hasn't come to light, so I can only presume that Bradley found it and destroyed it.'

'Oh,' Tina said in a small voice.

'But, as Mother intended me to have Anders and the castle has been in my family so long, I'm regarding it as mine until Bradley's will has been proven and probate granted. Then, unless I fight it through the courts, which may take years, it will be yours.'

She shook her head. 'That's just it—it won't.'

His head came up. 'What do you mean— it won't?'

'I'm not Bradley Sanderson's daughter. I couldn't possibly be. My parents had been married over a year when I was born.'

Wearily, he began, 'That doesn't—'

'I know what you're going to say. The fact that they'd been married over a year doesn't rule out the possibility that my mother had an affair with Bradley.

'But I don't believe she did. Apart from the fact that she'd been brought up to have good moral principles, she and my father adored each other. She would never have looked at another man.'

'What was she like? Do you take after her?'

Tina shook her head. 'She was small and dark, like the rest of her family, with a gentle face and big grey eyes.

'What about Bradley—what did he look like?'

'He was short and thickset. His hair was iron-grey when I knew him, but it had been dark and his eyes were brown.'

'My father is tall and fair and blue-eyed. Everyone used to say I was the spitting image of him. I have a photograph of us together and the likeness is unmistakable.

'So you see there's been some mix-up.'

Richard frowned. 'Dunbar isn't a particularly common name and the solicitors must have been satisfied they'd found the right woman.'

'Helen mentioned that they'd written to me and that you'd...intercepted the letter.'

'Yes.' He looked momentarily discomposed. 'I'm sorry, but I thought it necessary.'

'How did you manage it?' she asked curiously.

'I was at Cartel Wines, and I saw you leave your office at lunch time—'

All at once everything clicked into place like a blurred photograph coming into focus. 'So you were watching me...'

He didn't deny it.

'Go on,' she said tightly.

'I went in and noticed a letter lying on your desk with the solicitors' names stamped on it. I was thrown by the fact that they'd managed to trace you so quickly.

'When I looked at the letter and found you hadn't yet read it, I thanked my lucky stars.

'I was still wondering what to do for the best when, from your office window, I saw you coming back through the gates.

'I pocketed the letter and came down. I was considering taking the chance to speak to you.'

'So why didn't you?'

'A kind of gut instinct that the timing wasn't right. I decided to wait until after De Vere had given you the news.'

'So it was your doing. I suppose taking steps to see I had no job was a way of softening me up, making me vulnerable...'

'Partly,' he admitted honestly. 'Also I'd regarded it as one less avenue through which the solicitors could contact you.'

'I see... What I don't understand is why, that evening, you tried to scare me.'

He turned and looked at her, holding her gaze. 'I wasn't trying to scare you.'

'Then why were you in the warehouse watching me...?'

He shook his head. 'You were so long coming down I began to think I'd missed you. When the security man had finished his rounds I went back to check that you were still in your office and found you were just leaving.'

She looked down at her hands, unable to look up at him. 'So you followed me out to my car and ran into me on purpose. Why?'

He sighed, lifting her chin so their eyes met. 'Though I had several strategies in place, I'd banked on having considerably more time. And, even though I'd taken the letter, I knew it would only be a matter of days before you learnt the truth.

'I decided I had to take some action, and quickly. My hope

was to drive you home and try to get to know you. It was a sheer stroke of luck that you had nowhere to sleep. The rest followed on from there…'

At the thought of what 'the rest' had been, she was filled with such anguish that for a moment she was unable to speak or move.

The whole thing had been just a sham. Lies and deception. And all for nothing.

Gritting her teeth against the onslaught of pain, she asked, 'Do you still have the solicitors' letter? It might provide an answer as to how the identity mix-up occurred.'

'I doubt it.' He got to his feet and, opening a drawer in his desk, took out a letter and handed it to her. 'Solicitors are usually too cautious to give much away.'

The envelope was addressed to Miss V Dunbar and in a red rectangle, opposite the franking, were the names Barnard, Rudge and Fry.

It was still sealed.

Her fingers just a shade unsteady, Tina tore it open and froze. After a stunned few seconds she read the cautiously phrased request that the recipient should contact them as soon as was convenient. The letter added that, after the necessary proof of identity had been provided, she would learn 'something to her advantage'.

'Well?' Richard asked. 'Does it provide an answer?'

'All the answer I need.' She handed him the letter.

He glanced through it, then said, 'They appear to have your given name wrong—'

'That's it exactly,' she broke in. 'It's headed Miss *Valerie* Dunbar…'

'It could be a secretarial mistake—'

'But it *isn't* a mistake. Had the envelope been addressed to Miss Valerie Dunbar, I would have known straight away that it wasn't for me.'

Richard was staring at her, his dark brows knitted.

'Don't you see; it's my stepsister who's Bradley's daughter! My stepmother once told me that she already had Valerie when she married her first husband.'

'You told me your stepsister was called Didi.'

'The family have always called her Didi, while her friends all know her as Val. She hated the name Valerie and wouldn't let anyone use it.'

Richard's thoughts raced. It seemed the solicitors had found the right woman and it was his own detective who had got mixed up.

So was the dossier Grimshaw had drawn up a picture of Valerie or Valentina?

Almost certainly, Valerie. He felt an overwhelming gladness. He'd been misjudging Valentina from start to finish. She wasn't the 'anything goes' young woman he'd presumed.

And that explained so much.

The first night he'd taken her to bed and been startled into thinking he was making love to an inexperienced woman, he'd been right.

Not really needing confirmation, but deciding to dot the 'i's and cross the 't's, he said, 'Tell me about your stepsister. What's she like?'

'She's beautiful. Slim, about my height, blonde and blue-eyed.'

'Naturally blonde?'

'No. When she doesn't change her colour, her hair's quite dark.'

'What is she like in character? You told me you and she were very different.'

'We are.'

'In what way?'

Tina sighed. 'I was always the quiet introvert, whereas Didi was headstrong and reckless. While she was still at school she got in with the wrong crowd. Her mother was worried to death about her—'

'Drink and drugs and sex,' Richard said.

'How did you know?' Tina demanded.

'My detective checked back.'

Realisation dawning, she cried, 'And you thought it was me!'

'Yes,' he admitted steadily, 'I did at first. Though I soon realised that nothing seemed to fit. You just didn't correspond with the picture he'd painted of you.

'The woman he described was bed-hopping when she was barely sixteen and since then she appears to have had numerous men in her life. While the only man you've mentioned was your fiancé.'

Then, frowning thoughtfully, 'I gather from what you've told me that your stepsister was living with you while you were engaged?'

'Yes.'

Watching Tina's face, noting her change of colour, he hazarded, 'Presumably she had something to do with the break-up?'

'I came home early one night and found them in bed together,' she told him flatly.

'And that's why you gave him his ring back.' It was a statement, not a question. 'What about her?'

'She said she was sorry. It hadn't been planned; it had just happened.'

'So you forgave her.'

'I always thought of her as being amoral rather than immoral.'

'Has she a boyfriend at the moment?'

'No one special that I know of. Why, were you intending to try to seduce and marry her?'

His jaw tightened as Tina's arrow went whang into the gold, but all he said was, 'You told me she was at drama school. I wondered who was paying her fees and supporting her...'

Tina remained silent, but suddenly recalling her saying, 'I have financial commitments that make it necessary to find another job without too much delay', he had his answer.

Carefully, he asked, 'How committed is she to the bright lights and becoming an actress?'

'I doubt if she would want to keep the castle, if that's what you mean. She always hated living in the country.'

'So you think she'll sell?'

'I'm sure of it. She's got her faults—haven't we all?—but greed isn't one of them, so if you offer her a fair price I believe she'll take it...'

His sigh of relief was audible.

'No doubt she'd squander it... But at least you'll have your home safe.'

Suddenly desperate to get away, she jumped to her feet and said, 'Now, if you'll please give me back my mobile...?'

He opened the top drawer of his desk and handed her the phone.

'Thanks.'

She turned to the door.

'Where are you going?' he asked sharply.

'Back to London to visit some employment agencies.' With a bitter little laugh, she added, 'I suggest you fire your so-called detective. If it hadn't been for him you wouldn't have wasted so much time and effort and I wouldn't be looking for another job...'

Richard caught her arm and brought her to a halt. 'Valentina, I—'

A knock cut through his words and he asked tersely, 'Who is it?'

Hannah came in, looking anxious and unhappy. 'I'm sorry to bother you, Mr Richard, but Cook would like to know what to do about meals...'

'You'd better tell her to serve lunch as usual.'

'And Miss O'Connell is asking to see you… She seemed very upset, almost hysterical.'

After a momentary hesitation he said, 'Very well. Perhaps you'll show her into the living-room?'

As Hannah turned to go, Tina pulled her arm free and made to follow her out.

'Wait,' Richard said. 'I need to talk to you.'

'As far as I'm concerned, there's nothing more to talk about. I intend to ring for a taxi and leave as soon as I've packed.'

'Valentina, listen to me,' Richard said urgently.

But, blinded by tears, she fled across the hall and up the stairs.

When she reached her room, she dashed the tears away with the back of her hand and, switching on her mobile, brought up the number of the Home Counties taxi firm.

Assured that a cab would be there within fifteen minutes, blinded by fresh tears, she began to push things higgledy-piggledy into her small case, trying to ignore the wedding dress that glimmered, pale and ghost-like, in the depths of the wardrobe.

Her packing finished, she was fastening the case when the ring she was still wearing caught the sun and flashed fire. Pulling it off, she hesitated for a moment, wondering where to leave the lovely thing. But somehow it seemed only right and proper to return it to its box.

She crossed to the writing desk and, as Richard had done, reached into the recess. After a moment, at either end her searching fingertips found a small, slightly raised area no larger than the head of a drawing pin. She pressed them simultaneously and the secret drawer slid open.

Taking out the velvet-covered box, which had previously held the three rings but was now empty, she put the solitaire back and returned the box to the drawer. But when she attempted to close it, the drawer slid part of the way and then stopped.

Realising that she couldn't have applied an even pressure, she tried once more.

But again it failed to close properly.

Wishing, now it was too late, that she had simply left the ring on the bedside cabinet, she tried for a third time to close the drawer.

Without success.

Wondering what was stopping it, she bent her head and peered inside. A small pale triangle right at the back of the drawer caught her eye. Something seemed to be trapped. But there was no way she could reach it, unless the drawer came right out.

After a moment's careful manoeuvring, she found it did, sliding free into her hands. Placing it carefully on the desk, she peered once more into the dimness of the recess.

Wedged in the small space behind the drawer was some crumpled paper that must have been caught and carried over the back. It might have stayed hidden there indefinitely if it hadn't somehow moved, preventing the drawer from closing properly.

Reaching in, she fished it out.

Though it was badly creased, the date and the writing were perfectly legible, as were the signatures of the two people who had witnessed it.

All she could feel was vast relief that justice would now be done.

She put her bag over her shoulder and her coat over her arm, then, her case in one hand and the will in the other, hurried out. She had just reached the head of the stairs when Richard and Helen came out of the living-room.

Standing like a statue, she watched him escort the other woman across the hall. He had an arm around her and they appeared to be the best of friends once more. Opening the door, he stooped and kissed her cheek. She gave him a fleeting smile as he followed her out.

After a second or two, Tina heard the sound of a car engine.

She had just reached the second stair from the bottom when Richard reappeared and crossed the hall to stand in her way.

'I suppose you saw Helen just leaving?'

'Yes,' she said.

'We had a talk and I told her how things stood, how I felt about you.'

'You appear to be good friends again.'

'Friends… Nothing more. She wished me well and said she hoped you'd stay.'

Looking him in the eye, Tina told him, 'The minute my taxi gets here I'm going and you can't stop me. But first I wanted to give you this.'

She held out the crumpled piece of paper.

He took it from her and stared down at it for a moment, then he looked up, his handsome face suddenly alight. 'Thank you,' he said simply. 'Where did you find it?'

'It was wedged behind your mother's secret drawer. I was putting her ring back when I found it wouldn't close properly. When I looked to see why not, I found the will wedged in the gap behind the drawer and the back of the desk… So now you've got what you want…' She made to brush past him.

'Oh, but I haven't.' He thrust the will into his pocket and, taking the case from her hand, tossed it aside. A moment later her coat and bag joined it.

Then, sweeping her up in his arms, he carried her into the living-room and, dropping her unceremoniously on to the couch, sat down beside her, trapping her there.

'Let me go,' she said raggedly. 'My taxi will be waiting.'

He shook his head. 'It came when I was seeing Helen off and I sent it away.'

'How dare you send it away when I—?'

'Before you think of leaving, we need to talk.'

'I've already told you that, as far as I'm concerned,

there's nothing more to talk about. I insist that you let me go this minute—'

He swooped and covered her mouth with his, stifling the angry words.

Only when she was limp and breathless did he raise his head. 'As far as you're concerned there may be nothing else to talk about, but you're going to stay and listen to what I have to say.

'First, however, I want to ask you something. Why did you bring the will to me?'

She looked at him blankly. 'I don't understand what you mean.'

'I mean that instead of giving it to me you could have destroyed it and made your stepsister rich.'

Horrified, she cried, 'What kind of woman do you think I am? Bradley had no right to the castle and Didi had no right to benefit from his perfidy. She would have been the first to admit that.

'As I told you before, she has her faults but she's neither dishonest nor mercenary. And, as she knows nothing about it, she won't grieve over it.'

'Even so, it will be my pleasure to make sure that her future is financially secure.

'Now, in answer to your question, I think you're honest and loyal and brave, the kind of woman that any man would be fiercely proud of and want to have in his life. I want you in mine.'

'If you imagine for one moment that—'

He put a finger to her lips. 'You have every right to be furious. I've treated you abominably. I've deceived you and lied to you. But not about everything. When I told you I'd fallen in love with you at first sight, it was true.

'My main fear was that when you discovered the truth you'd leave me. My only hope was that *you'd* said you loved *me*.

'Even when I thought the worst of you, I still wanted to marry you, wanted you to be my wife and the mother of my children.

'If I hadn't loved you and meant the marriage to be a permanent one I would never have suggested using my parents' rings…'

If she had needed any further proof that he meant what he said, that would have convinced her.

But when he went on with obvious sincerity, 'Anders means a great deal to me, but you mean more…' the last of her anger and resentment vanished and her heart swelled with love and gratitude.

He took her hand and held it tightly. 'If you don't marry me and live here with me for the rest of my life, I'll only be half alive.

'Say you can forgive me and let me start all over again. I'm willing to wait, to take things slowly this time.'

'I don't want to start all over again.'

She saw the naked despair in his face, the desolation he couldn't hide, and, putting the palm of her free hand against his cheek in the tenderest of gestures, went on. 'I love you. We have a priest and a chapel, a wedding dress and rings, so why wait? After all, we don't want to disappoint—'

The rest of the sentence was lost as he pulled her into his arms and began to kiss her.

When they finally drew apart a little, he said, a shade unsteadily, 'If the ceremony goes ahead as planned, then we won't disappoint Hannah.'

'I wasn't going to say Hannah,' she told him mischievously.

'Oh?' He raised a dark brow. 'Who *were* you going to say? The Reverend Peter?'

She shook her head. 'Our bed.'

Laughing, he pulled her back into his arms and said, 'My love, the way we feel about each other, we'll give it a whole new tale to tell.'

DATING THE
REBEL TYCOON

BY
ALLY BLAKE

Having once been a professional cheerleader, **Ally Blake** has a motto: 'Smile and the world smiles with you.' One way to make Ally smile is by sending her on holidays—especially to locations which inspire her writing. New York and Italy are by far her favourite destinations. Other things that make her smile are the gracious city of Melbourne, the gritty Collingwood football team, and her gorgeous husband Mark.

Reading romance novels was a smile-worthy pursuit from long back, so with such valuable preparation already behind her she wrote and sold her first book. Her career as a writer also gives her a perfectly reasonable excuse to indulge in her stationery addiction. That alone is enough to keep her grinning every day!

Ally would love you to visit her at her website: www.allyblake.com.

To my baby Boo.
You own my heart, you crack me up,
you dazzle me daily,
and it is my absolute privilege
watching you become you.
Love Mum xxx

CHAPTER ONE

CAMERON Kelly opened the heavy side-door of the random building, shut it smartly behind him and became enveloped in darkness. The kind of inky darkness that would make even the bravest boy imagine monsters under the bed.

It was some years since Cameron had been a boy, longer still since he'd realised people didn't always tell the truth. When he'd found out his two older brothers had made the monsters up.

The small window between himself and the Brisbane winter sunshine outside revealed the coast was clear, and he let his forehead rest on the cold glass with a sheepish *thunk*.

Of all the people he could have seen—many miles from where a man such as he ought to have been while commerce and industry raged on in the city beyond—it had to have been his younger sister Meg, downing take-away coffee and gabbing with her girlfriends.

If Meg had seen him wandering the suburban Botanical Gardens, pondering lily pads and cacti rather than neck-deep in blueprints and permits and funding for multi-million-dollar sky-scrapers, she would not have let him be until he'd told her why.

So he, a grown man—a man of means, and most of the time sense—was hiding. Because the truth would only hurt her. And, even though he'd long since been cast as the black sheep of the Kelly clan, hurting those he cared about was the last thing he would ever intentionally do.

He held his watch up to the parcel of light, saw it was nearly nine and grimaced.

Hamish and Bruce, respectively his architect and his project manager, would have been at the CK Square site for more than an hour waiting for him to approve the final plans for the fifty-fourth floor. This close to the end of a very long job, if they hadn't throttled one another by now then he would be very lucky.

He made to open the door to leave, remembered Meg—the one person whose leg he'd never been able to pull, even with two adept older brothers to show him how—and was overtaken by a stronger compulsion than the desire to play intermediary between two grown men. His hand dropped.

Let the boys think he was making a grand entrance when he finally got there. It'd give them something to agree upon for once. He could live with people thinking he had an ego the size of Queensland. He was a Kelly, after all; impressions of grandeur came with the name.

'We're closed,' a voice echoed somewhere behind him.

He spun on his heel, hairs on the back of his neck standing on end. Though he hadn't boxed since his last year at St Grellans, in a flash his fists were raised, his fingers wrapped so tight around his thumbs they creaked. Lactic acid burned in his arms. It seemed fresh air, sunshine and tiptoeing through the tulips weren't the catharsis for an uneasy mind that they were cracked up to be.

He peered around the huge empty space and couldn't see a thing past the end of his nose, bar a square of pink burned into his retina from the bright light of the window.

'I'm desperately sorry,' the voice said. 'I seem to have given you a little fright.'

Unquestionably female, it was, husky, sweet, mellow tones

drifting to him through the darkness with a surprisingly vivid dash of sarcasm, considering she had no idea who she was dealing with.

'You didn't frighten me,' he insisted.

'Then how about you put down your dukes before you knock yourself out?'

Cameron, surprised to find his fists were still raised, unclenched all over, letting his hands fall to his sides before shucking his blazer back onto his shoulders.

'Now, I love an eager patron as much as the next gal,' the mocking voice said. 'But the show doesn't start for another half-hour. Best you wait outside.'

The show? Cameron's eyes had become more used to the light, or lack thereof. He could make out a bumpy outline on the horizon, rows of seats decked out auditorium-style. They tipped backwards slightly so that an audience could look upwards without getting neck strain, as the show that went on in this place didn't happen on stage but in the massive domed sky above.

He'd stumbled into the planetarium.

Wow. He hadn't been in the place since he was a kid. It seemed the plastic bucket seats and industrial carpet scraping beneath his shoes hadn't changed.

He craned his neck back as far as it would go, trying to make out the shape and form of the roof. The structural engineer in him wondered about the support mechanisms for the high ceiling, while the vestiges of the young boy who'd once upon a time believed in monsters under the bed simply marvelled at the deep, dark, infinite black.

Finally, thankfully, one thing or another managed to shake loose a measure of the foreboding that ruminating over rhododendrons had not.

He kept looking up as he said, 'I'll wait, if it's alright by you.'

'Actually, it's not.'

'Why not?'

'Rules. Regulations. Occupational health and safety. Fire hazards. Today's Tuesday. You're wearing the wrong shoes. Take your pick.'

He slowly lowered his head, glancing down at his perfectly fine shoes, which he could barely see, and he was a heck of a lot closer to them than she was.

He peered back out into the nothingness, but still he couldn't make her out—whoever she was.

Was she security, ready to throw him out on his ear? A fellow interloper protecting her find? A delusion, born out of an acute desire to change the subject that had shanghaied his thoughts since he'd caught the financial news on TV that morning?

'Go now, and I can reserve you a seat,' the honeyed tones suggested.

Management, then. And strangely anticlimactic.

'I'll even personally find you a nice, comfy seat,' she continued. 'Smack bang in the centre, with no wobbles or lumps, that doesn't squeak every time you ooh or aah at the show. What do you say?'

He didn't say anything. He could tell she'd moved closer by a slight shifting of the air to his left, the sound of cloth whispering against skin, and the sudden sweet scent of vanilla making his stomach clench with hunger.

Had he forgotten to eat breakfast? Yes, he had. He swore softly as he remembered why.

The appearance on the financial report on the TV news by the very man who had made him a family outcast many years before had not been a bolt from the blue. Quinn Kelly, his father, was a shameless self-promoter of the family business: the Kelly Investment Group, or 'KInG' as it was irresistibly dubbed in the press.

His father was the epitome of the Australian dream. An immigrant who had come to the country as a boy with nothing to his name but the clothes on his back, he had built himself the kind of large, rambunctious, photogenic family the press prized, and a financial empire men envied. Tall, handsome, charming, straight-talking, the man acted as though he would live for ever, and the world believed him— needed to believe him—because he had his fingers in so many financial pics.

Cameron hadn't realised he'd believed the man to be immortal too until he'd noticed the pallor make-up couldn't hide, the weight lost from his cheeks, the dullness in his usually sharp eyes that would only have been noticed by someone who went out of his way not to catch a glimpse of the man every day.

For that reason it was highly possible that not even the family knew something was very wrong with Quinn Kelly. The rest of the clan was so deeply a part of one another's lives he could only imagine they had not noticed the infinitesimal changes.

He'd lost hours trying to convince himself it wasn't true. And not for the kinds of reasons that made him a good son, but because he'd felt the sharp awakening of care for a man not worth caring about. Why should he care for a man who'd so blithely severed him from his family to save his own hide, and that was after laying waste to any naivety Cameron might have yet possessed about loyalty and fidelity? And at an age when he'd not even had a chance to make those decisions himself.

It wasn't even nine in the morning and already Cameron wished this day was well and truly over.

'The door is right behind you,' the only highlight in his day so far said.

Cameron pulled himself up to his full height in the hope the unwanted concerns might run off his back. 'While I'm enjoying the thought of you testing each and every seat for me, I'm not here to see the show.'

'You don't have to act coy with me,' she said, her teasing voice lifting him until he felt himself rocking forward on his toes. 'Even big boys like you have been known to find comfort in the idea that there might be something bigger and grander than you are, out there in the cosmos, that will burn bright long after you are a two-line obituary in your local paper.'

Surprising himself, he laughed out loud, something he had not expected to do today. It wasn't often people dared to tease him. He was too successful, his reputation too implacable, his surname too synonymous with winning at all costs. Perhaps that was why he liked it.

'Your expertise on the ways of big boys aside,' he said, 'I saw the show years ago in middle school.'

'Years ago?' the husky voice lobbed back. 'Lucky for you, astronomers hit a point at *exactly* that point in time when they said, "Well, that'll do us. We've found enough stars out there for a hundred generations of couples to name after one another for Valentine's Day. Why bother studying the eternal mystery of the universe any more?"'

He laughed again. And for the first time in hours he felt like he could turn his neck without fear of pulling a muscle. He had not a clue if the woman was eighteen or eighty, if she was married or single, or even from this planet, but he was enjoying himself too much to care.

He took a step away from the door. He couldn't see the floor beneath his feet. It felt liberating, like he was stepping out into an abyss.

Until he stubbed his toe, and then it felt like he was walking around in a strange building in the dark.

Something moved. Cameron turned his head a fraction to the left, and finally he saw her: a dark blob melting into the shadows. If she was standing on the same level as him, she was tall. There was a distinct possibility of long, wavy hair, and lean curves poured into a floaty calf-length dress. When he imagined seriously chunky boots, he realised he didn't have any kind of perspective to trust his eyes.

But he'd always trusted his gut. And, while he'd come to the gardens searching for the means to navigate his way around a difficult truth, the only real truth he had so far found was the voice tugging him further into the blackness.

'How about you turn on a light?' he said. 'Then we can come to an arrangement that suits us both.'

'Would you believe I'm conserving power?'

There wasn't a single thing about the tone of her voice that made him even half believe her. His smile became a grin, and the tightness in his shoulders just melted away.

He took another step.

'Not for even half a second,' he said, his voice dropping several notes, giving as good as he got to that voice—that husky, feminine voice. Mocking him. Taking him down a peg or two. Or three, if he was at all honest.

He—a Kelly and all.

Rosie kept her distance.

Not because the intruder seemed all that dangerous; she knew the nooks and crannies of this place like the back of her hand, and after stargazing half her life she could see in the dark as well as a cat. And from the lazy way he'd held his fists earlier, like he'd instinctively known nobody would dare take a swipe, she'd surely have been able to get in a jab or two.

She kept her distance because she knew exactly who he was.

The man in the dark jeans, pinstriped blazer, glossy tie and crisp chambray shirt poking out at the bottom of the kind of knit V-necked vest only the most super-swanky guy could get away with was Cameron Kelly.

Too-beautiful-for-words Cameron Kelly. Smart, serious, eyes-as-deep-as-the-ocean Cameron Kelly. Of the Ascot Kellys. The huge family, investment-banking dynasty, lived their lives in the social pages, absolutely blessed in every possible way Kellys.

She would have recognised that untameable cowlick, those invulnerable shoulders, and the yummy creases lining the back of that neck anywhere. God only knew how many hours she'd spent in the St Grellans school chapel staring at them.

Not that getting up close and personal or turning on the light would have rendered her familiar. She'd been the scholarship kid who'd taken two buses and a train to get to school from the indifferent council flat she'd shared with her single mum. He had attended St Grellans by birthright.

Post-school they'd run in very different circles, but the Kellys had never been far from the periphery of her life. The glossy mags had told her that dashing patriarch Quinn Kelly was seen buying this priceless *objet d'art* or selling that racehorse, while his wife Mary was putting on sumptuous banquets for one or another head of state. Brendan, the eldest, and his father's right-hand man, had married, had two beautiful daughters, then become tragically widowed, adding to the family folklore. Dylan, the next in line, was the charmer, his wide, white smile inviting every magazine reader to dare join the bevy of beauties no longer on his speed dial. Meg, the youngest, was branded bored and beautiful enough to rival any Hollywood starlet.

Yet the one Rosie had always had a soft spot for remained mostly absent from the prying eyes of the paparazzi. He'd played into the Kelly legend just enough by sporting fresh new consorts every other week: a fabulous blonde senator on his arm at some party here, a leggy blonde dancer tucked in behind him at a benefit there.

Yet the minute he'd appeared without a blonde in sight, her soft spot had begun to pulse.

'Rightio,' she said, curling away to her left, away from Cameron and towards the bank of stairs leading to the front of the auditorium. 'What are you doing here if not to once and for all find out who truly did hang the moon and the stars?'

'Central heating,' he said without missing a beat. 'It's freezing out there.'

She grinned, all too readily charmed considering the guy still seemed to have blinkers when it came to skinny, smart girls with indefinite hair-colour and no cleavage to speak of.

And now she was close enough to make out the subtle, chequered pattern of his vest, the fine platinum thread through the knot of his tie, and the furrowing of his brow as his eyes almost found hers.

She took two definite steps back. 'The café just up the hill has those cool outdoor furnace-heaters—big, shiny brass ones that have to be seen to be believed. And I hear they also serve coffee, which is a bonus.'

After much longer than was at all polite, his voice drifted to her on a rumble. 'The allure of coffee aside, the warmth in here is more appealing.'

Her knees wobbled. She held out both arms to steady herself. Seriously, how could the guy still manage to incapacitate her knees without trying to, without meaning to? Without even knowing her name.

She wrapped her russet beaded-cardigan tighter around herself, squeezing away the return of an old familiar ache that she thought she'd long since cast off: the sting of growing up invisible.

Growing up with a dad who'd left before she was born, and a mum who'd never got over him, being inconspicuous had come with the territory. Being a shy unfortunate in a school saturated with the progeny of politicians, moguls and even royalty hadn't helped the matter.

But since then she'd achieved a master's degree in astrophysics, run with the bulls, stood at the foot of the sphinx, spent a month on grappa and fresh air on a boat off Venice and surveyed the stars from every corner of the globe. She'd come to terms with where she'd come from. And now hers was a life lived large and not for anyone else to define.

Cameron took another step forward, and she flinched, then indulged in a good eye-roll. An eyelash caught in her contact lens, which was about all she deserved.

As she carefully pulled it free she told herself that, just as she'd evolved, this guy wasn't *that* Cameron Kelly any more—the Cameron Kelly who'd seemed the kind of guy who'd smile back if she'd ever found the pluck to smile first. Maybe he never even had been.

Right now he was the guy wasting the last precious minutes she had with the observatory telescope, before Venus, her bread and butter, disappeared from view.

'Okay, tell it to me straight. What do I have to say or do to get you to vamoose?' She paused to shuffle her contact lens back into place. 'I know Italian, Spanish, a little Chinese. Any chance "off you pop" in any of those languages will make a dent?'

'What if I leave and not another soul turns up?'

Rosie threw her arms out sideways. 'I'll…grab a seat, put my feet up on the chair in front and throw popcorn at the ceiling, while saying all the lines along with the narrator. It wouldn't be the first time.'

That got her another laugh, a deep, dry, rumbling, masculine sort of laugh. Her knees felt it first, then the rest of her joined in, finishing off with her toes curling pleasurably into her socks.

She remembered exactly what the smile that went along with the laugh looked like. Deep brackets around his mouth. Appealing crinkles fanning out from a pair of cornflower-blue eyes. And there was even a dimple thrown in for good measure.

Yikes, she hadn't waded quite so deep into the miasma of her past in a long time. It was time she moved the guy on before he had her remembering former lives.

Knowing he'd follow, she circled him to the left and herded him towards the exit. 'I thought you weren't interested in the show?'

'You should never have told me about the popcorn.'

He edged closer, and she could tell by the slightest amount of diffused light from the window in the door behind her adding colour to his clothes that she couldn't back away much further.

She glanced at the glowing clock on the wall by the ticket office. Venus would only be visible another fifteen minutes at most. If she wanted to finish the day's assessment, she'd have to get cracking. 'So, try a movie. Far more action.'

'More action than supernovas, red dwarfs and meteor showers?'

'You boys and your love of all exploding, fiery things,' she said. 'Thank goodness there are women in the world to appreciate the finer details of the universe. You should sit still and just stare at the moon once in a while. You'd be amazed at the neural pathways a little down-time can open up.'

'Maybe I will.' This time the lift of one blazer-covered shoulder was obvious in the hazy sunlight. 'I was holding out on you before. I have my own telescope.'

Damn it! There weren't many things he could have said to have distracted her, but even a passing interest in the one great overriding passion in her life was a pull she couldn't resist.

'What type?' she asked.

'It's silver. Not solid silver. Maybe not even silver. Silver looking.'

'The silver-look ones are the best. It comes down to the light refracting off all that extra shininess.'

His half-second pause as he decided whether or not she was taking the mickey out of him was a pleasure. So much of a pleasure it made her soft spot for him stretch and purr.

'To tell you the truth,' he said, 'All I remember from way

back when is the bit about the wormholes. And I'm man enough to admit I lost a couple of nights' sleep over them.'

His voice was low. Rough. Suggestive. Her bad, bad lungs contracted until the air inside her felt like it had nowhere else to go but out in a great, big fat sigh.

She played with a turquoise bead on her cardigan. It had been sewn by the hand of a woman she'd found on the way to Rosarito, Mexico. She'd lived alone in a shack made of things she'd found on the edge of the most beautiful beach in the entire world. It reminded Rosie that she'd been places, seen amazing things, and was not easily impressed.

Waxing lyrical in the dark with Cameron Kelly ought not to feel so much like a highlight.

She straightened up. 'Fine. Since you're not staying for the show, I'll let you in on the big climax. Pluto isn't a planet any more.'

'It's not?' he asked, genuinely shocked. 'Poor Pluto.'

This time she was the one to laugh. Loose, low and most enjoyable.

And then she realised, all too late, that Cameron was close enough now that she could see the sunlight brush over evenly tanned skin, a straight nose, a smooth jaw and deep-set eyes. Eyes that had become so used to the light that they'd finally found hers.

He wasn't likely to be able to see much more than their shape, and perhaps the curve where ambiguous grey met the dark edges of her pupils, which were no doubt dilated from the lack of light. But he certainly seemed keen to try.

When his eyes left hers, she breathed again. Unfortunately she was not to be let off so lightly.

His glance took in her hair, which was likely a mess, since she'd had it up, down, twisted in a knot and in plaits since she'd arrived a little before sunrise. Then there was her long, floral dress she'd thrown on that morning because it had been atop the clean-clothes basket, the cardigan she'd found in the back of her car, and the comfortable boots that had taken her all over the world and brought her home again in one piece—but did little in terms of being fashionable or flattering.

It was the briefest of perusals. Really no more than a flick of his gaze. But that didn't stop her from wanting to fix her hair, hitch her bra, and wipe fingers beneath her eyes to remove any traces of smudged mascara that several hours of awake-time would have left behind.

Thankfully his gaze cut back to her eyes.

All traces of thankfulness dried up smartly when those famously blue eyes remained fixed on hers. Her throat grew dry. She tried to swallow, only to find she couldn't quite remember how.

She had the distinct feeling time was running out on something she was meant to be doing, but she couldn't for the life of her remember what it was. She wished ultra-hard for a light-bulb moment.

And got one.

Fluorescent bulbs by the dozen flickered in the walls around them, strobing on and off like disco lights.

In between dark patches, Cameron's eyes locked with hers, deep, dark, determined. She wondered for a moment how she'd ever thought she knew him…

And then he smiled. Cheek brackets. Eye crinkles. Dimple. And she felt like she was fourteen years old, complete with glasses, funny clothes and a crush.

Her glasses had been exchanged for contacts, and her now mostly pre-loved wardrobe was probably still a little funny. But at least the moony kid she'd once been was no more.

With every flash of intense white light, Rosie made sure her feet were well and truly on the ground.

CHAPTER TWO

ADELE, Rosie thought, giving the word in her head all the oomph of a curse.

It had to be Adele who'd turned on the lights. She was Rosie's best friend, the astronomer in residence at the planetarium, the one who let her use the observatory whenever she pleased, and the woman she most wished to tie up and gag most of the time—now being one of those times.

'That puts a whole new spin on "let there be light",' Cameron said, looking around before his gaze landed back on hers.

Even her amazing night-sight wasn't enough to ready her for the true wallop those of eyes: bluer than blue; the bluest blue. Bordered by thick chestnut lashes the same colour as his perfectly scruffy hair.

As for the rest of him…

As tended to be the way of the gods, they had decided that the boy who'd once had it all would turn out even better for the ageing. The years had sharpened the smooth edges, filled out the willing frame and tempered the blazing confidence of youth so that intense self-assurance now wrapped tight around him like a second skin.

Which congruently, in all her loose-haired, comfy-shoed, laid-back glory, made her feel like something the cat had dragged in. She fought the need to rewrap her cardigan tighter again.

'Jeez, hon, you sure you're not becoming a vampire?' Adele called as she clumped up the stairs. 'All that night-time activity finally getting to you? Oh, sorry. I didn't know you had company.'

Rosie's eyes swept to her friend, who was grinning and raising her eyebrows manically and pointing a thumb at Cameron's back.

Rosie quieted her friend with a withering look as she explained, 'I was just failing miserably at trying to convince this gentleman that we were not yet open and that he ought to come back another time.'

'Cameron,' he said, stepping closer. 'The gentleman's name is Cameron.'

Rosie blinked into his eyes.

It took a second or two before she realised he had stretched out a hand for shaking. She placed her hand in his. Warmth met cool. Soft skin met skin weathered by manual labour.

Her eyes flickered back to his. Manual labour? She searched his eyes for something to answer the unspoken question, but no matter how hard she tried she couldn't see even a millimetre beneath the blue. Because he didn't want her to, or because he didn't want *anyone* to?

Cameron Kelly, clean-cut and preppy, had been yummy. Cameron Kelly with hidden qualities was a force to be reckoned with.

'Rosalind,' Adele called out, leaning her backside against a chair before noisily biting down on an apple. 'The lady's name is Rosalind. Like the eighth moon of Uranus.'

'Like the character from *As You Like It*,' Rosie corrected. 'The eighth moon of Uranus wasn't discovered until 1986.'

'Either way, it's a pleasure to meet you, Rosalind,' Cameron said, somehow making the antiquated name she'd only ever thought of as just another hurdle sound almost wistful, pretty, romantic. She found herself correcting her posture to match.

Then she realised that, even with her name attached, there was still not a glimmer of recognition in the cool depths of his gaze.

She quickly deflated back into her normal, regular, perfectly content self. She did not need any man to notice her in order to feel interesting—and she couldn't believe she was really having to remind herself of that.

Then Cameron said, 'I realise this sounds incredibly corny, but have we met?'

'Smooth,' Adele muttered from the sidelines.

Rosie shot her so-called friend a frosty glare, but Adele only pointed at her watch, meaning they were about to open to the public.

Knowing that to pretend she had no idea what he was on about would only make her feel even more foolish, Rosie said, 'We have. I'm Rosie Harper. I was below you at St Grellans. I took advanced maths with Dr Blackman the same time as you.'

The fact that she'd spent more time imagining what it might be like to kiss him than taking actual notes had led to a B- that had threatened her full academic scholarship.

It had been a watershed moment; proving she'd inherited her mother's propensity to fall hard, and indiscriminately, and with no thought of self-protection.

She now protected herself so vigorously, even the common cold had a hard time getting near.

'Small world,' Cameron finally said, almost hiding the fact that he still couldn't place her behind the charming, crinkle-eyed, dimpled smile that had likely got him out of trouble his whole life.

His hand moulded ever so slightly more snugly around hers. She'd forgotten they were still holding hands, while he held on with a purpose she was only now just beginning to fathom.

His smile warmed, deepened, drew her in, as he said, 'In the interests of remaining corny, what do you say we—?'

The door behind him slammed open before he got out another word, and a harried-looking woman burst inside.

Rosie sprang away from Cameron as though they'd been two teenagers caught *in flagrante*. She ran the hand he'd been holding across the back of her hot neck, only to find the hand was hotter still.

The anxious woman said, 'Sorry to intrude. I'm Miss Granger, Kenmore South grade-four class teacher. Please tell me I can send the kids in? Another minute in the open and they'll be beyond my control.'

The teacher somehow managed to smile through her stress. Probably because she directed her comments entirely towards Cameron, who did look more in charge in his blazer and tie than Rosie did in her vintage get-up—and that was putting a nice spin on it.

Or maybe it was that indefinable X-factor that meant every woman he ever encountered ended up inexorably spinning in his orbit. Rosie, it seemed, was destined to be within perilously close proximity to this particular heavenly body once every fifteen or so years.

Fifteen years earlier he'd been a beautiful boy who'd brushed shoulders with her once or twice in a crowd. This time round he was a fully grown man who saw something in her that made him rethink moving on just yet. She'd hate to think what another fifteen years might do to the man's potency. Or aim.

She glanced up after a good few seconds staring at his shoulders to find him watching her. Unblinking. Radiating authority and curiosity.

Break eye contact, her inner voice said; *back away, roll into the foetal position, whatever it takes to make him head back to his side of the street leaving you to yours*.

'Pretty please?' the teacher asked Cameron.

Rosie had a feeling the woman was asking a completely different question from her first.

Before Rosie had the chance to tell Miss Granger she was barking up the wrong man, Adele called out, 'Send 'em on in, hon! Who are we to turn away those ready and raring to learn about the mysteries of the universe?'

'Who indeed?' Cameron asked.

Rosie steadfastly ignored him and his rumbling voice as Miss Granger heaved the heavy side door-open again, letting in wisps of cool late-winter air and a throng of kids in green tartan school uniforms, half-mast beige socks and floppy wide-brimmed hats.

They slid into the arena like water spurting through a bottle neck. But at the first sign of a break Cameron slipped through until he stood beside Rosie, well and truly within her personal space.

She kept her eyes dead ahead, but couldn't ignore the tug of his gravitational pull, the scent of new cotton, winter, and clean male skin. She breathed in deep through her nose, then pinched the soft part of her hand between her thumb and her index finger in punishment.

'Any feet seen touching any chairs will be forcibly removed!' Adele said as she was carried away with the noisy crowd.

And all too soon it was just the two of them again. Alone, in the unforgiving fluorescent light that couldn't seem to find one bad angle on him.

'It seems you really do have to get to work,' Cameron said, a hint of something that sounded a heck of a lot like the dashing of hope tinging his words.

Rosie's heart twitched, and kept on twitching. She coughed hard, and it found its regular steady pattern once more.

'No rest for the wicked,' she said, turning to him, thus allowing herself one last look before she brought this strange encounter to a halt.

Looking was allowed. Looking at pretty, bright, hot things was her job. And as it was much safer doing so from a great distance she began backing away, thus setting in motion the next fifteen years until they crossed paths again.

'It was great seeing you again, Rosalind.' A glint lit eyes that she was entirely sure had been that exact cornflower-blue from the moment he'd been born.

A jaunty salute and she was gone, hitting the top step at a jog and not stopping until she reached the control room at the bottom, as from there she couldn't tell if he had turned and left or if he'd watched her walk away.

The outer door shut behind Cameron with a clang, sending him out into the cold over-bright morning.

He stood on one spot for a good thirty seconds, letting the winter sun beat down upon his face, savouring the pleasant, hazy blur that an encounter with an intriguing woman could induce.

Rosalind Harper. St Grellans alumnus. How had he managed to go through the same school without once noticing that soft, pale skin, those temptingly upturned lips that just begged to be teased into a smile and the kind of mussed, burnished waves that made a man just want to reach out and touch?

He took a deep breath through his nose and glanced at his watch. What he saw there brought him back down to earth. And lower still.

Into his father's world.

Quinn Kelly was a shameless, selfish shark who a long time ago had convinced Cameron to keep a terrible secret to keep his family from being torn apart.

He'd done so the only way he'd known how, cutting himself off from the family business. As he saw it, if the man was as unscrupulous in his business dealings as he was in his personal life, God help the stock holders. Quinn on the other hand had seen it as a greater betrayal, and had cut him off completely, which in the end made for a nice cover as to why the two of them couldn't be in the same room together.

It hadn't for a minute been easy, looking his mother, brothers and sister in the eye while knowing what they did not. In the end he'd worked day and night to establish his own career, his own identity, his own manic pace with nonexistent down-time in which to miss those things he no longer had, or yearn for things he'd learnt the hard way didn't really exist, or scratch himself, giving himself a reasonable excuse to decline attendance at enough family gatherings that it was now simply assumed he would not come.

There was the rub. There was no subtle way to sound the others out. The only way to know for sure was to ask the man himself.

The opportunity was there, winking at him like a great cosmic joke. His father's seventieth birthday was less than a week away, and that was one invitation he had not managed to avoid. Every member of his family had called to remind him, all bar the big man himself.

There was no way he'd attend. For if it gave that man even an inkling that deep down he still gave a damn…

The echo of a bombastic musical-score sprang up inside the domed building behind him, more than matching the clashing inside his head. The star show had begun.

Cameron looked to his watch again. It didn't give him any better news. He shoved his hands deep into his trouser pockets, turned up the collar of his jacket against the cold and jogged towards the car park, the diminishing crunch of pine leaves beneath his feet taking him further and further from the gardens.

He turned to watch the great white dome of the planetarium peek through the canopy of gum trees. Quite the handy distraction he'd found himself back there. With her sharp tongue and raw, unassuming sex-appeal, Rosalind Harper had made him forget both work and family for as long a while as he could remember doing in one hit in quite some time.

He hit the car park, picked out his MG, vaulted into the

driver's seat, revved the engine and took off through the mostly empty car park, following the scents of smog, car exhaust, money and progress as he headed towards the central business district of the river city.

And the further away he got from all that fresh air and clear open sky—and from Rosalind Harper, her bedroom hair and straightforward playfulness—the heavier he felt the weight bear down upon his shoulders once again.

The fact that she was still at the forefront of his mind five sets of traffic lights later didn't mean he'd gone soft. It simply wasn't in his make-up to do so.

His parents had been married nearly fifty years. They were touted throughout the land as one of the great enduring romances of the modern age. Such tales had filled newspaper and magazine columns, and at one time they'd even had a tele-movie made about them.

But, if the specifics of their marriage was as good as it could get, he wasn't buying. Even a relationship that to the world looked to be secure, long-lasting, deeply committed could be a sham. What was the point?

The short-term company of an easygoing, uncomplicated woman, on the other hand, could work wonders. A dalliance with the promise of no promises. Having the end plan on the table before the project began sat very comfortably with the engineer in him.

Rosalind Harper had been an excellent distraction, and he knew enough to know that behind the impudent exterior she hadn't been completely immune to him. The spark had sparked both ways.

He saw a gap in the traffic, changed down a gear and roared into the spot.

His stomach lifted and fell with the hills of Milton Road, and he realised if he was going to endure the next week with any semblance of ease a distraction was exactly what he needed.

* * *

That afternoon, after taking a nap to make up for her usual pre-dawn start to the day, Rosie sat on the corrugated metal step of her digs: a one-bed, one-bath, second-hand caravan.

As she sipped a cooling cup of coffee, she stared unseeingly at the glorious hectare of Australian soil she owned overlooking the Samford Valley, a neat twenty-five-minute drive from the city.

For a girl who'd been happy to travel for many a year, the second she'd seen the spot she'd fallen for it. The gently undulating parcel of land had remained verdant through the drought by way of a fat, rocky stream slicing through a gully at the rear. High grass covered the rest of the allotment, the kind you could lie down in and never be found. A forest of achromatic ghost-gums gave her privacy from the top road, lush, subtropical rainforests dappled the hills below and in the far distance beyond lay the blue haze of Moreton Bay.

But it was the view when she tilted her head up that had grabbed her and not let go.

The sky here was like no other sky in the world. Not sky diffused with the glare of city lights, distorted with refraction from tall buildings or blurred by smog. But *sky*. Great, wide, unfathomable sky. By day endless blue, swamped by puffy white clouds, and on the clearest of winter nights the Milky Way had been known to cast a shadow across her yard.

She wrapped her arms about her denim-clad knees, quietly enjoying the soothing coo of butcher birds heralding the setting of the sun.

A mere week earlier her work day would have been kicking off as Venus began her promenade across the dusk sky, masquerading as the evening star. Now that Venus had begun her half-yearly stint as the morning star, Rosie was still getting used to the crazy early starts to the day, and finding it tricky to know what to do with her evenings.

This evening she had no such trouble, filling it ably by

reliving her curious encounter with Cameron Kelly. The way one side of his blazer collar had been sticking up as though he'd left the house in a hurry. The way he still hadn't worked out how to stop his fringe from spiking out in all different directions. The way she'd felt his smiles even when he'd been little more than a Cameron-shaped outline. The way her skin had continued to hum long after she'd last heard his deep voice.

She sighed deep and hard, and figured she'd at least get some pleasant dreams out of it!

All of a sudden her bottom vibrated madly. When she realised it was the wretched mobile-phone Adele had made her buy when she'd moved back to Brisbane—lest they live within the same city but never see one another—she picked it up, stared at the shiny screen, and jabbed at half a dozen tiny buttons until it stopped making that infernal 'bzz bzz' noise that made her teeth hurt.

'Rosie Harper,' she sing-songed as she answered.

'Hey, kiddo.' It was Adele. Big surprise.

'Hey, chickadee,' she returned.

'I have someone on the other line who wants to talk to you, so don't go anywhere.'

'Adele,' Rosie said with a frown, before she realised by the muzak assaulting her ear that she was already on hold. 'Girl, I'm gonna throw this damn thing in the creek if you're not—'

'Rosalind,' a deep, male voice said.

Rosie sat up straight. 'Cameron?'

She slapped herself across the forehead as she realised she'd given herself away. If she hadn't been thinking of him in that moment it wouldn't have made a difference. Deep, smooth, rumbling voices like that only came around once in a lifetime.

'Wow, I'm impressed,' he said. 'Did your stars tell you I was going to call?'

'You're thinking of astrology, not astronomy.'

'There's a difference?' he asked.

Her skin did that humming thing which told her that wherever he was he was definitely kidding, definitely smiling.

'So you *are* an astronomer, then?' he asked.

'That's what my degree says.'

'Hmm. I did consider you might be a ticket-seller, but then when I thought back on how hard you were working to not let me buy a ticket I had to go with my third choice of occupation.'

'What was the second?'

After a pause he said, 'Well, it wasn't a choice so much as a pipe-dream. And I'm not sure we know one another well enough for me to give any more away than that.'

The humming of her skin went into overdrive, a kind of fierce, undisciplined overdrive that she wasn't entirely sure how to rein in. She went with a thigh pinch, which worked well enough.

'What's up, Cameron?'

'I just wanted to let you know how much I enjoyed my morning.'

She turned side-on so that her back could slump against the doorframe, and lifted her boot-clad feet to the step. 'So, you did stay for the show. Good for you.'

'Ah, no. I did not.'

Her brow furrowed. Then it dawned: he was calling to say he'd enjoyed the part of the morning he'd spent with *her*. Okay. So this was unanticipated.

When she said nothing, Cameron added, 'I couldn't do it. The wormholes, remember?'

She laughed, loosening her grip on her phone a little. 'Right. I'd forgotten about the wormholes.'

'I, obviously, have not.'

'If one was smart, one might have thought this morning might have been a prime opportunity to overcome such a fear, since you were already there and all.'

'One might. But I've not often been all that good at doing what I *ought* to do.'

First calloused hands, now rebellion. Where was the nice, well-liked Cameron Kelly she'd known, and what had this guy done with him?

'You were in Meg's year at St Grellans,' Cameron said. Meaning he'd been asking around about her.

Rosie unpeeled her fingers from the step and lifted them to cradle the phone closer to her ear. 'That I was.'

'And since then?'

'Uni. Backpacking. Mortgage. Too much TV.' After a pause her curiosity got the better of her. 'You?'

'Much the same.'

'Ha!' she barked before she could hold it back. She could hardly picture Cameron Kelly splayed out on a second-hand double bed watching *Gilligan's Island* reruns on a twelve-inch TV at two in the afternoon.

'No kids?' he added. 'No man friend to give you foot rubs at the end of a long day telling fortunes?'

Rosie didn't even consider scoffing at his jibe. She was too busy trying to ignore the image of him splayed across her bed.

'No kids. No man. Worse, no foot rubs,' she said.

'I find that hard to believe.'

'Try harder.'

He laughed. Her cheek twitched into a smile. She slid lower on the step, and told herself she couldn't get closer to being physically grounded unless she lay on the dirt.

'You're in a profession which must be teeming with men. How is it you haven't succumbed to sweet nothings whispered in the dark by some guy with a clipboard and a brain the size of the Outback?'

'I'm not that attracted to clipboards,' she admitted.

'Mmm. It can't help that your colleagues all have *Star Trek* emblems secreted about their persons.'

'Oh, ho! Hang on a second. I might be allowed to diss my fellow physicists, but that doesn't mean you can.'

'Is that what I just did?'

'Yes! You just intimated all astronomers are geeks.'

'Aren't they?' he said without even a pause.

She sat up straight and held a hand to her heart to find it beating harder than normal, harder than it had even when she'd been a green teenager. It had more than a little to do with the unflinching, alpha-male thing he'd found within himself in the intervening years. It spoke straight to the stubborn in-dependence she'd unearthed inside herself.

'You realise you are also insinuating that I am a geek?' she said.

This time there was a pause. But then he came back with, 'Yes. You are a geek.'

Her mouth dropped open then slammed back shut. Mostly because the tone of his voice suggested it didn't seem to be the slightest problem for him that she might be a geek.

'Rosalind,' he said, in a way that made her want to flip her hair, lick her lips and breathe out hard.

'Yes?' she sighed before she could stop herself.

His next pause felt weightier. She cursed herself beneath her breath and gripped the teeny-tiny phone so tight her knuckles hurt.

'I realise it's last minute, but I was wondering if you had plans for dinner.'

Um, yeah, she thought; *cheese on toast*.

He continued, 'Because I haven't eaten, and if you haven't eaten I thought it an entirely sensible idea that we make plans to eat together.'

Oh? Oh! Had Cameron Kelly just asked her out?

CHAPTER THREE

ROSIE looked up at the sky, expecting to see a pink elephant flying past, but all she saw were clouds streaked shades of brilliant orange by the dying sunlight.

To get the blood flowing back to all the places it needed to flow, not just the unhelpful areas where it had suddenly pooled, Rosie dragged herself off the step and walked out into the yard, running a hand along the fluffy tops of the hip-high grass stalks.

Dinner with Cameron Kelly. For most girls the answer would be a no brainer. The guy was gorgeous. She couldn't deny she was still attracted to him. And there was the fantasy element of hooking up with her high school crush. One of the invisibles connecting with one of the impossibles.

But Rosie wasn't most girls. She usually dated uncompli-cated, footloose, impermanent guys, not men who made it hard for her to think straight. She *liked* thinking straight.

The only time she'd ever broken that rule was with a card-board cut-out of a gorgeous A-list movie star Adele had nicked from outside a video store for her seventeenth birthday. He was breathtaking, he never talked back. Never stole the remote. Never left the toilet seat up. Never filled any larger part of her life than she let him. Never left...

She wrapped her hand round a feathery tuft of grass and a

million tiny spores flew out of her palm and into the air, floating like fireflies in dusk's golden light.

Her mother had been the very definition of other girls. She'd fallen for the wrong man, the man she'd thought would love her for ever, and it had left her with a permanently startled expression, as though her world was one great shock she'd never got over.

After years of thought, study and discovery, a light-bulb moment had shown Rosie that, contrarily, the way to make sure that never happened to her was to *only* date the wrong men—those who for one reason or another had no chance of making a commitment. She could then enjoy the dating part dead-safe in the knowledge that the association would end. And when it did she wouldn't be crushed.

So, back to Cameron Kelly. He was gorgeous. He was charming. But most importantly beneath the surface there was a darkness about him. A hard, fast, cool character that he was adept at keeping all to himself. He was fascinating, but there was no mistaking him for some sweet guy looking for love.

And, of all the men who'd asked her out, she knew exactly what she was up against. Cameron Kelly was the least likely man in the world Rosie would again make the mistake of falling for, making him the ideal man for her, for now.

'I haven't lost you, have I?' he asked.

You can't lose what you never had, she thought, but said, 'I'm still deciding if I'm hungry enough for dinner.'

'It's a meal, on a plate. I was thinking perhaps even cutlery may be involved.' His voice resonated down the phone, until cheese and toast was the last things on her mind. 'We can reminisce about average cafeteria food, bad haircuts and worse teachers.'

'When did you ever have a bad haircut?'

'Who said I was talking about me?'

'Ha! You know what? I don't remember you being this ruthless at school.'

'Have dinner with me and I'll do my very best to remind you just how bad I can be.'

Suddenly her hands began to shake. She wiped them down her jeans, dusting off the tiny fragments of plant residue. Then said, 'Where would we go?'

'Wherever. Fried chicken, a chocolate fountain, steamed mung beans; whatever you want, it's yours.'

'Steamed *mung beans*?'

She felt him smile, and even without the visual accompaniment it made her stomach tighten. But now that she'd reconciled herself to her attraction to him she let herself enjoy it. It felt…wonderful. A little wild, but she had a handle on it. This was going to be fine.

'I didn't want to be all he-man and impose my carnivorous tastes upon you,' he said. 'For all I know you might well be a vegan, anti-dairy carb hater.'

'So happy to know I give off such a flattering vibe.'

'Your vibe is just fine,' he said, his voice steady and low and, oh, so tempting.

She stopped brushing at her jeans and hooked her thumb tight into the edge of her pocket. 'Imagine me as the least fussy woman you've ever taken to dinner.'

'Then I know the place. It's so informal, it's practically a dive. They make the best quesadillas you'll ever have.'

'Mexican for grilled cheese, right?' *How ironic.*

It was his turn to pause. 'It seems I have failed in my attempt to impress you with my extensive knowledge of international cuisine. Mmm. I'll have to up my game.'

Rosie took a moment to let that one sink in. It left a really nice, warm glow where it landed; her hand clutched the fabric of her old black T-shirt against the spot. 'And I guess dinner would be one way of making up for the astrology jibe.'

'I admit, it was hardly gracious.'

'It was hardly original, either.'

He laughed again, the sound sliding through the phone and down her back like warm honey.

The distant tones of a warning bell rang in the back of her mind, but she was confident enough of him and of herself to say, 'So, yes. To dinner. Sounds fun.'

He gave her the time, and address of the place that made the exotic grilled-cheese, and they said their goodbyes.

When Rosie hung up the phone she realised her knees were wobbling like mad. She slumped down upon the metal step, hugged her arms around herself and looked up.

The clouds had moved on, the colour of the sky had deepened, and several stars had shown themselves. When she hadn't been paying attention, the world beneath her feet had turned.

The world turned some more until night had well and truly fallen upon Brisbane. The bark and bite of peak-hour traffic had subsided to a low growl, and Rosie pulled her caramel velvet jacket tighter around herself to fend off the night chill as she walked briskly down the city footpath. Late for her date.

A minute later the *maitre d'* at the Red Fox bar and grill pointed the way through the bustling bar crowd towards a table along the far wall.

A dive, Cameron had promised. The place was anything but. It was bright, shiny, cool, filled with men with more product in their hair than she had in her bathroom, and women wearing so much bling around their necks she wasn't sure how they kept upright. While she'd been in so many seedy places in her time she could practically write a guide, Cameron it seemed was still very much a Kelly.

She ruffled her hair, wished she'd washed it or put it up, or had a haircut in the past six months, and excused herself as she nudged a group of hot young things out of her way.

Her hand was still delved deep into her hair when she saw him sitting at the head of a loud, rowdy table peopled by ex St Grellans students.

Kids who'd been given sportscars for their sixteenth birthday while she'd taken on an after school job cleaning dishes at a diner. Kids who'd skipped class to shop but had still magically got into universities she'd worked her butt off to attend. Kids who hadn't given her the time of day when, having been accepted to St Grellans, she'd so hoped she'd finally found a place where she might shine.

Suddenly she couldn't for the life of her remember what it had been about Cameron Kelly that had made her convince herself dinner was a good idea. To put on lip gloss. To walk through a cloud of perfume. To wear her nice underwear.

She took a step backwards and landed upon soft flesh. A woman squealed. She turned to apologise, then glanced back at the table where several pairs of eyes were zeroed in on her chest. She wasn't sure if they were collectively less impressed by her lack of top heaviness or the rainbow-coloured peace symbol splashed across her black T-shirt.

But it wasn't so much their eyes she was concerned about as Cameron's. And she remembered why she'd said yes. He was standing, his eyes locked onto hers with a kind of unambiguous focus that was almost enough to send her hurtling towards him like an object falling from the sky.

But not quite.

He was beautiful. He was irreverent. He made her knees wobble in an entirely pleasant way. But she had no intention of going to a place where she had to perform cartwheels to feel remarkable. No man on the planet was worth that.

She offered him a shrug by way of apology then backed into the crowd.

Cameron's backside hovered several inches off his chair as he watched Rosalind disappear into the crowd.

His chair rocked, screeched, and he had to reach out to catch it lest it crash to the ground. His old schoolmate in the chair next to him raised an eyebrow in question.

Cameron shook his head as he brought the chair back upright, and then made a beeline for the front door.

He hit the pavement, looked right then left, and then saw her. In amongst the night owls in their barely-there attire, she stood out like a rare bird, striding down the city street in skinny jeans, flat shoes, a soft jacket nipped at her waist, a multi-coloured scarf dangling to her knees, her long, wavy hair swinging halfway down her back, everything about her loose and carefree. Unpretentious.

And, just as before, having her within reach he felt as though for now the weight of the world could be someone else's problem.

He took off after her at a jog. 'Rosalind!'

When she didn't turn, he grabbed her elbow.

She stopped. Turned. A stubborn gleam lit her eyes before she glanced pointedly at where he still held her arm. But if he was the kind of guy who got scared off by a little defiance he wouldn't be where he was today.

'What's with the hasty exit?'

Her chin tilted skyward. 'Would you believe, I suddenly realised I wasn't hungry after all?'

'Not even if you donged me on the head and hypnotised me before saying so.'

She kept backing away. He kept following, the sounds of the bar fading behind him.

It occurred to him that he didn't usually have to work this hard to get a woman to eat with him. In fact, he'd never had to work all that hard to get a woman to do *anything* with him. For a simple distraction, Rosalind was fast proving to be more difficult than he'd anticipated.

But he was born of stubborn Irish stock; he couldn't leave

well enough alone. The effort of the chase only made her vanilla scent seem that much more intoxicating, her soft skin that much more tempting, the need to have her with him tonight that much more critical.

'Rosalind,' he warned.

'Can't a girl change her mind?' she asked.

'Not without an explanation, she can't.'

The stubborn gleam faltered. She glanced down the block at the façade of the bar and bit her bottom lip.

When her teeth slipped away he found himself staring at the moistened spot, transfixed. And imagined pulling her into his arms and leaning her up against the building wall, and kissing her until the dark clouds hovering on the edge of his mind vanished.

He dragged his gaze to her eyes to discover she was still watching the bar, which was probably a good thing, considering his pupils were likely the size of saucers.

As casually as possible, he let her arm go and took a step back. 'So what gives?'

Her chest rose and fell. 'When you invited me to dinner, I thought you meant just the two of us. If I'd known it was to be a class reunion I might have pretended to be washing my hair.'

He followed her line of sight to find one of the guys chatting to a girl lined up outside the bar, but he knew the cheeky bugger was there to give word back to the group. His world was excessively intimate. Everybody assumed a right to know everybody else's business.

Which is why this girl, this outsider, with her refreshing candour and her easygoing, cool spirit was just what he needed.

When he turned back, Rosalind's arms were crossed across her chest and her hip was cocked. Her patience was running thin.

He reached out and cradled her upper arms; the velvet was freezing cold. On impulse he ran his hands down her arms to warm her up.

And at his touch her eyes finally skittered from the bar and back to him. Mercurial grey. Luminous in the lamplight. And completely unguarded. He saw her restlessness, her disharmony, and the fact that she was searching for an excuse to be with him rather than the other way round.

Arrested, he moved close enough to follow every glint of every thought dancing behind those amazing eyes, yet not so close he found himself caught up in the scent of her until he couldn't think straight. And he did his best to be as forthright in return.

'Rosalind, I invited you to dinner because I knew I'd enjoy a night out with you. I chose this place as it makes the best Mexican on the eastern seaboard. As to that lot in there, I had no idea they'd be here; I haven't seen most of them in years. It would have been far more sensible of me to have avoided them once I realised Meg's best mate Tabitha was there, as she can talk the hind leg off a horse, but another fellow is a union lawyer and, workaholic that I am, I saw my chance to talk business and took it. Scout's honour.'

Her eyes narrowed as she asked, 'When were you ever a scout?'

His laughter came from nowhere, shooting adrenalin through his body, putting every muscle on high alert. No longer much caring about keeping himself at a sensible distance from her pervasive scent, he moved in tight and said, 'It's on my to-do list.'

She watched him a few long, agonising seconds before she gave a little shrug beneath his touch. 'Okay, then.'

Okay, then. He took a few more moments to enjoy her sweet scent, her gentle curves leaning into him, and thought about suggesting they skip dinner after all.

He let out a long, slow breath and disentangled himself from Rosalind Harper's corrupting wares. Self-restraint was an asset. It separated men from monkeys, and Cameron from being anything like his father. He needed to get some food into him and soon.

He slid around beside her, placed a hand in the small of her back and did his best to pay attention to his two feet as much as he was paying attention to the swing of her hips beneath his thumb as he herded her towards the Red Fox's red doors.

'It's cold out,' he said. 'Come wait in the entrance while I get my jacket. Then we'll find somewhere else to eat.'

'After all the time you spent convincing me how great the quesadillas are? Not on your life.'

Well, he'd shot himself in the foot there. All he wanted was her. Alone. Distracting him senseless. Now he was going to be stuck in a place peopled by Dylan and Meg's mates, who knew enough about him to want to catch up, and not enough to know which subjects to avoid. 'There's a joint down the road where you can choose your own lobster before they boil it.'

She shook her head, no.

'You sure?'

Her mouth titled into a sexy half-smile as she said, 'Can't a girl change her mind?'

Somehow Cameron found the words, 'Right. Then we'll head inside, and say polite hellos on the way past as we find a table of our own as far away as it can possibly be. Sound good?'

'Sounds perfect.'

'Though, I must warn you, I fully expect them to throw potato wedges at us. If we're lucky they won't have dipped them in guacamole first.'

She snuck a quick look sideways. 'I like guacamole.'

He liked her perfume. He liked her lips. He liked the feel of her beneath his hand. And most significantly he liked the fact that when he was with her his mind couldn't for the life of it wander.

For that alone he promised her, 'Then guacamole you shall have.'

They reached the front of the queue and the bouncer looked up, saw Cameron then opened the velvet rope without hesitation.

Cameron nudged Rosalind with his shoulder and she skipped ahead of him, glancing back with a half smile.

The bar crowd closed in around them. She ran a quick hand through her hair, fluffing it up, and straightened her shoulders like she was preparing to enter a prize fight.

Before he let himself think better of it he took her hand, and as though it was exactly what she'd been waiting for her fingers wrapped tight around his. It brought her back to his side, where her warm body fit in against him.

Images of lips and backs against walls and hot hands rushed in on him so fast one would think he'd been a monk these last thirty-two years.

'Relax,' Cameron said, so close to Rosie's ear her lobe got goose bumps. 'They won't bite. Though, just in case, I hope you've had your shots.'

She tried to put some air between them, but the crowd kept jostling her back to his side. 'I don't know if you're trying to be funny, as I don't *know* any of them. I barely even know you.'

Her arm dragged behind her as he came to a halt. She let go of his hand and turned to see why.

He was rooted to the spot among the surging crowd, a half-head taller than everyone else, broader of shoulder, and more likely to make a woman tremble with one look than anyone else she'd ever met.

Talk about being remarkable without any effort whatsoever. Maybe once this unnerving-yet-irresistible night was finally over she would have learnt a thing or two about genuine cool.

He slid his hands into his trouser pockets and asked, 'What would you like to know?'

'The highlights so far will do fine.'

His eyes narrowed. 'The name's Cameron Quinn Kelly. Star sign, Aries. Six-feet-two inches tall, weight unknown. I like test cricket more than many consider natural, and can spend hours in hardware superstores without spending a cent and never consider it time wasted. I buy far too many useless things on eBay, because once I'm committed to an auction I can't stand to lose. I'm slightly reluctant to admit my favourite holiday destination is Las Vegas, and I have no shame in saying I have cried during *Dead Poets Society*.'

Rosie took a deep breath. Was it really possible to like a guy that much more after such a simple snapshot? 'You forgot your favourite colour.'

'Blue.'

She didn't doubt it. At some stage that day he'd lost the vest and tie, and the blue shirt hugging his chest was a perfect match for his eyes. It looked so good on him she was finding it hard to remember what else he'd said.

'Enough?' he asked.

She swallowed hard, then quipped, 'That was more than I know about my mailman, and I give him beer at Christmas.'

He bowed ever so slightly. 'Now, before I let you loose upon *my* friends, maybe I should know more about you too.'

Fighting the urge to cross her arms, she grabbed hold of both lengths of her long scarf as she said, 'Rosalind Merryweather Harper. Star sign, Taurus. I'm about five-eight. Weight, none of your business.'

His eyes dropped, lightly touching her breasts, her hips and her calves, before sliding neatly back to her eyes. Her pause was noted, and his cheek curved into the kind of smile that made a girl think of fresh sheets, low lighting and coffee in the morning.

Unnerving yet irresistible. Yep, that summed him up perfectly.

'Merryweather?' he asked.

She grinned. 'It's rude to interrupt. Now, where was I? I've been to Nevada twice, yet never seen Vegas. With all those lights it has to be one of the more difficult places on earth to see stars. My guilty pleasure is Elvis Presley movies, and I was born with seven toes on each foot.'

Cameron's smile wavered. Twitched. Stumbled. His eyes slid to her shoes.

Until she said, 'Gotcha.'

His eyes took their time meandering up her body before they returned to hers.

'Satisfied?' he asked, his voice deeper than the bass notes thumping through the bar.

'Getting there,' she breathed.

The shift of the crowd threw them together. The slide of his cotton shirt against her velvet jacket acted like a flint shooting sparks between them.

She pressed both hands against his chest. 'I'm almost certain somebody promised me dinner.'

He smiled. 'I'm almost certain you're right.'

Then for a moment, the briefest snap in time, she thought she caught a glimpse of the man behind the dark-blue fortress, and saw strengths, knowledge, experience, and hunger far deeper than she'd even imagined. Her fingers curled into his shirt as once again she felt like she was in some kind of free fall.

She didn't like the feeling one little bit.

She slapped him hard on the chest, twice, then with a thin-lipped smile turned away and slid through the crowd.

And then the St Grellans table loomed before her. She recognised a couple of faces—a school captain, a drama queen, the daughter of an ex–Prime Minister. Bless their hearts.

Rosie felt Cameron slide in behind her. 'Do you think for some of them school really was the time of their lives?'

'Was it the time of yours?'

Rosie scoffed so loudly she practically snorted. 'You reeeally don't remember me from back then, do you?'

His silence was enough of an answer. Then he had to go and ask, 'Do you remember me?'

She thought it best to let her own silence speak for itself on that one.

CHAPTER FOUR

AN HOUR and a half later, with the remains of a shared plate of nachos dripping in sour cream taking the edge off her flash-back-phobia, Rosie felt surprisingly serene.

Cameron was a great date—talkative, funny, attentive. And he didn't flinch when she ordered seconds of the quesadillas. That was during the sporadic moments in which they'd been left alone.

A round of drinks had appeared every half hour on the dot, followed by a rowdy toast from the other side of the restaurant. Just about everyone had come over to pay their respects as though Cameron was some kind of Mafia don. And Tabitha stopped by for a chat every time she went to powder her nose. During those moments Cameron held his beer glass so hard his fingertips were the colour of bruises.

Then, when she had him to herself again, he was a different man. The darkness abated, the clouds cleared and he was entirely present. That was the reason she'd sucked up her pride and entered the dragons' den.

In the end she was so glad she had. If nothing else came of the night, slaying some dragons of her youth had been a major plus. Even so, she half-wished they had gone some-where else after all so that she could have had a little more time with *that* Cameron Kelly.

'Glad we stayed?' he asked.

A fast song came on and Rosie had to lean in to hear him properly. Cameron took her cue and leaned in himself. He was close enough that she could see the ridges in his teeth, a small scar on the bridge of his nose and a slight shadow of stubble at his throat. Tiny imperfections that should have made him less attractive only made him more so.

She smiled. 'You were right about the quesadillas. If they plonked another plate in front of me there is no way I could send them back.'

'Good. Now, for the real reason I invited you to dinner. When do I get my free horoscope?'

She laughed, and flicked the back of his hand so hard he flinched. With reflexes like a cat, he grabbed her offending hand and held it, ostensibly to keep himself from harm, but when his thumbs began running up and down her palm she wasn't so sure.

She manoeuvred her hand away, then sat back and crossed her arms, crossed her legs and remonstrated with herself to keep her feet firmly on the ground where they belonged.

'Pay attention,' she said. 'Because I'm not going to tell you this again. I am a scientist, not a fortune teller. I study the luminosity, density, temperature and chemical composition of celestial objects. My speciality is Venus, the one planet you can still see in the sky after sunrise, about a hand span at arm's length above the western horizon. I am an authority in the field, and if you're not careful one of these times I might turn miss-ish and decide to get offended.'

Cameron looked deep into her eyes, seemingly deadly serious. 'So, tell me, are we alone in the universe?'

She threw out her arms and laughed until every part of her felt loose. 'Are you kidding me?'

'I'm interested in your expert opinion.'

'Here it is. In all my years searching the stars, I've never knowingly seen anything which I couldn't explain. But I'd feel way sillier ruling out the idea than flat-out believing we're alone. The universe is a great, strange and mysterious place.'

He smacked a fist on the table. 'I knew those UFO stories couldn't all be fakes.'

She picked up her napkin and threw it at him. He caught it before it landed in his food. And they sat there smiling at one another like a pair of goons.

An hour later Tabitha was back, perched on the corner of the table, prattling on and on about Dylan's high-school pranks, and Meg's spate of hopeless boyfriends; Cameron had had enough.

The fabulous distraction that was Rosalind Harper only worked when the life he was trying to forget wasn't being shoved down his throat quite so regularly. More to the point, he'd spent enough time with a table between them and an audience watching over them. He wanted to get her alone.

As though she'd sensed him watching her, Rosalind glanced at him over her left shoulder, frowned, then licked a stray drop of salsa sauce from the edge of her lip.

He tilted his head towards the front door. Her eyes brightened, she nodded, and he wished he'd done so a hell of a lot sooner.

He clapped his hands loud enough to cut through Tabitha's verbosity. 'Tabitha, the lovely Rosalind and I are away.'

Tabitha stood up. 'Oh, right. You sure? I just never get to see you any more. Meg says it's because you're always so busy with work, but—'

'Yep,' he said. 'Quite sure. Our after-dinner plans are set in stone. We have to leave immediately.'

Rosalind, trouper that she was, grinned and nodded through his fibs.

Tabitha backed up with a wave. 'Okay, then. Cam, maybe I'll see you at your dad's party on the weekend if you can drag yourself away from work. Rosalind, it was a pleasure. I'll say hi to Meg for you. Both of you.'

Rosalind gave her a wave back, then when she was gone slumped her forehead to the table, arms dangling over the edge from the elbows down. Cameron laughed as he caught the attention of a passing waitress and mimed the need for the bill.

'And why didn't we go somewhere else to eat?' she asked from her face-down position.

'The quesadillas.'

She clicked her fingers and lifted her head. 'Right. And you have to admit there was nary a projectile potato-wedge in sight.'

'The place should advertise as much.'

She grinned, her eyes sparkling, that wide, sensual mouth drawing his eyes like a lighthouse on a stormy night. It was on the tip of his tongue to tell her as much when the bill arrived.

Saved by the waiter, Cameron took out his wallet, which was closely followed by Rosalind's. He stilled her hand with his. 'Put that away.'

She slid her hand free and hastened to flick through compartments, searching for cash. 'I've got it covered.'

'Rosalind, stop fidgeting and look at me.'

She did as she was told, but it was obvious she was not at all happy about it. And again he got a glimpse of how stubborn she could be.

'I invited you out tonight, so it's my treat. Let me play the gentleman,' he insisted. 'It's not all that often I get the chance. Please.'

It was the 'please' that got to her. Her flinty-grey eyes turned to soft molten-silver and finally she let go of the death grip on her wallet. 'Fine; that would be lovely. Thanks.'

He threw cash on the table. As she eyed the pile, she brightened. 'But you have to let me look after the tip.'

'Too late; I've already added fifteen percent.'

'Why not twenty?'

'Fifteen's customary.'

'Tips shouldn't be just customary. They can make the difference between the underpaid kitchen staff, out there right now washing our dirty dishes, paying rent this week or not.'

Cameron blinked. Forthright, stubborn, *and* opinionated. He tried to reconcile that with the playful, uninhibited girl he'd thought he'd picked up at the planetarium, and found he could not.

What did it matter? Whatever she was, it was working for him. He said, 'So the tip comes to…?'

'Fourteen-ninety,' Rosalind said a split second before he did. She threw another twenty dollars on the table before he had the chance to try, and glanced at him with a half smile. 'Beat ya.'

'Geek,' he said, low enough only she could hear.

As she put her wallet away she grinned, then leaned in towards him. 'Let's blow this joint before Tabitha comes back.'

'Excellent plan.'

Cameron stuck close as he herded Rosalind back through the crowd, partly to protect her from the flailing arms of dancers and chatters alike, but mostly because being close to her felt so damn good.

'So, what now?' she asked.

He moved closer until he was deep inside her personal space. 'Lady's choice.'

She licked her bottom lip, the move so subtle he almost missed it. 'Okay. But dessert is most definitely on me.'

She turned and practically bounced ahead of him.

The image of her wearing nothing but strategically placed curls of chocolate was distracting in a way he might never get over.

Cameron waved a hand towards a large, red plastic toadstool in the universal courtyard outside the Bacio Bacio gelataria on South Bank.

Rosalind sat upon it, knees pressed together, ankles shoulder-width apart, sucking cinnamon-and-hazelnut flavoured *gelato* off her upside-down spoon.

He had straight vanilla. He'd been craving it all day.

As the rich taste melted on his tongue, he let out a deep breath through his nose and stared across the river at his city. His eyes roved over the three skyscrapers he'd built, the two others he now owned, and through the gaps which would soon be filled with more incomparable monoliths he had in the planning.

'Some view, don't you think?' he said, his voice rough with pride.

Rosalind squinted up at the sky and frowned.

Cameron said, 'Try ninety-degrees down.'

'Oh.' Her chin tilted and her nose screwed up as she watched the red and white lights of a hundred cars ease quietly across the Riverside Expressway. 'What am I missing?'

He held a hand towards the shimmer of a trillion glass panels covering the irregular array of buildings. 'Only the most stunning view in existence.'

She stared at it a few moments longer as she nonchalantly tapped her spoon against her mouth. 'I see little boxes inside big boxes. No air. No light. No charm.'

Cameron shifted on his spot on the toadstool. 'I am in the business of building the big boxes. Skyscrapers are my game.'

She turned to look at him, resting her chin on her shoulder, a lock of her long, wavy hair swinging gently down her cheek. 'Sorry.'

'Apology accepted.'

'Though…'

'Yes?'

'A city is a finite thing. Some day, in the not too distant future, someone like you will come along and tear down your building to make a bigger one. Doesn't that feel like wasted effort?'

He laughed, right from his gut and out into the soft, dark silence. 'You sure don't pull your punches, do you?'

Her cheek lifted into a smile—a smile that made him want to reach out and entwine his fingers in her kinky tresses.

Before he had the chance, she shook her hair back and looked out at the city. 'Growing up, my only chance at being heard was by having something remarkable to say.'

'I hear that. Big family?'

'Like yours, you mean? Ah, no. My mother and I did not ski together, or turn on the City Hall Christmas-tree lights together. My mum cleaned houses and waited tables and took in ironing, and I can't remember five times we ate dinner together. Much of the time she had other things on her mind.'

She glanced back at him, the reflection of the river creating silver waves in her eyes. And she smiled. No self-pity; no asking for compassion. Only Rosalind Harper just as she was, wide open.

While he sat there, the most mistrustful man on the planet. The secrets he'd kept had led him to play his cards close to his chest his whole life. Hell, he had three accountants so that no one man knew where he kept all his money.

She hid nothing. Not her thoughts, her past, her flaws, her quirks. He wondered what it might feel like to be that transparent. To leave it up to others to take you or leave you.

Oh, he wanted to take her. Badly. But though a level of shared confidence came with them having gone to the same school, and though he was attracted to her to the point of distraction, and though she made him laugh more than any woman he'd ever met, there was nothing he wanted bad enough to make him quit his discretion.

He tightened all the bits of himself that seemed to loosen around her, as he gave as little and as much as he could. 'Is this where you expect me to try to convince you how difficult my childhood was?'

'Cameron,' she said, white puffs of air shooting from her now down-turned lips. 'I have no expectations of you whatsoever.'

And, just like that, tension pulled tight between them. It was so sudden, so strong, he felt a physical need to lean away, but the invisible thread that had bound them together from the beginning refused to break.

He finally figured out what that thread was.

He'd convinced himself he'd been merrily indulging in an attraction to a pretty girl with a smart mouth. He should have known that wouldn't be enough to tempt him. He was a serious man, and, beneath the loose Botticelli hair, the uncensored wry wit and carefree, sultry clothes, Rosalind Harper's serious streak ran as deep as a river.

It would no doubt make for further unpleasant clashes; it would mean continuously avoiding the trap of deep discussions.

Unless he walked away now.

His shoes pressed into the ground, and his body clenched in preparation for pushing away. Then his eyes found hers. Shards of unclouded moonlight sliced through the round silver irises. She had never looked away, never backed down. Who was this woman?

The wind gentled, softened, and took with it a measure of the tension. It tickled at his hair, sending hers flickering across her face. Before he found a reason not to, he reached out and swept it back behind her ear. Her hair was as soft as he'd imagined, kinky and thick and silken.

Her chest rose, her lips parted, her eyes burned. Seconds ago he was ready to walk away. Now he wanted to kiss her so badly he was sure he could already taste her on his tongue. He let his hand drop away.

Rosalind turned back to face the river. She scooped *gelato* onto her spoon and shoved it into her mouth, as though cooling her own tongue. Then from the corner of her mouth she said, 'Am I alone in thinking that got a little heated for a bit?'

'That it did,' he drawled.

She nodded and let the spoon rattle about in her mouth. 'That wasn't me trying to be particularly remarkable.'

'Mmm. I didn't think so.'

She laughed through her nose. 'Thank goodness, then; neither of us is perfect.'

Cameron had to laugh right along with her. It was the best tension-release there was. The best one could indulge in in public, anyway.

Rosie gripped her spoon with her teeth and said, 'Speaking of not being perfect…'

Cameron gave in, stuffed his napkin into his half-finished tub and tossed it in the bin, the makeshift-sweet bite of vanilla no longer cutting it when he had the real thing right in front of him.

She watched the cup with wide eyes. 'What on earth did you do that for?'

'Because I get the feeling I'll need both hands to defend myself against whatever's coming next.'

She held a hand over her mouth as she laughed to hold in the melted *gelato*.

'Come on,' he said, beckoning her by curling his fingers into his upturned palms. 'Get it off your chest now while I'm still in a state of semi-shock.'

She lifted her bottom to tuck her foot beneath, her body curling and shifting, the fabric of her T-shirt pulling tight across her lean curves. 'Okay. Sharing family stories shouldn't be like flint to dry leaves; it should be in the normal range of conversation on a date.'

He pulled his gaze back up to her face and reminded himself she was no intellectual small-fry. 'I like to think a normal range includes favourite movies, a bit about work and a few *double entendres* to keep it interesting.'

Her wide mouth twitched. 'I get that. But people are more than the movies they've seen. We're all flawed. Frail, even. We make mistakes. We do the best we can under the circumstances we've been given. So why not just put the truth out there? I admit I have no dress sense. My dad was never around. My mum was unfit to be a parent. I can't cook. Your turn.'

He broke eye contact, looked across the river and anchored himself in the integrity of concrete and steel, of precise engineering and beautiful absolutes. Everything else he'd once thought true had turned out to be as real as the monsters under his bed. 'You want my confession?'

'No. Yes. Maybe. It sure as hell might make sitting here with you a lot less intimidating if I knew you actually had something to confess.'

He turned back to her, monsters abating as she took precedence again. 'You find me intimidating?'

She raised an eyebrow. 'No. You're a walk in the park. Now, stop changing the subject. I've had the highlights, now give me the untold story before I start feeling like a total fool for thinking you might be man enough to hack a little cold, hard truth.'

God, she was good. She had his testosterone fighting his reason, and no prizes for guessing which was coming out on top.

He kicked his legs out straight ahead to slide his hands into the pockets of his jeans. The moonlight reflected off the water, making the glass buildings on the other side of the river shimmer and blur, until he couldn't remember what they were meant to signify any more.

All he knew was that when his car swung into the botanical gardens that morning he'd been on a search for the truth. And he'd found her.

Maybe he'd regret it, maybe it was the wrong thing to do, but, with his mind filled with that siren voice calling for him to give himself a break, to admit his flaws, to confess…the words just tumbled out.

'What would you say if I told you that I have spent my day certain that my father is gravely ill, and that I've kept it to myself?'

CHAPTER FIVE

THE second the words came out of his mouth Cameron wished he could shove them back in again. Rosalind was meant to be distracting him from worrying about the bastard, *not* inducing him to tell all.

'That the kind of thing you were after?' he asked.

'I was kind of hoping you might admit to singing in the shower,' she said with a gentle smile. But her voice was husky, warm, affected. It snuck beneath his defences and spoke to places inside him he'd rather she left alone.

'Tell me about your dad,' she said.

He ran a quick hand up the back of his hair and cleared his throat. 'Actually, I'd prefer we talk about something else. You a footy fan?'

'Not so much.'

He clamped his teeth together, betting that his stubborn streak was wider than hers. She leaned forward and sat still until he couldn't help but make eye contact. The beguiling depths told him she'd give him a run for his money.

'Look, Cameron, I don't always have my head in the stars. I do know who you are. I get that it might be difficult to know who you can trust when everybody wants to know your business. But you can trust me. Nothing you say here will go any further. I promise.'

Cameron wondered what had happened to a promise of no promises. Then realised things had been at full swing since they'd caught up, and he'd yet to make that clear.

'Unless you'd really rather talk about football,' she said, giving his concentration whiplash. 'I can fake it.'

Her eyes caught him again, and they were smiling, encouraging, empathetic, kind. He couldn't talk to his family; he couldn't talk to his friends or workmates. It seemed the one person he'd taken into his life to distract him from his problems might be the only one who could help him confront them instead.

He ran his fingers hard over his eyes. 'He was on TV this morning, talking oil prices, Aussie dollar, housing crisis and the like. He flirted with the anchorwoman, and ate up so much time the weather girl only had time to give the day's temps. Nothing out of the ordinary. And for the first time in my life he seemed…small.'

'Small?'

He glanced sideways, having half-forgotten anyone was there. 'Which now that I've said it out loud seems ridiculous. Look, can we forget it? We don't have to talk footy. We can talk shoes. Glitter nail-polish. Chocolate.'

'I want to talk about this. You know your dad. He didn't seem himself. Worrying about him isn't ridiculous. It's human. And you know what? It kinda suits you.'

'Worry suits me?' he asked.

'Letting yourself be human suits you.' She closed one eye, and held up a hand to frame him. 'Mmm. It mellows all those hard edges quite nicely.'

Cameron rubbed a hand across his jaw as he looked harder at the extraordinary woman at his side. He wondered what on earth he'd done right in a former life to have had her offered up before him this morning of all mornings.

She opened her squinting eye and dropped her hand. Those

eyes. Those wide, open eyes. Attraction mixed with concern, and unguarded interest. No wonder he hadn't been able to resist.

She looked down into her melting *gelato*. 'Are your family worried?'

'I'm fairly sure they don't suspect.' If they had, there was no way they wouldn't have all been on the phone to him, telling him to get his butt over there.

Her brow furrowed as she tried to fit that piece into the puzzle. But all she said was, 'And your dad? Have you asked him straight out?'

Cameron breathed deep through his nose. *In for a penny in for a pound...* 'That's a tad difficult, considering we haven't spoken in about fifteen years.'

One edge of her bottom lip began getting an extreme workout by way of her top teeth. His physical reaction made him feel all too human.

Eventually she asked, 'On purpose?'

How the hell did she know that was exactly the right question to ask? That no living soul knew how hard he worked to keep clear of the man in question without letting his family know why?

Slowly, he nodded.

'Then why did I think you worked for him?'

'Brendan does. Dylan does. I never have.' *Never will.*

'But you were planning to, right? Economics degree here, then Harvard Business School?' Her mouth snapped shut and her cheeks pinked. Then her mouth drew up into a half-smile. 'My turn again. I confess I overheard you talking to Callum Tucker about it once in the canteen. Of course, it only stuck with me because he said he was going to become a roadie for a rock band.'

Her smile was infectious. A bubble of laughter lodged in his throat. 'Callum is an orthodontist. And I didn't go to business school. I became a structural engineer. After several years in the field, I moved into property development.'

'Impressive.' She blinked prettily. 'Callum Tucker's an orthodontist.'

The bubble burst, and Cameron's laughter spilled out into the night. Her half-smile bloomed, full and pink and blushing. And, while her hair still whipped lightly about her face in the wind, it had been some time since he felt the cold.

She asked, 'What is a structural engineer, exactly?'

'I warn you, most people tend to go cross-eyed when I start talking structural systems, lateral forces and the supporting and resistance of various loads.'

'Like I don't get blank faces when I get excited about the chemical composition of celestial objects?'

'Sorry,' he said after a pause. 'Did you say something?'

She lifted a hand and slapped him hard across the arm. 'Not funny.'

'Come on, it was a little bit funny.'

She snuck her foot out from under her and placed it next to the other one on the ground, facing him. 'Why not just stick with the engineering?'

'Ego.'

She shot him a blank stare.

'The more things we Kellys see with our name upon them, the happier we are. It comes from having been born out of abject poverty. Generations ago, mind you.'

'How's that? No freshly churned butter on your crust-free organic toast-fingers every second Sunday?'

Cameron grinned. 'Something like that. Ironically, business school would have saved me half the time it took to become profitable when I went out on my own.'

'Nah,' she said, flapping a hand across her face. 'School can only get you so far. In the end you have to throw yourself at the mercy of the universe and take pride in your own ride.'

Cameron let that idea sink in. He was a meticulous planner, demanding control, assurance and perfection from himself and every employee he had. Then again, as a seventeen-year-old kid, he had broken free of the only world he'd ever known. If he hadn't done so he would not be the self-made man he was today.

He nodded. 'I'm damn proud of my ride.'

'Well, then, good for you.'

Her eyes softened, and her smile made him feel like he'd been covered with a warm blanket.

The need to touch her again was overwhelming. Pushing aside her hair would not be enough. He wanted so badly to sink his hand into the mass, pull her in and kiss her until he could taste cinnamon. So, what the hell was stopping him?

The fact that she knew the worst about him certainly didn't help.

Rosalind broke eye contact to eat another mouthful of melting *gelato* and the moment was gone. And, without her striking grey eyes holding him in place, he remembered: there was something wrong with his father. And worse: after a decade and a half spent keeping his whole family at arm's length because the bastard had given him no choice, he still gave a damn.

He blinked, clearing the red mist from his vision and letting Rosalind fill it instead. At first glance, she seemed a 'just what it says on the tin' kind of person—playful, slightly awkward, with an impertinent streak a mile wide. But those eyes, those changeable, mercurial eyes, kept him wondering. He could have sworn she'd changed the subject back there, knowing it was what he needed.

Then, in the quiet, her hand reached out to his. It took him about half a second to give in and turn her hand until their fingers intertwined.

For the first time since that morning Cameron felt that everything was going to be all right.

He frowned. He'd managed to figure that out on his lonesome time and time again over the years. And at the end of the day, when they parted ways, he'd once again only have himself to count on. To trust.

He gave her hand a brief squeeze before pulling his away and leaning back to rest on the toadstool, cool, nonchalant, like nothing mattered as much as it had seemed to matter moments earlier.

'Cameron—'

'You done?' he asked, gesturing to her melting *gelato*.

She licked the inside of her lips as though relishing every last drop of the delicious treat. But her eyes pierced his as she asked, 'Are you?'

He didn't pretend not to understand her. 'Well and truly. I didn't invite you out tonight for a therapy session.'

'So, why did you invite me again?' she asked, with just the perfect amount of flirtation in her voice to make his fingers spontaneously flex.

'It was obvious you were the kind to appreciate the finer things in life.'

'Quesadillas and *gelato*?'

'God, yes.'

He stood.

She did the same, threw her empty container into the bin, pressed her hands into her lower back, then closed her eyes tight and stretched. 'First, I'm a geek. Now I'm obvious. You sure know how to make a girl feel special.'

'Stick around,' he said, his voice gravelly. 'The night is young.'

She stopped stretching and looked him in the eye. Attraction hovered between them like a soap bubble, beautiful, light and with a limited lifespan. Just the way he liked it.

'I could do with walking some of that off.' Cameron patted his flat stomach. 'You game?' He held out a hand.

She stared at it. Then she wiped her hands on her jeans and, after a moment's hesitation, put her hand in his.

Holding hands made him feel like he was seventeen again. But, then again, the fact that he couldn't remember the last time he'd held a woman's hand unless it was to help her out of his car made it feel far more grown up than all that.

As Rosie strolled beside Cameron down the length of South Bank, they talked movies, politics, religion and work. She made fun of him loving a sport that managed to keep a straight face while giving a man a job title of "silly mid-on", while he utterly refused to admit he believed man had ever really set foot on the moon.

But she couldn't get her mind off the elephant in the room; Cameron and his father must have had some kind of falling out. She'd never heard about it in the press or on the grapevine. Yet he'd confided in her. She was caught between being flattered, and being concerned that what had started out as a fun date had become something more complicated so very quickly.

It would be okay so long as she remembered who she was and perhaps, more importantly, who *he* was. He might have fled the nest but he was still a Kelly. He walked with purpose even if that purpose was simply to walk. He had that golden glow that came with the expectation of privilege, while she knew what it was like to struggle, to trip over her own feet and her own words, and to feel alone even in a room full of people. They were manifestly wrong for one another.

They dawdled along the curving path. Moonlight flickered through the bougainvillea entwined in the open archway above. A group of late-night cyclists shot past and Cameron put an arm around her to move her out of their way. Once they were free and clear he didn't let go.

Against her side he was all bunched muscle and restrained strength. His clean scent wrapped itself around her, and it took everything not to just lean into him and forget everything else.

To reforge the natural boundary between them, she asked, 'So, what is it like being a Kelly?'

'What makes you think there is only one way?'

'I'm not sure. Terrible instincts. Stumbling about in the dark only to find the electricity has been cut off. No, wait—that's how it is to be a Harper.'

His steps slowed until they came to a stop. 'Right. Let's stop talking around the real question, shall we?'

Rosie bounced from one foot to another, wondering what can of worms she'd inadvertently fallen into now. 'And what's that?'

'If you were such a poor unfortunate in your youth, while I was given every opportunity, how *did* you work out twenty percent faster than I did?'

Her head fell back as she laughed into the night. She bobbed her head in the general direction of the Red Fox, wondering briefly if everyone else had made it home to their nice warm beds. 'Don't beat yourself up. Spending time with that lot, how could you not revert to your teenage IQ?'

His eyes narrowed. 'I'm not entirely sure that was in the slightest bit complimentary to any of us.'

She looked him dead in the eye and said, 'Well, colour me surprised. You're not as slow as you seem.'

His cheek slid into the kind of smile that would melt the icy crust of the moon Europa. No wonder she couldn't stop moving. He was always so switched on, he made her feel like there were ants in her shoes.

'So, how did a smart mouth like you end up in such a dry field as astrophysics?' he asked, lifting his foot to lean it against a log on the edge of the garden beside them.

Rosie clasped her hands together behind her back. 'I used to wish upon every star I saw. When I didn't get a trip to Disneyland for my eighth birthday, I gave up on them.'

'Stars?'

'Wishes. Stars I couldn't let go of quite so easily. So, while you hunkered down in your seat shaking like a little girl at the animated wormholes on your planetarium visit, I paid attention. I learnt about Venus, about how she always appeared alone, separate from all the other planets, and only at the most beautiful times of day, sunset and sunrise. That afternoon, I sat in the kitchen window of our apartment block and there she was—bright, constant and unblinking. A free show, for anyone in the world to see. That was the beginning of a beautiful love affair that has lasted til this day.'

Rosie came back to earth to find Cameron standing very still, his eyes dark, intense, with the kind of absolute focus she was certainly not used to being on the receiving end of. She'd been balancing on her toes. She bounced back to her heels with a thud. It didn't help. Those deep, blue eyes looked just as hot from a lower angle.

She started walking again; no dawdling any more. Assuming he'd follow, she said, 'Did you know Venus is the only planet in the solar system named after a woman?'

'I think I'd heard that.' His voice told her he was close.

'And, with a few exceptions, all surface features take their names from successful women.'

'That I did not know.'

'And that, if you weighed one-hundred kilos on Earth, you would weigh about ninety on Venus?'

'I feel like you're trying to sell me an interplanetary timeshare.'

She glanced back and wished she hadn't. When she looked into his eyes she forgot herself. Forgot that their time together was one of the universe's crazier anomalies. And she found herself wishing again. Just for the briefest moment, but each and every time.

He asked, 'So are any other planets allowed a look in, or is this an exclusive relationship?'

She looked up, and the tightness in her chest ebbed away.

'I'm a one-planet woman. Earth and Venus are the most similar in size of the planets in our solar system. They came into being around the same time with nearly the same radius, mass, density and chemical composition. But she has clouds laced with sulphuric acid, a surface hot enough to melt steel, and her surface pressure is equivalent to being a kilometre under the sea.'

'She's one feisty broad.'

'Isn't she?' Having built up a safer distance, she spun to face him, and, walking backwards, said, 'Sorry you asked?'

'Not in the least. So, how long have you been working at the planetarium?'

She fell into step beside him, figuring it best to keep her eyes on the path ahead. 'I don't. I've known the manager there—Adele, who you met yesterday—since uni, and she lets me camp out in the observatory whenever I like. I travelled a lot after school, and now, being back, having the observatory on hand means I can mix things up.'

'And it's a living?'

She shot him a sideways glance. 'As Australia's pre-eminent Venus specialist, I've given talks at international conferences, guest lectured at universities, and even talked on TV about her. And I've worked freelance for NASA for yonks. So, yeah, I do just fine.'

'You're a humble little thing, aren't you?'

'The humblest.'

He moved alongside her, close enough she could feel the whisper of air from his swinging arm brushing her jacket against hers. Their footsteps found a rhythm; her heart on the other hand felt like it was skittering all over the place. It was a feeling she'd never experienced before, comfortable and sexy all at once. She wondered if he felt that way all the time, if being with him she would too.

Rosie slid her arm out of Cameron's grasp, feigned having

to unhook the back of her shoe from her heel, then walked on with a good foot's distance between them.

They hit the end of a row of cafés at the southern end of South Bank, then veered around in a one-eighty-degree arc and headed back towards the Victoria Street Bridge. Towards their cars.

Towards the end of the night.

And Rosie's relief and disappointment at the thought of their date coming to an end ran pretty much neck and neck.

On the other hand, Cameron was feeling strangely content. He would have expected by now to be over the elation that came with revelation, and to have moved on to disappointment with himself for giving into a moment's weakness.

But instead his mind was completely filled with the fact that he was out on a stunning winter's night with a beautiful woman. And, having given up so much of himself, he found himself wanting more from her. To restore the balance? That was the reason he was most comfortable admitting to.

He said, 'What's your relationship with your father like?'

She tilted her face towards him; her hair shifted against his shoulder, long, soft, kinky, fabulous. He breathed in deep to stop himself from ravaging her then and there. She really tried his self-control, this one.

'You ask that question like it should have an easy answer.'

'Complicated man?'

She shrugged beneath his arm. 'I wouldn't know. He and my mum met, married, he left, then she had me.'

Cameron's neck tensed. Not in surprise, but in disillusion at the levels to which some men would sink in the grips of their own self-interest. 'That can't have been easy on your mum.'

'Not for the whole time I knew her. They knew one another less than a year, but she dropped out of uni when she met him and never went back. It was as though she always thought one day he'd come back, and she wanted everything to be the same as when he left.'

'So where did a grown-up daughter fit into that?'

Her smile was as rich as always. Could nothing floor her? 'With difficulty, and tantrums and killer grades. Whatever it took to break through the fog. Mum passed away a few years ago when I was overseas. I wish she was still around so that she could see that I've landed on my own two feet. Him too, actually—which is the nuttiest thing of all.'

Her voice was strong, as though she was telling a story she'd told a thousand times. But Cameron was close enough to feel the tremble beneath the gusto.

'Cousins? Grandparents?'

She shook her head. No blood ties. No fallback. No choice about whether or not to turn her back on the man who'd hurt her...

'But I've known Adele since I was seventeen. She's as bossy as a sister, as cuddly as a grandparent, as protective as a dad ought to be. So as far as family goes, I'm more than covered.'

He held out an arm, an offer, and she sank into him. It took a whole other kind of strength not to lean against her, not to kiss the top of her head.

'Argh!' she said, curling away all too soon. 'The last thing I meant to do was get slushy. You just happened to hit a soft spot.'

She slid round in front of him, out of his embrace, though her hand stayed resting on his arm as though she couldn't break all contact. 'Can I poke at one of yours?'

Okay, so she was touching him because she knew he might try to get away. 'You're asking this time?'

She tilted her head, not to be brushed off. 'You have the kind of family some of us only dream of.'

'You know those suburban news reports when a neighbour says "they always seemed like such a nice family"?'

'I never assumed they were *nice*. They might all be stark raving mad for all I know. Nice seems such a bland word to describe…' She waved a hand at him, her eyes touching on his shoulders, his chest. She blinked quickly as they scooted past the zipper of his jeans.

'Nevertheless there are many members of your family. Talk to them about your dad. Talk to your dad. And soon.'

He jawed clenched so hard his back teeth hurt. 'I have my reasons not to.'

'Which are?'

'Impeccable.'

She stared him down, wanting more, but there was no more he would give.

When on that dark day many years before he'd discovered his father had been cheating on his mother, he'd realised that the man his family held up with such reverence and esteem— the cornerstone of everything they represented, everything they were—didn't really exist. And, even if he wanted to explain any of that to Rosalind, unburdening himself would only hurt the others.

When she realised it would take more than silence for him to talk, she said, 'A few years back my mum accidentally let on that she'd been in contact with my father again. He was living in Brisbane. Had been for years. In all that time, he'd never once bothered to look me up. He passed away before she did, and, ridiculous as I know it is, today I still wish I'd had the chance to meet him—to know him, for him to know me—no matter what kind of man he might have been. I'd really hate for you to one day wake up feeling that way.'

Her big, grey eyes were bright in the lamplight. Dazzling with resolve. Could she really be as staggeringly secure as she seemed?

Either way, this conversation was over. 'I give up,' he said, deadpan. 'You win.'

She rolled her eyes and then bent double from the waist,

as if he'd finally exhausted her determination. 'It wasn't meant to be a contest. It was meant to be a cautionary tale!'

'You don't like winning?'

She brought herself back upright and grinned at him. 'Depends on the prize.'

Back on solid ground again, on territory in which he was far more comfortable, it took very little effort for Cameron to think of about a dozen prizes he'd happily provide without breaking a sweat. Or, better yet, sweating up a storm.

'Here we are again,' she said.

Mmm, there they were again.

It took a moment for him to realise she was being literal. They'd reached the end of South Bank, and turning left would take them back to the Red Fox and their cars.

He could do as he'd originally planned, kiss her cheek, thank her for a most enlightening night and get on with his life.

Considering the awkward particulars she now knew about him, and perhaps even more importantly what he knew about her—that she was no more the easy, lighthearted-dalliance type than he was a court jester—that would be the smart thing to do.

But it seemed tonight he'd left his smarts behind at the office.

'Thirsty?' His heart thundered harder than he could have anticipated as he awaited her answer.

'What did you have in mind?' she asked, the matching huskiness in her voice making him feel an inch taller.

'The casino's only two blocks away.'

She looked up at him, all luminous eyes, wide lips, sparkle and street smarts, pluck and temptation. He wondered, and not for the first time, how he'd managed to get through high school without noticing her. He'd been seventeen. Maybe that was enough.

Her nose creased; she nibbled at the inside of her bottom lip and picked at a fingernail, and took her sweet time deciding. He had the feeling she might be smart enough for the both of them.

'So, what do you say to one more stop?' he asked, promising himself it would be the last time.

But then her wide, open eyes gave him his answer even before she said, 'There's a tiny corner lounge on the second floor of the casino where they make hot chocolate to die for.'

CHAPTER SIX

ROSIE'S body clock told her it was some time after midnight by the time Cameron walked her from the beautiful old Treasury Casino to her car. Which meant that barring a cat nap in the afternoon, she'd been up for around twenty hours.

No wonder she'd been delirious enough to agree to hot chocolate. Okay, so if he'd suggested they walk the city til they found a greasy kebab van she would have said yes.

She unlocked her old runabout before Cameron reached down to open the driver's side door.

She threw her bag over to the passenger seat and turned to find him standing close, still holding her door, trapping her in the circle of his arms. Close enough so the street lights above created a glow around his dark hair and kept his face in shadow. But the determined gleam in his eyes could not be hidden by a mere lack of direct illumination.

'Tonight was…fun,' he said.

'Which part? The stream of your friends interrupting dinner. Me annoying you so much you had to throw out half your gelato. Or the bit where I tripped on the stairs at the casino and almost broke your toe?'

One dark eyebrow raised. 'I saw the look on your face when you had that first sip of hot chocolate. You were having x-rated fun.'

'Fine,' she said. 'The hot chocolate was heavenly. For that I will be forever in your debt.'

That was the moment she should have waved goodbye, ducked into the car and hooned home. But, even though she felt her life complicating with every new glimmer of light that fractured the darkness within him, she couldn't will herself to leave.

Heck, after she'd let slip that both she and her mum had worked behind the scenes in restaurants, he'd surreptitiously left a crazy-monster tip for the guy who'd served them their hot chocolate when he'd thought she wasn't looking. How was any girl supposed to just walk away from a guy like that?

Wrong. How could Rosie *not* walk away?

While her will played games, her body came to the rescue as she was forced to reach up and stifle a yawn. 'I'm so sorry. I have no idea where that came from.'

'It's after two in the morning, that's where.'

'It can't be!'

He took her wrist, and turned it until the soft part underneath was facing upwards. A small frown appeared between his brows. 'You don't wear a watch.'

She shrugged. 'Even when I used to wear one it never occurred to me to look at my wrist. So I gave up.'

His gaze travelled up her arm to her face. 'I must look at my watch a thousand times a day.'

'Think what you could have done with your lost time if you hadn't been so centred on knowing what the time was.'

Even in the darkness she could sense the sexy grooves dinting his cheeks as he smiled at her. 'You have a strange way of looking at the world, Miss Harper.'

'I look at it exactly the same way you do, Mr Kelly. Just from a few inches closer to the ground.'

'Perhaps. Though what happens to that information when it gets beyond those gorgeous eyes of yours and hits that wild, wily brain, I'm sure I'll never know.'

Rosie hadn't heard all that much past 'gorgeous eyes'. Dangerously familiar and long-since buried parts of her began to unfurl, warm and throb.

When Cameron ran a careless thumb over the raised tendons of her inner wrist, he created even more havoc within her. If he thought her mind a wild and wily place, it had nothing on the state of her stomach.

'Rosalind,' he rumbled. Boy, the guy had a way of saying her name…

'Yes, Cameron?' she sighed.

He closed his hand about her wrist and tugged her away from the protection of the car door. The sigh became a moan, thankfully quiet enough that he would have had to be two feet closer to have heard. Two feet closer would mean his lips would have been close enough to kiss.

She stared at them a while in silent contemplation. A good while. So long a while that the night stretched between them like a tight rubber-band, and if somebody didn't speak soon Rosie was afraid it would snap.

'I'd really like to see you again,' he said.

Snap! Rosie's eyes flew north til they met his. Deep, blue heaven… 'Seriously?'

He laughed. She bit her lip.

Just because he used her full name in such a deferential way, and how more than once she'd caught him looking at her like she was the most fascinating creature on the planet, didn't mean she should go forgetting herself. On the contrary, she never intended on being just who she seemed in someone else's eyes.

He said, 'Do you want a list of reasons why, or would you prefer them in the form of a poem?'

She shook her hair off her face and looked him dead in the eye, tough, cool, impassive. 'Is that the best you can offer? No wonder you had a blank night in your calendar.'

'Who says it was blank?' he rumbled.

Rosie's heart danced. She blamed exhaustion. She knew that taking guidance from one's heart was as sensible as using one's liver for financial-planning advice, having witnessed first-hand what listening to the dancing of your heart could do to a woman. If she needed any further reason to call it a day…

And then he had to go and say, 'What are you doing tomorrow?'

Her heart did the shuffle. She tried to concentrate on her liver instead. But it seemed every organ was on Cameron-alert.

'Tomorrow?' she said. 'I'll be sleeping. Eating. Watching telly. Looking up. The usual. You?'

'Working. Working. And working some more. Though I too will need to fit some eating in at some stage.'

'What a coincidence.'

'Dinner, then?' he insisted. 'This time just the two of us.'

The two of them. Didn't that sound nice? She looked skyward, but couldn't for the life of her see a star above the canopy of cloud and bright city-lights with which to anchor herself.

She took care to get her next words just right. 'How about you check you diary, and down the track, if you have a window, call the planetarium and they'll get a message to me, and I'll get back to you if my window matches up, and we'll see how we go?'

He let her wrist go which gave her a moment of reprieve before he brushed a lock of hair from her cheek, his fingers leaving trails as light as a breeze across her skin.

'I need a diary,' he said, 'Like you need a watch. And it would make things simpler if you'd just give me your home number.'

He brushed a lock from the other cheek, leaving his hands resting on either side of her neck, leaving her feeling extremely exposed. She'd had to work so hard in her youth to be seen, she'd never had the need to develop a poker face. But she needed it now. All she could do was look at the top of his shirt, where a triangle of tanned skin peeked out from the expanse of blue.

'Can't do that,' she said.

'Why not?'

'Don't have one.'

'You don't have a home phone number?'

'Too difficult, considering…'

'Considering?'

She paused then, wondering quite how to put it in such a way that a man who'd likely never felt a need to deny himself pleasure for the sake of reason would understand. In the end she really saw no choice but to say, 'I live in a caravan.'

Instead of flinching at the very thought—oh, it had happened to her before!—Cameron laughed. Uproariously. As though she'd turned into all the comedians in the world combined.

Her eyes flew up to clash with his. 'What's so funny about living in a caravan?'

'Nothing at all,' he said, his voice still rippling with amusement. 'I think if you owned some suburban Queenslander or lived in a flash city-apartment I'd have been disappointed.'

He'd moved closer, his face now lit by the reflections in a shop window behind her. 'So, tomorrow night. Dinner. Just the two of us. I'll call the planetarium with a location.'

'You could do that.' She bit the inside of her lip only to find that, now he was within the required proximity, it was practically swollen with the desire to lock with his. 'Though I do have a mobile phone.'

His voice was low and dry as he said, 'Do you, now?'

'I never remember to take it with me,' she justified. 'And it's so ridiculously small that I lose it four days out of seven, so I rarely bother giving the number out. But it's there. If you'd like it.'

'That'll do just fine.'

She bent into the car and fumbled through her bag for her phone, and the slip of paper on which her number was written, as she didn't for the life of her know what it was. Then realised she was giving him a fine view of her tush, and stood up so straight she hit her head on the doorframe.

Pretending she hadn't, she jauntily threw him her phone. He punched her number into his, and when she looked at him blankly he did the same for hers. It made her feel like she was nineteen again, in a nightclub, half-hoping the cute guy would call, half-hoping he'd leave her be.

She shoved her phone back into her bag so roughly her knuckles scraped on an inner zip. She then looked up and directly into his eyes from barely a foot away. Those relentless blue eyes…

Kiss me, she yearned inside her head.

No, don't kiss me. Yearning led to pining, which led to languishing. And that was not for her.

He leaned in.

God, yes, please kiss me!

His warm breath slid past her ear as he pressed firm lips against her cheek. With an undisciplined sigh her eyelids fluttered shut, and she let herself open up just a little, just enough so that she could truly feel the moment. His touch, his scent, his strength. The way he made her feel feminine and desirable just as she was.

When he pulled away, her whole body swayed with him. Her eyelids darted open to find his eyes focussed on her lips with such intensity it took her breath away.

Her tongue darted out to wet her lips, and his eyes clouded over, so dark, so hot. She had two choices: throw herself at him, or remove herself from a situation which suddenly felt like it was getting out of her control.

She slid deeper inside the cover of the car and swung the door between them.

Coming to as if from a trance, Cameron growled, 'I'll talk to you tomorrow.'

'It is tomorrow.'

The darkness brightened but the heat remained as his eyes shot to hers. 'So it is.'

'And time I got home to my nice warm bed.'

His accompanying smile was so broad she had the perfect view of a pair of sharp incisors.

'And you to yours,' she added.

This time his growl came without words.

She took that as the opportune moment to give a noncommittal wave before diving into the car and buckling up while he closed the door for her. The fact that she remembered which pedal was the accelerator amazed her as she drove into the night.

Her head throbbed, her knuckles stung, and the voice in the back of her head pointed out she'd lived in one spot for a while now, and Peru was nice this time of year…

An hour later, after Rosie had realised she was too wired to get any sleep, she took a shower and got changed from her pyjamas back into jeans, a warm jumper, and her mangy brown boots in preparation for heading out to the edge of the thicket in which she often spent her early mornings with a tent, a sleeping bag and her favourite old telescope.

She put the TV on while she made herself some jam on toast, not sure how she hadn't keeled over from a sugar rush from the amount she'd already eaten the night before.

The name Quinn Kelly barked from her TV, and she spun and leaned her backside against her tiny kitchen bench.

She didn't know the man, but he was about the most famous personality in town. A charismatic man, with a deep Australian drawl overlaid with enough Irish lilt for it to be unforgettable. He was outrageously good-looking even with his seventieth birthday just around the corner. She recognised him the moment he came on screen in what must have been a repeat of that morning's financial-news report.

She looked through the crooked smile and stunning blue eyes for a sign that all was not well. Or, more truthfully, for signs that Cameron had been wrong and his father was fine. But, as though Cameron was sitting beside her pointing out the subtle nuances of pain etched across his father's face buried deep beneath the infamous smile, she knew something wasn't right.

She'd lived through the sudden loss of one parent and the permanent loss of another, and she wouldn't wish either situation on anyone. Especially not on the man who'd asked the barista at the casino to put extra marshmallows in her hot chocolate just because he thought she might like it.

She picked up the remote and jabbed at the off switch. The small screen went black. 'They were marshmallows,' she blurted at her reflection in the small, black screen. 'Get a grip.'

She grabbed her backpack and headed out into the frosty darkness.

That next evening Rosie arrived at the mid-city address Cameron had invited her to, only to find there was nothing there. Just a cold sidewalk with a handful of newly planted trees looking drab and leafless in the winter darkness, and grey plasterboard two storeys high lining the entire block.

She banged the soles of her knee-high boots on the ground to warm them, and wished she'd brought a cardigan to wear over her floaty paisley-purple dress. But obviously she'd lost her mind the second she'd agreed to come.

She looked up and down the block. A group of bright young things in even less clothing than she wore skipped merrily across the road, arms intertwined. Their voices faded, then it was just her once more.

Her and her chatty subconscious.

What if he was stuck at work? What if he was alone somewhere, trapped under something heavy? Or, better yet, what if he was about to prove how beautifully unavailable he was, how ideal a choice for a first date, by standing her up on the second?

Just as she was about to give herself a pat on the back for being immensely gifted at picking the right wrong men after all, a concealed doorway opened up within the wall of grey, revealing a figure silhouetted within the gap. A figure with sexily ruffled hair, broad shoulders and shirt sleeves rolled up over the kind of sculpted forearms that made her think this was a guy who knew how to fix a leaky tap.

Cameron. Even cloaked in darkness there was no doubting it was him.

'I'm late. Again,' she said, her voice gravelly.

He pushed the hole in the wall open wider. 'You're right on time.'

She shook her head and hastened across the path. When she was close enough to see his eyes so blue, like the wild forget-me-nots scattered throughout her wayward back yard, he said, 'You look beautiful.'

'So do you,' she admitted before she even thought to censor herself.

'Why, thank you.'

She tucked her hair behind her ear and looked anywhere but at him. 'Where are we?'

'We're not there yet.'

Cameron shut the hole in the wall and locked it with a huge padlock, then passed her a great, hulking, orange workman's helmet.

'You have to be kidding,' she said.

'Put it on or we go no further.'

'I'll get hat hair.'

He glanced briefly at the waves that for once had been good

to her and curled in all the right directions. 'While inside these walls, you're not taking the thing off.'

'Jeez, you're demanding. You could try a little charm.'

'Fine,' he said, putting his own helmet on and only ending up looking sexier still in a strong, manly, muscly, blue-collar kind of way. '*Please*, Rosalind, wear the helmet lest something drop on your head and kill you and I have no choice but to hide your body.'

She grimaced out a smile. But all she said as she lugged the thing atop her head and strapped herself in was, 'You're lucky orange is my colour.'

He stepped in and reached up to twist it into a more comfortable position, then looked back into her eyes. He said, 'That I am.'

He smiled down at her. She felt herself smiling back, hoping to seem the kind of woman who could get those smiles on demand. It seemed eighteen hours away from him hadn't made her any more mindful. She wondered if it was too late to feign strep-throat or the plague.

She hoisted her handbag higher on her shoulder and gripped tight on the strap. 'Is this going to be some kind of extreme-sport type of dinner? Should I have brought knee pads and insurance?'

'Stick close to me and you'll be fine.'

Said the scorpion to the turtle.

He tucked her hand into his elbow so that their hips knocked and their thighs brushed, and Rosie felt nothing as straightforward as fine as they tramped over tarpaulins, beneath scaffolding and past piles of bricks and steel girders, until they reached a lift concealed behind heavy, silver plastic sheeting.

Rosie said, 'I feel like a heroine in a bad movie with people in the audience yelling "don't go in there!"'

He waved her forward. 'Go in there. Trust me.'

She glanced at him, at the come-hither smile, the dark-blue eyes, the tempting everything-else. Trust him? Right now she was having a hard time trusting herself.

She hopped in the lift, and for the next one and a half minutes did her best not to breathe too deeply the delicious scent of another freshly laundered shirt. Or maybe it was just him. Just clean, yummy Cameron.

She hoped this date would go quickly. Then at least she could say she'd given it a good old try. And know she could still rely completely on her judgement.

As the lift binged, Rosie flinched so hard she pulled a muscle in her side. Cameron moved to her, resting a hand against her back, and she flinched again. Then closed her eyes in the hope he hadn't noticed.

She felt the whisper of his breath against her neck a moment before he murmured by her ear. '*Now* we're here.'

'Where, exactly?'

'CK Square.'

The lift doors swished open, and what she saw had her feet glued to the lift floor. 'Holy majoly,' Rosie breathed out.

They had reached the top floor of the building, or what *would* be the top floor. The structure was in place, but apart from steel beams crisscrossing the air like a gigantic spider-web there was nothing between them and the heavens but velvet-black sky.

Cameron gave her a small shove to the left, and that was when she saw the charming wrought-iron table set for two around which candles burned on every given surface, their flames protected by shimmering glass jars. A cart held a number of plates covered in silver domes, and a bottle of wine chilled in an ice bucket to one side.

It was all so unexpected she felt as though the lift floor had dropped out from under her.

'Cameron,' she said, her voice puny. 'What have you gone and done?'

'I needed to make up for the farce at the Red Fox.'

And, it seemed, for every mediocre date she'd ever endured in her lifelong pursuit of cardboard-cutout companions.

Cameron guided her round neat piles of plasterboard and buckets of paint to the table. Only when his hand slid from her back to pull out her chair did she realise how chilly it was.

She let her handbag slump to the floor and sat, knees glued together, heels madly tapping the concrete floor.

The second he'd finished pouring her a glass of wine, she grabbed it and took a swig. For warmth. He caught her eye and smiled. She downed the rest of the glass.

'So, how was your day?' he asked, and she laughed so suddenly her hand flew to her mouth lest she spit wine all over the beautiful table. 'Did I say something funny?'

She put down the glass, and with her finger pushed it well out of reach. 'Well, yeah. We're currently sitting atop the world, surrounded by what looks to be every candle in Brisbane. And you're actually expecting me to remember how my day was?'

She looked down, picked up a silver spoon and polished it with her thumb. 'Of course, you've probably had dinner here a hundred times, so none of this is in the slightest bit unusual for you.'

She put down the spoon and sat on her hands. He poured himself a glass of wine slowly, then refilled hers just as slowly. Maybe he didn't feel the tension building in the cold air. Maybe she was the only one second guessing why they were here.

As he pushed her glass back towards her, he said, 'I have eaten Chinese takeaway atop a nearly finished building many, many times when the deadline came down to the wire and every second of construction counted. But my only company has been men in work boots. I'm not sure candles would have been appropriate.'

She slid her eyebrows north in her best impression of nonchalance. 'Did you just compare me with sweaty men? I may just swoon.'

Cameron's eyes narrowed, but she caught a glimpse of neat white teeth as a smile slipped through. 'Eat first, then swoon. I'm afraid this will be a shorter meal than last night. The fact we are here at all at this time of night without supervision means that we are breaking enough laws and union rules to get me shut me down.'

Rosie tried to do a happy dance at the "shorter meal" remark, but alas she found mischief even sexier than smooth talk. She clasped her hands together, leaned forward and whispered, 'Seriously?'

He put the bottle down and leaned close enough that she could see candlelight dancing in his eyes. 'Bruce, my project manager, just about quit when I told him what I had in mind.'

'Just about?'

The eyecrinkles deepened and all breath seeped quietly from her lungs.

'Though he looks scary, Bruce is really a big softie. He huffed and puffed and made me promise we'd wear helmets, and then promptly forgot I ever let him know what I was planning.'

She realised then that this would have taken a lot of planning. Meaning he'd been thinking about dinner, and more importantly about her, for much of the day.

What had happened to the hard, fast, cool character she was meant to be dating? And why was she so damn stubborn that she wasn't running scared right now?

He lifted his glass in salute. She took hers in a slightly unsteady hand and touched it to his. The clink of fine craftsmanship echoed in the wide, open space.

She said, 'Here's to Bruce.'

Cameron gave a small nod and took a sip, his eyes never once leaving hers. The urge to laugh had been replaced by the urge to scream. This was all so unreal, the kind of thing that happened to other girls. Nice girls. Not pragmatic girls who'd deliberately ruined every semi-meaningful relationship by walking away before the other shoe had a chance to drop.

She allowed herself the luxury of screaming on the inside of her head, and it helped a little.

'Hungry?' Cameron asked.

'Famished,' she said on a whoosh of air. Her eyes drifted to the silver-domed platters. 'So, who else did you bribe tonight?'

'A friend owns a place at Breakfast Creek Wharf.' He opened up the first dome to reveal a steaming plate of something delicious-looking. 'Scored calamari-strips in capsicum salsa, topped with quarters of lime.'

Rosie flapped her hands at him. 'Gimme, gimme, gimme.'

Cameron did as he was told and she dove in. At the first bite the taste exploded on her tongue, sour and sweet, fresh, salty and juicy. Plenty to keep her mouth full so she didn't have to talk. And didn't have to hear him say anything else to make her warm to him even more.

Her eyes shifted sideways to the four other domes, a move he didn't miss.

'Lobster-tail salad with truffle oil,' he said. 'Followed by apple and rhubarb tart with homemade vanilla and cinnamon ice cream.'

She warmed a good ten degrees.

A while later, after she swallowed her last mouthful of what had been the most heavenly, delicious apple pie ever created, Rosie let out a great sigh, folded her napkin on the table and looked up to find Cameron sitting back in his chair watching her.

She wiped a quick hand over her mouth, in case she had a glob of melted ice cream on the edge of her lip. But that wasn't it. He was watching her like she'd watched the lobster tail: with relish for what was ahead.

Those blue eyes of his, so like his dad's.

Her heart squeezed for him so suddenly, she held a hand to her chest. But knowing how it felt to have no father at all was one connection she couldn't will away. She wondered what might happen if someone stuck his father and him in a room together and locked the door. It couldn't hurt, but would it help?

Or should she just mind her own business and be glad he was ever so slightly aloof? Aloof was a good thing. Aloof meant there was no chance of any real deep connection being made. Which was fine. Great, even. Perfect.

Cameron's mobile phone rang, and she jumped.

He glanced at it briefly then ignored it.

It rang and rang, and Rosie ran a finger over the last of the melted, cinnamon-flecked ice cream on her plate, licking it off her finger. 'I think that might be your phone making all that racket.'

'It's my brother Brendan,' he said, jaw tight. 'He's the least likely person in the world to call unless he wants something.'

If she'd thought him aloof before, that was nothing compared with the thick, high wall blocking all access to him now. But it didn't help her situation one bit. If there was one thing she didn't like more than feeling emotionally unchecked, it was being made to feel invisible.

'Unless, of course, it's an urgent family matter,' she said, her voice as rigid as his change of behaviour.

His brow furrowed as he glanced at his phone, already a million miles away from her. 'Do you mind?'

'Not in the least.' She stood, snaffled a sugar-sprinkled strawberry from a bowl and took the opportunity to give herself some much-needed breathing space.

CHAPTER SEVEN

ROSIE had no idea how long she sat on a box crate, nothing between her and the edge of the building but fresh air, watching the world below her winding down.

The Brisbane River curved like a silver snake around the city. White boats bobbing on the river surface looked like little glow-bugs; dark patches dotted within the sparkly array marked out gardens and parks. And ragged mountains in the distance barely altered the gentle curve of the horizon.

The world was whisper-quiet, bar the shoosh of the wind. And above? The moon was hidden behind patchy, leopard-print cloud, and delicate, multi-coloured stars beamed intermittently through the gaps.

A wall of warmth washed against her back. She tensed and turned to find Cameron, his face lit by the quiet moonlight. 'Everything okay?'

'Fine,' Cameron said, in such a way that she knew it was not. She knew it was about his dad. The moment heaved between them. She itched to ask, to know, but the truth was for her the less she knew about him the better. That always made it easier when the time came to kiss cheeks and walk away.

'So what do you think of the view?' he asked, sliding a crate next to hers.

She hugged her knees to her chest and wrapped her floaty dress tight about her. 'Apart from it giving me a case of adult-onset vertigo?'

He laughed. 'Apart from that.'

'The view is…lovely.'

'Just *lovely*? Not magnificent? Not unmatchable? This floor will be rented out for so much money it makes *me* almost blush.'

'It's pretty. But kind of unreal when surrounded by so much concrete and steel. You really want to see something? Stars so bright, so crisp, so shiny and perfect, that you just want to hug yourself to keep all that beauty locked up tight inside of you.'

As her little flight of fancy came to a close she realised he was watching her with that inscrutable intensity that swept her legs out from under her. Lucky thing she was sitting.

'Where, pray tell,' he asked, 'Can a man see such stars?'

'You're mocking me.'

'I am. Only because it makes you blush, which is a view to match even this one.'

She thanked her lucky stars that he was yet to figure out her blushing had nothing to do with his words, and everything to do with his…everything. As his eyes searched hers, she looked back out into the night.

'Around three a.m. is best,' she said. 'At exactly this time of year. Five-hundred metres down the road from where I live, there's a dirt track leading to a plateau where the land drops away on three sides into Samford Valley. If you look to the south-east you can see the city in the distance. But you won't; you'll be looking up. And you'll truly understand why it's called the Milky Way.'

He breathed deep. 'You'll be there tonight?'

'I'm there every night. Though I must admit, I lasted about an hour this morning before I fell asleep.'

His deep, warm voice skittered across her skin as he asked, 'Tired you out, did I?'

'Hardly. I'm just not as gung ho as I used to be.'

She glanced back at him, and regretted it instantly. The guy was like a strong drink: just one taste and the effect on her body, and mind, was debilitating.

He asked, 'And what are you hoping you might find up there in the sky to be out so late at night?'

She nudged her chin against her shoulder. 'I'm not hoping to see anything. I saw what I needed to see long ago.'

His voice was low as he asked, 'What did you see?'

'That my trifling concerns don't matter all that much to anyone but me.'

'Hmm.' Cameron closed one eye and squinted at her with the other. 'I was brought up believing my family was the actual centre of the universe.'

'You do know the geocentric model went by the wayside around the sixteenth century, right? You've really got to see one of Adele's shows at the planetarium.'

Cameron laughed, and Rosie did too. The sounds joined for the briefest of moments before being carried away on the air.

'Until then, take this home with you—the fault is not in our stars, but in ourselves, that we are underlings.'

Cameron waited a beat before saying, 'Where have I heard that before?'

'Eleventh-grade Shakespeare.'

He blinked blankly.

'Now, come on, you can't tell me you never compared some poor, lovestruck and less-rigorously-educated young thing to a summer's day?'

He leaned forward until his face was a relief map of dark and light. She could see the shape of his hard chest as the breeze flapped his shirt against him, and the worry lines that never truly faded even when he smiled.

Thus she was blithely staring into those dreamy blue eyes

when he turned to her and said, 'Thou art more lovely and more temperate.'

Several seconds passed in which she said nothing; she just sat there, desperately searching for the humour that ought to have laced his words. Try as she might, she found none. Instead she found herself drowning in his voice, his words, his eyes, in his possibilities.

But that's not why you're seeing him, she told herself slowly, as if approaching an unknown and possibly dangerous animal. *You might be revelling in the invigorating slaying of invisibility demons of your childhood, but he is still the greatest of all impossibilities.*

She uncrossed her arms and grabbed hold of the edge of the crate, let her feet drop back to the concrete floor and dug her toes into her shoes. 'It's getting late.'

Cameron nodded. 'After Brendan rang, my project manager buzzed.'

'Good old Bruce.' The pleasure that skipped through her when he smiled made her wish she'd kept her mouth shut.

'I promised him my whim had been appeased and we were already on terra firma. Unscathed. I got the feeling he was lying in bed awake awaiting that news.'

He held out a hand. She took it. She didn't realise how cold hers was until it was enveloped in the warmth of his. He lifted her easily to her feet, and time folded in on itself as together they walked through the maze of building materials, blowing out each of the candles.

When they reached the table he scooped up her handbag and lifted it onto her shoulder, and then with her hand still snug in his he led her to the lift.

'Shouldn't we take some of that stuff back downstairs?' she asked, giving one last, longing look at the romantic little alcove before, for the sake of every future date, she did her best to forget it had ever existed.

'It'll be taken care of in the morning.'

'There you go again,' she said, shaking her head. 'Thinking yourself at the centre of the universe.'

He lifted his chin. 'You know what? I'm thinking I might hang onto that thought a while longer yet. The pay's good, and the benefits are beyond compare.'

The lift door closed on the concrete and steel, unlit candles and glowing horizon, and Rosie had to admit the guy probably had a point.

They reached the plasterboard wall and Cameron glanced at the top of Rosie's head and held out a hand. It was only then that she even remembered she'd been wearing the orange protective helmet the whole time.

She groaned inwardly. All those longing glances she'd imagined—the moments his eyes had locked on hers, and she'd seen things therein that had made her feel warm all over and scared her silly—she hadn't even noticed his helmet; she'd been so caught up in the rest of him. All the while she must have looked an utter treat.

'If you are hoping to keep it as a souvenir—'

'No, of course not!' She slid it forward, ran ragged fingers across her scalp and tied the length into a hasty knot at her nape, not wanting to know what kind of red marks were shining across her forehead as she spoke.

'Where did you park?' he asked.

She motioned vaguely with her shoulder. 'Down the street.'

He moved in closer. Or had the moon shifted behind a cloud and made everything suddenly seem more intimate? 'Where? I'll walk you there.'

'I'll be fine. These boots might not be steel-capped but I know where to aim them if I get in any trouble.'

The word 'trouble' almost lodged in her throat. Trouble was the look in Cameron's eyes. Trouble was the slip and slide of desire keeping her from backing away as he inched ever closer. Trouble had become her new best friend the moment Cameron Kelly had re-entered her life.

She leapt up on the only thing she could think of that might give her time to find a reasonable, last ditch, way out. 'I've been meaning to ask—what *were* you doing in the planetarium yesterday morning?'

He paused. She took a thankful breath.

'I'm not sure I should say,' he said.

'And why not?'

'Because it's not going to flatter me any.' And it wasn't enough to stop him any longer. He moved in closer.

Rosie lifted a hand to his chest. 'Try me.'

His eyes narrowed. The weight of him pressed upon her hand. His voice was as low as she'd ever heard it as he said, 'I was hiding.'

'No! Yes? Seriously? From whom?'

'My sister Meg. She was there having coffee with a couple of mates, one of them Tabitha.'

Rosie's laughter split the quiet night. 'Tabitha on caffeine? I don't blame you for hiding.'

His eyes slid down her face to settle upon her lips. Her heart shot into her throat. She shut her mouth. But it was no use; every part of her buzzed in expectation of what it would feel like to have his lips on hers.

'Did you know Venus is the hottest planet in our solar system?' Okay, so she was getting desperate.

He paused about three inches from touchdown.

She went on, 'And, while Venus was the Roman goddess of beauty and love, in Greek mythology she was named Aphrodite, and Ishtar for the Babylonians?'

'That I'm sure I knew. I went to a very good school, you know.'

He was so close now; he breathed out, she breathed in, and the sweet taste in her mouth was his.

'Did you ever see that movie—? *Ishtar*? What was the name of that French actress?'

'Rosalind.'

'I don't think so. I wouldn't have forgotten her name if it was the same as—'

'Rosalind,' he growled.

'Yes, Cameron?'

'Shut up so I can kiss you.'

'Yes, Cameron,' she whispered, but it was lost as his lips finally, finally found hers.

She'd heard how some people claimed they saw their lives flashing before their eyes as they were about to pass over. She'd never really believed it could happen until that moment.

Memories of past kisses faded to dust. Every other man she'd ever thought she'd been attracted to melted into a grey, shapeless nothingness, and the blank slate inside her head filled with everything Cameron as emotion upon emotion crashed over her so fast she couldn't keep up.

She tucked a hand along the back of his neck, letting her fingers delve into his soft, springy hair as she pulled him close. His hands bunched into the back of her dress. And together they shifted and turned until every part of them that could touch did.

The kiss deepened, warmed, and took her breath, her sense and her mind until she curved against him like a sapling defenceless against a strong gale.

Helpless, unprotected, lost…

The wind in her ears began to decelerate as the kiss gentled and fell away. It took a few seconds longer before she was able to clamber her way back to the surface, only to find Cameron's smouldering eyes looking deep into hers.

'You busy tomorrow night?' he asked.

She blinked heavily, trying to remember where she was, what day it was, who she was… 'You need some new material.'

'My material is just fine. Are you free?'

She still needed a moment to gather the last few strands of sense that had not been unravelled by his kiss. She'd known it would be amazing, but she hadn't expected anything could be so stunning that it could sap her of every ounce of judgement so that she stood there wide open, wanting more, taking more, any tiny little bit she could get her hands on.

She licked her lips, took a breath, then said, 'I'm busy every night. Busy busy busy, stargazing and the like.'

'Too busy to have dinner with me again?'

'It's certainly possible.'

'I've never known a woman make me work so hard to pin her down for a simple dinner-date.'

He ran a fast hand through his hair, mussing it up, making him look like he'd just tumbled out of bed. The pure, unadulterated sexual energy that careened unimpeded through her brought her out of her trance quick-smart.

She pulled away just enough so that she could feel where she ended and he began. 'The thing is, Cameron, dinner with you has never *been* simple.'

He trailed one hand up her back to unhook her knot of hair, sliding his fingers through it until it fell down her back. Then he twirled a curl around one finger and let it go. Again and again and again.

He said, 'If you like simple, "yes" is a simple word. Only three little letters.'

Heck, if she was looking for simple, the word 'no' only had two letters. So why was it so very hard for her to say? Because cracks the likes of which she'd never experienced before were appearing in her resolve. So far she was coping okay. She was keeping her feet, she was sticking up for herself. What she couldn't be sure of was at what point the damage would be irreparable.

Or perhaps Cameron Kelly was to be the man who would help her prove to herself just how strong she could be, and how the hard work she'd put into herself to make sure she wouldn't make the same mistakes her mum made had truly paid off.

Less than certain of her reasoning, she still said, 'Fine. Yes.'

His forehead unknotted, and she hadn't even realised how tight it had been as he'd awaited her answer. Unless it was evidence of other concerns, which in the midst of her internal toing and froing she had all but forgotten he had.

'Cameron, is…?' She shook her head, searched for the words that would least likely bring the shutters slamming down between them. 'I'd understand if you wanted to make time for your brothers and sister tomorrow night instead, to talk about…things. Or maybe even to go see your dad in person. I know I'm being presumptuous, but with twenty-twenty hindsight that would be my next move.'

'Being with you tends to keep me more pleasantly occupied.' He said it with the kind of smile he knew could make a girl's knees go weak. But she wasn't falling for it, not when she'd glimpsed what it felt like to really be with him on the other side of the wall. It was enough to keep her pushing.

'So that would be a no to visiting your dad?'

Cameron's cooling smile said it all.

'Did you even talk to Brendan about it?' she pressed.

His eyes narrowed.

She just raised an eyebrow in return. 'You're not going to scare me off the subject. Being an obnoxious teenager prepared me too well for dealing with stubborn men like you.'

A glint lit his eyes, and the corner of his mouth lifted. 'I'm beginning to see that. Fine. He made no mention of my father's health, but he was quite vocal about the fact that if I don't come to the birthday bash this weekend I may as well relinquish my surname for good.'

His hand on her back slid upwards, the shift of fabric made her body melt back against him.

'Them's strong words,' she said, her voice husky.

He pushed the hair he'd been playing with behind her ear. 'Brendan's been around the longest. He's been indoctrinated. He doesn't know any other type of words.'

'Poor Brendan,' she whispered.

'Poor, poor Brendan.'

He leaned in and placed a kiss just below her ear, and she half forgot what they were talking about. And when he moved to nibble on her earlobe itself she forgot the other half.

An age later when he pulled away all she could remember was that they had agreed to a third date. 'So, where to tomorrow? A spaceship? No, a submarine. It better be your basic, run-of-the-mill submarine or I'm out of there.'

'I was thinking of taking you to the first place I ever built.'

She bit back a yawn. 'Fine. But they'd better serve coffee. Three nights out in a row, and I'm afraid I might fade to a shadow.'

'If that's what it'll take.' With that he pulled her close and kissed her again. This time it was slow, soft, tender, mesmerising. He tasted of white wine and strawberries. He made every inch of her feel toasty warm. In that moment the word 'yes' felt like the easiest word in the entire world.

When he pulled away, he did so with discernible regret.

He groaned, spun her on the spot, gave her a small shove in the direction of her car and said, 'Now get, before today becomes tomorrow and we both turn into pumpkins.'

As Rosie walked down the street she felt Cameron's eyes on her the whole way. He obviously hadn't believed her about her ability with her boots. Or maybe he just liked the view.

She added a swagger for good measure.

CHAPTER EIGHT

THE sun was just beginning to rise but Cameron's backside had already been parked atop a dry, paint-spattered stool for an hour as he earned his keep playing diplomat between Bruce, the project manager, and Hamish, the architect. With a month to go before completion, things were tense.

He slid a finger beneath his hard hat to wipe the gathering sweat from his brow, and was hit with the image of Rosalind wearing one the night before.

With those big, grey eyes and her long hair hanging in sexy waves beneath the orange monstrosity, she'd looked adorable. And he was entirely certain she'd had no idea. As a short-term distraction she was proving to be all he could have hoped for.

'Kelly!' Bruce called out, slamming Cameron back to earth with a thud.

'What?' he barked.

'Where the hell have you been for the past five minutes? You sure as hell haven't been on Planet Brisbane.'

Cameron frowned. But Bruce was right. Spending every spare moment with Rosalind was proving to be mighty helpful at distracting him from obsessing about his father. He just didn't need that distraction spilling over into other areas of his life.

Since he'd been thrown out on his own, his business was

his everything. It filled his waking hours, and many of his sleeping ones as well. It was his fuel, his drive, his passion. While on the other hand, Rosalind was…

'Earth to Cameron,' Bruce said, shaking his head.

Cameron mentally slapped himself across the back of the head. Enough, already.

'I'm here,' he growled. 'Keep going.'

Bruce leant against a column and crossed his arms. 'I was just telling Hamish here about your little tryst upstairs last night. Candles? Seafood?'

Cameron all but threw the handful of papers in his hands into the air in surrender.

Hamish pulled up a stool so that he was in Cameron's direct eyeline. 'Please tell me the big man's been telling tales out of school. You did not bring some woman here after hours without proper supervision. Not a month out from signing off?'

Cameron stared hard at his mate. Hamish—who had known him since university, therefore knew him only as the ambitious, focussed, blinkered entrepreneur he had become—stared right on back.

'God, Cam,' Hamish drawled. 'You had to be breaking a good dozen laws, not to mention union rules.'

'You think I didn't tell him that?' Bruce asked.

But Hamish wasn't done. In fact there was a distinct glint in his eye as he crossed his arms and leant back on the stool. 'Cam,' he said. 'The last of the honourable men, brought thudding back to earth by a mystery woman. Who the heck is she?'

Cameron closed his eyes and ran his index finger and thumb hard across his forehead. 'She's no-one you know. And this subject is now closed.'

'Fine with me.' Hamish held both hands in the air, then glanced at his paint-splattered watch. 'I have somewhere else to be.'

'We have work to do, McKinnon,' Bruce cried. 'Where else could you possibly have to be?'

'I have a date waiting for me on the exterior-window cleaning trestle. She should be at about the thirtieth floor by now, so I'll just go grab the champagne and get harnessed up.'

Cameron didn't even bother telling Hamish where to go, he just slid from the stool and walked away.

'Where's he think he's going?' he heard Bruce ask as he reached the lift door.

'If he's trying to cut in on my date,' Hamish said, 'It'll be pistols at dawn.'

There was a pause, then Bruce said, 'I thought you were kidding about the girl,' as the lift doors closed. Cameron was only half-sorry he missed Hamish's response.

He reached the top floor before he knew it. The lift doors opened to a cacophony of noise as glaziers, construction workers and plasterers chatted, banged, drilled, swore and gave the place the kind of raw energy that usually invigorated him.

It meant progress. Honest work, honestly executed by honest men. Sweat of the brow stuff. He was proud of the healed blisters on his own hands for that exact reason.

But as he hit the spot on the roofless penthouse floor, where the night before Rosalind had sat upon a crate, looking out over his city, and with her mix of ruthless candour and subtle beauty had managed to smooth over his perpetual dissatisfaction, the noise faded away.

He leant a foot against the edge of the roof and looked out over the horizon where streaks of cloud were just beginning to herald the rising of the sun.

He held out his hand at arm's length and a span above the horizon; just where she'd said it would be, there it was: Venus. A glowing crescent in the pale-grey sky.

His hand dropped. Somewhere out there, beyond the borders of the noisy, thriving city he loved, she would be sitting somewhere quiet looking at the exact same point in the sky.

And while she was thinking trajectories, gas clouds and expanding universes, he was thinking about her. About seeing her again tonight. It would be their third date in as many nights, which was more time than he'd spent with one woman in as long as he could remember. More time than he ever let himself see Meg or Dylan.

A thread of guilt snuck beneath his unusually unguarded defences. He'd kept those he loved most at the greatest distance so as to save them from being tainted with the hurtful knowledge about his father's weak character he always carried with him. But something Rosalind had said made him wonder: was keeping them at bay hurting them as much?

If he really wanted to see them he knew where they'd be that weekend, all in the one place at the one time, which was usually an impossible feat.

He ran a hand over his mouth. If he went to his father's birthday party, he pretty much knew what would happen. Brendan would swagger, Dylan would win money on a bet he had made somewhere about the date of his return home and Meg would squeal, leap into his arms, then try to set him up with a girlfriend. And his mother would probably cry.

His stomach clenched on his mother's behalf. The clench turned to acid as he thought of how shabbily she'd been treated by the one person who was meant to care for her. The idea of putting on a show at a celebration of that man's years on earth turned to dust in his throat.

He needed to put it out of his mind for good. He checked his watch. Twelve hours to go before he was due to pick Rosalind up at the planetarium. Not soon enough.

'Cam?'

He turned to find Hamish standing in the lift, holding the door open.

'Anything else you want to go over before I do head off?'

Cameron had to think, the usually crisp, clear list in his head squished at the edges, having been pushed aside by other pressing thoughts. 'If there is, I'll call you.'

Hamish nodded and stepped back into the lift, where he held the door open. 'Unless, of course, you need a different kind of advice. I have some moves the likes of which you could not even imagine.'

'I've got it covered,' Cameron said, his voice gruff.

Hamish nodded. 'Good to know.'

Cameron stretched his arms over his head and shook out the looseness that invaded his limbs, and the woolliness that infiltrated his head whenever Rosalind Harper was on his mind.

He did have it covered. He just needed to find some perspective. His business was his life. His family his cross to bear. Rosalind Harper was a delightful but temporary distraction. Tonight he would make sure those boundaries were clearly redefined.

By the time he joined Hamish in the lift, he was clear-headed and ready to act like the head of a multi-million-dollar business.

When after several seconds the lift had yet to move, he realised he'd forgotten to press the button. He reached out and jabbed it so hard his finger hurt.

As the lift doors closed, Hamish said, 'If you're this scrambled, I'm thinking redhead.'

Rosalind's face swam before Cameron's eyes—her wide eyes unguarded, her smile heartfelt, her kiss like heaven on earth.

'Hair like caramel,' he said. 'Skin like cream, legs that go on for ever.'

Hamish swore softly and Cameron grinned.

On the other side of the city, Rosie peeled her eye away from the planetarium's telescope then stared unseeingly at her open laptop.

The cursor blinked hopefully on a blank screen. Her daily notes about Venus's position, colour, opacity, flares, shadows, and any other nuances her dedicated study was meant to bring forth, were lost within the muddy mire of her mind.

She glanced through the gap in the domed ceiling and stared at the distant patch of sky where Venus's crescent had been before streaks of cloud slid across the view. Though, truth be told, she wasn't entirely sure how long she'd been staring at cloud rather then planet.

She leant her hand on the telescope, leant her chin on her hand and stared at a blank spot mid-air about an inch from her nose. Her mind wandered happily back to the top floor of CK Square. Was Cameron there now? What was he doing? Who was he with? What was he wearing? Was he thinking about her at all?

'Mornin' kiddo!'

At Adele's voice, Rosie jumped so high she landed awkwardly and clunked herself on the chin. She rubbed the spot with one palm and asked, 'What time is it?'

Adele perched on the corner of a desk and shrugged. 'Seven-ish.'

Rosie groaned and let her face land against her forearm, where she got a mouthful of red-and-grey-striped wool poncho. She waved a hand in the direction of her laptop and her voice was muffled as she said, 'I've been here since five-ish and have literally achieved nothing.'

A crunching sound brought her head up to find Adele eating a packet of corn chips. Rosie clicked hungry fingers at her friend.

Adele stood. 'Uh-uh. Not while you're within breathing distance of my telescope. I've already had to explain to the board why we needed to have the mirrors cleaned twice last month. A third time and they'll start looking closer.'

Rosie packed up her gear and dragged herself after her

friend into the nearby office, where she slumped into an old vinyl chair. She grabbed a handful of chips then hooked her boots over the edge of the chair.

'So,' Adele said, swinging back and forth on her office chair, eyes narrowed. 'How is it that you, Rosalind "stars in her eyes" Harper spent two hours sitting at that thing without making a single note?'

Rosie licked cheese-flavoured salt off her fingers and stared at her friend wondering what, if anything, she should say. Could say. In the end she went with, 'My mind was otherwise occupied.'

It took less than half a second for Adele to join the dots. 'Who's the poor sod?'

She baulked. It wasn't as though she'd kept her dates from her best friend because they felt too precious; she just hadn't found the time. So if that was true why was she hesitating now? She closed her eyes tight and blurted, 'Cameron Kelly.'

When Adele didn't shoot her down with a snappy comeback, Rosie opened one eye.

'Cameron Kelly,' Adele said. '*The* Cameron Kelly who was here the other morning?'

Rosie nodded.

'Well, fair enough too,' Adele said. 'Those thighs, that voice, those eyes; I've been having some nice dreams ever since myself.'

Rosie nibbled at her lower lip and let her legs slide back to the floor. 'The thing is it's kind of gone beyond nice dreams. We've been out the past two nights. And he's picking me up here to take me to dinner again tonight.'

'So why don't you sound as over the moon about that fact as I feel you should?'

'He's just not the kind of guy I usually go for.'

'Um, he's gorgeous and sexy. And you usually go for gorgeous and sexy. Think about the blond who hung around here every morning last summer, making the place smell like sunscreen.'

'Jay was following the waves down the east coast. His job was over at nine in the morning.'

'Right, well, he was gorgeous and sexy. And last winter…?' Rosie thought back. 'Marcus.'

'Right! The American professor playing job-swap for three months. Super-duper cute in a leather elbow-patch, reading-Emily-Dickinson-to-you-in-bed kind of way. So what makes this one so different?'

Rosie shrugged.

'Is there something wrong with the guy you're not telling me? Some physical flaw hidden beneath the designer duds? Some personality deviation one would never expect? It's okay; I can take it. I have fantasy guys in reserve.'

'Well…no. Okay, it's like this—he has that inviolable, lone-wolf aura that makes some men always get chosen captain of every team they join, which I really like. He's resilient, self-reliant, and far too focussed on the intricacies of his own life to even think about searching for the girl of his dreams.'

'He sounds just like you.' Adele nodded along. 'Except the liking girls part.'

'In that respect, I guess, yeah. But then in the spirit of full disclosure he's shared with me intimate details of his private life. And he's the kind of man who opens your car door without being asked. I didn't know they even existed any more. Is a nice streak a personality flaw? No, I'm clutching at straws there. Because the way he kisses…'

Rosalind's voice petered away as she became lost in memories of his sultry, liquefying, unnerving, transporting kiss. There had not been one moment of that kiss that could be blandly described as 'nice'.

'Hey!' Adele called out. 'You seem to have drifted off there at the best part.'

'Use your imagination,' Rosie said.

'Oh, I shall.'

Rosie hunched inside her poncho and wondered about Cameron's best parts. Somehow she knew she hadn't even scratched the surface. And that was fine; he could hardly help it if he was naturally fascinating. It was the ferocity with which she found herself longing to know those parts, and to let him get a glimpse of hers, that had her in a twist.

She began nervously flicking at a crack in the end of one short fingernail. 'So, do I see him tonight or quit while I'm ahead?'

'I'm sorry, was Miss Independent looking for my humble opinion?'

Rosie glanced up. 'I ask your opinion all the time.'

'Sure you do, when you want to know which science journals might suit whatever new paper you've whipped up.'

'I'm not that bad.'

'Ah, yeah, y'are. Hon, you're a rock.'

Rosie stared at her friend, who stared right back. She bit the inside of her lip as she said, 'Yeah. I am. I'm just used to looking out for myself, is all.'

Adele reached out with her foot and gave her a nudge on the leg. 'I know, hon. It's cool. Now, do you really want my opinion?'

'I really do.'

'You said this was your third date?'

Rosie nodded.

'Well, then, yeah you're seeing him tonight!'

The friction between Rosie's jiggling knees suddenly had nothing on the warmth invading her cheeks and her palms, and the searing coil deep and low in her belly.

'Adele, the third-date rule is rubbish. Nothing ever happens in life that you don't allow to happen.'

'So you don't want to sleep with him?'

'I didn't say that, I—'

'Then let it happen, for Pete's sake! Jeez. To think if only I'd been at work ten minutes earlier that day it might have been me having this conversation. Actually, no; it wouldn't. I don't believe in the third-date rule either. The second date is fine with me.'

'Adele!'

Adele held up a hand. 'Can I just say one last thing before I zip my lips for good on the matter?'

'Please,' Rosie said.

Adele bit her lip for a moment, just a moment, but just long enough so that Rosie knew she wasn't going to like what she had to say.

'You like the guy, right?'

Rosie nodded, and Adele patted her on the hand.

'Then consider this,' Adele said. '*He* may be an island, but his family is an institution in this town. Unlike your professor or your surf pro, who both came with convenient expiry-dates built in, Cameron Kelly isn't going anywhere.'

Rosie waited for the heat in her belly to cool to room temperature. But for some unknown reason the idea of Cameron being around a while longer than her normal guys didn't scare her silly.

Which of course only scared her out of her mind.

That evening, as they snaked up the steep cliff-face of exclusive, riverside Hamilton in Cameron's MG, Rosie kept doggedly to her side of the car, arms crossed beneath her poncho, knees pointed towards the outer window, feet bouncing against the low-slung floor.

She'd been pacing outside the front door of the planetarium when he'd appeared through the trees, gorgeous in dark low-slung jeans, a black T-shirt under a designer track-top, sleeves pushed up to his elbows, revealing his strong, sculpted forearms that she found so irresistible. His hair was ruffled, his cheeks slightly flushed from the cold. His heavenly blue eyes had been on her. Focussed. Unwavering.

He'd kept an arm about her waist as he'd guided her to his car, then had hastened to put the soft-top up, reminding her how spontaneously nice he was. Then, just before she'd hopped in the car, he'd pulled her close to kiss her hot, hard and adamantly, and she'd remembered how beautifully *not* nice he could be.

Yet all she could think the entire time was that he was gorgeous. It was their third date. And he wasn't going anywhere.

They turned down a street where mature palm trees lined the perfectly manicured footpath and all the houses were hidden behind high fences and brush-box hedges. The MG slowed to a purr as Cameron pulled up in front of a cream rendered-brick wall. A double garage door whirred open and they slunk inside.

Golden sensor-lights flickered on at their arrival, revealing a simple room with polished-wood floors and just enough room for two cars. Or in Cameron's case a car, a mountain bike, a jet ski and three canoes suspended from the far wall.

He took her hand and helped her out of the car.

When he let go she snuck her hand back beneath her poncho and eased round him to give herself space to breathe.

Cameron twirled his keys on the end of a finger as he opened the unassuming doorway to the left and waved her through. 'Welcome to my humble abode.'

On the other side of the door, at the bottom of a tall, curved floating staircase, lay an open-plan room with shiny blonde-wood floors, a far wall made up of floor-to-ceiling windows and a dramatic two-storey canted ceiling. On the right, a raised granite-and-oak kitchen with a six-seater island bench rested beneath a charming skylight the size of a small car. In a living area on the left was a soft, cream leather lounge-suite that would easily seat ten, and a flat-screen TV that must have been six-feet wide. The fireplace in the corner was filled with half-burnt logs and fresh ash. Outside the windows she could see a large, dark-blue, kidney-shaped pool.

Rosie stopped cataloguing and swallowed. 'You built this?'

'It gave me blisters, took a toenail and dislocated a shoulder, so I wouldn't forget. It was the best education for a guy who would one day have labourers in his employ. My empathy when they whinge is genuine, as is my insistence that if I could do it so can they. Come in,' he said as he placed a hand in the middle of her back and encouraged her to get further than one step down.

Her feet moved down the stairs, past the lounge and to the windows as she stared at the view. Beyond the smattering of orange-tiled rooves meandering down the cliff-face below, established greenery bordered the Hamilton curve of the Brisbane River. Half-baked shells of what would one day become multi-million-dollar yachts rode the water surface. In the distance the Storey Bridge spanned the gleaming waterway, and the city glowed in the last breath of dying sunlight while the moon rose like a silver dollar between the towers.

This place was more than just a building; the personality, the warmth, the lovely, lush detail made it more than a house. It felt like a home.

For a girl who took enormous gratification in the fact that the place in which she slept was just that—a place to sleep, with no history, or memory, or attachment, nothing she would fear losing. It was an extraordinary feeling.

Extraordinary and emphatic. Adele was dead right: Cameron Kelly may appear a lone wolf, but he was a man with roots as deep as his city was tall.

'Rosalind?'

'Do you sleep on thc couch?' she said overly loudly, to cut him off.

'My bedroom and the study are in the level above. More bedrooms, wet bar; games room below.'

She nodded. 'Your home is really beautiful.'

'Thanks.' His voice rumbled through the wide, open room, but he might as well have whispered them into her ear, the way it affected her.

He was different from the guys she usually dated in more ways than she'd let on to Adele. No surfer's body or profcssor's poetry had ever brought her to this state of permanent anticipation and awareness of every detail around her, every tactile sensation, every natural beauty. And worse, neither had the dedicated life she'd led alone.

She gave herself a little shake and decided a change of subject was what was needed if she had any chance of finding her feet again.

She turned with a plastered-on smile. 'So where's this telescope you claim to have—still in its box? A figment of your imagination? A falsehood with which to impress the science girl?'

'It's…unpacked. Though honestly it's always been more decorative than functional.'

She stuck a hand on her hip. 'So it's an expensive dust-collector?'

He winced. 'The night I moved in, I looked through the thing. The trees were upside down. I gave up and watched the cricket match instead.'

'Ever heard of an instruction manual?'

He stared back at her. She let her gaze rove over the glassware in his clear kitchen-cabinets, anywhere but at those hot, blue eyes.

'Some refractors work that way. You just have to remember that in space nothing's upside down or the right way up. Only your thinking makes it so.' She glanced back at him as she said, 'Your problem is the "centre of the universe" thing you have going on.'

'I have the feeling if I keep you around long enough you'll eventually knock that out of me.'

The very idea created a knot deep in her belly. How long was long enough? How long was a piece of string? How long until she relaxed, for Pete's sake?

She tugged on the fingers of one hand until a couple of knuckles gave helpful cracks. 'So where is it? I can give you a quick lesson.'

'It's in my bedroom.'

'Of course it is. Is there any better place from which to spy on your neighbour's trees?'

'There's only one way to find out.'

She tugged her fingers so hard something popped that she wasn't sure ought to have popped. 'I'll take your word for it.'

She stretched out her tense hands, and again didn't quite know where to look—while he stood at the bottom of the stairs clean-shaven, handsome as they came, oozing cool, calm and collectedness. Pure and unadulterated Kelly.

And in that moment Rosie knew she'd been kidding herself; she'd bitten off far more than she could chew.

Cameron was secure in the lifestyle he'd been born to, while it had taken her half a lifetime and a lot of fight to become half as comfortable in her own skin, and she was still very much a work in progress.

If the two of them came together in the kind of collision she felt was on the horizon, he'd not show a dint, while if genetics counted for anything she could well be damaged beyond repair.

When he threw his keys into a misshapen wooden bowl on a chunky hall-table at the bottom of the stairs, the sound made her jump.

She blew out a stream of air, her eyes scooting over the table to find that it was covered in clutter—a baseball cap, a couple of loose computer back-up-stick thingies on brightly coloured lanyards, a camera bag tipped over and empty, a coffee cup with remnants on the rim and a messy pile of opened envelopes in need of throwing out.

The flotsam and jetsam of a real life. And a reminder that Cameron wasn't just a name, or a bank balance, or an alma mater, or an archetype she could shove into some pigeon hole that suited her.

Above all else he was a man. A real man. Possibly the first authentic man she'd ever known.

Warmth curled throughout her insides, loosening all the immobilised places inside her. The feelings that tumbled in its wake came too thick and fast for her to even hope to herd them somewhere safe. She just dug her toes into her shoes and waited for the waves to stop.

Thankfully Cameron was in the kitchen by that stage, with his back to her and his head deep in the fridge, one hand wrapped about the edge of the door, the other wavering near the top shelf, letting out the cold air and not giving a hoot.

'I had a crazy day today,' his muffled voice said. 'One level of chaos after another, starting with some attitude from your friend Bruce. It's made me so hungry I'd eat the fridge if I had a knife sharp enough.'

Rosie was so addled; if he came out of there with a lasagne he'd cooked for her himself, she thought she might just faint.

He ducked his head round the door and his cornflower-blue gaze caught hers. She blinked and stared right back.

He was gorgeous. And this was the all-important third date. But was she willing to yield to everything that concept entailed, even knowing that afterwards he wouldn't be going anywhere?

As though he knew the exact nature of her thoughts, the corners of his mouth lifted lazily, creating the sexiest creases in his cheeks, adorable crinkles around his eyes and such a provocative gleam in those eyes it was as good as an invitation.

Maybe she hadn't bitten off more than she could chew. Maybe she just had to adjust her perspective on who he was and how much of him she could handle. She just had to trust herself that she'd absolutely know the moment to pull out before she'd gone too far. Or maybe, just maybe, he was worth going over the edge for.

'I have no idea what I was hoping I might find in there,' he said. 'There's not a single thing I know what to do with. How does Chinese takeaway sound?'

Rosie let go at the breath she felt like she'd been holding for the past half an hour. 'Sounds perfect.'

CHAPTER NINE

AN HOUR later Rosie sat at the kitchen bench, three of the four white boxes of noodles empty. She abandoned the final unopened box before leaning against the chair back and laying her hand over her stomach.

Beside her, Cameron laughed. 'For a moment there I thought I might have to throw myself in front of the leftovers to save you from yourself.'

'No fear. I know when to quit.'

Cameron's laughter subsided to an easy smile. And Rosie smiled back. The freak-out that had afflicted her early in the evening had faded to a reminder to take care. Once she'd mentally adjusted the limits of what she could handle, she'd begun to relax into Cameron's effortless company.

He'd long since ditched his jacket, and Rosie her poncho and shoes. A CD played softly in the background. A fire crackled in the hearth. And the conversation fell into a natural lull.

Rosie's naked toes curled around the bottom rung of the stool and her eyes blinked slowly. All snug and warm, the past few nights finally threatened to catch up to her.

'You have a little smudge…' Cameron said, his voice low and soothing.

She opened her eyes to find him staring at her mouth, a

hand hovering so close to her lips that they began to tingle. Her tongue darted out to swipe at the left corner of her mouth.

He smiled, frowned, then gently wiped a half-centimetre lower. Whatever speck of sauce he found there he proceeded to lick off his finger. And suddenly sleep was the last thing on her mind.

She leant her elbows on the bench and leant her chin on her upturned palms. 'Of all the places in all the world one can be, how is it that a guy like you ended up staying so close to home?'

His eyes narrowed. 'It's not that close.'

The edge in his voice had her shifting to face him. 'St Grellans is five minutes from here,' she shot back. 'And your parents' house is, what, two suburbs over?'

'The fact that I wanted to live in the finest part of town isn't reason enough?'

'Nope. Not for you.'

He picked up his beer and took a slow sip, watching her over the top of the glass. 'How many days ago did we meet up?'

'Two,' she said.

'But this is our third date?'

She nodded. His cheek twitched, and he took another long sip, his eyes never leaving hers as he let that thought sink in. Her leg began to jiggle beneath the bench.

He put down his glass, but kept hold of it as he looked into the amber bubbles. 'I grew up in Ascot. Meg's still at home, though she stays at Tabitha's bachelorette pad in town half the week. Brendan's in Clayfield, close to his daughters' school. Dylan's place is neck-deep in cafés in Morningside. So you're right; we are all a stone's throw from home.'

She crossed her ankles to stop the jiggling and shoved a hand into her hair as she let her upper arm sink against the bench. 'So why didn't you move to the other side of the city when you had the falling out with your dad? Or the other side of the country, for that matter? Or the world. I've done it, several times over. It's too easy.'

He tipped his glass and let it fall back upright before pushing it away and giving her his full focus once more. 'And imagine where you might have ended up had interplanetary travel been on the cards. I hazard a guess that this place wouldn't have seen you for dust.'

Three dates. That was as long as they had really known each other. She thought she had him figured out, but it hadn't occurred to her til that moment that maybe he had her figured out too.

She wrapped her hands about her shoulders, her fingers sliding against the white cotton T-shirt and digging into soft flesh. 'But we're not talking about me.'

His hand slid along the bench to tap her elbow. 'How about we do?'

She shook her head slowly. 'No need. Unlike yours, my life is all figured out. No more analysis necessary.'

He watched her for a few long seconds before sliding his hand beneath her elbow, and turning her on the spot until she was looking out the window at the view of the Brisbane skyline.

His low, rumbling words brushed the hair against her ear as he said, 'That view of that city is what inspired me to do what I do. I can see almost every building I've built from here, and I spend way more time than I ought to admit to sitting by the pool, fantasising about where the next one should go. And that view reminds me that, while I am creating the future of the city, I need to be mindful not to take anything away from the aesthetic created by those who came before me, and hope one day another developer will do the same for me.'

As Cameron's words came to an end, Rosie felt like she was stuck in a kind of suspended animation. Her eyes were locked on the peaks and valleys of the teeming metropolis glittering brightly in the dark distance. And with his deep words echoing in her ears for the first time she saw the profound beauty he saw. In what he did. And in who he was, the true man deep down inside the fortress.

He swung her back round to face him, one eye closed, his divine mouth twisted in chagrin. 'Was that the biggest load of egotistical clap-trap you've ever heard?'

She shook her head slowly, wondering if he had a single clue how at risk she was to his smiles in that moment. 'That wasn't what I was thinking at all.'

'No?'

'I was thinking that, no matter how much you might like people to think that you consider yourself to be the centre of the universe, you really don't. I'm not sure that you ever have.'

He opened both eyes and lost the humble grin. He let his hand slip away from her elbow, ostensibly to grab his drink, but she knew better. Even before he said, 'Whatever gave you that idea?'

'Why skyscrapers? Why not mini-malls or housing estates or parking garages?'

'The bigger the building, the bigger my…income.' He grinned. Gorgeously.

'See, now you might think you can dazzle me with your jokes,' she said, waggling a finger at his nose, 'And your fancy noodles, but I've realised something.'

He leant a forearm along the counter-top and inclined his head towards her. His voice was deep, dark and beguiling as he said, 'Enlighten me.'

'The pragmatic black-sheep, lone wolf, tower of strength, big boss, cool-as-a-cucumber thing you have going on is all an act. You, my friend, are a romantic.'

Well, now, that was the last thing Cameron had ever expected to be called.

Demanding, ruthlessly ambitious, with tunnel-vision.

He'd been labelled all of the above at one time or another. But *romantic*?

Rosalind was so mistaken it was laughable. But by the sureness in her wide grey eyes, and the heavy air of attraction curling out from her and enveloping him, he knew laughter was definitely the wrong response.

Needing a moment to find the right way to let her down easily, he slid from his seat, collected the takeaway paraphernalia, slid the chopsticks into the sink and tossed the cartons into the recycling bin.

Then he stood on the other side of the island bench from her and placed his palms on the granite worktop.

'Now, Rosalind, don't you go getting any funny ideas about the man you might think I am. You'll only set yourself up for disappointment.'

Her lips pursed ever so slightly but her eyes remained locked on his. She was swimming against the current, against all evidence that he was as unyielding as he made himself out to be, but she refused to bend.

His voice was a good degree cooler as he said, 'I'm thirty two and single, and there's good reason for it. I don't have a romantic bone in my body.'

She shook her head, refusing to hear him. 'You create things that by their very definition scrape the sky, each one greater and more awe-inspiring than the last. I might look at the stars every night, but you are reaching for them. Just think about it. Let the idea just seep on in under your skin. You'll find I'm right.'

The light in her eyes… He'd never in his life seen anything so bright. And it hit him then that, though she appeared to be as blithe as dust on the wind, though her bluntness made her seem tough, inside she was as soft as they came. Her absent father, and her mother's inability to let go, had wounded her, and she walked through life with a heart prone to bruising, and he had no intention of being responsible for that kind of damage. It would make him no better than his father.

He grabbed a tea towel and wiped his hands clean. He'd been here before. Well, not exactly here, nor quite so soon, but surely near enough that he knew what he had to do.

Looking into those beautiful eyes had been his first mistake. He moved around the bench and took the edge of her chair and spun it to face him.

Giving in to the overwhelming need to touch her, to tuck a silken wave of hair behind her ear, to make her realise that what he was about to do wasn't her fault but his—that he'd been selfish in letting things flow as they had—was his second mistake.

She leaned into his touch, infinitesimally, but enough that her warmth seeped into his fingertips, infused him with her natural heat. Gave him signal upon signal that she wanted him as much as he, for days, had wanted her. Tempted him beyond anything he'd ever felt before.

Feeling like it might be his last chance before he could stop himself, he placed a hand either side of her face and kissed her hard.

Hating the very sight of himself, he closed his eyes tight, which only made every other sense heighten.

She tasted of honey and soy. Beneath his hands she was warm and soft and everything delectable. And beneath everything else she was struggling. He could feel it in her lips as she let in his touch, but nothing more. Nothing deeper.

Earlier she'd claimed she knew when to quit; it seemed neither of them was that astute.

Cameron pulled back, only so that he could kiss her again, more comprehensively, longer, slower. He had no intention of letting up until she kissed him right back.

It didn't take long.

With a sigh that seemed to tremble through her whole body,

Rosalind sank back so that the kiss could deepen. And deepen it did, until all he could see behind his eyelids were swirls of red and black, deep, desolate darkness with no end in sight.

She snuck a soft hand behind his neck, lifted herself from her seat and melted against him. The world of sensation inside his mind lit up until he felt as hot and bright as the surface of the sun.

He held her tighter, fisting a hand into the back of her T-shirt, running another over her bottom, the exquisite softness of old denim making his fingers clench, pulling her closer still. His eyes were shut tight, head spinning, and he was kissing her for all he was worth until he couldn't remember ever doing anything else.

As do all good things, it came to an end.

Rosalind pulled away first, her lips slowly sliding away from his, as though it took every effort she could muster. Her head dropped and she rested her forehead against his chest, her hands splayed over his abdomen.

Cameron opened his eyes, the bright, sharp light of reality slamming him back to earth—the reality of what he'd done and what he'd been about to do.

He laid a gentle kiss on her soft hair as his eyes focussed hard on the perfect precision and crisp, true angles of the floating staircase in the distance, looking for his centre as a builder looks to a spirit level.

But all he could think of was lifting her into his arms, carrying her to his bedroom and making love to her all night long. Hell, once there he knew he'd be happy not to come up for air for days.

This woman was giving him a lesson in the lure of temptation, of the lengths a man might go to in order to satiate the want of the one thing his reason and sense and experience and moral centre told him he shouldn't want.

That pull of dangerously destructive desire, a dimension he'd always feared he might be genetically predisposed to possess, was ultimately why he tucked a finger beneath her chin and lifted her head, and waited until her soft dilated eyes were focussed on his.

And in a firm voice he said, 'Might I suggest after tonight we slow things down?'

There, he'd done it, on the back of the kind of kiss that made a guy unable to think sensibly for hours after. That way she'd know it wasn't as merciless as it had sounded.

Her skin paled and went blotchy all at once. She looked at him as though she'd just been slapped. And the shock in her eyes...

His fingers recoiled guiltily into his palm, then uncurled to touch her face. But she'd already disentangled herself to bolt into the lounge, frantically searching for something in her handbag. Whatever it was he could see by the tension in her neck that it wasn't coming to the surface quick enough.

'Rosalind.'

She held out a hand, which as good as told him to shut the hell up.

Ignoring it, he tried reasoning with her, 'Three dates in three days was pure overindulgence on my part. And you can't tell me you're not exhausted. I saw you trying to hide a yawn not ten minutes ago.'

When she lifted her eyes to his, he was fairly sure all she saw was red. She held her mobile phone to her ear and said, 'Which is why I think now is the perfect time to call a cab.'

'Don't be ridiculous. I was always going to take you home.'

'Really? Was it diarised? Kiss Rosie at nine. Dump her at nine-fifteen. Drive her home by ten. In bed by eleven.'

She turned her back, put in the order for the taxi, then threw the phone into her bag.

'Rosalind. Come on. Nobody's dumping anybody. All I'm saying is that we be sensible and look at where we are going here with open eyes.'

She closed her eyes, took a breath and her shoulders relaxed. Somewhat. But that warm, husky voice that he'd become so used to turned as cold as the river at night as she said, 'You want me to be sensible? Well, you obviously haven't been paying close enough attention. If I'd been sensible I would never have agreed to go out with the guy I had a crush on through high school. That is obviously one fantasy best left unfulfilled.'

Cameron's heart slammed hard and fast against his ribs. She'd had a crush on him? And fantasized about him? His voice was deep and dark when he said, 'Come back, sit down and talk to me.'

She waved a frantic hand across her eyes. 'Please. You were right. I'm just overtired. I get it; we've both monopolised one another's time so much these past days. You're busy and I'm busy, and neither of us ever meant for this to be more than it has to this point been. It's fine.'

In the end all she could do was shrug.

If he wanted out for good, this was the moment. He had no doubt she was just waiting for the word—goodbye. It was a simple enough word. Benign, unambiguous, final.

But he couldn't do it. He couldn't be that cool with her. Unlike every other woman he'd ever dated, she'd never been cool with him. She'd given him nothing but the complete truth, and she deserved the same.

'Rosalind, it's not you.'

'Where the hell's the damn cab?' She paced to the bottom of the stairs. He followed.

'Rosalind, I need you to hear me out.' He knew it was manipulative, but in order for her not to leave feeling hurt and angry he needed her to hear what he had to say, so he said it anyway. 'Please.'

At the 'please', she turned back to him. Her jaw was tight, her eyes wild with emotion. But at least she stopped walking away.

Having to ground himself if he was really going to say this, Cameron parked his backside against a corner of the lounge and looked out across the city view.

'I was in the eleventh grade when I saw my father come out of a city hotel with a woman who wasn't my mother. As I stood on the opposite side of the street, on my way to meet him at his office after school, he kissed her. Right there on the footpath, in front of peak-hour traffic—my father, who the whole city knew by sight. No thought for discretion or propriety or the woman the world thought he'd been blissfully married to for the previous thirty years…or anyone but himself.'

He blinked, dragged his eyes from the city view and looked to her. She stood still as a statue, those grey eyes simply giving him the space to keep going. Deeper. To places he'd never let himself go before.

'My mother… She had to put up with a lot, being married to a man like my father. The long hours, the ego, having to raise his four headstrong children in public. She did so with grace, humility, and love. So the fact that he could show such contempt towards her, to all of us…'

His fingernails bit into his palms as he fought down the same old desire to take a swing at his father the next time he laid eyes on the man.

'Why I am telling you this, what I'd *like* you to take from this,' he said, 'Is that I won't be like him. I'd rather see you walk away now—right at the very moment I can barely think straight for how much I want to continue what we started back there in the kitchen—if that means not hurting you by giving you false hope that I might one day offer you anything more. I can't. Not when I know that even the most solid relationships ultimately fail beneath the weight of secrets and lies.'

He came to an end and needed to breathe deep to press out the sudden tightness in his lungs. His eyes locked onto hers, her strength keeping him amazingly steady.

'Cameron,' she said on a release of breath, 'You expect *far* too much of people.'

'Only what I expect of myself.'

'I was including you too.'

He shifted on his seat. 'You think loyalty and good faith are too much to expect, even after how your father treated you and your mother?'

A muscle in her cheek twitched but her steady gaze didn't falter. 'For some people they are too much.'

He shook his head hard. 'I'm sorry, but I can't accept that.'

'Then that's a real shame.'

Cameron shot to his feet and ran a hard hand across the back of his neck. This wasn't how this had been meant to go. He'd hoped that by being forthright and upfront with her he'd feel justified in slowing things down, like he'd done right by her. Instead she was somehow making him feel like he hadn't done right by himself.

She tugged her poncho over her head, flicking her hair out at the end and running fingers through it until it fell in messy waves over her shoulders.

His response was chemical. His insides tightened and burned with a need to have her lose layers, not put them back on.

The doorbell rang; her taxi. She slipped her feet back into her shoes then looked back at him.

Her eyes said, *ask me to stay*.

But her tilted chin and tense neck said, *let me go*.

He went back to her eyes. Those beautiful, sad, grey eyes, so wide open he felt himself falling in, wanting more than he knew he could give. He pulled himself back from the brink just in time to say, 'I'll call you.'

She nodded, gave a short smile that held none of the mischief and humour he was so used to seeing therein, and jogged up the stairs without looking back.

CHAPTER TEN

ROSIE was exhausted. Which was naturally manifesting itself in a complete inability to sleep.

The minute the clock beside her bed clicked over to a quarter to three, she dragged herself out of bed.

She wouldn't be able to see Venus until about an hour before sunrise, but it had to be better outside than staring at the low ceiling of her caravan, wondering how on earth she'd let herself get to the point where she'd decided she might be able to allow Cameron deeper into her life at the precise moment when *he* had decided he wasn't sure that he wanted her in his.

She ran her hands over her face, then through her hair, tugging at knots in the messy waves, then trudged into the bathroom to splash water on her face. As she wiped it dry, she caught sight of her reflection in the mirror. Eyes dark. Mouth down turned.

She blinked and for a moment saw herself at fifteen, locked in the bathroom of the tiny flat she'd shared with her mum, and this feeling, the same familiar, cutting pain, crawling beneath the surface of her skin. It wasn't the pain of a girl pining for a man in her life. It was the pain of a girl who'd never been bright enough, good enough, devoted enough to fill the subsequent hole in her mother's heart.

How could an invisible girl like that ever hope to be enough to fill anyone else's heart?

Rosie licked her dry lips, then wiped fingers beneath her moist eyes. Time to go. Focussing on the colossal mystery of the universe would render her woes less important. It had to.

Too cold and too miserable to get completely naked, she pulled her clothes on over the top of her flannelette pyjamas— a fluffy wool knee-length cardigan she'd picked up in a thrift shop years before, a thick grey scarf, a lumpy red beanie with two fat, wobbly pom-poms on top, and the jeans she'd worn the day before. She didn't bother with her contacts, leaving her glasses on instead.

The hike to the plateau with her massive backpack was not in the last bit invigorating. It was cold, uncomfortable, and when she hit the spot the night sky was covered in patchy cloud.

She popped up the one-man dome tent which was just tall enough for her to stand up in, threw in all her stuff to keep the dew away and laid a canvas-backed picnic blanket upon the already moist grass. She set up her telescope. And turned on the battery-operated light attached to her notebook.

She sat on the ground cross-legged, waiting for the cloud cover to open up, revealing a sprinkle of stars.

Time marched on and the sky gave her nothing.

No mystery, no majesty, nothing to take her mind off the world at her feet and all the heartache that came with it. She slumped back onto the rug and closed her eyes.

She and Adele had both been wrong. Cameron wasn't really any different from any of the others. They all left her eventually; location had no effect on the matter.

She heard a twig snap, and her eyes flew open.

It could have been a possum. Or there had long since been rumours of a big cat loose in the area. And crazy axe-murderers were a genuine fear for some people for a good reason.

Rosie was on her feet, spare tripod gripped in her hands,

eyes narrowed, searching the shadows, when Cameron appeared through the brush, tall, imposing, stunning. It was as though a girl could simply imagine a man like him into existence through sheer wishful thinking.

'What the hell are you doing here?' Rosalind cried, waggling a big black metallic object Cameron's way.

He snuck both hands out of the warm pockets of his jacket and held them in front of him in surrender. 'I tried calling your mobile several times but you didn't answer. So I called Adele.'

'*Adele?*'

'She gave me her home number when I first rang you at the planetarium. I assumed in case of emergencies.'

Rosalind glowered, but at least she was lowering her weapon at the same time. 'Sounds like her. Though you've got her motives dead wrong.'

'Either way, she told me how to find you in the dead of the night in this crazy middle-of-nowhere place, where anything could happen to you and nobody would ever know.'

He stepped forward, shoes slipping in the soft, muddy earth. By the look in her eyes—behind glasses that made her look smart enough to be an astrophysicist, yet somehow still her usual effortlessly sexy self—she was far from happy to see him.

He didn't blame her. He'd acted just the way Dylan had when they'd been boys, wiping the chess board clean at the first sign the game wasn't going the exact way he'd intended it go.

After she'd gone, he'd lasted about three hours before his furniture had begun mocking him. The stool she'd sat upon when he'd kissed her stuck out from under the bench stubbornly. The beige rug on which her pink shoes had been haphazardly dumped, and the cream couch where her bright poncho had been suggestively draped, had seemed drab and bare. Even the fire had hissed at him, and, whereas for her it had been roaring, for him alone it had crumbled into a sorry pile of ash.

He'd told himself he felt like there were ants crawling under his skin because she was out there feeling upset and it had been his fault. But the truth was his home had felt empty because she wasn't in it. Because he'd expected more of their night together. Before he'd acted like such a lummox, he'd planned on having more time to familiarise himself with her soft skin, to let her sexy hair slide through his fingers. To know those lips as intimately as he could. And the rest.

He needed boundaries, but they also had unfinished business he hoped to take care of—if he could convince her.

'Can you put down the truncheon?' he asked. 'It's making me nervous.'

Rosalind bent at the knees, set the metal object onto a backpack and stood up, her dark-grey eyes on him the whole time. 'You've told me how you got here, not why. And hurry up. I have to get back to work.'

He picked a reason that she couldn't say no to. 'I was watching the sky through my bedroom window when I remembered you telling me that I hadn't seen stars until I saw them from this spot. I thought, what the hell? I'm awake anyway, let's see what the fuss is all about.'

She glared up at him over the top of her glasses. 'So what do you want to see?'

He was looking at it. But he said, 'Show me something spectacular.'

'You've picked a rubbish night.' She dragged her eyes away and looked up into the clear heavens. 'Huh, well, what do you know? Five minutes ago you were all hiding. But in *he* waltzes and there you all are, all bright and shining and cheerful. Capricious brutes, the lot of you!'

She glowered back down at him. 'Well, go on, then. There it all is for your viewing pleasure.'

Cameron looked up into the clear sky, and there it all was,

the Milky Way, spread across the sky like someone had scattered a bag of jewels on a swathe of black velvet.

He looked down at her; her nose was tilted skywards, her chin determined, her long, pale neck and wavy hair glowing in the moonlight. He breathed out through his nose. *Spectacular.*

As though she sensed him watching her, she turned her head just enough to make eye contact. She blinked at him, then leaned down towards the eyepiece and found a bearing using the naked eye. She twirled knobs, gently shifted the lever, changed filters, then with both eyes open pressed one eye to the eyepiece and carefully adjusted the focus.

A minute later she stood back and made an excessive amount of room for him to have a look. He took her place, looked through the lens, and the view therein took his breath away.

She'd given him the bright side of the moon. Craters and plateaus in stark white-and-grey relief faded into the creeping shadow of the dark side. So far away, yet it felt so close.

He pulled away, blinked up at the white crescent high in the sky and said, 'I also came here because I don't like leaving a conversation unfinished.'

He felt Rosalind cross her arms beside him. 'Oh, I think we both had ample opportunity to say what we wanted to say.'

'Can I ask…if I hadn't kissed you…?'

She shivered, and this time he knew it wasn't the cold. He wanted to wrap her up in his jacket, but he knew she wasn't near ready for that. Not yet.

'What do you want from me, Cameron?'

'Truth?'

'Always.'

'I didn't like watching you walk away tonight.'

She said nothing. The conversation it seemed would be all up to him.

'I've been having a great time being with you. I get a kick out of your frankness. You must have noticed that I have huge trouble keeping my hands off you. And none of that has changed. All I've ever hoped is that we might continue to enjoy one another's company for as long as it's enjoyable. And not a minute longer.'

He felt her breathe in. Breathe out. 'And who gets to decide when that minute's up?'

'You can, if it needs to be that way.'

'And if I think that minute has already passed?'

'Do you?'

He looked down to find she was no longer staring at the moon; she was watching him, her eyes wary, calculating, her mind changing back and forth with every passing second.

'I don't want to hurt you,' he said.

Her chin lifted. 'I don't plan on getting hurt.'

She was talking in the present tense. And, though she wasn't smiling at him, neither was she scowling. He'd done enough. Relief poured through him, its intensity rather more than he would have expected.

'Aren't you cold?' she asked.

And he realised he was shivering. She might have been rugged up like she was about to spend a week on Everest but he was still in his jeans, T-shirt and track top.

'I'm absolutely freezing,' he said. Now he'd noticed it, he really noticed it. He rubbed his hands down his arms and stamped his sneaker-clad feet before they turned to ice.

'You have to make the most of your body heat.'

He stopped jumping about like a frog and asked, '*My* body heat?'

'*One's* body heat,' she reworded.

'I was going to say, that was a line I hadn't heard before.'

'Hey, buddy, I have no agenda here. I was out here minding my own business. You came looking for me.'

Still no smile, but the bite was back. Attraction poured through him like it had been simply waiting to split the dam behind which he'd held it in check.

'I did, didn't I?'

She stared at him, the wheels behind her eyes whirring madly. Finally she demanded, 'Get inside the tent, unzip the sleeping bag, and wrap it around you. It's thermal. You'll be toasty in a matter of minutes.'

'Who knew you had such a Florence Nightingale side to you?'

'You're too heavy for me to carry you back to your car if you freeze to death,' she muttered, then gave him a little shove.

From outside the tent Rosie watched as Cameron's head hit the roof as he snuck inside.

He'd come looking for her. In the middle of the night, along unmarked roads and through wet, thorny bushland, he'd come. That was an entirely new experience. Men had left before but none had ever come back. Not one.

She hadn't had any past experiences from which to extrapolate the right course to take. All she'd been able to do was follow her instincts. They'd gently urged her to let him back in. To understand that his dad's betrayal ran deep and that had caused his panic. And that, now that the boat had righted itself, things would be as they were.

She didn't have time to decide if she'd been cool and sophisticated or simply stupid, as right then his elbow slid along the right wall of the tent, making an unhappy squeaking sound against the synthetic fabric. The next loud 'Oomph,' meant she had to go in after him in case he managed to break any equipment worth as much as her caravan.

He turned and saw her there.

Moonlight glowed through the tight mesh, creating glints in his eyes. Though she soon realised the glints would have been there even if they'd been in pitch blackness.

The pom-poms on top of her beanie brushed the ceiling, while he had to bend so as not to stick his head through the top. She glanced up, saw his hair catching and creating static, went to tell him so, but he reached out to her, grabbed a hunk of her cardigan and pulled her to him. Her breath shot from her lungs in a sharp whoosh as her chest thumped against his.

She desperately clambered for her instincts, hoping they might come to her rescue again, but they were as immobilised as she was.

He dropped to his knees and she came with him. They were nose to nose, the intermingling of warm breath making her cheeks hot. Her heart thundered in her ears. She felt light-headed. Little tornados curled about her insides.

And she knew, as well as she knew her own name, that she'd done the right thing. Their minute wasn't up.

He snuck a hand along her neck, his thumb stroking the soft spot just behind her ear. Her whole body responded, opening to him like a flower to the sun. She immediately contracted in fear at exposure of how much she wanted this. Wanted him. Was willing to tell herself whatever she needed to hear to have him.

But then he leaned in and kissed her. Gently. Slowly. And all the last bits of her that hadn't melted finally did so. She sank into him and kissed him back.

Sensation so astronomical overwhelmed her until she could only pick out pieces to focus upon lest she drown in the delectable whole.

The subtle strength of his hand cupped the back of her head. His breath tickled the column of her neck before he rained kisses over every inch of her throat. Her cardigan tie slithered across her back as he undid it.

She came to from far, far away when suddenly it all came to a cruel halt.

She opened her eyes to find him staring at her chest. Her chest wasn't all that impressive without a lot of help.

'What on earth are you wearing?' he asked.

She looked down to find his fingers enclosed over a fat, furry, pig-shaped button on her pink flannelette pyjama-top.

She slapped a hand across her eyes. 'My pyjamas. Oh God, I was cold, I was lazy. I was feeling sorry for myself.'

'Rosalind.' *The way he said her name…*

She let her hand slip away and looked up into his eyes. His deep, dark, bottomless, persuasive blue eyes.

He slipped the first button from its hole, and her breath caught.

And when he kissed her again she felt so frail she believed she might just shatter into a thousand pieces before the night was through.

Hours later, Rosie stroked slow fingers over Cameron's naked chest while his fingers played gently with her hair.

The rising sun washed beams of gold through the opening of the tent, leaving his beautiful profile in sharp relief, while she was shielded from the beams' touch by his large form.

So it had to be. No matter how much they each struggled against their true natures, he would always be a child of the light, she of the dark.

Perhaps the only moments they could simply still be together were the in-between moments, right at dawn or dusk, when everything seemed softer, gentler, quieter. When nothing, past or future, mattered more than the moment itself.

A great sadness overwhelmed her. Why, she didn't know. After the night she'd had, she should be feeling anything but sad.

She rested her chin on the back of her hands and in the rosy half-light her thoughts spilled unchecked from her lips. 'I've come to the brilliant conclusion that you're the human equivalent of Alpha Centauri.'

He opened his eyes and her sadness slipped away. He turned his head to watch her, a quizzical smile only adding more character to his beautiful face. 'Would it be in my best interests to ask why?'

She grinned from the top of her mussed hair to the tips of her bare toes. 'I'm gonna tell you anyway. Alpha Centauri appears as a single point of light to the naked eye, but is actually a system of three stars.'

'You think I have a split personality?'

She held up a stilling finger. 'I think there's more to you than the face you show the world. You're also bright, eye-catching and seem much closer than you really are.'

'Eye-catching, eh?' He closed one eye. 'And how long were you lying there coming up with all that?'

She shrugged, her upper body sliding deliciously against his. 'Not long.'

'Mmm.' He lifted a heavy hand and trailed it down her naked back, sending goose bumps popping up all over her skin. 'So how far away is my heavenly twin right now?'

'Four-point-three trillion kilometres.'

His laughter lifted her as it echoed through his ribs.

Rosie buried her blushing cheeks in a mound of sleeping bag. 'I'm sorry. I just compared you with spheres of hot gases. And after all the nice things you just did for me. And *to* me. It seems to have opened neural pathways better left closed.'

'I only have myself to blame.'

She lifted her head and rubbed a knuckle across the end of her cold nose. He lifted his head to kiss the spot.

This was bliss. This made it all worth it. Surely…

She looked directly into his disarming eyes as she said, 'All that Alpha Centauri stuff—I just meant that you've turned out to be not quite who I expected you'd be.'

'A man ought to do his best to exceed expectations wherever possible.'

'Maybe a man ought to, though in my experience not all that many bother to try.'

'Your experience?' he rumbled. 'Now, there's a subject I could warm to.'

He waggled his eyebrows, and Rosie felt like she'd blushed enough for one day. Any more and her cheeks might stay that way.

'This is *not* the time for that conversation.' She dragged herself into a sitting position. She slipped her flannelette pyjama-top on, and quickly added the beanie and scarf, suddenly cold now that she was no longer wrapped in Cameron.

His fingers slunk beneath her top and trailed down her back, creating a slip and shift of heat that made her want to give in and stay, talk, confess, believe…

But, like Alpha Centauri, the four-point-three trillion ways he made her feel safe and secure and precious were illusions all. At the end of the day, she was all she had. And that was fine. She could enjoy him in the in-between times. And that would be enough. If she told herself enough times she might even start to believe it.

'Then how about we put it right up front during a Saturday night drink before my dad's birthday party?' he said.

'Before your who and what?' she asked. Her head whipped round to stare at him, to find him leaning on one arm, bare chest rippling with manly gorgeousness that made her sure the canoe, bike and jet ski in his garage weren't the dust collectors his telescope was.

Her mouth watered. She dragged her eyes back to his— like that had ever made anything any easier!

'My father's seventieth,' he said. 'Something you said has been percolating for a while now. And last night, as I cleaned the floors of my house with my hours of pacing, I made up my mind. I'm going.'

'What did I say?'

'That you spent too long wishing you'd had the chance to know your father, no matter what kind of man he might have been. I need to face the man, to ease my mind. And, since you're the one who convinced me as much, I thought you might like to tag along.'

Rosie breathed in and out. In and out. Not eight hours earlier he'd wanted to cool things down. Now he was making plans whereby she would meet his parents. His whole family. She tried to figure out what he was playing at, but all that beautiful, warm skin was making it hard for her to see the bigger picture.

'Saturday? I can't,' she said, searching the end of the sleeping bag with her feet for her jeans and sighing with relief when her toes hit denim.

'It'll be one hell of a party.'

'I'm sure it will.'

The sleeping bag around her bare thighs slid away as Cameron sat up, and it pooled low around his hips. Staring at the bland wall of the tent, she whipped on her cardigan and did the bow up tight.

He leaned in and pushed her hair aside, laying a small, soft kiss on her neck.

She closed her eyes and tried to ignore the warmth washing across her skin, the grip of his gravitational pull tugging her into oblivion. But it felt too good. He felt so good. So difficult, so dangerous, but so very good.

'Cameron…'

'The truth is, I need you there.'

She squeezed her forehead tight, trying to push away how wonderful those three words—*I need you*—felt.

Once upon a time all she'd wanted was to feel needed, wanted, loved. She'd been a good kid, she'd studied hard, and she'd silently hugged her mum whenever she'd found her crying, even when deep down she'd known it would never be enough.

Since she'd been on her own in the big, wide world all

she'd needed was fresh air, food, water and basic shelter. She'd never once felt that need to be needed by anybody else.

Yet now those three little words danced behind her eyes, waving streamers and skipping through fertile fields, singing at the top of their lungs. It had been so long since she'd shoved the wish down so deep inside that the moment it came to the surface it was intoxicating.

'I'll think about it.'

'Don't think, just come,' he murmured against her shoulder.

She extricated herself from his wandering hands and slipped out of the tent, happier to be half-naked beneath the open sky than to see how much more he could get her to promise him from just a simple touch.

'So, I'll pick you up at your place around eight,' he called out.

She found her functional white, cotton briefs hanging provocatively over her tripod, and shoved them into a pocket of her telescope bag. 'Oh, for Pete's sake, fine! I'll go. Are you happy now?'

'Now I am happy.'

All her fidgeting stopped. He might have been playing like he was flirting, but the thread of truth lacing its way beneath his words got to her like nothing else.

She glanced back into the tent to find Cameron was lying back with his arms over his head, his biceps cradling his head, watching her.

'It's black tie,' he said with a grin.

Her eyebrows lifted so fast she almost pulled something. 'Are you intimating *that* might be a reason for me to back out?'

His gaze meandered down her crazy get-up. 'Not at all. So far you haven't found it at all difficult to just say no to me when you really wanted to say no.'

'You have no idea,' she muttered.

'What was that?'

She wrapped the tie of her fluffy cardigan ever tighter.

'Cameron, I'll go with you to your father's party because I'm madly proud of you for listening to my words of wisdom. No hidden agenda. Nothing more. As agreed last night.'

He stared at her for a few moments, then nodded. She was mighty glad he believed her, as she wasn't even close to sure that she believed herself.

She shielded her eyes and looked to the sun, which had risen, making it some time after seven in the morning. The faint crescent of Venus had been hovering above the horizon for some time without even getting a look in.

She said, 'Shouldn't you get going? Don't you have minions to boss around at the worksite? Won't Bruce be lost without you?'

'I'm not so worried about Bruce right this second. How about you?'

'Bruce isn't high on my list of priorities either.'

He smiled. A smile so stunningly sexy that Rosie's knees forgot how to work.

'I meant, do you have anywhere else to be,' he said.

She blinked down at him, arms crossed. 'Um, no. I don't. Because this is my place of work.'

Cameron didn't move a muscle. He simply lay naked in her tent, while she realised that from the minute he'd walked into her glade—all gorgeous and conciliatory, talking of how he couldn't keep his hands off her—she hadn't given her work, her time, her warm bed, her breakfast, or anything else usually so important to her, a single thought.

Warning bells began to chime inside her head, telling her to finish getting dressed. To get moving. To just let him keep the damn tent.

'Then what are you doing out there in the cold when it's still so warm in here?' he asked, flapping open the sleeping bag, leaving room for her.

That was all she'd done for him too—left room. And if that

meant having a little less room for herself then maybe that was the price a girl had to pay for getting a man who came back for her.

Rosie bit her lip, weighed her options, became trapped in his eyes, then said, 'Oh, what the hell,' as she tore off her beanie and threw it over her shoulder before she dove back into the tent.

'Now, tell me more about this crush you had on me in high school,' he muttered as he stripped her down.

'I *think* it was you I had the crush on. You were the captain of the footy team, right?'

'No, I was not. Now, stop sassing me and tell me about the moment you first laid eyes on me and your teenaged heart went pitter-pat.'

'Cameron Kelly,' she said on a sigh as he went to work, 'You'll have to do much better than that if you think I'm ever going to spill a single detail.'

He did better. Like a lightweight, she spilled.

And, just as she'd hoped, the warning bells were soon drowned out by the symphony of sensations only this man could make her feel.

CHAPTER ELEVEN

MOST of that next day and night Rosie slept like a log. Saturday morning she woke late, crinkled, ruffled, and blissfully replenished in every which way.

It was after lunch by the time she stood staring unseeingly at the window of the designer boutique on the top floor of Queens Plaza.

Adele was puffing when she arrived at her side. 'Sorry, sorry. Lipstick disaster. Don't ask.' Puff, puff, puff. 'What's the big emergency?'

'I have to buy a new dress to wear tonight.'

'I know a dress from a pair of trousers, so I'm your girl. Do you have any maybes as yet?'

'Not exactly. I have yet to venture inside.'

Adele turned to stare into the window at the shimmery, wispy, frothy frocks hanging off obscenely thin mannequins. 'Any reason you're looking in *this* particular window?'

'It's for Cameron's father's birthday.'

In the reflection Adele's eyes shimmied down a mannequin whose dress was low cut in places, high cut in others and barely worth putting on, it covered so little flesh. 'Happy birthday, Quinn.'

Rosie slapped her on the arm without even turning her head.

'Ow. So I take it you and the great and wondrous Camster are still on?'

'We're not *on*,' Rosie said, running her thumb hard down the middle of her palm to stop the tingle that had spread up her fingers at the memory of his hands touching her cheek, getting lost in her hair, stroking her naked back. 'We agreed that our relationship only extends so far as dining together on occasion, and now we are attending an event in tandem.'

Adele's eyes left the dresses to turn slowly her way. Her voice was impassive as she said, 'Heck, Rosie, I've never seen you so very giddy.'

Rosie squinted. 'I don't do *giddy*, and you know it. It's just new. He's different. And… Oh, shut up.'

Adele grinned. 'Mmm. Now he's invited you to his father's biggest-bash-Brisbane-has-ever-seen birthday party, where you will meet his whole family including his parents. Sounds ultra low key to me.'

Rosie scowled. 'Just help me find a dress.'

Adele's mouth quirked as she looked back at the window. 'Have you seen the price tags hanging off those there garments?'

Rosie shrugged. 'I can afford it.'

'That one costs as much as a small car.'

'There are side benefits to living in a caravan.'

'So it would seem.'

Rosie stared at a more demure black, shimmery sheath. It was beautiful. It was what someone who Cameron Kelly took to a party would be expected to wear.

She hadn't been kidding when she'd told Cameron how proud she was that he was going to face his dad. And she knew how hard it would be. She wanted to be there for him. And if she was truly honest the more she thought about it the more she wanted to be there, like she could somehow vicariously live through his experience now that it was too late for her to do the same with her own father.

And if that meant straightening her hair and pumping up her assets with chicken fillets, and stuffing herself into some dress that she'd never in a million years have picked out if she'd had the choice, could she do it? Should she do it? Was every new decision going to mean making room for him? Was it either do that or lose him?

'So, are we going in?' Adele asked. 'I'm fairly sure the sales assistant won't bring them out here unless you flash a platinum Amex.'

'Give me a minute,' Rosie said.

Adele rubbed a hand down her arm. 'Kiddo, you're starting to look a little flushed. Are you feeling quite yourself?'

And then it hit her.

She was as different as a person could be from the kind of date Cameron Kelly usually had on his arm at parties— She, in her unapologetic hand-me-down glory, with her *au naturel* hair desperately in need of a cut, and the big trap she couldn't keep shut. And he knew that.

Yet of all the women who would have jumped at the chance to be on his arm dressed in designer clothing, he'd asked *her*.

Rosie grabbed Adele's hand, tucked it into the crook of her arm and tugged her away from the shop window. 'I'm done here. We're going to the Valley.'

Adele tugged against her hand. 'No, Rosie! I'm not going to let you find some sad old second-hand prom dress to wear to Quinn Kelly's birthday bash. Please, for me, for the sake of the future princes of Brisbane you may one day be able to introduce me to, no!'

Cameron drove up Samford Road, one hand loosely working the steering wheel, the other running back and forth across his top lip.

Within hours he'd be face to face with his father for the first time since he was a teenager.

He could have given his mother a believable excuse. None of the family would have been surprised. But now that he'd committed he was not backing out.

A familiar National Park sign had him turning left towards Rosalind's. He breathed deep and pressed the accelerator to the floor. Even the whisper of her name helped relieve the pressure building inside his head.

Their night together had been beyond anything he could have expected. It was the most intense, affecting and wicked night of love-making of his young life. And right then he couldn't have been more impressed with himself for having had the mettle to go after her.

As he drove up her dirt driveway he was forced to slow, to shift his mind to focus on the matters at hand so that the low-hanging trees didn't scratch his car, and so he didn't land in the same great hole in the ungraded path in which he'd almost lost himself when he'd dropped her home the morning before.

That made it almost thirty-six hours since he'd last laid eyes on her, since he'd left her at the door of her crazy caravan, with its hills, sun and flowers painted all over the sides like some leftover relic of the seventies. Since he'd touched her hair, and held her tight, and kissed that spot on her lower back that made her writhe.

The tyres jerked against the wheel, and he concentrated fully on finding a path that led him to her door relatively unscathed.

The ground was dry, so his dress shoes didn't collect any mud as he picked his way up the path made only by her daily footsteps rather than by any kind of design.

He looked for a bell, but found nothing of the sort. At a loss for a moment, he lifted his hand to knock thrice on the corrugated door.

Shuffling was followed by a bump, then a muffled oath. Then, when she didn't appear in an instant, he tugged at his tie and hitched his belt so that it was perfectly set just below his navel. He straightened his shoulders and cleared his throat. He had no reason to be nervous. So why did he feel like he was seventeen again, and picking his date up for the senior dance?

The door whipped open, and that was where all fidgeting stopped.

Backlit by the warm, golden light of a small desk-lamp, and helped along by the thin moonlight falling softly through the clouds above, Rosalind stood in the doorway looking like she'd stepped out of a 1930's Hollywood movie-set.

Her shoulders were bare, bar a thin silver strap angling across one shoulder. Lilac chiffon fell from an oversized rosette at her chest and swirled about her long, lean form like she had been sewn into it. Several fine silver bangles shimmered on her wrist. And her hair was pinned at the nape, with soft tendrils loose and curling about her cheeks.

He'd never once in his entire life been rendered speechless—not when one of his mates had streaked during the debate-team final. Not when he'd made a three-hundred percent profit on the sale of his first property. Not even when his father's only response to his declaration that he could never work for a man with so little backbone had been that, as long as he didn't work for the Kelly family, he was not welcome in the Kelly family home.

But Rosalind Harper, in all her rare, noble, charming loveliness, had him at a complete loss for words.

'Hi,' she said, her voice breathy, and he knew it had nothing to do with her rushing about before she opened the door.

She looked at him like she'd be happy to keep looking at him for as long as she possibly could. Like he was all she'd ever wanted, and all she would ever want.

His heart raced like a jackhammer. He felt the boundaries he'd set being smashed left, right and centre and he had no idea what to say, or do or think.

But then she let out a long, descending whistle and flapped

her hand across her cheeks, and her eyes ran coquettishly down his dinner suit. His skin tightened every place her gaze touched, and his heart eased.

He snuck a hand to her waist, the fabric sliding against his palm until he connected with the curve of her hip. It took all of his self-control not to throw her over his shoulder, take her back inside her crazy home, close the door behind them and forget about the rest of the world.

Instead he leaned in and kissed her on the cheek, letting her sweet vanilla scent wash over him like a cure-all.

'You,' he said, his voice gruff, 'look like a dream. And that dress; there are quite simply no words.'

The smile he wrought lit her from the inside out. 'What,' she said, swinging from side to side, 'this old thing?'

Her tone was wry, but he knew she half-meant it. For nothing that romantic could ever have come from today.

'Are you ready?' he asked.

She held up two fingers. 'Two seconds. I'm still missing an earring. You'd think in a place this small that wouldn't be a concern, right?'

She turned and raced inside. He followed, intrigued at just how much Rosalind's home might reveal about the woman whose layers seemed to go on and on.

At one end an ajar door revealed the corner of a double bed which all but filled the space. It was covered in a soft, worn, pastel comforter. It was unmade. One pillow lay in the centre of the bed, dented where her head had lain. She was used to sleeping there alone. So far, the insights were entirely positive.

In the middle where he stood was the kitchen. He looked for photos of family or friends, but there were none on show. No knickknacks had pride of place on the pleasantly scuffed bench. It was almost as though she was on holidays rather than living in the place. He wasn't sure what to make of that.

He glanced up. In lieu of a chandelier was a home-made mobile of the solar system made from bent wire-hangers and string, planets made from chocolate wrappings, balls of rubber bands, and an old squash-ball pitted with teeth marks. He'd asked for insight and he'd been given a fanciful, inventive, dynamic mind. No surprise there.

He counted. No Pluto. Poor Pluto. He was in, then suddenly one day he was out. Cameron felt an affinity with the little guy. He only hoped Pluto was out there in the universe, kicking butt and taking names.

'Found it!' Rosalind called out from deep in the other end of the caravan.

In the bathroom, perhaps? He took a step in that direction, and out of the shadows a face peered back at him. Against one wall rested a life-size cardboard cut-out of a musclebound actor in a wetsuit. And just like that all the good the single pillow on her bed had done to his ego was wiped out. *By a piece of cardboard.*

He stepped back into the relative safety of the more conservatively decorated kitchen. His head brushed against something. He turned and came face to face with a line of string, over which had been hung a collection of skimpy lace underwear, quite different from the androgynous knickers she'd had on under her layers upon layers of clothing the other night.

He swallowed hard, wondering just what she might or might not be wearing under her diaphanous dress. The answer would be his for the taking if he wanted it, of that he was sure. And try as he might he couldn't imagine a situation in which he would not.

Before he had the chance to interpret the thought, Rosie appeared from the other end of the van, pinning the back on a dangly earring at her left lobe, saw where he was standing and came to a screeching halt. And blushed.

It wasn't even the loveliness of the blush that got him deep in his gut. It was the fact that, even after he'd already seen every inch of her beneath the underwear, she still managed to blush at all.

Their eyes caught. And locked. Her sparkling grey depths were warm, questioning, unguarded as always. But this time he felt like he was teetering on the edge of a most important discovery, when she closed her eyes and spun away, and it was gone.

'It's getting late,' she said, grabbing a clutch purse and a fake-fur wrap the same colour as her hair. 'Your family will be expecting you. How good does that feel?'

He let her lead the way, and paused when she simply shut the door and kept on walking.

'You're not locking up?' he asked.

She shot him a quick smile as she backed towards his car. 'No need. You met my faithful protector, didn't you? Serious eyes, big muscles, made of cardboard. He keeps me safe from harm.'

His eyes narrowed and he stalked to catch up. Not able to go even ten seconds without touching her, he slid an arm around her waist.

'Seriously,' she said, leaning away from him as though he was holding her as some form of punishment rather than for his own satisfaction. 'If anyone is brave enough to head into my woods at this time of night, they're welcome to whatever they find.'

When they reached the car he spun her to face him, holding her by the hips, his nostrils flaring as her sweet scent caught on the wind. 'Promise me when you come home tonight you'll lock that door behind you.'

Her eyes smiled. 'It's an old van. You can't open that front door unless you know exactly how to jiggle it. Nobody's getting in there, bar me or anyone I choose to let in.'

She kissed him on the lips, softly, lingeringly, with a prom ise he couldn't quite discern, then she slid into his car.

It took a moment for Cameron to collect himself before he rounded the back of the car, slid into the driver's seat and curled his way down her drive.

He kept half his focus on the road, half on preparing himself for the momentous evening ahead. Yet, even with all that to contend with, somehow he was never quite able to take his mind off the woman at his side.

By the time the front gates of the Kellys' family home loomed, Rosie was so nervous she could barely feel her toes.

Meeting the infamous Kellys was only half the problem. She was here for Cameron, and so long as she was herself and did her all to support him in his quest then she couldn't go wrong. But from the second he'd shown up at her door looking so suave, so sexy, so dark and delicious in his black tie, she had found it hard to remember how it was that she had promised him that she would be just fine when one day it all came to an end.

Cameron pulled up to the front gates, which opened in time for him to slide the car through. The charcoal-coloured drive- way, embedded in a swirling pattern of white quartz, curled around a pristine green mound sprinkled with neat rows of white and orange roses.

Rosie pushed herself an inch off the seat. 'You have to be kidding me. Is that an Irish flag?'

Cameron didn't even need to glance at the garden to know what she was talking about. His mouth quirked into a smile. 'Welcome to Kelly Manor, where nothing is done by halves if it can be done twice as big.'

They drove on down the long, straight drive through an archway of oak trees which opened out to reveal a three- storey, dark brick, and cream trim, Edwardian-style home that looked like something out of an English period film.

Cameron pulled his car to a stop at the top of the circular

drive. A liveried servant held the door open for Rosie, then took Cameron's keys in order to park the car goodness knew where, as the whole front drive was clear.

'Is this an intimate gathering?' she asked.

'Of course. Only a few hundred of my father's best friends.' There was no mistaking the tinge of bitterness in his voice.

She snuck her hand into the crook of his arm. 'You are doing the right thing. I meant it when I said if I had the chance to sit down and talk to my dad, to get things off my chest and let him explain himself in his own words, I'd take it.'

'You are a magnanimous woman, Rosalind Harper.'

'Well you, Cameron Kelly, are an amazing man. With a family who obviously want you to be a part of their lives. Don't blow it or I might never forgive you.'

'We can't have that, can we?' He tucked her hand close, and she could feel him drawing from her strength. It was a heady feeling indeed. One she found she liked very very much.

Fearing he might see in her eyes how much this was all affecting her, how much he was affecting her, she looked over her shoulder to find a Bentley cruising up the drive. 'This place is where the Thunderbirds got all their ideas, right?'

His laughter rumbled through her. 'Now what on earth are you talking about?'

'The cars. Where do they all go? I mean, the whole house opens up and there's an underground car-park beneath it all, right?'

Cameron unhooked her hand from his arm and snaked his arm around her hip as he guided her up the front steps. The move was possessive and sensual, sending her nerves spiralling up into the sky.

'You watch too much television,' he murmured against her ear, a wisp of hair tickling her cheek.

She leaned back into him. 'I work odd hours. I have an excuse.'

Cameron pressed the doorbell, and Rosie turned away to fix her hair, lick her top teeth in case of lipstick smudges and generally take in as much oxygen as she could before she entered the kind of rarefied air she had not had to endure since St Grellans.

'Everything okay?' Cameron asked, his hand touching her elbow in reassurance.

Over the top of the box hedges, Brisbane twinkled in the distance. 'Everything's fine. And for the record the view from your place is *way* better than this.'

Cameron grinned as the twelve-foot front door swung open, and he guided her inside. 'I knew I brought you for a reason.'

If the Kelly family had intended the front of their home to be imposing, it had nothing on the ballroom in which the party was being held.

Rosie's cold hands gripped the edge of a curling wrought-iron railing as she looked down from the gallery into the main room below.

Over two hundred people in evening dress milled about the massive rectangular space. A gleaming parquet floor shone in the light of six crystal chandeliers hanging from the multi-vaulted ceiling; a string quartet played in one corner of the room, a jazz band was setting up in the other, and white roses tumbled from every surface available.

She felt a sudden need to hitch up her dress.

'Come on,' Cameron said.

He took her hand and practically dragged her down the staircase and through the crowd so fast that he didn't have to stop and talk to anyone, and onto the dance floor, where several couples were swaying to the beautiful music.

He took her in his arms, pulled her close and together they danced.

With a blinding flash that had her losing her footing for a

second, Rosie found herself deep in the middle of a memory she'd long since forgotten.

She was at the only school dance she'd ever attended. She'd been invited by a boy in her science class—Jeremy somebody. He'd been two inches shorter than her, and had always worn his trousers too tight, but in those days even to be asked…

Halfway through the night, dancing alone within the pulsating crowd, she'd turned to find herself looking into a pair of stunning blue eyes brimming with effortless self-belief. Cameron Kelly. A senior. She'd looked and she'd ached, if not to be with him then to be like him—content, fortunate, valued. He hadn't looked away.

And like that they'd danced with one another for no more than a quarter of a song before one of his friends had dragged him away for photos with the gang.

Cameron pulled her closer and drew her back to the present, just in time to hear him say, 'If only you'd let me dance with you this close all those years ago then who knows what might have happened?'

Rosie snapped her head back so fast she heard her neck crack. 'Excuse me?'

He pulled her back into his arms and wrapped her tighter until her cheek was back against his chest, and she could feel the steady beat of his heart as he twirled her around the floor.

'My senior-year dance,' he said, the sound rumbling through her. 'You were there, weren't you?'

She closed her eyes lest he realise what she could no longer deny—that she was still very much the young girl with the naïve, wide-open heart that had seen something exceptional in him all those years ago.

'You remember,' she whispered.

'Mmm. I remembered a couple of days back, actually. I forgot to mention it til now.'

Her knees wobbled in recognition of the smile in his voice. Her poor, struggling heart wobbled right along with them.

'Skinny black jeans,' he continued. 'Hot-pink tank top, enough eyeliner to drown a ship. And I might be getting this part wrong, but did you have your hair in two long plaits?'

Rosie's hand lifted off his shoulder to slap across her eyes. 'Oh no, I'd forgotten that part. That was my "separate myself from the preppy, pastel suburban princesses before they separate themselves from me" phase. You know what? I'm not sure I ever grew out of that.'

Cameron slipped a finger beneath her chin and didn't slide it away until she was looking into his eyes. Those beautiful, corn-flower, soulful, sexy, smiling eyes. 'I'm glad. And for the record you looked adorable. And scary as hell.'

She blinked up at him, her brow furrowing. 'Scary?'

'God, yeah. I was mucking about, pretending to dance with my mates, and when I turned there was this stunning creature right under my eyes, chin up, eyes fierce, daring the world to even try telling her off for simply being herself. I was fairly sure that girl must have thought me ridiculous.'

'Ridiculous?' she repeated, beginning to feel like a parrot, but it was either that or say something she'd never be able to take back. That, in that moment, she'd been fairly sure she was looking at the most beautiful boy in the whole world.

She gripped his shoulder a tad too tightly, but he didn't seem to notice. He just looked deep into her eyes with that barely there smile lingering upon his mouth.

'It didn't take any kind of genius on my part to know you were far too cool for the likes of me.' He reached out and slid a finger under her fringe, pushing it off her face until he cupped her cheek. 'You know what? Nothing you've said or done this week has made me think any differently. Only now I'm old enough not to give a damn.'

And then he kissed her, so softly, so gently, her heart turned inside out.

'Well, if it isn't little Cam Kelly. I'm not sure I believe my own eyes,' a deep male voice drawled.

Rosie dragged herself out of the bottom of a beautiful dream and blinked into the warm light to find they'd stopped dancing.

And Cameron was no longer all hers.

His shoulders were stiff, his back straight, his neck tense as he stared at a taller man with slick hair and cold eyes.

'Brendan, this is my friend, Rosalind Harper,' Cameron said, his voice so cool if felt like the exhilarating warmth that had enveloped them both only moments earlier had all been in her imagination. 'Rosalind, this is my brother, Brendan. He is the heir apparent to my father's empire.'

Brendan gave her a short nod with a smile that didn't light his eyes. She smiled back and offered a tiny curtsy. His eyes narrowed, but his smile broadened, and Rosie caught a glimpse of Cameron's charisma therein.

'Which by the old joke makes our Dylan the spare,' Brendan said. 'And what does that make you, brother?'

'Delighted to be my own man.'

Feeling like she was in the middle of two lions circling one another, hoping to bite the other's head off, Rosie disentangled herself from Cameron's hold and waggled his little finger. 'I think I'll take a look around, see what there is to eat. Give you boys the chance to do what you need to do.'

'I'll come back for you soon,' Cameron said.

Rosie smiled, but a shiver ran down her back as she thought it would be asking too much to have the same good luck twice. 'Nice to meet you, Brendan.'

'Likewise,' he said, and this time she believed him.

As she walked away through a crowd of people she'd never met, and didn't particularly want to, she glanced back to find Cameron and his brother already deep in heated conversation.

She'd brought him here, she'd made his first step bearable. Was that as far as she was needed? She kept walking straight ahead and ignored the sadness that had once again begun to settle in her chest.

It was all she'd ever known how to do.

CHAPTER TWELVE

TEN minutes later Rosie leant against a marble column in the corner of the room, a champagne glass in one hand, a couple of *hors d'oeuvres* secreted within a linen napkin in the other. The food hadn't done much to ease the tightness in her chest; the champagne, on the other hand, had.

She watched Cameron and Brendan holding court with two politicians, a tennis pro and a guy with so many shiny medals on his chest she figured he was an army general.

For a guy who'd supposedly turned his back on all this guff, Cameron was in his element—while she was hiding lest she was forced to have another conversation about yachting, or golf, or the medical benefits of rhinoplasty.

'Rosalind Harper, right?'

Rosie blinked and spun to find Meg Kelly at her shoulder, her chocolate-brown curls bouncing about her perfect pink cheeks, and her petite figure poured into a glittery copper number that could not possibly have been worn as well by another living soul.

'Hey, Meg.' Rosie clamped her fingers around her glass to stop herself from checking her hair, from tugging at her dress, from feeling awkward and gangly and everything Meg Kelly was not.

'Having fun?' Meg asked.

'The mostest fun,' Rosie said. 'You?'

Meg's face twisted in the way that only someone who somehow knew she would never wrinkle could twist her face. 'I hate these things. So many ancient VIPs trying to kiss Dad's butt. I mean, if they had vodka cruisers rather than this dry, old champagne then maybe, just maybe, these nights might not make me feel so much like my youth is just slipping away. You know what I mean?'

Rosie sipped her champagne and smiled with her eyes.

'So how do your people celebrate birthdays?' Meg asked.

Rosie spluttered on her drink. 'My people?'

'Your friends and family.'

Rosie mentally kicked herself. Cameron was from *good* people. His friends were at heart good people. It stood to reason Meg would be good person too. Just because this night had wrenched up some latent feelings of inferiority and doubt, that wasn't her fault.

'Pizza,' Rosie said. 'Beer. Ten-pin bowling. Birthday cake with used candles. Pressies under thirty bucks a pop.'

'So, no ice-sculptures then?' Meg asked.

They both turned to look at the six-foot-tall melting bust of Quinn Kelly's head in the centre of the twenty-foot long head table.

'Ah, no,' Rosie said. 'Not that I can remember.'

'And don't you now think those parties were the poorer for it?' Meg's voice was deadpan, but her eyes were sparkling.

Yep, she thought, *Meg Kelly is one of the good ones*. She could barely imagine how hilarious she and Adele would be together.

'So,' Meg said, just as Rosie started to relax, 'You and my brother are together.'

'I think you'll find your brother is over there,' Rosie said carefully, 'While I'm over here.'

Meg tapped the side of her nose. 'I'm with you. Don't want to jinx things.'

Rosie made to correct Meg, but then realised she had no way of defining what they were that would make sense to anyone outside the two of them. Actually, the longer she spent alone, she was finding it hard to make sense of it herself.

Suddenly Meg stood straight as a die. 'Will you lookie there?'

Rosie's gaze shifted back to Cameron, to find that his father had joined the group, and her relationship with Cameron once again moved to the back of the line.

Her eyes darted between the two men. They seemed civil, at least from a distance. Profile on, they looked so similar— both tall, both straight-backed, both broad and ridiculously good-looking. Princes among men.

Only she knew Quinn Kelly was a man who liked to keep secrets. Secrets that could destroy those who loved him and needed him most. Secrets that had already destroyed that part of Cameron that was open to trust.

She had to loosen her grip on her champagne glass for fear it might smash in her hand.

All she could do was stand on the sidelines and wait. Wait for him to sort himself out. Wait for him to come back to her. The irony of her situation in comparison with her mother's wasn't lost on her. And the rest of her champagne was downed in three seconds flat.

'I truly never thought I'd see the day those two would manage to be in the same room together without shooting laser beams at one another with their eyes. Ever since Cam told dad he wasn't going to work for KInG, it's been the battlefield of Brisbane. What did you say to get him here?' Meg asked.

'Me?' Rosie said, lifting her napkin to the rosette on her chest.

'Yeah, you,' Meg said with a smile. 'It's only since you came on the scene that he's gone all soft and gooey around the edges. He called me twice this week. I don't remember a time he called me that often in a month!'

Rosie's stomach turned soft and gooey in half a second flat. But then she remembered that Cameron had not shared his fears about his father's health with Meg. It was more likely he'd been fishing and the timing had been coincidental.

Then again, maybe not. Maybe the timing was everything. She stared into her champagne. Maybe everything in his life was backwards this week because of the situation with his dad.

An older couple who smelled of talcum powder and diamonds came wafting past, and Meg said just the right things to have them smiling and on their way.

'You make it look so easy—the schmoozing,' Rosie commented, her voice a tad breathless.

Meg sighed. 'I sing rock songs in my head, imagine them all wearing suspenders and fish nets and carry a flask wherever I go.'

She tapped her bag, which clunked with a metallic sound, patted Rosie on the arm, winked and boogied back into the crowd, air-kissing along the way until she found Tabitha, and then together they danced like they were at a rave.

But Rosie had the distinct feeling that Meg Kelly was no more the ditzy socialite she appeared to be than Cameron Kelly had been the carefree, lackadaisical golden boy she'd once thought he was. Or the dark, hard character she'd thought he'd turned into.

'What the hell is wrong with my brother, leaving you all alone in this crowd of vultures?'

Rosie turned to find Dylan Kelly leaning over her shoulder. She would have recognised him anywhere; he graced the social pages more than the rest of them combined. Fair, dashing, roguish, he grabbed her last *hors d'oeuvre* and popped it in his mouth.

'There is nothing wrong with your brother,' she said, snatching her near-empty champagne away lest he went for that too.

He grinned at her with his mouth full. 'Meg was right—soft and gooey. The both of you.'

'Sorry to disappoint,' she said. 'I don't have a gooey bone in my body.'

He leant against the side of the column, close enough for her to smell his aftershave. It was nice, but it was not Cameron. Just the thought of Cameron's clean, linen scent made her gooey, gooey, gooey.

'And what do you know of my brother's body?' Dylan asked.

'Are you absolutely certain the two of you are related?' she asked. 'Because I just can't see it.'

Dylan's laughter rang in her ears, and she wondered how Adele, Meg *and* Dylan would be in a room together. Add Tabitha, and it would be such a riot she'd be able to charge admission.

Her chest expanded expectantly at the thought that, if things continued to go well, her friendship circle could triple overnight. And all because Cameron had chosen to include her.

The second she had the chance, Rosie sought him out. To her eyes he stood out like a lantern on a foggy night. His dinner jacket was open, his left hand in his trouser pocket, his right hand lifting and falling as he told a story which held the group enthralled. Though his eyes never once touched on his father, who stood quietly to the side focussed completely on his youngest son, she knew Cameron knew he was there.

Dylan was mistaken; Cameron hadn't left her alone. She hadn't been rendered invisible once her work was done. She'd kept herself away, giving him the space she knew he needed.

Right?

Cameron's mind wandered, and not for the first time. Only once his gaze found Rosalind, and he knew she was being entertained—that she was smiling, happy and in safe hands—could he begin to relax.

Right now she was being entertained by Dylan, a guy he'd never been stupid enough to leave alone with a date even without the added benefit of trust issues. But seeing his brother with Rosalind...

Nothing.

It wasn't ambivalence he was feeling. Quite the opposite. He *knew* Rosalind was with him even when she wasn't with him. His trust in her was absolute. And, in a night filled with extraordinary moments, that was one of the more unexpected.

Dylan leant in close to her to point out something on the ceiling. The guy took the opportunity to place a hand on her waist, feigning a need for balance.

And in the blink of an eye Rosalind had hold of the offending hand, bending his fingers back ninety degrees, and his brother was begging for mercy.

Cameron's first thought was, *that's my girl*.

That was the moment he felt his father slide in beside him.

'Nice girl,' Quinn said—the first words that had been spoken directly to him by the man in years. He couldn't have been less surprised.

'Nice doesn't even begin to cover it,' Cameron said, turning to look his father in the eye.

He looked older. Thinner. In person there was the same air of gravitas and power about him that there had always been. But he couldn't deny he'd seen what he'd seen, felt what he'd felt. There was no point in putting it off any longer.

'You're sick, aren't you, Dad?' His voice was dry. Emotionless. He had no idea how, as the words burned the inside of his throat as he said them.

'Wherever did you get that idea?' Quinn asked, smiling for his audience of hundreds.

'Dad,' Cameron pressed. 'Come on. This is me you're talking to—the one person on the planet who knows better than to fall for your line of bull. So tell me what's wrong?'

Quinn blinked at him as though not only seeing him for the first time in a decade and a half, but really *seeing* him for the first time.

'Nothing major. Just a couple of minor heart-attacks.'

Knowing had been one thing, having that thing confirmed was a whole other level of hell. Somehow he managed to keep his cool. 'How minor?'

'Minor enough I was able to call for Dr Carmichael myself when I felt them coming on. He brought me round both times without the need for anything so gauche as an ambulance. Just as well; those drivers would have sold some trumped up version of events to some shoddy paper within the hour.'

'So you've had no treatment apart from Dr Carmichael?'

'Not necessary.'

Cameron took a breath. 'Dr Carmichael is ten years older than you, and barely strong enough to hold a syringe, much less resuscitate a man your size.'

'Proving I was fine.'

'He has no other job but keeping you well. The guy wouldn't tell you it was serious for fear you'd fire him!'

'Which I damn well would. The man has no idea what a health scare would do to KInG. You, on the other hand, are smart enough to figure it out. So I trust you'll keep your concerns to yourself.'

Cameron scoffed. 'I've heard those words before.'

His father's face turned red, the kind of red that went with high blood pressure and too many whiskeys over too many years. Cameron's fingers stretched out to touch his arm, to stay him, to make sure he was okay—but Quinn jerked away as though one show of vulnerability would be enough to let the crowd in on the truth.

'Son,' he barked, 'It's not your secret to tell.'

'Well, then, that's a pity, because I've recently discovered the healing quality of letting secrets go.'

'Think of your mother,' Quinn warned.

Cameron got so close to his father he could count the red lines in the man's eyes. For that reason alone he kept his voice as calm as he could as he said, 'You're the one who needs to think of my mother a hell of a lot more than you ever do. I don't give a flying fig about the business, or the press, but I do care about the family. They may think you're a god, but I know that you are just a man. And I'm not keeping this secret—not from them—because if something happened to you and they didn't see it coming they'd never forgive you. So I'm back. Today's a new day for the Kelly clan.'

'Cameron?'

Rosalind's soft voice was enough to bring him off his high horse and back down to earth.

'Cameron?' she said again. 'I'm so sorry to interrupt, but Meg was looking for you. She needs you for a reason I can't mention in front of the birthday boy.'

Her hand clamped down on his forearm, gently but insistently. His vision cleared enough to tell him they had an audience. She'd just saved him from telling everyone in the room what even the family did not yet know.

Her other hand slid around his back, sliding along the beltline of his trousers, slow, warm, supportive. Vanilla essence, purely feminine warmth. Rosalind.

'Quinn,' she said, 'Happy birthday. And can I steal him away?'

His father nodded, then looked back to him, the slightest flicker of sadness damping his sharp, blue eyes before it disappeared behind the usual wall of invulnerability. But it was something. It was regret. It was a beginning.

'Happy birthday, Dad,' he said, leaning in to give his father a quick kiss on the cheek before turning and walking away.

'Oh God!' Rosalind whispered. 'I so apologise if that was

the exact wrong moment, but you looked like you were about to bop him one. I thought you might need a distraction.'

The woman was a mind reader. He took a deep breath, wrapped his arm about her waist, leaned over and kissed the top of her head. 'Thank you.'

'For what?'

For what? For far too many things for him to extrapolate right now.

'Just thank you.'

'My pleasure. And your dad?'

He held her tighter and set his gaze straight ahead. 'I was right. Heart problems. Certainly worse than he is making out. The man simply won't admit weakness no matter what it costs.'

'And your family?'

'Know nothing. But not for long. I'll let them have tonight, but tomorrow I'll be back to tell them all. Give them the chance to make their peace.'

'Good man.'

Rosalind looked up into his eyes. She'd meant it when she called him a good man. And with it he felt the last of the places inside him that had been hard, fast and immovable for so very long melt away.

'Now Meg really *does* need you,' she said. 'Are you up for it? Whatever it is?'

'You bet.'

And as they joined his brothers and sister in an ante room he couldn't keep his eyes off Rosalind standing quietly in the doorway, watching the interplay between the four musketeers with a wistful smile on her face.

Tonight, rather than her distracting him from his family's dramas, his family's dramas had been distracting him from her. Being with her was where he constantly wanted to be. The words gathered in his throat, but not in any order he recognized, so he swallowed them back down.

'Cam!' Meg called out, clicking fingers in front of his eyes. 'Pay attention, Bucko, or I'll make you jump out of the cake instead of me!'

He blinked, then stared at his sister. 'You are not jumping—?'

'No.' She grinned. 'I'm not. But pay attention so we can get this done, and then, my little friend, the rest of the night is yours to do with as you please.'

He couldn't help himself. He looked to the doorway, only to find Rosalind had gone.

Happy Birthday had been sung by the world-famous St Grellans Chorale. A cake the size of a piano had been wheeled out by Quinn's four children, and a line of people had snaked around the room as everyone awaited their chance to get a piece of cake and slap some Kelly flesh.

Rosie stayed in the gallery, leaning on the railing and watching the proceedings from a more comfortable distance.

'You must be Rosalind.'

Rosie spun from the rail to find herself face to face with Mary Kelly, the matriarch of the Kelly clan, as petite as Meg, but overwhelming all the same—resplendent in a royal-blue gown, her ice-blonde hair swaying in a sleek bob. She was so elegant Rosie had to swallow down a raging case of stage fright.

And then the woman smiled, and Rosie knew where Cameron's natural warmth had come from. She couldn't help but smile right back.

She held out a hand. 'Rosie Harper. It's a pleasure to meet you, Mrs Kelly.'

'Rosie. Please, call me Mary.' Mary clasped Rosie's hand between both of hers. 'And the pleasure is all mine, I assure you. You're the girl who finally brought my Cameron home.'

Rosie realised how hard she was shaking her head when a lock of hair fell from her up-do and stuck to her lip gloss. She peeled it out as she said, 'Really, you've all got to stop saying that. I promise, it was all Cameron's idea, his attachment to you guys, that made him come. I was just the lucky girl who got a party invite.'

She could tell by the steely resolution in the older woman's eyes that she was having none of it. But before Rosie could press her case home—to somehow explain what they were, or maybe more easily what they weren't—Mary turned to glance out over the crowd, every inch a queen surveying her land and peoples.

'My Cam's always been a stubborn boy. He'd never accept help with his homework. Never come in from playing outside until he'd achieved whatever sporting milestone he'd set out to accomplish. He can want a lot from others, but is much harder on himself. Much like his father.'

Don't tell him that, Rosie thought.

'I'd never tell him that,' the woman said with an eloquent smile. 'Though it's why the two of them could never see eye to eye. They are both bull-headed. Determined. Competitive. Ambitious. And sadly unforgiving of human limitations.'

Rosie stopped nodding along when she hit the final word. Her skin broke out in a splatter of goose bumps as the whole truth dawned: her husband's infidelity, his current illness, Mary Kelly knew it all.

What she didn't know was that her youngest son knew it all too. If she had, Rosie had no doubt she would have done everything not to let him suffer being an outcast to protect them all.

The fiercely independent side of her nudged her towards feeling sorry for the woman. But really Rosie just thought her immensely brave.

Mary Kelly's valiant choices had shaped four formidable children. Rosie had witnessed how naturally close they were in the ante room downstairs. If she'd still believed in wishing on a star, her wish would have been to be a part of that. To be able to tap into Meg's humour, Dylan's confidence, Brendan's strength, to be cushioned by that much unconditional devotion.

But she especially wanted to hug Mary Kelly for creating Cameron—a man who might well be bull-headed, but then so was she. While he was also gentle. Gentlemanly. Incredibly strong. Generous. Funny. Attentive. He had a huge heart and the soul of a dreamer.

Her cheeks began to warm. She'd never let herself list his good points in one go before, as though deep down she'd known that all together they would be overwhelming.

When she realised Mary Kelly was awaiting her response, she casually fanned her cheeks with her clutch bag as she said, 'Thank goodness for the renowned Kelly charm, then. I'd bet it gets them both out of a lot of trouble their mulishness gets them into.'

Mary smiled. 'Thank goodness for that. And for the fact that they are both men who have always known who they are. And what they want. That's a rare thing indeed.'

Rosie smiled back. All the while her mind spun and spun.

Cameron Kelly was a rare man. A man who worked hard and played hard, but above all wanted to be a good man. He *was* a good man. The best man. That such a man had pursued her, looked out for her, desired her, *needed* her…

And right there, standing next to Cameron's mother, it dawned on Rosie with the gently rising glow and warmth of a winter sunrise that it had taken a rare man to give her—a woman who had been certain that she would go a lifetime without knowing love—all the room she'd needed in order to know one thing with all her heart.

Rosie loved him. She was in love with Cameron Kelly. She loved him with a mad, aching, tumbling, soaring, absorbing, textured, lovely love.

Her lungs filled so deeply that the resultant burst of oxygen made her feel lightheaded, weak-kneed and tingly all over. Trying to find some kind of centre, she repeated the words over and over again in her head.

She loved him. She was in love with him. Rosie Harper loved Cameron Kelly.

After a while the words stopped making sense.

How could they? How could she have let herself love this man of all men? Cameron might have come here to broker a peace, but the cuts from his father's betrayals ran deep. They had screwed with his sense of gallantry so much that, even if a miracle occurred and he ever came close to loving her back, his critical fear of hurting those he loved would be one great reason for him to let her go.

That was what he'd been trying to tell her that night after the Chinese at his place. He'd been warning her. Subconsciously he'd seen this coming, even if she had pretended she was fine.

Her flutter of instinct when she'd been with Meg had been spot on. While Cameron had thought he'd found himself an easygoing girl who would know better than to fall for him, Rosie had gone against character and done just that.

She'd fallen head over heels in love with the one man who could never be hers.

Punch drunk, Rosie inhaled deeply, but this time the air felt like it barely touched her lungs. There were too many people. Crowding into her personal space. Making it impossible to breathe.

'It's been lovely to meet you all, Mrs Kelly. You have an amazing family,' she managed to get out without choking. 'Please excuse me.'

She blindly stumbled onto one of a dozen half-circle balconies leading off the gallery, towards fresh air. And open sky.

Looking up into the infinite stars—all of them seemingly serene and quiet, yet crashing, imploding, living and dying out of control right before her eyes—she managed to get air into her lungs once more.

Cameron leant in the frame of the balcony doorway, watching Rosalind.

Her hair flickered in the soft breeze. Her dress clung to her subtle curves. His blood warmed as he imagined wrapping himself about her again tonight. Celebrating with her. Taking her with him to the heights he was feeling, and finding solace in her arms as he came to terms with his father's mortality. And his own.

Her long, lean fingers gripped the columned balustrade, her eyes looking up.

That was one of the many things that drew him to her: her restless energy. She was hard to satisfy. He felt exactly the same way. At least, he had for years.

But looking at her now, her delicate shoulders braced to take on whatever her stars might throw at her, he felt something inside him shake free and settle.

The three steps that took him to her felt like they took an eternity. He slid his arms around her waist, leant his chin on her shoulder and kissed the tip of her ear.

She melted against him, a perfect fit, and he felt her whole body sigh.

But then her hands clasped down on his; she peeled his hand away from her waist and stepped away.

She glanced at him from beneath her lashes, and he realised she was upset. Soft swirls of wet mascara bore witness to the tracks of her tears.

His fists clenched, ready to take on Dylan or Meg or Brendan or whoever had said something to make his big, brave girl so distressed.

He went to touch her again. 'Rosalind, honey…'

She held up a hand, and he stopped mid-step.

'What's wrong?' he asked.

'I can't do this any more,' she whispered between her teeth.

'Do what?' he asked. But while his fists unclenched all of the newly settled places inside him began to squeeze in expectation.

'This.' Her arms flew sideways, taking in the balcony, the ballroom, the immaculate grounds.

'Fine,' he said. 'I've done what I came here to do. Why don't we go home?' He wasn't sure where that would be, his place or hers, but as long as she was with him he didn't really much care.

He reached out to take her hand, which even in the beginning had always felt like the most natural thing in the world. But she pulled her hand away as though burnt.

'I can't,' she croaked. 'No more. Enough is enough.' Two fat tears slid down her blotchy pink cheeks. She swiped them away in frustration. 'Why did you even bring me here?'

He opened his mouth to tell her, then realised what a complicated question that really was. Less than a week earlier she'd been a welcome distraction. But tonight…

'This was always going to be a difficult night, and knowing you were here with me, for me, made all the difference. I could never have done this without you.'

He took another step. She shook her head so hard her curls drooped.

Realising she was more than upset—she was so distraught he wasn't sure she even heard him—he thought harder, went deeper. 'Asking you to come was not a decision I made lightly.'

Her eyes were like chipped ice when she looked up at him. 'Neither was my agreeing to come.'

He slid his left foot back to meet his right, keeping space between them while he tried to figure out what was happening.

It had all seemed to be going so well. Meg thought her fun, Dylan thought her hot, she'd earned his father's respect in an instant, and his mother had merely kissed him on the cheek and smiled, which told him everything. What had happened during *Happy Birthday*?

'Rosalind, I'm sorry, but I'm at a loss as to what's going on here.'

'It's *Rosie*,' she shot back. 'Just plain old Rosie. Which is exactly why you asked me here. But that doesn't make me some oddment you can flash about to get a rise out of your father. Or a diversionary girl to get Meg and Dylan off your back. Or a false hope for your mum. That's just not cool. I don't deserve that.'

She was so upset her voice was catching on her words, as though she could scarcely draw breath. It physically pained Cameron not to gather her up in his arms and make everything better.

But the truth was she was spot on—from the beginning he'd used her. Even when he'd realised she was too smart, too clued into him, not to figure it out. Now he'd hurt her when he'd promised himself he would never hurt anyone he cared for.

His only chance was to show her, and himself, that deep down he wasn't the cold, calculating man he'd been acting like for the past week.

'This has been a night for fresh starts,' he said. 'Maybe we could take a leaf out of that book and try for one ourselves.'

She laughed, but it was tinged with bitterness, the likes of which he'd never felt from her. He felt it like a slap across the face.

She said, 'You are on a high, and I get that. I am honestly so happy for you that you have that. But let's be honest— you've never pretended that you had any intention of committing further time and energy to this than you absolutely had to. Don't start messing with me now.'

God, but the woman was stubborn! His hands clenched into fists rather than reaching out and shaking her. 'You want me to be brutally honest?'

His frustration came through his voice. She glanced up at him, her eyes like silver charms in the moonlight.

'Why the heck not?' she said.

'Fine. Then here it is. You are honestly the most difficult, defiant, demanding woman I have ever met. And I think you ought to try to find it in you to give me a break. Now, do you really want to talk about commitment?'

'Yeah. Let's.' She crossed her arms and glared at him. She was so fierce it brought about a growl deep down inside his chest. He would have grabbed her and kissed her had it not been for the fact that she was driving him so damned crazy.

He said, 'As far as I can tell, apart from some far-away planet that can't answer back, you've never committed to a thing! Not to a job that isn't freelance. Not to a home that you can't up and move with an hour's notice. Not even to your own name.'

The heat in her eyes made his lungs burn as he breathed deep to keep from saying any more; his skin felt a hundred degrees. And he'd never been so turned on in his whole life. Not by success, or power, or by being the one man in town gutsy enough to build the tallest, greatest, most spectacular buildings his city had ever seen.

'Fine,' she shot back. 'If I'm the world's greatest hypocrite, then you are the most wilfully pig-headed man in the universe. Do you have any kind of clue what you have? You are surrounded by people who love you so much.' Her eyes flickered from his for a moment before slamming into him again. 'Family who need you, who want you in their lives no matter what. You have roots in this place a mile deep, and you've done everything in your power to chop them off. One of these days they might not grow back, then you'll have the faintest clue what it truly feels like to be alone in the universe.'

Two fat tears slid from her eyes and peeled pathetically down her cheeks. The ache it created inside him knocked him sideways. He wished he knew how to tell her. He wished she would let him hold her, kiss her, show her, so that he didn't have to find the words—as he wasn't even sure he knew what the words should be. But she let him off the hook by staring hard at her shoes.

'Can you please thank you mother for a lovely party? Give my regards to the rest.'

She looked up and captured his eyes with hers. He felt like his whole life had led him to this one minute in time. The defining minute of his life. Was he really a good man after all? Would a good man get on his knees and tell her how he felt, or would a good man realise he'd hurt the woman enough and let her go?

All of a sudden an explosion of sounds startled them both rigid. A half-second later fireworks burst and sparkled in the sky over the river.

The balcony quickly became crowded with guests, oohing and ahhing, and Cameron felt Rosalind being tugged from him. It wasn't until he lost her within the sea of faces that he realised she'd been the one doing all the tugging.

Suddenly she was gone.

And, though he was surrounded by people, including the family he'd taken back into his life this night, he already felt more alone than he'd even known it was possible to feel.

CHAPTER THIRTEEN

CAMERON had ditched his jacket and tie, his sleeves were rolled up past his elbows, his forearms leant against the cold stone of the ballroom balcony and he watched blue turn to pink as morning came round.

Venus was already up, steadfast in the sky. Unlike the other heavenly bodies that had set with the moon, there was no unsteady flickering, no distracting twinkling. She was constant, unwavering, enchanting and all alone.

Something hard and heavy thumped behind his ribs, and not for the first time in the past twelve hours. In fact, the thumping and heaviness had come over him the moment Rosalind had left him standing in this exact place.

The hours had passed. He and his family had retired to the library once all the guests had gone, and he had told them all about Quinn's heart attacks and stubborn refusal to seek treatment, and together they had fought, reconciled, laughed and cried—and he'd come to realise that he'd never in his life been really alone.

But Rosalind had—solitary in her work, isolated in her home, alone even in her family. And it didn't matter any more that she might have done everything in her power to keep at arm's length those things that could provide her the same easy comfort he'd enjoyed; he finally understood the reason.

Loving something, then losing it, hurt like hell.

Was she out there hurting right now? Hurting and alone, because of him? Because he'd been too stubborn, too scrupulous, too disenchanted to take on the mess that came with the good in any real relationship?

A good man would suck up his pride, put himself in the unpleasant position at being rejected twice in twenty-four hours and do what he had to do to to make sure the person he cared about knew she would never have to be alone again.

He glanced at his watch. The hour was nearly polite enough. Home, a shower, a change of clothes; he pushed himself upright, stretched his tight arms over his head then felt in his pocket for his car keys.

If she slammed the door in his face afterwards, he'd never darken her door again. If her eyes confirmed how deeply he believed she cared, if she opened the door wide and let him in…

The rush of his next thought was stripped from him as a hard hand slapped down upon his shoulder. Dylan sidled in beside him, dressed much the same way as Cameron since none of them had yet been to sleep.

'So this is where you've been hiding since the big brouhaha?' Dylan said.

Cameron slapped a hand around his brother's shoulder and turned them back inside. 'You know as well as I do there are far better and darker places to hide in this monstrosity than on an open balcony.'

Dylan grinned. 'I'm thinking right about now Dad would pay good money to know just one.'

They meandered through the upper level, gravitating towards the kitchen as they had a thousand times before. It didn't feel like he'd spent years away from this place. It just felt like home.

And there was one person he had to thank for showing him the way back. He glanced at his watch again, restlessness beginning to take hold.

Dylan held open the swinging door of the massive white-and-wood kitchen, but not quite so far that Cameron could slip through.

His dress shoes came to a squeaking halt, and he looked up at his brother in time for Dylan to say, 'Thanks, mate.'

'For what?'

'For opening our eyes. For not letting the old man twist your arm. For giving us all the chance to remind him that he was the one who always told us to put family first, and it's about time he remembered that. It's tense in there right now, but once everyone calms down they'll realise the air in this place has never seemed so clear.'

Dylan let the door swing closed to give him a hug. Cameron hugged back, wondering how the hell he'd forsaken this all these years. Not for one more day would he forsake his own happiness for the sake of some cold, loveless principle.

When Dylan let him go and headed into the kitchen, Cameron looked to his watch again. It was nearly seven. She was a morning bird; she'd be up.

Not for one more day? He wasn't going to deny himself the chance at happiness another minute.

Dylan grabbed a slice of birthday cake and a glass of milk from the fridge. 'You staying for breakfast?'

Cameron shook his head, his mind a million miles away from there already. 'Not this time.'

'Damn it. I was itching to find out what new bombshell you might drop over waffles—Brendan's gay? Mum voted Labour? Meg's adopted, as she always hoped? No? Fine; so what *are* your plans for this fine day? Tell me they involve that fabulous young thing who accompanied you here last night and I might forgive you.'

Cameron took a swipe of icing. 'I have high hopes.'

Dylan paused. Then said, 'How high, exactly?'

'Ridiculously, I'm afraid.'

'Do tell.'

'She accused me lately of having no staying power, and I am of a mind to prove her wrong.'

'Wow. Don't tell me you're in need of the little blue pills yet? You're younger than me.'

Cameron elbowed his brother neatly in the solar plexus and was rewarded with a satisfying, 'Oomph!'

He slipped the icing into his mouth, and the sweetness exploded on his tongue. Then he said, 'Rosalind knew I was making excuses. What I didn't realise was that with her I didn't need to.'

'She's figured you out, then?'

Cameron breathed in deep through his nose. Then he pushed away from the island to head to the door leading outside, to his car, to her. 'That she has.'

'Excellent,' Dylan said with a chummy grin. 'It seems I may have a bombshell to drop over breakfast after all.'

Rosie sat on Adele's couch, staring unseeingly at the shifting yellow stripes on the wall left by the early-morning sun spilling through the wooden blinds behind her. Her feet were tucked beneath her, her legs covered in the blanket beneath which she'd slept—kind of. A bit. Not really.

In fact she'd been awake pretty much all night having deep and meaningful conversations with herself across a range of matters that had all led back to the one crucial fact: that she had gone and done the most stupid thing she could ever do and fallen for Cameron Kelly.

About three minutes after the cab had pulled out of the Kelly Manor driveway, the words, 'Turn this cab around right now!' had crowded her throat. Shouldn't she at least have allowed herself the chance to be loved back?

A deep breath, a sharp tug of the hair at the back of her neck and an extra five kilometres distance, and she'd been certain that she'd been on the verge of unashamedly setting herself up for heartache again, and again, and again…

Repeat one-hundred times, and that had been her night.

Adele came into the lounge with a tray of coffee, cake, chocolate, salt-and-vinegar chips, and lollies in the shape of milk bottles.

'How you doing, snook?' Adele asked, pouring her a strong cup of coffee.

'Better.' She uncurled her legs before they got stuck that way, and let her toes scrunch into the coarse, woven rug at her feet.

Adele's eyebrows rose. 'All better?'

Actually she felt like a walking bruise. She wrapped her hands around the hot mug and glanced at Adele over the top. 'Thanks for letting me stay.'

Adele blinked down at her several times before saying, 'Thank me later.'

Then the doorbell rang.

Adele jumped. She glanced at the door, back at Rosie, then back at the door. She said, 'I think I left the iron on. Can you get that?' And then shot from the room.

The doorbell rang again.

Rosie dragged herself from the couch, ran fingers through her thicket of hair, rubbed her hands hard over her face to make sure all the bits were where they were meant to be and trudged to the door in her borrowed pyjama bottoms, T-shirt and bare feet. The delivery guy would just have to suck it up and pretend she didn't look like a one-woman freak show.

She hauled open the door and found herself face to face with a crumpled khaki shirt with rolled up sleeves, revealing the greatest pair of forearms God had ever created. And on the end of them…

'Cameron!'

'Hi,' he said.

She swallowed. It seemed his name was the most she could hope to say.

His hand reached up to cup the doorframe, as though she might be about to slam the door in his face—like he couldn't see that her irrational heart was trying its best to leap from her chest and into his beautiful arms.

'Can I...?' He cleared his throat. 'Rosie, can I come in?'

Rosie... Had he just called her Rosie?

She curled her toes into the hard wood and, no matter how hard she tried to resist, all the stagnant, decided places inside her began to flutter back to life. Which was ridiculous. He was likely there because she'd left something behind, and he was so damned civilised he was returning it by hand.

Needing an anchor, someone on her side, she glanced over her shoulder but there was no sign of Adele.

Then he said, 'I tried calling you last night. Many, many times.'

She closed her eyes, swallowed hard then looked back to him. His hair was mussed. His jeans unironed. Stubble shadowed his jaw. She'd never seen him so sexily rumpled.

She licked her dry lips and tugged at her T-shirt, and amidst the fidgeting it occurred to her that beneath the sex-god rumples he also looked tired, grey around the eyes, like he hadn't had much in the way of sleep either.

Her hand shook and she gripped her T-shirt tight. 'I left my mobile at home.'

A crease came and went in his cheek. 'I managed to somehow convince myself of that after the first dozen times you didn't answer. So I called Adele. She told me you were here. That you were still...upset. And that I should give you time.'

Rosie glanced at the angle of the sunlight on the porch outside. 'It can't yet be eight o'clock.'

He didn't even need to look to his watch before he said, 'It's not.'

She blinked at him once, then turned and walked inside. The soft click of the door told her far less than her next breath, which was filled with his clean, male scent.

Her knees wobbled plenty before she plopped back onto the couch. Cameron sat next to her. Close. Her scrunched-up blanket had the other third all to itself.

'Rosie—'

'Coffee?' she asked, her voice overly loud. She as yet needed time to collect herself. To protect herself.

He nodded. She poured.

'I'm not sure where Adele has gone; she was here a minute ago.'

'She gave me a goodbye wave over your shoulder when I first arrived. I'm assuming this place has a back door.'

Rosie swallowed hard. And nodded. They were alone. She would have no choice but to anchor herself.

He said, 'I'll get straight to the point, then, shall I? Which would be a first, I'm sure. We do seem to have an uncanny ability to lay things on the line without ever really getting to the point of what we are trying to say.'

Her hand shook. She stopped pouring halfway, lest she end up with more scars for her troubles. Then she pushed a mug in front of him, but his hands remained clasped on top of his thighs.

He waited til she looked him in the eyes, those deep, dark-blue eyes, now so solemn, so serious. She nodded. She was as ready as she'd ever be.

'So, last night on the balcony, you accused me of not appreciating what I had. And I want you to know that I think you were absolutely right.'

Rosie swallowed. This was not what she had expected at all.

He went on, 'I've put so much time and effort into my work, and my home, the parts of my life that don't offer any form of opposition. And not because it was right, but because it was easier than facing the truth—that I have been taking for granted those things which should have been more important the whole time.'

As he spoke, as he confessed, his stunning, searching, blue eyes never once left hers, not a for a second. If she had an ounce of faith left in her judgement she might have fancied he was talking about her. But that boat had sailed the minute she'd said yes to a date with a guy no sane woman could know and not love.

Needing a distraction, she grabbed a handful of milk-bottle lollies and nibbled on the end of one. His gaze finally left her eyes and rested on her lips before they slid back up.

He rolled his shoulders once, then continued. 'I thought my life was good. But now I see that it was completely untethered, all the separate parts unconnected, because I was afraid that I might one day slip up, word would get back and my family would be hurt. Then you came along, and I slipped. Over and over again. And you know what?'

'What?' she asked, her chest lifting as she breathed in deep.

'The world didn't end. And last night I began the process of joining the dots. I have reconnected with old friends. I have spoken with my father. I have my family back.'

She smiled a wobbly smile. Because she was happy for him. She really was. Not so happy for herself...

Until a hand reached out and took hers, its fingers curling around hers until they were indelibly knotted together. Reconnected.

'Rosie,' he said, and her heart beat so hard she heard it in her ears. She lifted her eyes to see that he was smiling too. 'Sweetheart, the glue that brought it all together was you.'

Her heart rate had nothing on the blood rush to her head. She shook it to try to clear the haze, to pick out the truth from the hope that was blurring everything. 'I'm not glue,' she said. 'I'm the opposite of glue. I don't even have any dots to join. You said it yourself—I work freelance, I live in a van, there is nothing in my life I couldn't walk away from given a moment's notice. I know nothing about being glue. All I do know is that the easiest way to break a person's spirit is to take away the things they love. I didn't want that to happen to you.'

'You were too late. It already had. But look at me. I'm still here.'

Cameron was still there, the strength of his spirit radiating from every pore. 'So here's what I think about all that—a spirit can be broken only if it's prone to breaking in the first place. And Rosie, honey, you are a force of nature. Your spirit is so vibrant, so fresh, so honest, I am certain there is nothing in this world that could ever break you.'

She blinked hard, then down at their entwined hands. It was true, her spirit still raged inside her even after the night she'd had. She felt sorry for her mum, angry at her dad, proud of Cameron. So she might not be broken. But that didn't mean that the cracks didn't feel like they were being held together with old gum.

'Cameron—'

'Cam,' he said, cutting her off. 'Those closest to me call me Cam.'

Her eyes were drawn back to his like magnets to steel. His smile remained, urged her to really listen. He was telling her that she was his glue. That he considered her a person close to him. That, even after she'd run scared the night before, he was still here.

Rosie felt the moment heave between them, draw breath and wait. Her world, her universe, her past, present and future felt as though they were teetering on her next words.

'Cam,' she said on a release of breath—and the smile that had been hovering on the corner of his mouth broke free, beaming as bright as morning sunshine, until all she could do was bask in the glow.

'Yes, Rosie?'

'Actually,' she said, 'I don't so much mind if you call me Rosalind.'

His brow furrowed, and she didn't blame him. She wasn't sure where she was heading either. Her mind was a blank page, untinged by history or expectation. All she could do was anchor herself in the warmth of his hand wrapped around hers and give him as good as he'd given her.

She snuck a foot beneath her and faced him. 'I am Rosie. Rosie who camps out in a van, loves comfortable boots, clothes with a past, and sleeps when regular sorts are awake and vice versa. But since I met you...'

Her voice caught.

'Since I met you, Rosalind—the girl I was, the version of myself I kept at bay all these years—came back. That part of me craved affection, wanted nothing more than to feel special, wanted to know what it was like to be the centre of someone's attention. Rosalind isn't afraid to hope.'

His other hand lifted off his thigh. She held a finger near his lips. He held his breath and stared at it. Though she had no idea what was coming next, all she could do was let the flood of words carry her til she found land.

'Since I met you, since I met your friends and your family, I finally knew what it must be like to have kinship— be a part of a collective spirit, of something enveloping, warm, vital. Watching you, Meg, Dylan and Brendan mucking about with your dad's cake, I would have given my left leg to have been allowed into that inner sanctum for just one more day. I hope you understand, I had to, *have* to, walk away. Taking it away from me any later would have been too much to ask.'

'Who's asking?' he asked, his voice deep, warm, encouraging.

Then the edge of his mouth kicked up into the whisper of a smile. His thumb found her palm and began running up and down the centre, sending goose bumps all around her body, inside and out.

She closed her fingers around his thumb and twisted it away. 'I… I'm not exactly sure what you're intimating. In all honesty, I'm kind of hazy about a lot of things right now. I've been up all night. I'm wearing someone else's pyjamas. I haven't showered.'

He took her hand back in his, turned it over and pressed his warm lips upon her palm. 'You smell great.'

A slow build of warmth settled low in her stomach. 'I smell like milk-bottle lollies and mothballs.'

'You smell like you.'

The warmth began to seep into her limbs, into her head, giving her ideas that maybe, just maybe, the only thing she'd left behind at the party had been him.

'Cameron,' she breathed.

He held up a finger to her lips, not stopping short, letting the calloused tip brush against her soft mouth.

'Rosalind,' he said, her name rolling off his tongue as poetically as it was meant to be. 'One of the many things I have long since found so irresistible about you is that, while you are such a champion of human frailty, you are determined to deny your own.'

'I don't. I—'

'Shush. Really. For your own good. It's my turn again.'

He took a deep breath and let it out through his nose, and Rosie realised that he wasn't just tired—he was nervous. He was wide open and unguarded. She opened her ears and listened.

'The night I suggested we slow things down…' He waited for her to nod along, his hand again holding hers tight. 'I was following a pattern I had followed time and time again. A whiff of getting too close, I put on the brakes. But when you left I realised it wasn't you getting too close that panicked me, it was *me*. It was so unanticipated that I took a long, hard look at my life without you in it and I didn't much care for what I saw.'

Just to make sure she was right there with him, he reached out and cupped her cheek. But she was there; she was all there.

'I had thought heading into the bush in the middle of the night to find you was enough of an admittance of my feelings, and that all I had been trying to do was protect you from every possible harm, including myself. I look back now and wonder what time and anguish I could have saved had I just had the guts to tell you straight. Like last night...' His eyes burned, as though he'd been sliced with a red-hot poker. 'I should never have let you walk away before we'd managed to have this exact conversation. Thankfully this week I've learnt not only how easy it is for all men to make mistakes, but how easy it can be to forgive them.'

He slid his hand into her hair, caressing her ear, drawing her closer. His beautiful blue eyes smiled into hers. Her heart danced. Her liver forgot itself. And the rest of her insides skipped and tumbled, and hoped more than they'd ever hoped in their life.

'Forgive me,' he asked.

Her voice shook when she said, 'I never gave you a chance. Forgive *me*.'

He slid his hand into her hair, drawing her closer. 'Since we are both extremely adept at complicating the heck out of everything, how about I try something new and make things really simple?'

'It's worth a try.'

'Rosalind,' he said, his voice almost as shaky as hers. 'My Rosie. I need you to know that I am very much in love with you. That I have loved you for some time. And I have no doubt that I will love you as long as I can draw breath.'

The second he'd said her name, warm tears streamed down her face, but she couldn't possibly lift a hand to wipe them away. She thought she might have to resort to using a shoulder when Cameron leaned in and kissed them away, one side then the other.

Before things kept moving in the direction it was obvious they had to, she stilled him with a hand at his chest. She looked from one eye to the other, until she was certain she had his attention completely. 'Last night, watching you wield the kind of strength that most men don't even know is possible, I knew I loved you too.'

His eyes glinted, his chest swelled, and the hand in her hair drew her in. 'Funny way you had of showing it,' he murmured.

'As it turns out, I am a funny girl.'

He grinned. 'Lucky me.'

And then he kissed her. She melted into his arms as he pressed her back against the couch. Her delighted hands slid up the back of his shirt, her legs entwined with his, and she kissed him until she saw stars; she was lost. Wholly and completely and beautifully lost. The sensation filled her, overwhelmed her, and didn't scare her in the least.

For she had not actually lost something, she'd finally found herself again in him.

Eons later, when they pulled apart, Rosie's lungs burned, her lips were hot and swollen and her whole body felt heavy and languid. Cameron on the other hand had admirable strengths. He lifted her back upright until she was sitting across his lap.

His sexy eyes narrowed as he asked, 'You did say that you loved me, right? That was one hell of a kiss, and could have been enough to have made me imagine it.'

'I do love you,' she repeated, the liberation of the words, of the feeling, of what it would bring her, making her feel sky high.

'Excellent,' he said. 'Then, before we go ahead and christen Adele's couch, I have one more thing I have to get off my chest.'

Rosie pushed a scruff of hair off his forehead, and allowed herself the crazy luxury of playing with his hair. 'This is *really* not the moment to confess you have a secret love of boy bands. Or that you already have three wives and they're all called

Rosalind. And there is no way I'm ever giving up my cardboard cut-out; he was a gift, and is a collector's item, so—'

'Rosie.' His eyes narrowed, but the sexy grin that accompanied it only made her want to curl up and purr. 'You're going to have to answer your phone when I call.'

She blew a raspberry, and continued playing with his thick, beautiful hair. 'That's asking too much.'

He pointed a finger at her nose. 'If I have to call Adele every time I want to see you or talk to you, or tell you I love you, or when I get the sudden urge to talk dirty to you in the middle of the day when I'm all hot and sweaty at the work site and you're wrapped up snug under your comforter in bed, then I guess that's how it's going to be. It's you, me and Adele for ever.'

The hot and sweaty talk had her turning her attentions to the top button of his shirt. 'Or…?'

He reached round behind him and pulled out a small silver box wrapped in a big white bow. She'd been so caught up in the fact that he was there at all, she hadn't even noticed him bring it inside.

'For me?' she asked.

He nodded.

She opened the box, realising she had no clue what kind of gift a man like him, a man who knew everyone, who could get his hands on anything, would…

'Oh, Cameron.'

On a bed of soft silver paper lay a mobile phone. It wasn't gleaming, new, expensive, complicated and demanding—it was simple, easy, and just retro enough for her to fall in love with it in a heartbeat.

She ran her fingers over the big, bumpy buttons. 'Oh Cameron, she's beautiful.'

He slid the phone from her hand and she whimpered. 'What's beautiful about it,' he said, ignoring her, 'is that I've programmed it already with all the numbers I could think of that you might need in the near future.'

She snuggled in beside him so they could look at her beautiful new-old phone together. 'Show me.'

He showed her. 'There's the planetarium's number. Adele's. I tracked down the number for your supervisor in Houston.'

Rosie lifted her head to stare at him.

'I had many hours to kill last night, remember.'

His cheeks pinked—tough, sharp, skyscraper builder Cameron Kelly pinked—then dragged her back into his arms.

'Meg, Dylan, Brendan, and my parents are all there.'

She blinked. It was as if he'd known how much that would mean to her. It was as if he knew her better than she even knew herself.

'And last but not least,' he said, 'Press the one button then send.'

She did, and up came the first number on her speed dial. His mobile number, and the name *Cam*.

No fanfare. No dibs on himself. No Mr Cameron Kelly, esquire, builder of skyscrapers, Prince of Brisbane. Just her self-assured guy who knew her and loved her, and wanted to be the first person she'd ever think to call.

Rosie looked up at him and said the first words that came to mind. 'Will you marry me?'

He tilted his head to kiss her, slow, soft, deep, for ever, before saying, 'It would be my pleasure. How does tomorrow sound?'

She smiled against his lips. 'Fabulous. But I'm sure we have to register, and it takes like a month in case we change our minds, and—'

'First, I'm not changing my mind. Once I commit to something, that's it. And, more importantly, I'm a Kelly. I can do whatever I want.' He grinned. 'I knew one day that would come in handy.'

She moved to kiss him some more, but he edged back.

'One problem. You're going to have to get a bigger caravan. I've seen your current bed and I'm far too big for it.'

'That's okay,' she said, turning away to bury her head into his shoulder while she scrolled through her chunky phone's limited options. 'I don't think I can live another winter in the van now that I know all about that fireplace in your house. Even if you'd said no to marrying me, I was thinking about squatting. The place is so big you might never have noticed.'

Cameron grabbed her phone and threw it on the far sofa, where it bounced once and landed face up on a cushion.

'Well, thank God you did that,' she said, turning into his arms to kiss him. 'I didn't have the heart.'

The next time she came up for air, Cameron looked so deep into her eyes she felt like she could happily drown in them.

'I promised myself,' he said, 'if you turned me away at the door today I'd let you go. But I was kidding myself. If you'd slammed the door in my face I would have climbed through the window, down the chimney, up a drain pipe, to get to you. Not because I'm used to getting my way, but because I can no longer picture my way without you there beside me.'

'That's lucky. Because that's right where I plan to be.'

Air was overrated, Rosie thought as she settled back into his embrace. Kissing Cameron was not.

By the time Adele got home an hour later, the house was empty. And the two full coffee cups were on the coffee table. Unnoticed, untouched.

It seemed the couple they were meant for had been far too distracted to remember anything but one another.

THE PLAYBOY
TAKES A WIFE

BY
CRYSTAL GREEN

Crystal Green lives near Las Vegas, Nevada, where she writes for Mills & Boon® Cherish™ and Blaze.® She loves to read, over-analyse movies, do yoga and write about her travels and obsessions on her website www.crystal-green.com. There you can read about her trips on Route 66 as well as visits to Japan and Italy.

She'd love to hear from her readers by e-mail through the Contact Crystal feature on her web page!

To Mary Leo and Cheryl Howe:
the best two pals a workaholic could ever have.

Chapter One

The minute Lucas Chandler stepped out of his limousine and onto the hard-packed earth of Rosarito, Mexico, he was swarmed.

Flashbulbs assaulted him, and so did the questions—most of them encouraged by an introduction to this press gathering from David, his half brother and the CEO of The Chandler Organization, otherwise known as TCO.

"How much money did you donate altogether to get Refugio Salvo running, Mr. Chandler?"

Flash.

"Why the sudden interest in an orphanage, Mr. Chandler?"

Flash.

"Can you comment on what happened in Rome with Cecilia DuPont and the police, Mr. Chandler?"

Yeah, there it was—the kind of query into Lucas's party-hearty lifestyle David had been attempting to circumvent.

Lucas forced a smile for the next photo, already sick of today's charade. What he wanted to do was get inside the orphanage and leave the cameras in the dust. And, no doubt about it, there was plenty of *that* covering the dilapidated buildings around them.

But one glance at stone-faced David told him that this was only the beginning of Lucas's new life: the turning over of a fresh public-relations leaf.

Why the hell had he agreed to this again?

Oh, yeah. To be a decent person. And then there was also the small matter of saving TCO.

Slipping into his most comfortable disguise—the charming act—Lucas shot his brother a brief glance, then dived in to answer questions. David, for his part, stood back, hands folded behind him, as cool and smooth as the Italian designer suit he was wearing.

Lucas ignored the confinement of his own suave wardrobe, all but boiling under the many layers of material. It was warm for December down here.

"Ladies and gentlemen…" Strategically he flashed his dimples, making the lone female reporter light up with a blush. "Thanks for being here. And, when I tell you that I won't be divulging dollar amounts, I'm sure you'll understand. Suffice it to say, that we gave a lot to the Angeles Foundation here in Mexico to buy the land, construct the orphanage and supply them with everything they'd need to keep the children in safe comfort. You can be assured that Refugio Salvo will be well taken care of in the future, too. There're also plans for more sites farther south, but that's still on the drawing board."

One of the male journalists raised his hand. "Rumor is that you'll be cliff diving in Acapulco after you visit the orphanage. You gonna take some orphans with you, or what?"

Ah, the Funny Guy. There was one in every crowd and one in every backside.

As Lucas reined in his temper, most of the other reporters lowered their cameras and notebooks, laughing. Even David, whom Lucas believed was made mostly of granite, smiled. But the gesture was more rueful than amused.

The female journalist answered for him. "That's great, Denham. Why don't you give Mr. Chandler a little credit, huh? He's got enough sense to keep the kids away from all that 'daredevil playboy' stuff." She glanced at Lucas hopefully.

Did they think he was some out-of-control idiot? Obviously. Maybe it was good that he'd promised David that he would lay off all his notorious thrill-seeking for a while.

Still, even the female reporter—Jo, that was her name—didn't look as though she truly believed he could behave himself.

"Thank you, Jo," he said, knowing he could use her as an ally. She was from one of TCO's media outlets, a newspaper that consistently tried to balance out the tabloids and the other entertainment sources that covered Lucas's colorful adventures.

At the reporter's modest shrug, Lucas turned to the others. "This is a time to find some serious answers for the troubles these orphaned boys are having. *That's* why I'm here—to check up on the progress and make plans for even more."

It wasn't the entire truth. He was also trying to show off the "new and improved" Lucas Chandler. TCO required it and so did—

Lucas tensed. *Don't think about the old man,* he told himself. *You're doing this for business and business only.*

Riding a crest of deep-seated frustration, he added, "I'm here to provide aid for these kids who might otherwise end up on the street without any education or vocational skills."

Censured, the reporters subjected Lucas to more pictures, and he tolerated it like the man his family had always expected him to be. The man he really wasn't.

Flash. Pop. Each burst of illumination needled into him.

Finally, a pleased David made his way over, putting a hand near his mouth so the reporters couldn't see what he was privately saying to his brother.

"Good start. Just so you know, they're running late in the orphanage because of a greeting the children have put together for you. They'll be ready in about twenty minutes."

Lucas presented the journalists with his back. "In twenty minutes, I'll need five shots of tequila."

Out of the corner of his eye, he saw some nuns wearing wimples and stark long skirts with white blouses. They disappeared behind a stucco wall of the orphanage.

Disappear, Lucas thought. What he'd give to be able to take a breather behind that wall, too.

David cleared his throat to regain Lucas's attention. When he had it, he fixed his ice-blue eyes on him. Funny how a twenty-eight-year-old genius could put a man who was three years older in his place with just a condescending reminder.

"Don't tell me," Lucas said, "that I should be used to this kind of attention. I can handle the paparazzi, but this is different. This is business."

"Yes, I know it's not your thing, but we agreed."

"Yeah, yeah." Agreement, sha-mee-ment.

"Mr. Chandler?" called an impatient reporter.

Something snapped in Lucas. No more questions, dammit. No more apologies for his recently abandoned lifestyle or justifications for "the playboy's trip to the orphanage."

"You take over," he muttered to David while walking away.

"Luke—"

"Buddy, you're the brains of this outfit, so dazzle the crowd with 'em." Lucas winked, just to convince David—and himself—that he had his position as the "face" of TCO under control, that he was still the pretty boy who fetched publicity while David actually ran the place.

But it was about *good* publicity this time, Lucas thought.

Too much of his PR had been negative. Especially

lately, with all those nonfamily-friendly wild-romance-
in-the-streets-of-Rome scenarios he'd been enjoying
with Cecilia DuPont, this month's starlet. Impulsive
scenarios that shed a red light on TCO.

As he left the media circus and headed toward the
spot where the nuns had disappeared, he heard David
assuming control of the press. Good man. He knew how
much of this crap Lucas could handle before blowing.

Shortly after arriving at the wall, he ducked behind
it, finding a cast-iron gate. In back of that, there was a
flagstone path strewn with vivid pink flowers. A fountain burbled in the near distance. Sure sounded peaceful
to him.

Opening the gate, he slid behind it before he could
be spotted by anyone, then walked over the path toward
the running water.

The fountain was in a side courtyard where red
bricks and iron benches hinted at a mellowness Lucas
had been craving. Like a collapsing wall, he crumbled
onto one of those benches, loosening his tie and rolling
his head around to work the cricks out of his neck.

Now this was more like it. No damned cameras, no
pressure. Just for a second—

A soft giggle hit the fragrant air.

He cocked an eyebrow and glanced around at the
thick foliage surrounding the courtyard.

"Peekaboos," said a child's voice from one of the
bushes.

An orphan? Lucas couldn't help grinning. Hell, as long
as the kid didn't have a lens aimed at him, he could deal.

A devilish titter followed. It reminded Lucas of how

he used to laugh when he was younger. Everything had been a joke to be told, a riddle to be solved, a game to be played. He still sort of subscribed to that theory, even if it got him into trouble more often than not.

Suddenly a woman's voice came from behind the bushes. "Gabriel? *Dónde está?*"

The foliage rattled as Lucas spotted a few strands of black hair spiking out from the leaves.

Two nuns scuttled into the courtyard. They chattered in Spanish, seemingly panicked.

"Gabriel!"

They stopped as they saw Lucas rising to a stand, hands in his pants pockets. He merely grinned and shrugged, hating to give the kid's position away.

One exasperated nun addressed him in English. "A guest? You are to come in the front door, sir! Not the back."

Thrilled that she hadn't recognized him, Lucas eased her a grin. "Sorry."

The nun raised a finger to say more, then stopped, reconsidered and sent him her own sheepish smile. "It is okay, sir."

It worked every time, Lucas thought. The Dimples.

Meanwhile, the other nun—a woman with chubby cheeks and a lively gaze—had caught sight of the little boy's hair. She parted the bushes, only to jump back when a golden-skinned child with wide brown eyes exploded out of the leaves, squealing. His hair splayed away from his head, wild and free, just as playfully ornery as Lucas suspected the rest of him was.

Much to the nuns' horror, Gabriel climbed into the

fountain and proceeded to splash around, sending waves of water at them while they tried to approach. The boy's defense worked wonderfully, because it seemed that the nuns thought they would melt if they got water on their clothing.

Finally he took pity on the ladies. They were, after all, of good quality, even if they didn't appreciate the fine art of child's play.

Approaching Gabriel from the back, Lucas scooped him up, putting a stop to all the shenanigans. Water dripped from the child's clothes, but Lucas didn't mind. His suit would dry.

"Hey, little guy," he said, "time to stop being a squirrel."

The child looked up at him, and Lucas blinked back. In those dark eyes he saw the same troublemaking, misunderstood expression that stared back at him from the mirror each morning, the glint of rebellion in a confused gaze.

Another female voice rang through the air. "Gabriel?"

"*Now* she comes," the first nun said, checking her skirt for water damage.

The chubby-cheeked nun merely caught her breath and flapped a hand in front of her face.

Gabriel squirmed, but Lucas wasn't dumb. He kept a hold of him, spinning him around to stand on one of the benches.

The boy held up his hands and laughed. "*Mucho gusto!*" He had mile-long eyelashes, chubby, round, smudged cheeks and a secondhand shirt splashed with water and old dirt.

A tweak of sympathy—that's what it was—forced Lucas to reach out and ruffle the kid's hair. Cute bugger.

"Gabriel," said the more exasperated nun, "please speak your English. And you are soaking and dirty. How will you be ready for the show?"

The boy stubbornly shook his head, turning to Lucas. "No show," he said, repeating the nun's word.

English. Suddenly Lucas remembered David's preparatory briefing: part of the orphanage's educational program included ESOL—English for Speakers of Other Languages.

A sound investment of the company's money, David had said, because it would allow bilingual children more opportunity and make TCO heroic.

Lucas liked the sound of that. It was a solid deal, even if a boy as young as Gabriel might not have learned that much since Refugio Salvo had only been running for about nine months.

His thoughts were interrupted by the arrival of that third woman. She was out of breath, her head bare, black hair curled in disarray down to her shoulders. Her light brown skin was flushed, her dark gold eyes wide.

She dressed like a nun but...no wimple. Maybe she was one of those novices or whatever they called them.

As they locked gazes, she held a hand to her chest, as if surprised by something.

Lucas's blood zinged and swerved through his veins. Instinctively, he took things up a notch and offered what the papers called "the smile to end all smiles," the ultimate way to charm any woman who caught his fancy.

Even a wannabe nun? he wondered. Say it ain't so.

Her stark clothing couldn't conceal the lush curves of her body. Around her wrist a charm-laden bracelet gleamed. Maybe this order wasn't traditional, choosing to forgo dressing in regular habits and accessories.

At any rate, Lucas thought, she's off-limits. *David, Dad and the board of directors would go ballistic if you outdid yourself and big-bad-wolfed a future nun, of all people.*

In welcome, she broke into her own smile, blushing while she allowed her hand to fall to her side as she gathered her composure. The color of her cheeks brought even more animation to her delicate, innocent features: a gently tipped nose, full pink lips and dark angel-wing lashes.

"I see you've met Gabe," she said breathlessly. Her English was very good, with barely the trace of an accent.

The cranky nun interjected. "Lord, help the man now."

"Sister Maria-Rosa…" said the chubby-cheeked one. Then she turned to the newcomer. "We were all playing 'Splash the Authority Figure,' and Gabriel was the winner."

The woman nodded. "It seems you put up a good contest, Sister Elisabeth."

"I always do." The nun looked like some kind of cherub as she rolled her eyes in resignation.

The new woman walked toward Gabriel. The boy was fairly hopping with excitement at her presence.

"You having fun with your friend?" she asked, frowning slightly at the boy's drenched clothing.

Gabriel reached out for a hug. The woman freely gave it to him, not seeming to mind that she would be dampened, too. When she pulled away, Lucas tried to keep his eyes off a wet blouse that was now hinting at the lines of a simple slip underneath.

Future nun, nun, nun, he told himself.

After she helped Gabriel down from the bench, it took her only a few seconds to realize that she was less than fully covered and she awkwardly crossed her arms over her chest. Good thing, too, because Lucas had been dreading having to embarrass her by pointing it out. It'd been tough enough to keep his gaze averted.

"Gabriel," the nun named Sister Maria-Rosa said, "we need to change your clothing now." She sighed. "What are we going to do with you?"

The novice stepped forward, arms still protecting her front. "I can—"

"No, Alicia—" Sister Elisabeth said, gently taking Gabriel by the hand and leading him away "—You already have many responsibilities. Don't worry about Gabriel."

They hadn't addressed her as "Sister," but maybe that was typical for a wannabe.

The nuns nodded at this woman named Alicia—a four-syllable name as opposed to three, Lucas noted— as they left. The little boy turned around and waved back at them.

"*Adiós,* Miss Alicia. Bye-bye, man."

Lucas waved, too, along with four-syllable Alicia.

"He's really a good boy." She looked at him, blushing an even deeper red, then glanced away. "Most of the time."

Lucas didn't know what to say, because if Gabriel was anything like *him,* as he suspected, she was dead wrong.

"But you were handling him very well," she said, raising a brow and grinning.

Damn.

He laughed, just to set himself back to balance again, to send away the thrust of a taboo attraction. "But I don't have to control him twenty-four hours a day."

Her face fell, and he realized that maybe she'd been sizing him up for a possible adoption.

Right. *Him.* That was a funny one.

He shrugged off his coat and offered it to her. With a grateful nod, Alicia took it.

"You don't mind?" she asked. "I don't have an extra change of clothes here and—"

"I don't mind a bit." Well, yeah, actually, the hound in him *did* mind, but Lucas wasn't about to admit to any carnal thoughts around someone bound for the church.

"Thank you." She put it on, bringing an end to the best thing that had happened to Lucas all day.

She tilted her head, gauging him again. Then, as if he'd passed some kind of test, she stuck her hand out.

"I'm Alicia Sanchez and I'll be your group's guide and hostess. We're so pleased to have you at Refugio Salvo, sir."

As he took her hand in his for a greeting, his skin tingled, sizzled.

Attracted to an angel, he thought. It was definitely something new, even for him.

* * *

As the stranger's hand enclosed hers, Alicia's heart kicked at her chest. It'd been doing that since the first instant she'd seen him, and she still hadn't recovered.

Unable to get enough of looking at him, she noted every detail: Fancy tie, shirt, shoes. Well groomed. His jacket smelled good, too, like spicy soap, clean and heady.

He was a lot taller, so much that she was forced to lift her chin to meet his gaze. The color of his eyes startled her—a deep violet, just like the flowers that had grown in the small garden of her *abuelita*'s house back in San Diego. His light brown hair was a little long and ruffled, carefree in the breeze. His body…

Alicia tried not to look, but she couldn't help noticing that he was strong, wide-shouldered and muscled like an athlete.

His grip tightened, and she realized that she'd been staring, her skin goose-bumped and flushed from the inside out.

Quickly, she let go of him, gaze trained on the ground. She shoved the hand that had been holding his, into a jacket pocket, wishing it would stop blazing with heat.

Then, donning a civil expression, she distanced herself from the visitor. Right away she saw the glimmer in his eyes fade a little, as if he were second-guessing something. Then he also took a step backward.

"You're with the billionaire?" she asked, making conversation. Easy enough, with his affable personality.

It was obvious that he was here with Lucas Chandler.

She knew the reporters were out in front now, taking pictures and asking questions before they all came inside Refugio Salvo. But why wasn't he with the rest of the crowd?

He gave her an odd glance, then sent her a high-wattage smile in answer. She just about pooled into herself right then and there. What was happening? Dizziness, flushed skin, a giddiness she couldn't explain…

"I'm looking forward to meeting him," she said, ignoring the blasts of heightened awareness shooting through her.

"Because he's so handsome?" He was teasing.

"Well, that's what the female cooks here say, among other things."

Cocking an eyebrow, he sat on a bench, looking pretty entertained with her comment. "They say that, do they?"

"It's not all that important. I'm not one for TV or tabloid nonsense, anyway. But still…" She blushed, laughing at her all-too-human curiosity. "I am wondering about him."

Especially because he had money. Wait—that sounded wrong. It wasn't that *she* wanted any of it. If Mr. Chandler were in another charitable mood, the orphanage itself would be much better off after another donation.

He was smiling at her again. Dimples. My, my.

They were such nice, deep dimples. Semitrucks could park in them.

Yet…was this man sort of flirting with her? Alicia

wasn't sure, but she should put a stop to it. *Now.* No, really, *now.* She wasn't a nun, but she might as well have been with all the promises she'd made to herself. No sex before marriage—never again. As a volunteer who worked side by side with the women of Our Lady of the Lost Souls at the orphanage, she did her best to be a good role model for the children.

And then there was also a very personal need to remain chaste....

"So the nuns volunteer at the orphanage, too?" he added, interrupting her musings.

Press time. She put on her best PR voice. "Yes, the order teaches academics and sees to the boys' spiritual needs. Regular workers—" like her "—run the facility and oversee the ranch work since each boy, whether he's just old enough to start chores or mature enough to work with the horses, has scheduled responsibilities and training."

"You're all a very caring group of people."

Why did he suddenly seem so...sad? Or did he look guilty? Alicia couldn't be sure.

The splashing of the fountain became the only sound. She rushed to cover the tension, wanting everything to run smoothly.

"It's our pleasure," Alicia said. "We're really happy to love and be around these children."

Months ago, she had volunteered to work here, renting a small house off the profits from the impetuous sale of her deceased grandparents' home. She had pleaded with the orphanage's director to be the one who played

hostess to the billionaire, to be the one who secured a
bundle of money for their needs.

She had to succeed in her goal for the orphanage today, to do whatever she could to be a decent person and
fight for their requirements. *Had* to. The more money
she raised, the more she could forget about the stain on
her soul left by her *abuelo's* dying words.

"So you've met him?" she said to the visitor, testing
the waters. "Lucas Chandler? Do you think he's a kind-
hearted sort of guy?"

The man seemed taken aback, but then he fought a
smile, clearly knowing something Alicia didn't. "Kind-
hearted? I suppose that depends on when you catch
him."

"Oh." Heaviness settled on her shoulders.
"What?"

He leaned forward, encouraging her. From just
his smallest movement, Alicia's pulse kicked, sending
a swirl of scrambled yearning to her chest. But passion
wasn't on her daily schedule. Not when it was so important for her to wait for a respectable marriage; it was
the only way to experience what came between a man
and woman. Marriage made sex pure and right.

She drew the jacket closer around her body. "Truthfully? We were hoping that he's one to part easily with
his money."

Well, that had come out wrong. Maybe she was just
too flustered around this man; Lord knew she was more
articulate than this. She'd meant to say that she hoped he
would be generous to the children, that's all.

And she could tell that she'd surprised him with her

words—her greedy-sounding, awful words. Well done, *muchacha,* well done.

His shoulders had stiffened. She rushed to correct herself but was interrupted.

"Alicia!"

She turned around to find Guillermo Ramos, head of the orphanage, rushing toward her. His crown of salt-and-pepper hair fluttered with the speed of his gait and his slender mustache twitched. Someone was in a snit.

"It's not quite time to start the greeting," she said in English, not wanting to leave their visitor out of the loop. "The children should be ready in a few more minutes."

"No, we are clearly starting now." Guillermo stopped suddenly, hand to heart. "Mr. Chandler, I am Guillermo Ramos. We have talked on the phone."

Alicia glanced at the stranger, who had gotten to his feet, hand outstretched toward Guillermo.

Mr. Chandler?

Good heavens, she was crushing on the billionaire?

"Good to see you, Señor Ramos," he said.

Gulp.

Alicia anxiously fiddled with the charm bracelet she always wore, but Guillermo was all smiles.

"I see Senorita Sanchez has been entertaining you during our delay—which I apologize for profusely," he said.

"Our future Sister Alicia's been doing an exceptional job." The stranger—no, *Lucas Chandler,* the billionaire—turned to her. Now, with the title and money, he seemed…different. More imposing and definitely even more off-limits. "We were just small talking."

Yes, she thought. Due to her ill-chosen words at the end of their conversation, she had obviously gotten smaller and smaller in his estimation.

And…future Sister Alicia? Who did he think *she* was?

"I am glad to hear it," Guillermo said. "But you must know that Senorita Sanchez is not with Our Lady of the Lost Souls." Here he laughed a little. "She is not even a Catholic, but we are fortunate that she is working in our company."

At those words Lucas Chandler's eyes lit up, changing him from an average visitor to everything the other orphanage employees had been whispering about.

Playboy. Ultimate bachelor. Devil in disguise.

"Excellent." He leveled that lethal dimple-edged smile at Alicia once again. "That's some excellent information to know."

She swallowed hard, feeling as if he'd whipped the jacket right off her.

Exposing everything she'd been covering up.

Chapter Two

As the Chandler party returned from the horse stables on their grand tour of Refugio Salvo, Lucas kept his photo-op smile in place. The cameras caught it with their freeze-frames, trapping him in the flashes yet again.

Alicia was at the head of the group, leading them toward the main building, which had been sparsely decorated for the upcoming holidays. There they'd be having an informal meet and greet with the children, who had already welcomed Lucas into their home with a sweet rendition of "What a Friend We Have in Jesus" before Alicia had guided them onward. They'd seen the state-of-the-art school building with its computer room, the mini gymnasium with basketball hoops and hardwood floors, the library stocked with the most recent and popular titles, the cozy quad-occupancy rooms in the cottages.

Money. It could work wonders.

Lucas stuck his fists in his pockets. Idly, he watched the way Alicia moved, her hands clasped behind her back, her hips swaying under the oversized jacket and full, dark skirt as she traveled the dirt path that led from the paddock to the main house. The mild air, scented with hay and sunlight, toyed with her black curls. When one strand of wild hair tickled her cheek, Lucas imagined smoothing it away, tucking it behind an ear and receiving one of her gorgeous smiles in return.

But she hadn't been smiling so much during the tour. Not after she'd told him the real reason she was interested in Lucas Chandler.

We were hoping that he's one to part easily with his money.

Join the club, honey, he thought.

He'd tried to forget how his chest had clenched when she'd said that. But why was he surprised? People liked him for what he could supply, whether it was cash, amusement or a good headline to laugh over in a tabloid.

That was all anyone had ever expected of him, so what was the big deal?

Hell, maybe he just wanted more from a woman who'd at first seemed a little different from the rest.

They arrived at the casa's back door, where one of the older boys—a teen with slashing eyebrows, crooked teeth and long scraggly hair—greeted them.

Camera flashes bathed the teen and Lucas as they shook hands.

Then, as everyone started entering the building, Alicia thanked them, inviting the crowd to eat and mingle.

The journalists wasted no time in attacking the spread: burritos, small tostadas, punch and cookies placed carefully on plates over the paper tablecloths. The boys stood nervously around the poinsettia-strewn room, plastic cups in hand, waiting to play host to their patron.

While going inside, David gave a laconic nod to Lucas. His brother was obviously happy about how today had gone. A flare of satisfaction caught Lucas in its spotlight and he glanced at the ground, hiding his reaction.

After the teen had entered, too, that left Lucas, who had stepped back outside to hold open the door for Alicia, the last of their group.

She hadn't moved from her hostess spot. In fact, Lucas got the feeling that she'd been watching him the whole time. He could tell by the intelligent depth of her gaze, the tilt of her head that maybe she'd gleaned something about him that he wanted to hide. Something that most people never caught on to.

He shut the screen door, arming himself with the Dimples to throw her off the scent of what she might've seen: Lucas's need to get this right, his fear of always being a joke.

"A job well done, Ms. Sanchez," he said lightly.

Narrowing her eyes a little, she held his jaunty stare. "I've been waiting to apologize to you. For the entire tour, I kept wondering what you must think of me."

"Don't sweat it. You thought I was a regular guy, I thought you were going to be a nun...."

"I'm talking about my comments. Please don't let my failure to say what I really meant reflect on the orphanage. We really are grateful for everything you've done. I hope you don't believe we aren't appreciative."

Caught by her honesty—Lucas wasn't really used to it from anyone except David—he leaned against the casa's stucco, the texture scratchy against the fine weave of his shirt.

Before he could answer, a preteen bounded out of one of the cottages, his all-white clothing spotted by colors.

"Ay, Roberto," Alicia said, stopping him. She laughed, glowing, as she straightened the boy's wardrobe. "Did we interrupt your painting?"

Roberto nodded, shooting a glance to Lucas, who shrugged in confederacy with the boy. Being late was cool with him.

"You." Alicia sent Roberto off with a soft, good-natured push. "Just don't let Sister Maria-Rosa see you."

After Roberto tore off, Lucas watched Alicia. She was still smiling in the wake of the boy's presence.

How could he ever doubt this woman's intentions? She seemed so openhearted, so guileless.

But...damn. It wasn't as if Lucas had great insight into character. There was a lot of anecdotal evidence that could prove his lack of judgment.

"Well..." Alicia said, whisking her hands down over her skirt, removing the imaginary wrinkles. "I suppose we should be getting inside."

Disappointment dive-bombed him. "Yeah—" he adjusted his tie "—I suppose we should."

Neither of them moved.

Instead, they waited as the wind hushed around them, the sun sinking closer to the horizon.

Both of them laughed at the same time, a quiet, intimate admission that neither of them felt like going anywhere.

"I've had it with reporters," Lucas said.

"I can tell."

"Not that I don't want to greet more of the kids. Don't get me wrong."

"Of course."

His eyes met hers and, for a moment, everything around them stopped—the wind, the rattle of branches.

For the first time in his life, Lucas didn't know what to say to a woman. But he didn't really want to be talking, anyway. In this pocket of stolen time, he was content just to look at her, to see the gold in her eyes shift with thought and sunlight. How had she come to be here, wearing these frumpy clothes and hanging out with nuns?

As if reading his mind, she looked away and touched her bracelet, almost as if it gave her something to concentrate on.

"So what's your story?" he asked softly. "What made you decide to volunteer for this kind of social work?"

Another strand of hair grazed her cheek, her lips. Lucas couldn't take his eyes off her mouth, the lush promise of it.

"I've found," she finally said, "that I'm good at working with young people."

"I can see you enjoy them."

The startling hue of his eyes seemed to press into her, digging for more information. She fidgeted, her skin too aware, too flushed with thoughts she shouldn't be having.

The forbidden nature of them kicked her brain into high gear; all the impulsive reasons she'd moved from the only home she'd known in the States to come down to the resort area where her parents had met.

"When my grandparents passed away, I realized what I needed to do with my life," she said, voice thick with emotion. She missed them so much, wanted them back so badly. "They raised me in San Diego, but, after they died, staying there didn't appeal to me." She swallowed, tacking on a harmless falsehood just to cover the reminder of why she was really in Mexico. "Not when I realized there was so much to be done down here."

"Your grandparents raised you?"

Alicia flinched, crossed her arms over her chest. "My mom and dad…passed out of my life. A long time ago."

Another adjustment to the truth.

Lucas Chandler stood away from the wall, so devastatingly handsome, so confusing to her. Couldn't her body just ignore those dimples, that inviting gaze?

He ambled closer, a growing hunger in his eyes, his interest in her so obvious that it almost took her breath away.

Closer…mere inches away.

Inhaling his scent, she got dizzy. Her head filled with scenarios, hints of fantasies—

Skittish, she took a casual yet significant step away.

She didn't want to offend him by assuming he was hitting on her, but she was trying to be a careful girl. Especially lately, after her view of life had been so blasted apart by what her grandfather had told her as he lay dying.

From a few feet away, she heard Lucas chuckle. When she chanced a look at him, she saw a vein in his neck pulsing.

Stop him from getting close again. "I think it's time to go inside now. The children are waiting and—"

"We shouldn't be standing out here by ourselves." His grin wasn't amused so much as wry. "I know. One photo with me and there goes your reputation. You're obviously held in some esteem around here, and we don't want to ruin that."

"That's not what I meant."

But he was right. The last thing she needed was this man standing only a few tension-fraught feet away from her, his skin giving off heat and the smell of musk and soap. She'd been around enough to know his type; he could make a girl think that whatever trouble they could get into was right.

Back when she was sixteen, she'd learned this well. Swayed by an older crowd—one her grandparents didn't know about—she'd given in to peer pressure on a summer night with a boy named Felipe.

And she'd liked it. So much. Too much.

Afterward, she'd been dogged by all the moral lessons she'd learned from church and her grandparents;

she'd even wondered what was wrong with her that she'd enjoyed it so much.

Needing some kind of stabilizer, Alicia had made a vow to wait for intimacy again until marriage. Then she could be a good wife, and sex would be respectable with her husband.

She was no angel—not even close. But now, more than ever, she tried her best to be.

There was a cryptic flicker in Lucas's eyes. It seemed to make him change his mind about being so close to her, because he grinned tightly and nodded while he turned away. Like the gentleman she'd seen all day, he held open the door for her to enter the building, his gaze suddenly a million light-years distant.

The sound of happy chatter greeted her, and she was drawn to it—charity, a cleansing of the soul.

But as she passed by Lucas Chandler, she met his gaze, seeing that it was anything but removed. Seeing that it was so filled with a lingering admiration for her that she couldn't help picking up her pace and fleeing.

An hour later, most of the boys had retired to their rooms, signaling the end of the reception. The reporters had been ushered away by David long ago, when the food had become less than a novelty and they'd gotten itchy to take pictures again.

Thank God for their absence, because Lucas was done with business for today. Come to think of it, he'd actually lucked out by avoiding the press in his more private moments. He'd all but lost his head out there with Alicia, almost forgetting what a picture alone with him would've cost her.

He really *hadn't* been thinking clearly, not with the way his body had been reacting to hers, growing more responsive with every step he'd taken toward her. And he was used to getting what he wanted from women too easily not to be miffed by her reluctance.

Still, he'd respected her refusal to turn their alone time into something more, had seen the warmth in her eyes when she'd talked about being with the kids. Lord knew Lucas didn't hang out with many people who had ambitions beyond planning the next party or acquiring the next "big thing" that would make them a Donald Trump overnight. She was refreshing, so why change her into one of his social casualties?

Especially since he was supposed to be turning over that new leaf.

As David summoned the limo and took a phone call outside, the last of the orphans said goodbye to Lucas. Gabriel, the kid who'd been so friendly at the beginning of the day, had seemed oddly shy at the reception, adhering to Alicia—who'd kept her distance from across the room—the entire time.

But, now that the excitement had died down, the dervish Gabriel was back, zipping over to Lucas with the verve of a tightly packed hurricane. He was carrying the jacket Alicia had been wearing.

"Hi," he said, giving the material to Lucas and shuffling from foot to foot.

Alicia followed him over, and Lucas perked up even more.

"He's practicing English on you," she said, acting as if he hadn't invaded her personal bubble earlier.

Maybe her polite cheer would force Lucas to be a good boy around her.

"Well, then…" He hunkered down to eye level with Gabriel. "Hi, back to you, too."

That was the boy's cue. Gabriel started to rattle off a breathless description of all the food he'd eaten today, and Lucas listened attentively. Somewhere in back of him, an enterprising reporter clicked away with a camera. Obviously, at least one of them hadn't gone home, after all.

Photo op. Lucas had stumbled into a nice one, hadn't he?

It wasn't until Gabriel stopped chatting and started watching him with those big dark eyes that Lucas realized his throat was stinging with an emotion he couldn't identify.

What the hell?

Brushing it off, he chalked it up to seeing evidence of the good those English lessons had done.

He abruptly stood, averting his face, ignoring thoughts of all the numb days that had been linking his existence together.

His sight settled on his brother, who was lounging by the doorway, tucking his phone into a suit pocket, face pensive.

Keep it together, he told himself.

By the time Gabriel tugged on Lucas's pants, Lucas had collected himself enough to turn around again.

The child stood there, dark eyes wide and playful. "Come on, come on. Hide-and-seeks."

As the child jumped up and down and tried to lure Lucas out of the casa, a nun from across the room called to the boy.

"It's time for chores, Gabriel. Say goodbye now."

The child frowned, looking as if he didn't comprehend why the fun had to end. Then, without warning, he turned to Alicia and fired a barrage of upset Spanish words that Lucas couldn't translate. His tone was choked, his hands fisted in front of him as he punched the air.

Lucas's chest tightened with concern, with empathy.

But when Alicia patiently reached out to smooth Gabriel's spiky hair, just the way you would your own child, the boy paused, at first shaking his head and denying her. But as she spoke soothing words, Gabriel allowed her to get closer, closer.

Carefully, she drew him to her, continuing to murmur as she hugged him and smoothed a hand up and down his back.

Thank God, within a few seconds, Gabriel had stopped, his head resting on her shoulder, one hand fisting the material of her blouse.

In his eyes Lucas saw those reflections again, the painted shadows of his own heart buried beneath this kid's chest. The need to find someone who could help him, too.

The words slipped out before Lucas could rein them in. "We'll hide-and-seek next time, Gabe, huh?"

He didn't know why he'd said it. Dammit, when would he ever be coming back here?

But then that beautiful smile lit over Alicia's lips, and Lucas knew it wouldn't take much more persuasion.

"See you soon, then, Mr. Chandler," Alicia said, leading Gabriel away and acting calm enough to fool him into thinking that nothing dramatic had just happened with the kid. "Thank you for everything."

Lucas nodded, unable to stop himself from appreciating the way her curvy hips swiveled under that shapeless skirt. She gave real nice form to it, that was for sure.

Before reaching the door, she sent him one last glance, and the power of it just about bowled him over. All she did was smile a little, and his world tipped.

What was it about her? In that smile it seemed as if she could read his mind, slip beneath his skin, whisper inside his head.

I know you're hurting, he imagined the smile saying. *And I understand.*

After they'd left, Lucas finally took a breath.

Realizing that he'd been holding the same one for what seemed like hours.

David had already gone outside by the time Lucas had said his farewells to the orphanage director. The Brain was waiting for his brother near the limo, where they had a view of the property: the main building, the annexes and the cottages, the chapel, the stables.

Arms crossed casually over his chest, David assessed Lucas, eyes a cool blue. With his stoic/casual pose, he looked like a stone-carved cowboy.

"Guess who called?" David said.

Lucas knew the answer before being told. "What's the damage from the old man this time? Or is he announcing another future stepmom who's two years older than I am?"

Well practiced in this line of conversation—one that never went anywhere—David kept his silence. Instead, his body language said it all: the loose limbs that spoke of a man in control of his own destiny, the slight tensing of his jaw that hinted at tension between the brothers. David was a big fan of Lucas's hands-off business approach; he didn't mind running everything while Lucas flashed his smile to the world at large. It was Lucas's majority holding in the corporation's stocks— a contract-tight promise his father had made to his first wife that included always seeing that Lucas, the first-born, would own the company—that got to the Brain.

"Just spill it," Lucas said, tired of waiting.

"He wanted an update. Wanted to know if today's events were enough to impress Tadmere and Company."

Tadmere, the family-oriented American media empire they were trying to acquire. Owning them would revitalize TCO, as well as give them more of an avenue to compete with the print rags and news shows that made a living off stalking Lucas. But the current, very pious owners were balking at turning over "their baby" to a company supposedly led by a man of Lucas's reputation. It was Tadmere—and that scandalous Rome trip—that had prompted this whole personal PR campaign to make him look like a "nice guy."

"And what did you tell him?" he asked nonchalantly, as was his habit. His dad hated when he did that.

And Lucas thrived on it.

"I told him things went perfectly." David glanced at his Rolex and stood away from the limo. "He was happy about that, Luke. Really happy."

A splinter of euphoria stabbed at his chest, making him bleed a little. It happened every time the old man seemed to be coming around, ever since he'd survived the stroke. But, even now, Lucas wasn't about to get too giddy; Ford Chandler would return to prehealth-scare form soon enough. Lucas wasn't about to set himself up for a fall.

"I'm sure you can imagine the happy fireworks going off in me," Lucas said.

David sighed and shook his head. "Come on. You and I both know that, this time, maybe Dad will come around to appreciating you. I, for one, am sick to death of the way things are. And don't deny—" David held up a finger to silence Lucas just as he was about to protest "—that you are, too. Suck it up this time and don't get all rebellious against the guy. He's sticking out an olive branch, these days. Would you just take it?"

"And what would sucking it up entail, David?"

"Just doing more of what you did here today. That's all. Did it hurt so much?"

In the back of his mind, he heard Gabriel speaking English to him, saw all the boys lined up by the food tables and smiling in an effort to impress him.

Him—the notorious Lucas the Lover.

Respect, he thought. How would it feel to finally have it?

But it was impossible to come clean with David at this point. After all, it'd been tough enough to admit to his brother that he'd gone overboard in Rome with Cecilia DuPont and that he needed to cut the shenanigans.

And it'd been awful to admit it to himself, too. Admit that, more than anything, he craved one kind damn word from a father who didn't give out many of them.

In response to that, Lucas had made a career out of being apathetic about the business his dad had raised from the ground up with his heart and soul. TCO was the son Ford Chandler favored best, so why didn't he expect resentment from Lucas?

Resentment. God, it wore him out. He was weary from fighting a father who'd seemed to age fifteen years in the last month. The last time Lucas had seen his dad—hell, it was the day the competing tabloids had come out with that picture of Cecilia dancing in all her naked glory in a fountain, with a champagne-swilling Lucas cheering her on—the man had looked almost done. *Finito,* as Lucas's Italian buddies would've said.

His fed-up father had been in a hospital bed in the penthouse of one of his New York buildings, skin pale from the pains Lucas had brought on. That was the day Lucas had realized that he might not have much time to show his dad he could be an actual success—not the punchline of the family.

"I think we accomplished a lot here," Lucas said. "I wouldn't say no to doing more of it."

There. Underplay it. Don't let them know how much it would mean for you to be taken seriously.

A small grin lifted the corners of David's mouth, and Lucas knew he'd said the right thing.

"Today was just the first step," his brother said. "It'll take more than a few charitable photo ops to erase that bad-boy image you've got going."

The memory of his father's exhausted sighs and the slump of his shoulders—disappointment—edged into Lucas. He could do more, all right.

Still, he didn't want to seem too excited. He couldn't go that far yet. "You have something in mind, Einstein?"

"I've had some ideas today." David's eyes went a bit dreamy, the pose of many genius brainstorms that had kept TCO afloat. "It'd be perfect if you could do something to put the world's—and Tadmere's—doubts to bed for good. What we need to do is make you a pillar of society."

"We've had a good start."

"It goes way beyond the orphanage. I'm talking about a life change. A total tabula rasa so no one remembers Rome or Paris or the many screwed-up headlines you've inspired."

Lucas bristled, mostly because the words were coming from his younger sibling. Mostly because they were true.

"Mammoth task," he muttered.

"Not really."

David was watching something in the distance, so Lucas turned around.

Without warning, his heart pinged around his chest and jumped up to lodge in his throat. Alicia Sanchez was walking hand in hand with a work-clothing-garbed Gabriel to the stables, swinging arms and laughing together.

"You got along with her real well," David said. "And you're good with kids, especially that one."

Slowly Lucas turned back around, shoulders stiff and wary, his blood racing.

David held up both hands. "Trust me on this—if you could even do one thing like convince the public that you're capable of a stable relationship with a decent woman, Tadmere would be ours. It might take some time for them to see what a wonderful monogamous man you've become, but… What can I say? Love changes even the wildest of miscreants. Then maybe, in the future…kids."

"You've got to be kidding." But even as he said it, a part of Lucas—the one that'd felt numb today, the one who'd cried out for a father's respect—didn't completely shut out the idea.

"Think of how the world would look at you," David added. "A reformed rake. People love that."

Monogamy. *Respect.* A relationship. *Respect.*
Respect, respect, respect.

That was the bottom line, the one prize that had eluded Lucas for so long that it seemed like a dream.

"She's beautiful." David again, damn him. "If you could be paired with a 'nice' woman like her…pure gold."

"Yeah, and, if the public found out that this was just a relationship built on the need for good PR, I definitely would come off looking even worse than before."

"Lucas—" David cocked a stoic eyebrow "—think of those Rome pictures with Cecilia. How could you possibly come off as more of a rake? Besides, we've got our publicity machines to cover for us."

Embarrassed anew to have been caught nearly in flagrante delicto by the press, Lucas glanced over his shoulder. Alicia and Gabriel were disappearing behind the buildings.

But that wasn't the only reason he couldn't help looking.

Fantasy merged with reality just for one pulse-stopping moment: Alicia's smooth cheek against his palm, her curly hair between his fingers, her lips against his…

But then the rebuttals rushed in, pounding against his skull. Good girl. Playboy. *Right.*

"Forget it," Lucas said, his tone brooking no argument.

"Listen, celebrities do this kind of thing all the time for good ink when they want to polish themselves up. Can you imagine the great press, even from the sources we don't own?"

And it'd be just a business decision, Lucas added. *Nothing different from any of the other safe relationships—dead ends—that you've had with every woman up until this point.*

As Gabriel scuttled into the open, laughing and trying to break free, Alicia emerged to catch him, hugging him to her. Lucas's stomach somersaulted.

Why? Because… Well, hell, because he was having

doubts that he even had the ability to be a one-woman guy. All the press's snide opinions testified to that.

Right? That's the *only* reason he was feeling so weird.

"It wouldn't hurt to talk to her to test the waters and see how she might react to such an idea, anyway," David's voice said.

The words drifted over Lucas as he kept watching Alicia, the woman who intrigued him and, Gabriel, the child who he suspected was so much like him.

Something like a family, Lucas thought as an unfamiliar emotion filled up the emptiness behind his ribs. What if…

Lucas turned to his brother, ending the discussion with a lethal glare.

Yet that didn't mean he wasn't hearing David's logic over and over in his own mind as they drove back to his five-star resort room, where he ended up pacing the floor most of the night.

Chapter Three

When Guillermo Ramos had contacted Alicia last night, requesting that she entertain Lucas Chandler at the orphanage for one more day, her belly had scrambled with excitement.

She told herself it was more because she was *that* much closer to securing additional money for the orphanage than anything else—like, say, seeing the billionaire again.

Ridiculous, she thought now as they rode horses over the sun-dappled property. He was so far out of her league it wasn't even funny. Plus, she had more important things than flirting to think about.

She snuck a look at him, hoping he wouldn't notice. The same wind-ruffled hair. The same piercing eyes.

He seemed at home, sitting expertly in the saddle in his faded jeans, the reins threaded through his hand. Even though Mr. Chandler had told her that he wanted another gander around the place in order to see how additional donations could be utilized, Alicia found herself tongue-tied right now, unable to "sell" her own ideas about what Refugio Salvo could use.

But she would get over it…just as soon as she could overcome this strange shyness enveloping her. Was it because there were no cameras and the lack of them made everything much quieter, more real? Less like she was putting on a show?

"Look west, Mr. Chandler." She pointed in that direction as they halted their horses. It was an expanse of grassy land, much like what they were on now, but it was cut off by a barbed-wire fence with a sign that said No Trespassing in Spanish.

"Neighbor's property?" he said, easily controlling his roan gelding, Ackbar, who was dancing around.

"Yes, and possibly more land for the foundation to purchase for the ranch."

With one last glance at the land, he paused, then prodded Ackbar into motion again. She caught up to him, and they rode side by side. He seemed deep in thought, so she didn't bother him unnecessarily. She didn't feel the urgency to.

And that was interesting. Even though she hadn't spent more than a few hours with him, there was a certain comfort level in place. It was almost as if she'd known him before and they'd slipped right back into a companionable flow upon his return. Alicia had never experienced anything like it. She was naturally good with people, sure, and that's why Guillermo was using her as a hostess. Yet there was always that invisible shield with strangers—a force you didn't see but a barrier that was definitely there, all the same.

But not with Lucas Chandler. No, there was a different, unspoken something hanging over them…a humid atmosphere she'd been trying to avoid thinking about.

The sounds of chirping birds and moaning saddle leather accompanied them as he took the lead. He seemed confident in where he wanted to go, so Alicia went with it, ready to correct their course if need be.

"Ms. Sanchez," he said, his voice blending with the smooth, grass-laced air, "may I ask you a question? And, if you don't want to answer, that's fine."

She straightened in her saddle, friendly but on alert. "Ask away."

"I'm just wondering, Ms. Sanchez…or Alicia. May I call you that? Alicia?"

"Of course."

He smiled to himself. "I love how everyone says it down here. A-lee-see-a. It's like a song."

She laughed. "Was that your big question?"

"No. I'm just thinking about yesterday, especially when I asked you about how you came to be a volunteer here. The orphanage doesn't pay you? Sorry if that's too personal—"

"Don't worry. It's a part of how Refugio Salvo works, and you'd want to know." Pancho, her mount, nickered, and Alicia absently patted the horse's neck.

"The orphanage can afford salaries for most of the staff—administrators, cooks, groundskeepers. But the sisters consider their work here to be part of their calling, freely given. Just like I do."

"You should be compensated."

She flushed, thinking how a paycheck would definitely help in day-to-day living but would also take away some of the significance of what she was doing. Charity. With a salary, her intentions of giving without taking just didn't seem to count as much.

"Not to seem ungrateful, Mr. Chandler, but—"

"The money's coming whether you take it or not."

Alicia didn't glance at the man next to her, but she didn't have to. She felt his gaze on her. Her skin heated, flaring to confusion.

What was driving him to stick around to see the details of what the ranch needed? Some of the orphanage staff whispered it had to do with all the cameras that had followed him yesterday, but Alicia didn't want to believe that.

Maybe he was trying to make up for something he felt badly about, just as she was. Maybe he was attempting to find purpose, too. But there was one thing she could guarantee: his trip to Refugio Salvo hadn't been designed to allow him to hide from the reality of a life left behind. That was her own cross to bear.

Her father…her mother…her shameful past.

Many times she'd even wondered if the piety she'd been raised with was forcing her to punish herself for how she'd been born. For her parents' carnal crimes that her *abuelo* had told her about. There were so many times she thought that the circumstances of her birth made her less of a person....

Mr. Chandler had grown quiet in his own right as he gauged the land with narrowed eyes. He wore an expression that gave her pause—so serious, his brows drawn together, his lips tight.

"Is something wrong?" she asked.

"I'm just now realizing how much can still be done." A beat passed, then a mirthless grin settled on his mouth. "Now that the camera flashes have worn off, it's a clearer view."

"You've been a true supporter," she repeated. But somehow she doubted it was getting through to him.

"I haven't contributed half as much as you, and that's humbling, Alicia."

For a naked second, she thought she saw a chink in his armor. She'd detected it yesterday, too, but he'd closed it up so fast that it'd almost been subliminal.

"As long as we all do our part," she said, "the children will flourish, Mr. Chandler."

"Lucas. Just call me Lucas."

They resumed their ride, neither of them speaking. He was back to that thinker's pose, and she wondered what exactly was causing all the seriousness. He seemed to catch on to this, because before she could take her next breath, he sent a sudden, devilish grin to her, encouraging his mount to a trot.

What had that sudden change of mood been about?

Not to be outdone, Alicia urged Pancho ahead, laughing, then hunching over her horse's neck and signaling him to a gallop.

Almost immediately he did the same, until they were neck and neck, flying over the grass.

A bubble of amusement expanded in Alicia's chest, then popped. She urged Pancho on and soon she realized that Lucas was veering toward a massive oak tree, its bare branches spread like a canopy, a haven from the mild sun.

When they got closer, she saw that there was a picnic table covered with a red-and-white-checked cloth. Silver bowls and a vase of wildflowers dominated the china.

Flabbergasted, she dismounted, cooling Pancho down. Lucas followed her example, and she couldn't help glancing at the spread with contained anticipation.

Laughing at her obvious impatience, he came and took Pancho's reins, allowing her to sprint to the table to finally get a closer look.

When the horses had been taken care of, Lucas sauntered over, having given them freedom in the grass.

"A picnic?" she said, her heart just now returning to a semblance of normal thud, thud, thuds.

Then again, with every step he took closer, her pulse started picking up again.

"It's snack time." He went over to a silver bowl on top of a smaller table and washed his hands, drying them off with a fluffy towel. "Come and get cleaned up. I thought you might enjoy something flown in from Bella Sofia. It's an Italian restaurant I like in San Diego. You enjoy Italian?"

"Who doesn't?" Still stunned, she moved over to her

own silver bowl, the rim delicately etched with flowered patterns. It was filled with water, a lemon wedge floating on the surface. After washing, she used that fluffy towel, sighing at the softness of it. She'd never felt a towel so lovely.

"I also had the restaurant cater the boys' meals today," Lucas said. "And the workers will get their fill. Got to share a good thing."

Touched by his thoughtfulness, she came to the picnic table, where he helped her onto the bench just as if they were in a fancy restaurant and he was pulling out her chair.

What was really going on? Was he kind of flirting, just like yesterday? Or was this just an expression of appreciation for showing him around today? Or maybe he was hoping she'd brag about his kindness to reporters after he'd left?

All these questions she had. Couldn't he just make a nice gesture without any cameras around and that was that?

She decided that he was treating her out of the goodness of his heart. Just seeing how much he'd enjoyed and been genuinely taken with Gabriel and the other children yesterday told her that his gestures came from a decent place.

Integrity, she thought. Even with Lucas's reputation, she wanted to believe that he really did have it. In fact, ever since her *abuelo* had told her the truth about her father and mother—how Alicia was the product of a sleazy one-night stand, how they had both deserted her because neither of them had been responsible enough to even raise a child—she'd searched for it. The possibility of finding some in a person like Lucas Chandler made her want to grab on, allowing it to pull her out from all the layers of mortification she was buried under.

He was taking a bottle of wine out of a basket. "Comte Armand, a wonderful burgundy."

"I don't—"

"Drink?" Shooting her a teasing grin, he tugged another bottle out of the ice bucket, deserting the more expensive wine. "Or there's always sparkling cider. I got it for variety."

Touched, Alicia fingered the flower vase in the middle of the table. "You think of everything."

"All your hard work deserves a treat."

He poured for her, then him, then opened a silver-lined cooler—a heater, really—and presented her with a basket of breads. She took one with cheese melted over the top while he poured oil and vinegar onto a side plate.

The cheese, tinted with garlic and herbs, made her close her eyes in pure pleasure.

Too decadent for her…usually. But why shouldn't she enjoy it while it lasted?

She opened her eyes to find him watching her. If she didn't know any better, she'd say he was taking as much happiness as she was out of her meal. Warmed by his interest, Alicia shivered.

He doled out the salad for her. "Want to know what surprised me yesterday, among other things?"

"I can't even begin to guess."

"That mojo you seem to have going with our friend

Gabe. He got pretty upset at the end of the day, but you seemed to know just how to handle him."

At Gabriel's name, Alicia pepped up. "From the day he came to the orphanage I've worked extra hard to win him over. He's come around, but you should've seen him before."

"Even more hyper?" Lucas hadn't said it unkindly at all. In fact, she suspected he had a tiny soft spot for Gabriel's vivacious spark, just as she did.

"He is active." She tossed her salad with a fork. "He always has been. But, at first he exhibited a mean streak, lashing out at the other children and the workers, throwing tantrums. He feels more comfortable now that he knows there are constant people in his life, thank goodness. And that's exactly what he needed—security. We don't know much about him except that he'd been abandoned by his parents so his trust is shaky."

A muscle flexed in his jaw, and she didn't have to be a mind reader to know that he was disturbed by the boy's background.

Welcome to life, she thought.

"You know," she added, "yesterday was a good day for him, but he still has his moments. We've had a part-time counselor who's seen him, so that helps, but in the long run he'll need a special family to give him a lot of attention and love."

A shot of panic seized her at the thought of him ever leaving. She'd become attached to the child and she knew it wasn't smart, but it'd just happened. He was charming and ultralovable; that was a part of his mercurial personality, though. He was a challenge her heart couldn't resist, because every time he needed reassurance or extra affection, she felt the responsibility to give it.

"I think," Lucas said, "we all need special families."

When he caught her understanding glance, he polished off his salad, not looking at her.

He seemed on the brink of saying something else, so she kept her tongue. A few seconds later, he laid down his fork, appearing so serious that she stopped eating.

"Have you ever thought—maybe one day when you're ready, I mean—of adopting? That's if you even want a family…"

He watched her intently.

"Yes." She hadn't even hesitated. If she could make sure a child like Gabriel grew up with people who adored him—people like her—she'd do it. Trouble was, everyone at Refugio Salvo thought the boy would be a tougher child to adopt out than most. He might always be passed over for the quieter ones and never even have the chance for a normal life out of the orphanage.

"I'd give anything to have a family again," she added.

"Your grandparents and parents…you miss them a lot. That's real obvious."

A pang of loss hit her square in the chest. He had no idea how much she wanted a group of people to surround her with love.

She blurted out her next heartfelt words before she even realized she'd said them. "Truthfully, all I want is a family. I even have dreams of children, especially the ones who are already born and need parents."

"That makes sense. I can see you and Gabriel together."

She had to fight a lump in her throat before she could answer. "Me, too. I can imagine that very clearly. But first, before any children, there's a husband...."

Silence emphasized the moan of wind through the branches as she concentrated on her food. Admitting her dreams out loud had made them all the more distant. For her, a family would also include a partner, because she believed in raising children the traditional two-parent way.

Too bad she couldn't adopt a man who would love her and bring back her dignity, too.

Avoiding any further revelations, she glanced at Lucas, who was considering her with a scrutiny that dug into her.

"And how about *you?*" she asked, returning the conversation to lightness. "Would Lucas Chandler, the big tycoon, ever consider adopting?"

At her question, he became even more intense, leaning on the table, his posture deceptively casual. "Only under the right circumstances."

Why did that sound as if he could mean so much more?

And why, Alicia asked herself with a growing mixture of trepidation and excitement, was she hoping he was back to flirting with her again?

Alicia took another bite of her salad instead of responding, but Lucas waited her out, using the opportunity to absorb her. She was wearing another prim, neat white blouse with short sleeves and crisp jeans to ride in.

The charms on her silver bracelet sang with her every move.

Anxiety throttled him again and he shifted on the bench. He still hadn't come to any conclusions about David's plan, but Lucas couldn't help feeling out Alicia, anyway. Why not? His desire to gain stature was probably going to force him into some kind of other PR relationship, anyway—he might as well admit it. He wanted the respect badly…so badly he could taste it.

So he filed away the information about her really, really wanting a family. She was a good woman who would make a good mother. Extra PR points for that—

He cut off the thought, disgusted with himself for even musing about it.

When Alicia finished her salad, Lucas brought out the next course, fettuccine slathered with a creamy marinara and topped with honey ricotta. Heaven.

She must've thought so, too, because the first bite caused her to do a little wiggly dance in her seat. Damn, it was cute.

"Know something?" he said. "I'm pretty surprised you're not giving me the hard sell about adopting one of the boys now, like a spokeswoman usually would. I get the feeling you'd normally never let this chance go with anyone else who'd visit the property."

"It shouldn't be a pressured decision, Mr…Lucas." She smiled. "If adopting was in your heart, then you won't need to be talked into making it happen."

Ouch. But he recovered because he had to. "I think you just know when to let something lie."

She took a sip of her sparkling cider, then slowly put

it down. "My grandparents taught me how to do that. They were full of good advice and lessons to learn from."

Lucas thought about his own family. He'd learned by example from them, too, except it was to do the *opposite* of whatever his dad did.

"We weren't very well off," she added, "but my grandparents scraped up enough money to give me a great home and an education. I realized from them what was important in life—the basics. And they showed me it was necessary to be thankful for every one of them."

"College." He was genuinely interested to hear more about her. "Where did you go?"

"Oh, just a community school. And it turned out that it wasn't for me. So I decided to work as a receptionist and contribute to the household, just as I did when I worked waitressing jobs in high school until I knew what I wanted. But eventually my *abuelo* died."

A shadow seemed to pass over her face as she returned to eating.

She hadn't explained anything, really, had she?

"And how did *you* become the philanthropist you are today?" she asked, clearly changing the subject.

"Oh, you know…" He twirled some noodles onto his fork. "The usual rich-kid tales. The best schools, the best of everything. My mom divorced me and my dad when I was real young. She decided life as a socialite was too empty and she took off for parts unknown to take advantage of her anthropology degree, doing lots of fieldwork, from what I understand."

"You don't talk to her?"

"Occasionally." When Lucas took a bite, the food was suddenly tasteless. "She attempts to make contact from each of her research locations but, more often than not, she's in a village with no modern technology and bad cell-phone reception."

"So you don't know her very well." Alicia's soft gaze was sympathetic.

"Right. But that's okay. I've had a lot of stepmoms to take her place. Four, by my last count."

"*Four?* Are you close to any of them?"

"Nope. I did get a half brother out of the deal, though. Luckily, he's the only other child my dad bothered to have. Unleashing two cynical Chandler boys into society is enough."

"Cynical." Alicia laughed. "You?"

She wasn't being sarcastic. Not this straightforward woman who barely knew him. It was a nice change of pace for once.

"I'm afraid so. See, we were raised by a man who values cold, hard success above everything."

Alicia tipped her glass to her mouth, the rim resting against her bottom lip. Lucas found himself leaning closer, envying the glass.

She finally took another sip, ending his reverie.

"So, am I to think that your father soured you on marriage?"

Her words were a punch to the gut.

He swallowed, nerves screaming. "In the past, I thought I might avoid getting hitched. I didn't want to be a serial husband like my dad."

"And that's why you…" She gently swished around

her glass, seeking words, the cider spinning around like a liquid golden web.

"I what?" He wanted to hear her say it.

She smiled sweetly and his heart flipped.

"That's why you date all those women," she said. "At least, that's what they say."

Yeah, all *those* women. The ones who didn't have any interest in families at all. There was a cold comfort in that kind of emptiness. Security. And the more Lucas thought about David's suggestion that he find an "appropriate" woman, the more he came to believe that it wouldn't be much of a change from his previous relationships. He wouldn't *have* to invest emotion. It was a business deal, pure and simple. A situation that would benefit everyone all around. His girlfriend could spend his money any way she wanted to, especially when it came to taking part in charity work that would generate positive ink in the press. And Lucas would be a better man—at least in the eyes of the world.

Putting down her glass, Alicia then propped her elbows on the table and rested her chin on her palms. She was just as beautiful as David had said, even more so. Her physical appearance whipped his overused libido into a frenzy, but that's not what really tore Lucas up about her.

She had soul. A sincerity you had to travel far and wide to find. Something he'd never experienced.

"You want to know the truth?" he asked.

"What?"

Lucas pushed his plate away, appetite for food gone. So many other appetites stoked.

"I wouldn't mind finding a wife at all. Someday."

Her eyes had gotten a little wider, probably because his comment clashed with his reputation.

Before he knew it, he found himself laying the groundwork to take the next step in this plan—not that he was going to go further. Hell, no, he was still thinking about all the pros and cons. He wanted to measure the possibilities, that's all.

Measure *her* to see if she'd be a fit....

"I know you're doing your best to save the world in this small corner of the earth," he said, pulse picking up speed, "but what if you had the chance to make changes on a large scale? How far would you go to get that opportunity?"

She was getting curious about where he was leading. He could tell from her puzzled smile.

"How big of an opportunity are we talking about?" she asked.

"Getting loads of money to spend as you see fit, on any cause that would speak to you."

Her lips parted, her eyes going hazy, her head tilting

He fought himself, feeling his inner playboy stir: The guy who loved fine champagne and loud music. The guy who loved a good, dirty, heart-stopping off-road race in expensive mechanical toys.

The guy who'd surprisingly been struck with respect for this woman's apparent selflessness.

"I would do just about anything to get that kind of chance," she said, her voice almost a whisper.

Anything, he thought. Would she even sign on for a fake liaison with a billionaire? Somehow he doubted it. A person with such devotion to others would never hop into such a calculating situation and compromise herself like that.

So why was he even pursuing this subject?

The images overtook him again. A woman who would bring grace and charity to his name.

"But," she said in a dismissive tone, "this is just a hypothetical question, so why think too hard about it? I'll never see that sort of opportunity."

Something about the way she concentrated on eating her salad again made Lucas wonder how much she really did long for the chance.

And if she was worth the extra effort it would take to secure himself a perfect partner.

Chapter Four

Chapter Four

Over the next few days Lucas found himself taking every opportunity to be near Alicia, whether it was at the orphanage where he just "spontaneously" showed up for arts-and-crafts hour with the boys or even at mealtime, when he could sit with her and enjoy another conversation.

Even as he still mulled over David's suggestion, he found that he genuinely couldn't get enough of this woman—her sincerity, her genuine interest as they talked about everything from the places he'd traveled to the scrapbooking she liked to do as a hobby. He also found out that she was a history buff and that, if she watched TV at all, it was to tune in to programs about California's evolution or even World War II, which her

grandfather had been a veteran of. That made him remember his own deceased granddad; somewhere along
the line Lucas had heard that he, too, had been a soldier,
but in the Pacific theater, not the European one. It bothered him that he didn't know more.

And then there was Gabe, who, for some reason, always made a beeline for Lucas. Maybe it was because
Lucas tended to sneak those chocolates from his hotel
pillow out of the room and into the kid's waiting hand
while no one was looking. Or maybe it was because Lucas couldn't help laughing with the boy as he rocketed
around the dining area or the playground.

Or...God, maybe Lucas merely liked to sit there and
get lost in the sight of Alicia hugging Gabe just when
it looked as if he really needed it. Maybe that was what
kept Lucas coming back, because he could see how
happy it made the kid.

He could imagine what it would've been like if he'd
only had someone around who'd cared enough to do the
same for him, once upon a time.

During these visits, only two reporters had lingered,
and they were both from TCO-owned papers. Lucas
supposed the rest had left because he wasn't providing
much in the way of encouraging salacious copy that
would sell news. But, at least, he was making headway
with this whole "rebirth of his reputation" deal, and
that's what mattered.

Yet, it did occur to him that he could be making
even more if he could just decide whether or not to
pursue this crazy idea....

An instantly respectable man, he thought as he buttoned himself into a pressed linen shirt that felt like a coffin. Outside his window here at the renowned Playa de Realeza resort, the surf beat against the rocks. Each forceful pound worked at him, pushed him further back into a stifling hole.

There was a knock at his door and, when Lucas moved to open it, he found David.

"Dressed to thrill?" his brother asked, stepping into the room as Lucas closed the door behind him. He was garbed in the usual polished suit. The way it balanced on his frame, as if he'd been born to wear expensive threads, unnerved Lucas. "Or am I wrong about what you've been doing these past few days?"

"I've been doing what I've agreed to—getting good publicity."

"Sure. Right. It's got everything to do with that."

Without invitation, David made himself comfortable on a dark leather couch. Around him, the glass-topped table, original modern art and designer furniture all seemed excessive and totally unnecessary when Lucas thought about what Refugio Salvo needed but didn't have.

"Good PR is what we've been getting, though," David added, referring to the positive stories that had, indeed, hit the papers because of this trip. "But, in case you don't remember, I need to get back to New York tonight for a board meeting tomorrow, so vacation's over. As it is, we've overstayed."

At the notion of leaving, something rebelled inside Lucas, clamping inside his stomach.

Noticing Lucas's hesitation, David sat up, a slow smile spreading over his mouth. "I knew it."

"What're you talking about?"

"You don't want to go anywhere."

Lucas turned away from David, suddenly in search of the tie he hadn't planned on wearing or even a jacket he wouldn't need out in the nice weather—anything to make his brother think he was on the wrong track. "If I needed to be anyplace else, I'd go. But where would that be?"

David shrugged, acknowledging that Lucas had a token office that had been visited by its occupant maybe three times in all these years. And there was no question that Lucas couldn't be traipsing around the globe making headlines again.

So where *did* he belong right now? Where did he have to be if not here?

"Whether you admit it or not," David said, "I know what you're trying to do." He laughed. "So my idea wasn't so ridiculous, after all, huh? What made you change your mind?"

Alicia, laughing at his jokes and spending time with him, making him feel as if she didn't want to be anyplace else but here, either, especially with little Gabe pulling Lucas toward the playground and spouting cute nonsense like, "Come on! Let's go! Monkey boy, monkey boy."

"Who says I've changed my mind?" he ground out.

"Spare me." On his feet now, the CEO started pacing, arms crossed as he shifted into genius mode. "Does she have any inkling?"

"Of course not, because I'm not going to do it."

Bull, said the rusty angel on his shoulder whom he'd

never paid much attention to in the past. *Your nose is gonna hit the wall if you don't stop lying to yourself.*

David obviously agreed with the old conscience, because he ignored Lucas's refusal altogether. "If I were you, Luke, I wouldn't breathe a word of this—what should we call it?—*relationship of convenience* to her. With a little more work, you've got her. I've seen the way she looks at you when you're not aware of it."

A flash of desire lit through Lucas at this proof of Alicia's reluctant attraction. Sure, he'd suspected her interest, but she was so damned stuck on avoiding it that he'd almost talked himself into thinking he was wrong.

As he dwelled on the fantasy of it, a slow thaw ran down his body, just under the skin. It heated him up as he imagined catching her in one of those looks someday.

Still, Lucas kept his head on straight. "It's a long way from secret looks to a commitment."

"I give up." David walked toward the door. "If she's going to be so hard to win over, let's go another way. I can set something up with another decent candidate within the week."

Someone Lucas actually enjoyed being with?

Or, more importantly, someone who made him feel as if he was a decent guy for the first time in his life?

"If I'm going to dive into this situation," Lucas said, "it might as well be with a woman I like."

But his conscience was gnawing at him again, yet in a different way. How could he even think of fooling her into this?

Just concentrate on the longing in her gaze when you

asked her about doing charity work on a more wide-spread basis, his other side argued. *Just remember how happy you could make her with your money.*

Coming back to the moment, Lucas realized that David was still in the room. As a matter of fact, he was even staring at Lucas with a new respect.

"You'd really do this for TCO?" David asked.

Chest tightening with some kind of emotion that could've been either good *or* bad, Lucas reluctantly nodded.

"I was wrong, then," the other man said. "You just might be a man to be reckoned with, after all. Dad's going to be impressed."

The magic words. Ones that almost erased Lucas's misgivings.

But not quite.

"Ready…" Alicia shouted, her voice echoing against the sky as she poised the Wiffle ball to throw it. "And…go!"

She tossed the sphere into the air, where a crowd of overeager little boys raised their hands to clumsily catch it. The light ball sailed over Gabriel's head and, with a squeal, he turned around to Juan, a five-year-old who'd batted it down to the grass and was diving on top of it. Immersed in the fun, Gabriel fell on Juan while the other boys followed suit, piling on top of each other like puppies.

The younger boys were in the middle of playtime while the older children attended class in the school building, taught by nuns who were proficient in their chosen subjects. On the sidelines of this little game, Sister Elisabeth sat in a lawn chair, her long skirt spread around her as she crocheted. Her chubby cheeks glowed while she smiled at the children's exuberance.

"Whoa, there, young fellers," Lucas called out, jogging over to the pile and playfully helping Juan out of the mess of little-kid limbs. "Poor Juan's gotta breathe."

Laughing, Alicia watched as the billionaire set the five-year-old on his feet and mussed his hair. He was having as much fun as the children, distinguished from them only by his height, heft and expensive clothing. Where they were garbed in their modest T-shirts and jeans, he was wearing top-of-the-line pants and a fine button-down shirt.

It didn't seem right, she thought. Lucas Chandler was better suited to a more relaxed wardrobe. Yes, he'd loosened his collar and rolled up his sleeves, but she intuitively knew that this wasn't how he liked to dress. It was in the ruffled cut of his hair, the no-holds-barred joy of his laugh when he allowed himself to cut loose, as he was doing now.

Once again she felt the connection that had tugged at her right from the very start—an invisible line that seemed to draw some kind of understanding between them.

As she ran a hungry gaze over him, she caught herself. *Not before you get married, Alicia. You shouldn't even be thinking about it unless he were to get down on his knees and beg you to be his wife.*

As if that would ever happen.

She shook her head. Billionaires fell for antiflashy

home-and-hearth women like her all the time. She'd be a real asset to his lifestyle, wouldn't she?

"Heads up!" she heard him yell.

The impact of his voice on her body made her jerk to attention. As the ball spun through the sunshine, his tone melted through her like a physical thing, like a caress of heat through her bones.

The ball plopped onto the grass five feet away, inviting all the small boys to run for it.

With an excited "Eek!" Alicia joined in, pretending she was racing for the prize, too.

Gabriel, the most determined of anyone, snatched the sphere and held it to his chest. "Nice ball!" he shouted, laughing.

She applauded him, loving his obvious enjoyment. Gabriel seemed to require more validation than most, and once again, she wondered what kind of parents he'd had, how long it would take for him to get over their desertion.

He was already on his feet, throwing the ball. It was a good effort for a three-year-old, awkward but not without potential.

"Look at that arm," Lucas said, bending to his knees so he could retrieve the Wiffle from the ground. "I see major league in this kid's future."

He looked just as proud as Gabriel did, and Alicia's heart wrapped around the sight. Whether the playboy would admit it or not, he was meant to be a father. Every second around these orphans, especially Gabriel, proved it. There was something in his eyes that she didn't see when he was doing anything else, like posing

for pictures or riding a horse around the property.
Something she wanted to touch and absorb.

As Lucas grinned at the child, something primal
flickered within her—the recognition of a protector.
Her body grew warm, as if a furnace had been stoked
and lit. The heat grew sexual, spreading between her
legs and twisting there like a writhing flame.

And, a little higher up, she felt the slow ache of desire.

Lucas rose to his full height, holding the ball and en-
thusiastically glancing at Alicia. But when he saw how
she was staring at him—probably with clear appreciation written all over her face—his smile faltered and he
grew more serious.

As their gazes connected, a glass world seemed to
shatter between them.

"Throw!" one little boy yelled. "Throw!"

The other children joined in the chorus, pulling Alicia out of her stupor. Blushing at what had passed between her and the billionaire—a moment that had been
repeated over and over with every one of his visits—she
got back into the game, desperate to ignore the lure of
him.

"Throw!" Alicia chanted with the boys, clapping
her hands and becoming the distant hostess yet again.
"Throw, throw…"

For a second, Lucas squeezed the plastic ball as if
to throttle it. Brow knitted, he glanced down at the toy
as if it held some kind of answer to whatever he was
asking himself.

Are you wondering how sad I'll be when you leave?

she mused. *Because now that I've met you, I think I'm going to miss having you around.*

He excited her, made her realize that in many ways she'd been sleepwalking through life—until he'd shown up.

This was not necessarily a positive thing, either, because she didn't want to feel, didn't want to *need* a man who had no use for her in his high-flying life.

Gabriel began to jump up and down in front of Lucas and his frown morphed into a grin. At that moment, Alicia would've sworn that the little boy could talk the man into anything.

As if realizing it, too, he winked at Gabriel, then lightly tossed the ball while shouting, "Up for grabs!"

Alicia got into the action, teasing the crowd by saying, "I'm gonna get it, I've got it, I've—"

Gabriel pounced on the ball again. But now he imitated *Sesame Street*'s Bert doing The Pigeon, victoriously kicking out his leg in a weirdly endearing dance he'd learned during TV time.

What a boy.

Ending his display, Gabriel threw the ball, and Alicia caught it. The kids applauded her, just as she always did for them.

"Thank you." She made a tiny curtsy.

Out of the corner of her eye she saw Lucas run a hand over his mouth to cover a laugh, and a flash of goose bumps covered her skin.

Great, more lust.

She threw the ball, but in her determination to chase

away the sensations, her focus and, thus, her aim were slightly off.

The Wiffle bonked Lucas right in the *cabeza*.

The billionaire merely blinked his eyes in reaction as the ball thudded to the grass. He stared at it on the ground, a vengeful expression spreading over his face.

Oh-oh.

In the meantime, the boys had descended on the ball. Someone threw it again and the game went on.

But Lucas just stood there as he slid his gaze to her.

Her heartbeat began jackhammering.

"Sorry?" she said.

He shook his head slowly. The gesture was so steeped in the promise of something more adult than a Wiffle-ball game that the blood kicked through her veins.

As his gaze narrowed, Alicia's adrenaline took over. *Run,* she thought. *Run for your…what?*

Chastity? Life?

With a burst of giggling panic, she moved back an inch, then yelled, "Sister Elisabeth!" in an attempt to recruit a defender.

When she sent the nun a pleading look, she saw that the lady was giving her a This-is-your-business glance. Then she returned her attention to the boys, who were playing ball very nicely on their own. No help there.

Lucas angled his body toward her. "Was nailing me your way of getting my attention?"

She swallowed, her heart flittering. She offered a sweet smile and a shrug in answer.

"Because," he continued, taking a predatory step closer, "you don't have to work that hard for it."

At his frank comment, she stumbled back another step. But all that did was encourage him. Something flashed in his gaze, and she knew she'd better start running.

From more than just his teasing, too.

With a yelp, she gathered her midshin-length skirt and took off, heading toward a nearby hill and hoping he'd lose interest before she got there. The oxygen was thin and sharp in her lungs and she held back a girlish squeak at the thought of getting caught.

Nearer, nearer, almost there…

She didn't want to look back, even if seeing him was all she'd been craving. No, instead, she pumped her arms, laughing wildly as she crested the hill and began the descent.

But when her skirt tangled with her legs, she lost it, stumbling, reaching out her arms as the grass rushed up toward her.

"Whoa!" It was Lucas's voice, right at her back.

Before she could smack the ground, she felt his thick arm around her waist, flipping her over, her back to his front as he took the brunt of the fall.

They rolled to a stop, panting, the sun shining down on her face.

For a short eternity, she felt every muscle of his chest, his stomach, his legs against her. Something wicked and buried noticed how well they fit together with her rear end nestled against him.

Spooning, she thought, recalling how her high-school friends and her coworkers in San Diego had talked at lunchtime.

Breathless, she closed her eyes, feeling his chest rise and fall against her back, feeling his arm tightening around her.

Her belly flared with forbidden heat again, prickling the areas around it. Wanting him, needing him…

She felt his breath on her hair. His hand rested on her stomach, fingers splayed and infusing her with trembling desire.

One minute, she thought. Couldn't she enjoy this for one minute and then go back to her personal vows of celibacy?

Forgetting herself—oh, that's all she wanted to do— Alicia slowly turned her head, shifting ever so slightly to open her eyes and glance up at him.

His lips were right there, so close, so tempting…

Don't do it.

But she couldn't stop, not when she'd been fantasizing about this for a string of long nights.

With tentative wonder, she brushed her mouth over his.

It was as if a shock of raw static had fizzed through her, ripping her apart at every joint. She buzzed with the feel of him, filled herself with his scent and the scratch of whisker friction against her face.

Relaxed and tense all at the same time, she opened her mouth a little more, their lips fully connecting, warm breath mingling and moist. His arm pressed into her, his fingers digging into her stomach as if to draw her out of the mental shelter she'd hidden herself in.

More, she thought, dizzy and restless.

She wanted so much more.

But the sound of a child's voice in the near distance shook her to reality. Then other voices joined the first as laughter danced on the air.

Horrified, Alicia broke away from Lucas, too afraid to look at him to see what his reaction might be. Her heartbeat rumbled like rocks falling down a mountain. Lord, what had she done?

She didn't have time to answer, because the boys were upon them before she could fully scoot away from the man she'd just thrown herself at.

"Miss Alicia!" they cried, crashing into her and hugging her against them as if she were the Wiffle ball now.

"Hey, hey!" she heard Lucas saying as he was overwhelmed by them, too.

One of the better English speakers, Miguel, said, "Where you go, Miss Alicia?"

At that moment, Juan smothered her with an embrace, so she couldn't answer, thank goodness.

Then she heard Gabriel's voice. "No! Off, off!"

Suddenly Juan was blindsided by Gabriel, and Alicia sucked in a stunned breath. He was in one of his moods; you couldn't predict when they would happen, but obviously Juan's affection had triggered the boy's jealousy.

Gabriel screamed, tears gushing down his face while he held Juan in a clumsy headlock. The older child sent Alicia a helpless glance while pulling at Gabriel's arms. He'd been taught not to hurt the younger children.

"Stop it, Gabriel!"

But before she could physically intervene, Lucas

was there, separating the two. Freed, Juan scuttled away, distancing himself from trouble. That left Gabriel with his fists bunched, his face red as he kicked at the ground.

"Hey, there's no reason for this," Lucas said, tone firm yet gentle.

The boy raised his fists as if to strike out.

"Gabe."

At Lucas's voice, the boy stopped, fighting his tears and watching the man to see what he would do from here.

Alicia held her breath.

When Lucas tentatively rested a hand on Gabriel's head, the child began to cry again, sending the billionaire a heartbreaking look that Alicia translated as a plea to understand his frustration.

In response, Lucas merely stroked the boy's hair, his gaze going soft.

Weren't playboys supposed to run away at this point? she wondered, her throat stinging.

Sister Elisabeth appeared at the top of the hill. "Boys…"

Her voice was quiet, stern, tolerating no defiance. They all came to her within seconds, and she led them away with a backward sympathetic glance at Alicia. She was trusting her to deal with Gabriel, as most of the nuns always did.

Sometimes she wondered how Gabriel would fare if she weren't around to handle him.

As if to validate her concern, the boy turned his tear-streaked face to her.

"I'm still here," she said. "Don't worry, Gabriel."

Then she went to him, gathering him in her arms. Yet he also reached out to Lucas, holding the man's hand as if anchoring himself on both sides.

"Man," the child said between tears.

That must've been Gabriel's way of asking if Lucas would be around for a longer time, too. She glanced up at him, wondering the same thing.

How long will you be here?

At Lucas's troubled gaze, Alicia couldn't even begin to guess the answer. Instead, she started to shiver again.

Just as she did whenever he looked at her.

Chapter Five

An hour later, Alicia was still trying to pretend the kiss hadn't happened.

While she, Lucas and Sister Elisabeth had escorted the children inside for "quiet time," Alicia had done her best to find every distraction available, to busy herself with anything but Lucas and the puzzling emotions he stirred up in her. She'd lavished attention on the boys as they'd all shuffled off to their rooms. Then, when the Sister had mentioned that a two-year-old they called Jaime was a little fussy, Alicia had eagerly volunteered to lull him to sleep while Lucas and Sister Elisabeth took care of the others.

It'd granted her some time alone, an escape that was allowing her to get her head together.

Now she rocked Jaime and sang him a lullaby. The air in the family room, with its silent television, walls of books and neatly stowed games, was laced with peace, as well as the spices used for the chicken mole they would be having for dinner.

A clear head, she thought, watching the boy in her arms as he breathed in serenity. *I can finally think rationally again.*

Alicia didn't know how long she felt that way before sensing Lucas's presence and glancing up to find him.

He stood in the doorway, concentrating on the child in her arms, an odd look on his face.

Her starved libido seized the opportunity to secretly watch him; her body recognized the broad shoulders, the violet-hued eyes from all the dreams she'd tried to stifle at night. Yet, even during this battle to be immune to him, the last notes of her lullaby misted away as her mouth went dry.

When her gaze refocused itself, she discovered that he was visually devouring her, too. She'd been caught.

Time seemed to spin and change shape, confusing the minutes into what seemed like hours. In the taut void, she allowed him to enter her in some inexplicable way, warming her with all their unspoken words.

If I just gave him permission, she thought, *if I moved just an inch or said yes, even silently, he would know how much he tempts me, how much I want him.*

But that was impossible.

She heard her ailing *abuelo*'s final words once again as he lay pale in the hospital bed.

"Before it's too late," he'd said, "I must confess something to you, *mija*."

And, just like that, he'd unburdened himself of all the lies she'd lived under her entire life. Lies that had once covered her with security, like the one she'd been told about how her parents had died in a car accident.

The truth had been more than ugly.

Before she'd been born, her *abuelo* had said, Alicia's untamable father had moved down to Mexico after a terrible family fight. There he'd believed he could live cheaply and freely.

It'd broken their hearts to let him go, yet Alicia's father, Edgar, refused to change and his parents wouldn't tolerate his wild habits. They were at an impasse.

"We didn't know this," *Abuelo* had added, holding her hand weakly, "but Edgar fell on hard times and began to earn money by…" Here, he'd choked to a stop as Alicia sat in her bedside chair, frozen by what she was hearing.

Then he'd mustered some strength, finishing his sentence while watching Alicia with pity. "By servicing wealthy women at the resorts in order to earn his way."

That was when Alicia, strictly raised and sheltered, had floated out of body, listening to what must be a stranger's story. That's what she'd kept telling herself, anyway.

Her *abuelo* had continued relieving his soul, confessing how Edgar had accidentally impregnated an early forties, unmarried one-night stand. As a Catholic, the woman had decided to repent after she'd found out about the baby; she'd refused to terminate the pregnancy but had no problem talking a guilt-ridden, easily influenced Edgar into accepting the child after she'd given birth. Knowing the single, divorced mother wanted nothing to do with Alicia, especially since she'd refused custody of her other children, he'd turned to his parents, feeling too guilty to give his child up for adoption before he could beg his mama and papa to take the baby into their home.

They'd loved Alicia right away, *Abuelo* had said, and promised to help their son raise her. But they had one condition for him: that he change his ways and be a good father.

But it was too much to ask because, after two months, he'd buckled under the responsibility. On the day he ran away, he'd left only two things: his baby, plus a silver charm bracelet as a wish for his daughter to someday remember her papa.

All her life, her grandparents had claimed that her dead father had intended to give the jewelry to Alicia himself at her *Quinceanera,* a fifteenth-birthday celebration. But that had obviously been a lie, too.

Her father had never planned to come back at all.

Rocked by shame at these revelations, she'd buried the shocking truth while tending to her sick *abuelo,* who ultimately succumbed to his pneumonia by nightfall. But something had altered her self-perception. She didn't know who she was, anymore, aside from the fact that she'd been born out of sin.

In the fallout, the only thing she could think to do was mindlessly quit her job, sell the home she couldn't bear to stay in anymore since it reminded her of how she'd gotten there in the first place, then seek answers. Any answers.

Desperation had led her to Rosarito Beach's resorts, where her parents had met, but her journey had been a futile one. Neither her father nor her mother could be accounted for, leaving her with so many questions and fears about who they were and what kind of legacy they'd left her.

In the end, unable to track anyone or anything down, she'd felt lonelier than ever, wishing for her grandparents, for a home. She missed the stability of her old life.

Missed the comforting lies that had kept her emotionally safe for years.

And, yet, it was then she found her true path. While struggling with her turmoil, she'd experimentally attended mass near Rosarito, drawn by the comforting pageantry of the Catholic church and thinking their old rituals might hold some answer she hadn't discovered yet. That's when she'd talked to Sister Elisabeth and found some purpose during their casual chats. She'd clung to the idea of finding solace in charity and redeeming herself through kind deeds.

The encounters had also made her realize that her parents' story was even more reason to uphold the personal chastity vow she'd already made after losing her virginity. It was a balm, a way to make up for the bone-deep disgust at the sinful choices her parents had made. Publicly she could also convince everyone that she really was a decent person, no matter what her parents had been and no matter what she'd done by following in their footsteps with that teenage boy.

She'd grown up in a house of morals and had always been told by her grandparents that she was good. To lose that identity and admit that she was just like her actual parents was unthinkable....

Disturbed by the mere thought of it, Alicia pulled her gaze away from the intense promise of Lucas Chandler, steadying herself until her heart began thudding in regular cadence again. As she held tighter to the boy in her arms, the silver heart charms on her bracelet brushed the child's skin. Like a penance, the jewelry always served to remind her of why she'd left San Diego, clasping her wrist with the weight of what she needed to conquer.

As if thrown off balance, Lucas cleared his throat softly, then moved toward a timeworn couch to take a seat.

The situation felt oddly innocent, with the famous playboy sitting across a room just as if he were paying a harmless call on her, so she didn't run away as she probably should have.

But that made no sense. He had much more to accomplish here than dally with her. Even though there were no cameras around today, she knew he was at Refugio Salvo for business and no other reason.

He cleared his throat again, and she risked a friendly, hopefully neutral, smile at him, testing to see if that would get her back on track. And it did, thank goodness. Saved.

"You look so natural like that," he whispered, nodding at Jaime cuddled against her.

"When the time is right, it'll be even more natural." She laid her cheek against Jaime's head, listening to him breathe against her.

"And when will the right time be?"

His question was so direct that she almost stopped rocking in her chair.

Noticing her obvious discomfort, he whispered, "Sorry. I guess I'm too curious about you."

His gaze lasered into her, and she grasped for control once again. Why was he so interested in this stuff, anyway?

He took a breath, leaned forward in his seat, then braced his arms on his thighs. He seemed so focused that Alicia actually held on to Jaime a little tighter.

"I guess I'm just wondering how long it actually takes to realize it's the right time with someone," he said. "Does it happen after a month? A week?"

Yes, how long *should* it take?

As if in a dream, she saw herself pressed against Lucas Chandler, lifting her face to him as he bent down to fit his lips against hers. She imagined how powerful more of his kisses would be, how persuasive and deep, bringing back all the passion she'd repressed for so many years....

No. Lucas Chandler was the last person she should be trusting in this area.

But he wasn't necessarily talking about sex here, was he? It sounded more as though he was referring to love.

Why? What kind of possible interest could he have in that?

"I guess," she said softly, "I'll know when I know."

Unless she already did know....

Again, she stopped herself. The thought was too

rash—and hadn't that gotten her and her parents into trouble before?

Lucas pushed out a heavy breath, in his thinker's pose again. "Sometimes, I think you just *know,* even right away, what you need in your life. I'm not convinced it takes a lot of dithering around to be sure once you've found it."

The room seemed to be compressing against her. What was he talking about? She couldn't understand....

"Alicia..." He scooted forward a little. "I'm going to be leaving soon, you know—"

It was at that moment she realized that they weren't alone.

Thank goodness they weren't alone.

"Gabriel?" She spied him standing in the entry. Then she switched to Spanish. "What are you doing out of your room?"

His cheeks were flushed, his hair bed-headed. "The man." He turned to the billionaire as if he had Lucas radar and was helpless in its powers.

But, much to her surprise, Lucas seemed to have something pretty similar, too. He was already out of his seat, kneeling in front of the child. "I thought I'd hang around and bother Miss Alicia. What's your excuse?"

At the way he so easily interacted with Gabriel, Alicia ached. It was overwhelming seeing this supposedly fly-by-night man showing such care for the orphan who clearly worshipped him.

In response, Gabriel held up his arms, and, without pause, Lucas scooped him up. As if it were perfectly natural, the boy leaned his head on the man's shoulder and closed his eyes.

Touched, Alicia couldn't stop the images from suffusing her mind: Lucas holding Gabriel like this, in sickness and in health, every day. Lucas raising the orphan as his own child, providing him with all he would ever need, such as enough clothing, food, guidance, a college education.

Then, shockingly, she saw herself entering the fantasy's frame, walking up to Lucas and Gabriel to join the family picture.

Somewhere to belong, she thought.

But reality ripped the image apart. Instead, she realized that she was sitting across the room from the other two, removed and left behind.

"What a team," she said, nodding at them, wishing she could be a part of it.

Even though Lucas didn't say anything, his glance seemed to speak volumes.

Maybe we could be, it said. *Maybe we could be a great team.*

But maybe it was all in her starved imagination.

Lucas and Alicia managed to slip Gabe and Jaime into their beds before either boy woke up again. Yet, as soon as Gabe left Lucas's arms, the tycoon felt a little emptier than when he'd first walked into the orphanage today.

He couldn't pinpoint why. He didn't want to. All he knew was that Alicia *was* attracted to him.

Back in the family room, when he'd first picked up Gabe, Lucas had felt as if something had clicked into place, as if he'd found a part of himself that'd been missing, like a gear that helped a machine work properly. But, with Gabe snuggling up to him like that, it'd been easy to fool himself. And, when the kid had fallen back asleep right away, Lucas had even found it simple to believe that he had some sort of touch with him, just like Alicia.

That he could actually matter in someone's life.

As he'd held the kid, he hadn't needed his brother around to catch Alicia's surreptitious admiration. In a bared moment, he'd seen one of those looks she'd been keeping a secret: a soft longing in her gaze, a slight parting of her lips.

It'd taken all of his strength to keep from going to her and revealing everything.

Just come with me, he'd wanted to say. *We can have a good thing. We can make each other happy, even if it's all business.*

But…couldn't it be more? Especially after that kiss she'd given him earlier? Especially after the touch of her mouth on his had almost drilled him into the ground with an intensity he'd never felt before?

As he shut the door to Gabe's room and joined Alicia in the hallway, he told himself that he was very wrong. That he needed respect more than any kind of affection.

On track again, he reminded himself that this woman needed to be won over with emotion, not promises of luxury.

"I think Gabriel is really asleep this time," Alicia said.

Lucas saw the willingness written in her relaxed

posture, in the way she wasn't stepping away from him to create a polite boundary this time. No, his care with Gabe had changed something about the way she was receiving him now. Hell, after that kiss earlier, she'd barely been able to even look at him.

At the end of his limits, he deliberately reached out, not knowing exactly where he wanted to touch, just knowing he wanted to feel her skin under his fingertips.

But when her eyes widened, he reconsidered, changed tack and smoothed back a curl from her face. Yet he did it with deliberation, wallowing in the contact.

It was as if the air had gone dark, an exploded light that had robbed the room of illumination while providing way too much of it at the same time. A buzz of electric hunger zapped up his fingers, his arm, blasting through the rest of his body and making him realize how damned far he'd go to touch her again.

As she sucked in a breath, he kept his hand where it was, daring her to inch away this time, daring her to deny what she felt for him. He needed her to want him for so many reasons.

But what he especially needed, he told himself stridently, was for her to fall quickly for him.

When she stayed where she was, eyes hazed over with pure, unadulterated desire, Lucas's groin tightened.

Mine, he thought. *I want you to be mine.*

"What're you doing tonight?" he asked, voice graveled.

"I…"

"I want you to come to dinner with me at the resort. They have one of the best restaurants in the country."

"Lucas…" She seemed to sway toward him.

His fingers burrowed deeper into her thick hair.

Don't back away. Please don't.

But then she inhaled, as if coming to her senses. With a swallow, she straightened her spine then tucked back the strand of hair he'd caressed. For good measure, she ran her hands over her skirt as if she needed something else to do.

"I can't meet you for dinner or…anything," she said.

The bottom fell out from under him. She couldn't? He wasn't used to hearing that. But he donned a smile all the same, allowing the Dimples to cover his sharp disappointment.

"I understand."

She laughed civilly, touching her bracelet without seeming to realize she was doing it again. Nervous habit, he supposed.

"You do?" she asked.

"Sure. By now you've probably heard about all my colorful adventures in detail, so you're afraid that more than your reputation will get smashed to smithereens."

"Rumors don't matter. You've done—"

"I know. I've done so much for the orphanage. You still don't know the details about Cecilia DuPont? Or any of the others?"

She shook her head.

God, why was he going there with the gossip? Did he *want* her to start watching him with higher-than-thou judgment? Was he searching for a reason that would explain her rejection? Or maybe he was just ruining this callous plan before it could come to fruition.

"I'll have to show you the photos sometime," he said. "The reporters got a real good one of Cecilia with her dress—"

"Stop, Lucas."

His stomach was coiled so tightly he thought he'd explode. "You don't want to know?"

"I don't have to." She sighed, then gave him a shatteringly genuine look. "I think there's much more to you than those pictures could ever say."

He was still waiting for her to realize how wrong she was and, perhaps, to validate all the disgust he held for himself.

Couldn't she see the truth?

"Just…" Alicia shook her head. "Just believe me when I tell you that any more time with you alone is more than I can handle. There. I said it. And…please don't ask me to explain, because I won't."

She was nervous about something, but… God, she'd kissed him earlier.

Kissed *him*.

And…he had to get this straight. She was rejecting him because of *herself?* Now he really didn't understand. But, all the same, he wanted to respect her wishes. No one had ever made him feel that he could someday be better than what the press said he was and he didn't want to ruin that by forcing the issue and proving all the skeptics right.

So where did that leave him?

In the dust, he thought as Alicia quietly moved away from him, down the hall and out of his range.

Yup, he thought. Alone again and in the dust.

As he went the opposite way, toward an exit, he didn't know what to do next.

But he didn't have to wonder for long, because that's when word of the fire at an orphanage down the coast hit.

And his own problems didn't matter, anymore.

Chapter Six

Alicia would never forget the moment Guillermo Ramos caught her near the kitchen and urgently whispered the news about the fire, because it had been the prelude to the rest of her life.

The administrator had quietly yet efficiently spread the news to all the other employees, throwing Refugio Salvo into a contained frenzy. Taking care not to upset the napping younger children, the adults and older orphans sprang into action, preparing to accept the boys from a devastated orphanage miles away.

A fire had consumed that property and, although there'd been no deaths, there was so much damage that the children had to be parceled out to existing sites, even if the other orphanages didn't have the space or supplies to offer.

After an hour of harried work, Guillermo, with his frizzed salt-and-pepper hair all but standing on end, gathered the adults for a more complete briefing. Alicia noticed that Lucas wasn't among the crowd, but she still kept searching for him, just in case he'd stayed after she'd brushed him off back by Gabriel's room.

He was nowhere to be found.

Her adrenalized body felt the sharp disappointment of his absence, even if her brain was rushing in a hundred other directions. Right after rejecting him, she hadn't been able to shake his reaction: a barely perceptible slump of his shoulders, the forced smile. While she doubted many people would've been able to detect any of that, she could.

And it made her just as sad as he'd seemed.

As a flock of teens began to shuttle juice boxes out of the kitchen and into the main area for the newcomers, Alicia fidgeted. She wished Lucas were here; he would be able to help during this emergency perhaps more than anyone else.

Where was he? Didn't he know that now, more than ever, Refugio Salvo needed him?

That maybe other people might need him, too?

"We are not sure of the numbers yet," Guillermo was saying in Spanish, "but we could be taking in at least twenty boys. The girls from the fire will be directed elsewhere since this is not a coed facility."

"Where will they be sheltered?" Alicia asked.

"Our Lady of the Lost Souls, for the time being.

This means the nuns will be busy minding the girls at the convent, as well as relocating them."

Another volunteer from Rosarito Beach, a wealthy housewife named Sylvia, asked, "How will we handle this overflow without supplies and manpower?"

"There are food and medical items en route as we speak. Also, arrangements are being made for us to receive temporary mobile homes until new buildings can be constructed. We also have more volunteers on the way from the U.S."

They all just stood there gaping at Guillermo's mustache for a moment. How… What…

But then Alicia knew. She just did.

Lucas.

She bit her lip to hold back the gratefulness and adoration she felt for him as, somehow, she took in Guillermo's instructions for what each volunteer would be doing when the newcomers arrived.

Her heart seemed to grow to twice its size, swelling with a warmth she could barely contain. She waited until her boss dismissed everyone before asking to speak with him alone.

The older man impatiently smoothed down his wiry hair.

"This won't take long, sir," she said. "But I'd just like to… Is Lucas Chandler behind all of this?"

"The benefactor wishes to remain anonymous, Alicia."

She recalled the flashes of all those cameras around Lucas, the reporters following at his heels a few days ago. Why would he keep his kindness a secret now? Unless…

Her stomach felt hollow. Unless she was wrong and someone else was actually behind the donations.

But she wanted to think of Lucas as a hero because, in spite of all the gossip, that's what she saw in him; a man who hadn't been forced to tuck Gabriel into bed or to play checkers with the boys when the cameras weren't around.

Guillermo must've sensed her disquietude. And why not? She was probably wearing it like a wilted corsage.

The administrator patted her arm. "Between you and me, Mr. Chandler will be returning soon. As soon as I told him about the fire, he summoned his helicopter to take him to the damaged site so he could offer help. I hear the vehicle was also being used to evacuate the wounded to the nearest hospital on an unofficial basis."

Yes, a hero. There could never have been a doubt.

"Thank you," she said to her boss, already on her way out of the kitchen, powered by a pattering pulse, inspired by the validation of her faith in a man who couldn't seem to believe in himself half as much as she did.

Heart pumping, she helped set out food and supplies in the common area, items that had already been donated from nearby businesses. Then she aided in putting together the makeshift beds that the older boys had volunteered to sleep in until the newcomers could get their own quarters. As they all worked together, Alicia hugged and encouraged everyone, taking strength from the common bond of helping those in need.

It was almost enough to make her forget about how

Lucas was affecting her, how she couldn't forget who he was and, more importantly, who *she* was.

But when a cry of "He's here!" went up from the boys, she was jerked out of her determination to remain cool and removed.

As she hurried to where the children were gathered by the front windows, she heard Guillermo trying to organize everyone. From outside she could hear a faint chopping whir, and her chest seemed to expand with the throbbing of her heart.

The taller boys made room for her, resting their hands on her shoulders as they craned for a view.

"There's Señor Chandler," said Roberto the painter, pointing out the window to a helicopter that was landing in the near distance. It hovered over a hill, blades spinning, then landed.

Then carrying a blanket-wrapped child in his arms, Lucas emerged from over the hill, his light brown hair waving in the wind, his fine shirt and pants clinging to the muscles of his athletic body.

The moment seemed chipped in time to her, a mental snapshot that made her bones turn to liquid.

Six boys wearing tattered clothing and dark facial smudges followed Lucas as he led them toward the orphanage. While he approached, Alicia saw that he was holding a toddler, his thick arms wrapped around the child, one hand cradling the boy's head to his shoulder.

In that moment, she truly gave him her heart.

"Welcome our new brothers!" she heard Guillermo shout.

The boys at the window excitedly broke apart, but Alicia couldn't move.

She was still caught up in watching Lucas, the man who claimed he was nothing more than a walking bad reputation.

As he came closer, he glanced at the window, saw her standing there, then slowed his steps.

It looked as if he was seeing every one of her confused needs and emotions laid out bare on her face. And it looked as if maybe, just maybe, he felt the same way.

Time disappeared as if it didn't even exist, stopping her heartbeat, stopping all motion around her.

How she wished she could be held against him, too. She wanted to go to him, to tell him that all she really did want was to be with him, even if the mere thought was ridiculous.

The boys flung open the door, allowing in the sound of the chopper as it took off again, allowing in the first wide-eyed newcomers.

As the room spun into action, she remembered what was important right now—securing the newcomers. She tore her gaze away from Lucas and rushed to greet the boys. Fighting her trembling limbs, she bent to their height, welcoming them with smiles and reassurance—her specialties.

But the good-hearted older Refugio Salvo orphans wanted to welcome the new boys, too, and they ended up leading them away for snacks and drinks as two staff doctors waited nearby to begin checking the arrivals over.

The back of Alicia's neck tingled.

She looked over her shoulder to find Lucas standing there, the child clinging to him as if he never wanted to let go.

The man's eyes were dark, fraught with the twilight colors of something Alicia couldn't explain as he consumed her with his gaze. Overcome, she stood, facing him, caught in his magnetism, her body quivering.

"You took care of everything," she said, voice ragged with the happiness and terror of seeing him.

Lucas moved toward her, his presence swallowing her.

"I'll always take care of everything," he said. "Always."

The words were still ringing in Lucas's ears as Alicia's eyes widened.

When he'd heard about the fire, he hadn't thought to do anything but call his pilot to warm up the chopper, fly down the coast to the site of the destruction, then offer any help he could. On the way to his transportation, he'd also called David to see if he could work their connections to procure more volunteers and supplies. Then he'd gotten a hold of Guillermo Ramos to provide whatever he needed for Refugio Salvo, whether it was money, food, buildings or all of the above.

When David had mentioned getting some reporters over to the orphanage to cover this "jackpot," Lucas had denied him. This wasn't about PR—in fact, it hadn't even entered his mind until his brother had brought it up.

"And, if I see any cameras around," Lucas had said, "I *will* eat them for dinner."

David knew when his sibling was serious, so he hadn't called the press. At least, not as far as Lucas knew.

Obviously he hadn't analyzed his intentions, at first, but on the chopper ride back, as he'd taken care of the traumatized children, he'd realized just why it was so important to help in secret. He needed to do the right thing and to do it because he *wanted* to, just as Alicia would have.

Maybe, that way, he'd actually deserve this woman who stood in front of him now with her heart in her eyes.

He was so mired in what this tragedy had brought on that being direct with her seemed the only way to communicate. Back at the other orphanage, he'd seen the smoldering foundation of what had once been a home. He'd seen some of the orphans who'd lived there choppered to the hospital with third-degree burns, had seen the staff weeping because they were so grateful that no one had died.

"Life is short and sweet," an old man with burns covering his hands and face had said to Lucas as he'd helped him onto the first chopper out. He'd tried to smile even around his charred skin. "I'm so lucky to still be alive."

Still alive, Lucas thought, hugging the orphan. *So make the most of life while you have it.*

As he and Alicia faced each other, the room bustled around them: orphans getting to know each other, little boys crying from the horror of the fire as others attempted to console them. Lucas had even called in counselors who would arrive tonight, because he meant what he'd said to Alicia.

He could take care of everything. And he would.

Guillermo Ramos came over to take the new orphan from Lucas. As the boy was lifted away, Lucas held out a hand as if it felt too empty without anything to fill it anymore.

But then, as if Alicia knew just what he needed, she enfolded his fingers in hers.

The contact was so profound that Lucas almost lost it. He'd never craved a touch so much—her touch.

He held her hand against his heart. At the contact, it pumped double-time.

As if shocked, Alicia froze, her gaze confused.

Right, Lucas thought. *She told me she can't be alone with me. I remember now.*

Firmly back in reality, the rest of the room came into focus. Gabriel, with his tousled hair, darted out of the hallway and across the floor, from group to group, handing out juice boxes. Lucas's pulse jumped at the sight of the child, an orphan who could've just as easily been caught in that fire and hurt—or even worse—today.

Shockingly, he realized he couldn't stand the thought of not having the boy around. Lucas felt so much more like an actual human being when Gabe was smiling at him, shooting him that gaze that said he thought Lucas was pretty decent.

Alicia noticed the little host, too.

Still touching her hand—could she feel the vibration of his pulse through it?—he squeezed it, connecting with her over their fondness for the boy.

"Gabriel's in his element, isn't he?" she said.

Her voice was rough, as if she were forcing it out of her.

"Alicia…"

Maybe it was the way he'd said her name, because she interrupted.

"I know I'm not supposed to be aware of what you've done today, but…thank you so much. You—" She shook her head. "You've gone above and beyond. Why don't you want anyone to know about it?"

It sounded as if his simple activities had made her admire him even more. He glowed with the confidence she had in him.

"It's nothing anybody else wouldn't do," he said.

"Oh, no," she said, head tilting as she seemed to look into him with a gaze that was just this side of reverent. "Don't tell me you're not buying into your own heroics?"

Looking at her, he could *almost* believe he was that savior.

Not knowing how to react, Lucas watched as Gabe gaily approached one of the lightly burned children who was waiting for medical attention. Then, with the open curiosity only the young could get away with, he inspected the boy's wounds. The disturbing sight of Gabe's smooth, unblemished skin against the other boy's injuries made Lucas fist his hands until his nails dug into his palms.

"Life can be so short," he said softly, realizing what was really important now. Realizing he had it right in his hands.

She'd also turned to glance at Gabe and the other child, but now, biting her lower lip, she turned back to him. He knew she understood just what he'd seen down at the fire site.

She slowly raised her other hand toward him, hesitated. Then something flared in her eyes, golden and open, and she reached the rest of the way toward his face, cupping his jaw.

He shivered at the power of her touch.

She paused, seeming to trip on her words, but then finally released them. "I missed you."

Jarred with surprise, Lucas leaned his cheek into her palm.

In a flash of all-consuming light, he knew what he wanted. His mind swam, blocking common sense, barring anything but a deep need his instincts knew how to feed now, only with the threat of tragedy hovering over his head.

He saw his future in front of him: a gentle, loving woman who believed in him the way Alicia did, a family—a son?—to complete what didn't necessarily have to be an illusion...

Do it, his impulse urged. *With people who believe in you, you can do* anything.

He looked into Alicia's eyes, drowning in them. On this surge of adrenaline and fear, his crazy emotions seemed like tiny epiphanies merging into an inevitable burst of reason.

He'd wanted her from the first second he'd seen her. He'd seen lives explode today. So why wait to grab what he already knew he needed?

"How much?" His words sounded distant, as if spoken by a better man. "How much did you miss me, Alicia?"

She bit her lip, closed her eyes.

He spoke his heart before his brain could catch up. "I want you to come home with me. I want you to—" holy crap, he was really saying it "—always be with me."

At first, the words didn't register. *Always be with me?*

They swirled, mixing with all the scenarios she'd created about home, hearth, Lucas and Gabriel.

What was he saying?

I'm wondering, Lucas had told her earlier today, *how long it actually takes to realize it's the right time with someone.*

Her temples were beating in time to her pulse. "I'm not… I don't…"

He seemed feverish as he led her into the hallway, where they had more privacy. During the short trip there, Alicia stumbled, halfway breathless with disbelief. What was happening?

When they got to a quiet spot, he turned her to face him, hands on her shoulders. His touch seemed to burn through her blouse.

"Alicia, I know how I feel about you. Time's not going to convince me of any more."

And how's that? she wanted to ask just to be sure. But her tongue was still tied.

He rushed on. "I'm going back to the States, but

something happened down here…things, day by day, that have made me realize what I'm missing in my life. And now, seeing how it could all disappear in a bunch of flames…I want you to be with me. Especially since—"

He cupped her face with his hands, his touch warm, the embodiment of all her nighttime dreams.

"Since I want Gabe to be around, too," he said.

Several things hit her: Joy that her favorite orphan— one everybody thought was unadoptable—had found a father. Happiness that Lucas had discovered something he was missing.

And that something was her. Right? Because she still couldn't believe what he was saying. How? Why?

Lucas bent closer in the dim light, eyes wide and wild, as if he were having a fervid dream. "I want us to be a family, Alicia. I want you to *marry* me."

It was as if a fist had reached into her and jerked, stripping out the wires that held her together, making her spark with excitement and fear.

"We barely…" She stopped because she didn't have enough oxygen to continue.

"I realize that. But I also know that you and Gabe belong in my life."

She thought of how she'd nearly imploded after he'd appeared from behind the hill, thought of how she just might feel that way every time he stepped through the door of their home.

A home, she thought, trembling.

"This is all moving so fast," she said, "I can't think—"

"Don't think," he said. "*Feel.* And I know you do feel something for me, Alicia."

Heat engulfed her. He knew. She hadn't been able to hide her affection at all. So why was she still fighting it?

Something unfettered by rules, something instinctive, wondered why she couldn't just take a chance, as she'd done when she moved down here from San Diego. She'd been born with that impulsiveness, even if she'd squashed it under a need to control her life. And he was offering her everything she wanted, so why not seize the day?

Use common sense, she thought. *Your parents dived in, and look what happened.*

And she wasn't them. Not if she could help it.

"Happiness has its price," she said, touching her charm bracelet, her souvenir from a father who'd been impetuous, too.

"And they call me the cynical one?" He laughed, stroking her hair back now. His voice was low, rough with emotion. "Happiness is having a real family you can depend on. Happiness is having enough money at your disposal to give to any charity that you want."

The picnic under the oak tree rushed back to her. He'd asked what she would do for the opportunity to have an endless amount of money for good works, for more redemption.

Had he been thinking of marrying her then? Had this been love at first sight for him, just as…

She flinched. Just as it had been for her, too?

It was true. Undeniably, shockingly true.

"Don't say no," he said, stroking his thumbs over her cheeks. "I can't—I *won't* leave without you. I can't imagine going back and never seeing you again or leaving you here while we trade e-mails or phone calls or… Alicia, just come with me."

She wouldn't choose to go a day without him or Gabriel, either. But… "I won't live in sin with you, Lucas."

He stiffened. "I would never ask you to do that. I know this is so fast, but leaving you and Gabe behind is out of the question. I'd rather marry you down here and take you back home as my wife. Come with me. You know this is right for all of us."

Her mind was whirling, her chest heavy with the weight of what he was laying on her.

She didn't even argue about the option of him staying in Mexico. When it came right down to it, this wasn't her real home, so she would never ask it of him. She wanted to settle in a place full of love, and that would be wherever Gabriel and this man were. Location wasn't the issue. Besides, staying down here while Gabriel was with Lucas…

She couldn't imagine it.

He must've taken her hesitation as a lead-up to rejection, because his shoulders seemed to slump a little. But then he seemed to stiffen, as if taking a big breath and jumping in.

"You make me a better man," he said quietly, voice racked with emotion so naked that she couldn't fully absorb it. "Can't you see that?"

In the dim hallway, she could barely discern his features. But she didn't have to. His tone told her everything: that he didn't believe in himself, that maybe she was the only one who'd ever given him the chance to make something more out of a tarnished reputation. It broke her heart.

"I swear to you," he said, "No more playboy or daredevil. Just a good husband and his angel."

Angel.

She slipped her hands up his arms, wanting so badly to comfort him, wanting so badly to be that angel. His muscles clenched under her palms, and she recalled how these arms had held that orphan as he'd come out of the helicopter, how he could hold her and Gabriel like that, too.

There were so many reasons to say yes.

But one thought kept echoing through her: respect. Marriage could erase the sins of her father and prove that she, his daughter, could live a decent personal life. It would show him, wherever he was, that she was nothing like him at all.

So tempting—the answer she'd been looking for. The solution to everything.

"Miss Alicia?" called a little voice. As it echoed down the hallway, she saw the shadow of a boy appear. "Miss Alicia!"

Gabriel, the son of her heart. The boy she could provide for if she only said yes.

He began running toward her. Toward *them*.

The people who could be his family.

In spite of her doubts about this going too fast, in spite of the shock she knew her spiritual advisors would display, an answer to Lucas's proposal rushed out of her, riding on pure emotion.

"Yes," she said. "Yes, I'll marry you."

Dios. Too risky, too—

He took her hands and, with an ecstatic laugh, pulled her to him. His chest was wide and firm, his arms like a haven that would keep trouble away.

Gabriel crashed into both of them.

As it was always meant to be, Lucas swooped the child into their embrace, and Alicia felt the borders of her heart fully connect, as if completed.

But panicked common sense screamed at her to take it back, to be real about this....

"Guess what, Gabe?" Lucas said, pointing to him and then her. "You're going to have a mommy and daddy!"

His meaning must've been obvious to the love-starved child, because he hopped up and down, squealing and hugging both of them.

As Lucas drew her into a hug with him and Gabriel, she thought that, yes, sure, certainly this *was* the best choice she could ever make.

Even if she still couldn't believe she'd made it.

Chapter Seven

T wo days later, Lucas lingered just outside the main building of Refugio Salvo where the orphans had first welcomed him with refreshments and shy smiles.

But today, under a clouded screen of sunshine, there were canapés instead of burritos and petits fours instead of cookies. There was a piñata hanging from a nearby tree, amusing a crowd of children, including the ringleader, Gabe. There was a mariachi band in traditional dress, singing in full-throated abandon while strumming their guitars. Guests wore flowered dresses and suits while sipping champagne and posing for pictures for carefully selected photographers.

His wedding reception.

He'd actually said the vows, Lucas thought, still a

little shell-shocked. Now that the flood of emotion from the fire had worn off, he was able to think clearly about what he'd done: married Alicia. The big *M*.

Funny thing was, he'd believed every word he'd been persuading her with at the time—he'd felt that she really was his salvation and he'd warmed to the spontaneous notion of having Gabriel with them. He had a soft spot for the child and he could do so much for him—much more than even an orphanage.

But then reality had hit. He'd realized that, for Alicia, this was true affection. He knew it from the cloud-nine smile she'd been wearing for the past couple of days, ever since he'd proposed so dramatically. So many times, Lucas had wanted to correct what he'd done, to be a big man about this and make up for the heat of a whirlwind moment....

But then David had heard the news and congratulated him. He'd even looked at Lucas with something like awe, marveling that he'd taken the relationship suggestion and gone "the extra mile" for TCO with a wife and a child, to boot. Lucas hadn't explained that everything had come from a moment of madness. No—he'd *liked* the admiration from his normally superior brother, even as he'd felt dirty and dishonest. And, when his father had called to congratulate him in a tone that didn't include derision or impatience? Game over.

Now, more than ever, Lucas knew Alicia would help him wash the dirt off. Their marriage really could be the cure-all for his misspent life.

In the aftermath, Lucas and David had pulled many a string to cover the details as soon as possible, since

the Brain believed practical Alicia might come to her
senses and cancel the whole thing soon. While Lucas
had bristled at that because it was niggling at him, too,
he also knew Alicia would never go back on her word.
Not after they'd promised Gabe in the heat of the moment that he was going to have a family.

The last thing Alicia would ever do, was break her
favorite orphan's heart. Lucas would swear to that.

But, he thought, there was something else that was
keeping her true to the proposal.

All I want is a family, she'd told him during their oak-
tree picnic. And then there was the way she watched
him, the way she'd kissed him.

God, what had he done?

They'd been so damned busy with this whirlwind
event, as well as getting the new orphans settled, that
they'd barely spent time together. Not the way they
used to, anyway, with privacy, intimacy, even that shy
kiss. Lucas missed it and he even found himself wondering when he'd feel her lips against his again, when
he'd get to be a true husband to her.

But…one thing at a time. He was determined to
leave the physical decisions to Alicia. His conscience
wouldn't allow any other option, even if his sex drive
was raging at him.

While she'd spent the past couple of days putting
together her wedding finery, David had brought an
army of TCO assistants to arrange everything from
the flowers decorating the area, to the cake, to securing a couple of handpicked reporters to cover the
event. One assistant had even flown in the Chandler

family's regular preacher for these last-minute out-door nuptials.

"We'll have an even bigger wedding any way you want it after we get settled in New York," he'd promised Alicia. "A church, the works. I just want you to be with me and Gabe as soon as possible, that's all." And he'd meant it.

She'd agreed to the rushed ceremony, not wanting to "live in sin," as she'd told him before. But he detected hesitation, nonetheless.

He knew that her nun friends had been emphatically arguing for her not to go through with this so soon, but she seemed to be forging on against their advice. Maybe it was because every time he saw her, he stressed the urgency of their union, how quickly he wanted them to become a family and make Gabe happy. He'd even en-listed TCO's best attorneys to facilitate the marriage and fast-track the adoption, utilizing every powerful, politically connected Chandler family resource to allow Lucas and Alicia to bring their new son home to the States.

And his hard-sell marriage idea—his ticket to respect—was working, even if reluctance did pass over her features before he kissed her forehead in a chaste farewell and blasted off to make more arrangements.

Lucas's searching gaze found her as she emerged from the building, surrounded by other female orphan-age volunteers. Even though they were all celebrating with his new wife, Lucas could tell they were worried about this quickie marriage, too. Every look they shot him said, *You'd better take good care of her.*

But he would. In fact, all he wanted to do was make her happy.

As she walked down the stairs, a headpiece sans veil collecting her upswept curls, he couldn't take his eyes off her. His chest ached at the sight of his bride holding a bouquet of white flowers and wearing a simple, roomy, long white dress. It had scalloped sleeves and embroidery, lending the outfit an old-fashioned dignity. Her ample curves filled it out, and his belly heated with pure…lust.

Yup, lust. That had to be all there was to it. He didn't love her. He couldn't. And, somehow, he'd gotten around ever having to say it to her.

Was that because she just assumed how he must feel? How? He couldn't have shown her any evidence of it because it didn't exist in him. Chandler men didn't know how to love.

Images and feelings from the night of the fire came barging back: The sublime joy at seeing her again; the loving look on her face as she'd been watching his approach through the window; the crazy thought that life is short and she would make his own existence so much better….

Alicia had stopped halfway down the stairs, the other women continuing to walk past her until they filtered into the rest of the crowd.

"Listen, listen!" yelled Guillermo Ramos as he climbed up the steps to stand next to Alicia.

He'd assumed the responsibilities of host, even though Lucas suspected the man wasn't fully convinced this wedding was the best choice for his diligent worker, either. But, like Lucas, the man clearly wanted her to be happy, so he was throwing himself into helping.

Alicia seemed to have that effect on everyone.

Guillermo had the crowd's attention, except for the boys smacking the piñata with a stick in the background. He'd spoken in English for the sake of the groom's U.S. guests.

Truthfully, Lucas didn't know most of them because David had invited family friends he'd flown out on one of their jets for appearances' sake. Lucas's "friends"— party buddies, mainly—hadn't been invited.

Sad thing was, Lucas didn't really miss them much.

"Thank you again for attending this celebration at Refugio Salvo," Guillermo added.

Amidst the applause, the administrator swept his hand around to indicate the grounds, and Lucas smiled to himself, knowing how proud Guillermo was of his hard work.

"We have experienced hard times here," he continued, "but they have been met with determination and great love from our staff and our patron, Lucas Chandler."

Here, Guillermo turned to Lucas, raising his glass of punch in salute.

In his corner, Lucas merely nodded, needled by the secrets he was keeping from his bride, the woman who was also raising her glass to him, her face flushed, her eyes full of adoration.

It was as if she were inside Lucas, nestling into a place that had always been meant for her.

He broke eye contact, knowing he didn't deserve the affection. He didn't deserve her, period.

"Join me," Guillermo added, turning his attention back to the guests, "in recognizing our patron and our beautiful Alicia, who has volunteered so much of her time to us and, she has reassured me, will continue to do so from afar."

"Hear! Hear!" someone in the crowd said as they all toasted, then drank. Soon afterward, one of the female orphanage volunteers started lobbying for Alicia to throw her bouquet. Lucas wondered how he was going to get through this.

He pictured the end of the party, when he could finally relax as the sun set. He'd fall into bed, close his eyes and…

An unexpected element entered that picture: Alicia snuggling against him, Gabe burrowing against his other side.

The thought should've panicked him, but he actually felt calmer. He held the picture in his head, allowing it to lead him to the end of the day.

"Woolgathering?" said a soft voice beside him.

Lucas shook off the fantasy, finding Sister Elisabeth standing there. Always freshly scrubbed, her skin smooth, her cheeks rounded, she was one of only two nuns who'd attended.

She'd requested to talk with him for the past couple of days and he'd deftly managed to avoid any chats. So he was thrown off balance by her approach.

A cheer went up as Alicia threw her bouquet. The flowers bounced off a guest's head and into another nun's arms. Sister Maria-Rosa, the strict one. She seemed stunned to be holding the bouquet as the crowd laughed and applauded.

"I've got a lot to think about," he said to Sister Elisabeth, making an attempt at joviality.

"I suppose you do and I'm here to show support for that very notion." The nun glanced over at the piñata, where Gabe was hopping up and down, waiting for his turn to take a whack at the colorful mock donkey. "You're taking on quite a bit, Mr. Chandler. Both you *and* Alicia."

He watched Gabe, too, thankful that the boy was in a good mood today. "I'll hire a top-notch child psychologist to help him along and to give us advice on parenting."

"Gabriel will need more than that. Are you ready to sacrifice all the time you enjoyed as a bachelor?"

Sacrifice. Even though Lucas had no delusions about how much effort Gabe would take, he'd never thought of the investment as a sacrifice. It was easy to admit that he dug the boy, faults and all. Every kid needed someone to feel that way about them or else…

Lucas thought of himself, of all the nannies who'd raised him and David, of all the social events he'd been forced to go to where he'd been a miniature man in a tiny suit who was expected to be seen and not heard. And, when he hadn't obeyed, there'd been hell to pay.

He wouldn't let that happen to Gabe. He'd never try to kill the love of life in him, just help to make it manageable—just as he was learning, himself, right?

The sound of silverware against glass caught Lucas's attention, and he glanced over to David, who'd emerged from skulking about the fringes and was calling for a kiss between the bride and groom. Lucas's hackles went up because he knew his brother wasn't just drunk and celebrating.

He'd taken over, reminding Lucas of what today was really about. Reminding Lucas, as well, that their father had supposedly been too ill to make it to the wedding....

"Kiss! Kiss!" yelled the guests.

Sister Elisabeth touched his arm. "God be with you. Even if this is abrupt, I've got a lot of faith in you."

Although her honesty nagged him, he nodded, glancing at the steps, at Alicia, who was blushing amidst the clamor.

Blushing. He'd never known someone to do it so much. It touched a nerve, made him feel protective of a woman who still had such innocence.

Too bad he was the biggest threat to that.

He came to stand a step below his bride, bringing them almost face-to-face. Her lips were so red, so desirable. Her perfume slid its way into his pores, his every sense, invading him with the warmth of musky flowers.

He realized that, with all the pomp and circumstance, they hadn't been this close since their chaste wedding kiss.

"Hi," she said.

"Hi." The word seemed to scrape his throat.

This near, guilt was flaying him bare, revealing the tender streak that had felt so natural the other night, when he'd proposed.

"Kiss, kiss..."

"Guess we've got to quiet them down," he said softly.

She pressed her lips together, her gaze on his own mouth. It was as if she was already tasting him.

"Kiss, kiss..."

Even though he moved toward her slowly, the staccato of his heartbeat made time rush. Just before he made contact, he heard her inhale, and his veins seized up, stopping his pulse.

As he pressed his lips to hers, he went deaf. Nothing existed but being with her, the kiss enclosing them in something like a snow globe, a fantasy world where nothing else could get in. Heaviness flowed through him, over him, washing him clean and infusing him with passion.

Without thinking, he slid his hand behind her head, then down to the graceful slant of her neck. He felt the bump of her nape, the softness of her skin.

In the comforting darkness of his desire for her, he saw a flash. Felt it rip through him. Then another. And another.

Cameras, he thought hazily. *We're not alone.*

Reluctantly, he broke away, his opened eyes greeted by those flashes. His hearing came back, ushering in loud cheers.

He pretended to recover by slipping an arm around Alicia's shoulders and waving to the crowd, even though he was shaken to the core.

A kiss, he thought. One damn kiss.

"Smile, angel," he heard himself saying. "Just keep smiling."

She stiffened, and he sympathized, holding her closer in the glare of the camera flashes.

Protecting her from himself.

* * *

At the airstrip, dust blew through the air as Alicia entered the tiny terminal, where she headed for the restroom. She'd told Lucas and Gabriel that she needed to freshen up before the reporters arrived to take pictures of their departure, but that had been a lie.

Angel, she thought again, the word running through her like an alarm that had been set to go off every hour since the reception. *He keeps calling me angel.*

She busted into the bathroom and rested her clutch purse on the metal shelf under the mirror. Bracing her hands on the sink, she peered into the looking glass, wondering just who was reflected back at her.

A crazy woman she barely knew, curls still held at bay by a pearl barrette, cheeks colored with two spots of red, body encased in a formfitting off-white two-piece suit that one of the TCO stylists had purchased for her.

The *new* her?

Alicia turned on the water and splashed her face. No, she was still the *old* her, the one who'd made this wild decision that was scrambling her life. The girl who'd spent the last couple of days busying herself with wedding preparations because she'd been racked with guilt about telling Lucas who he was really marrying.

No angel. That was for sure.

Water dripped from her face and into the sink. Every sound was a poke to her conscience. What would Lucas do if he knew she was tainted? He wouldn't love her, that's what would happen. He could have any woman in the world, yet he'd chosen her because she made him a better man.

She almost laughed at that. If only he knew. She doubted it would take him two days to realize he belonged with one of his own set.

But she was going to make it up to him in spades because no one could take away the family she'd finally found. She'd be the perfect wife and live up to every expectation he had for her. Deep down, she believed he wanted the same thing—love. True love.

Yes, she'd definitely made the right choice. Definitely. Especially where Gabriel was concerned.

At the thought of the boy they were adopting, Alicia perked up, thinking that the end justified the means. As soon as Lucas's money rushed the adoption papers through, Gabriel would get his stable home and so much more. She would give him all the love in the world while doing the same for Lucas, another person whom she suspected needed someone to just understand him.

Renewed for the time being, she dried her face, grabbed her purse, then strode out of the restroom, determined to confront her new responsibilities.

But when she heard a voice echoing through the small, quiet lobby, she paused. Lucas?

With a burst of beatitude, she went toward the sound, turning the corner with a smile so wide it almost hurt.

Her heart fell when she saw it was only David, his back to her, a cell raised to his head and a finger plugging his other ear. She wasn't sure what to think of Lucas's hard-as-nails brother, yet, and now wasn't the time for her to sort it out.

Before she could leave, she caught a piece of his conversation.

"Oh, yeah, she's our secret weapon with the demographic here. She's gold."

Demographic? What was he talking about—an employee with TCO?

Feeling like a little girl who'd walked in on an adult discussion, Alicia took a couple of steps away, backtracking around the corner. But when David started turning around while unplugging his other ear, she automatically pretended she was just rounding the wall.

"Oh..." she said, feigning surprise.

Cool as silk, David nodded to her. "Uh-huh, uh-huh," he said to the person on the other end of the line.

She held up a hand in acknowledgment of him, then pointed to the tarmac, where the family jet was waiting. The other, larger one, which had transported some wedding guests, would depart tomorrow morning.

Without sticking around for David's response, she headed for the exit.

TCO business. David had been talking about one of his female employees, that's all. The corporation had interests all over the world, including Mexico...

At least, that's what she kept telling herself.

She spotted Lucas by the stairs that led up to the jet's entrance and her brain futzed, like a television station that had closed down for the night.

He was bending to Gabriel, brushing some dust or grime or whatever the heck the child had gotten into off his leg. But Lucas wasn't chiding him as one of the nuns would have. He was smiling, as if he enjoyed the chore. As if understanding that children got dirty and that was okay.

She approached them. "Damage control?"

When he looked up, her pulse jammed, veins tangling.

"Gabe here decided to pretend he was an ant crawling on the ground with food on his back." Lucas stood, tweaking the boy's cheek as Gabriel glowed up at him. "I already tried to get the grit out of his pants."

With one look, she saw that Lucas hadn't been too successful.

"Gabriel, you're so funny," she said, joking with him in a pattern they'd established long ago.

"*You're* funny, Miss Alicia."

All of them laughed and, for the first time in hours, she felt good. They'd returned to how everything had been before the chaos of the last few days. It was almost as if they were playing Wiffle ball again or as if they were laying Gabriel down for a nap.

A warm glow settled in her, nesting.

"Ready to go to your new home?" Lucas asked the boy, hefting him up into his arms.

Gabriel's mouth pursed as he went, "Hmm." Alicia knew that meant he was confused and he didn't know how to express himself, so she translated into both Spanish and child speak.

The boy lit up. "Yes. Ready."

"Yes, *Papa*," Alicia said, without thinking. Then the weight of reality settled on her. "You can call him Papa now."

Lucas seemed to realize what was going on at the same time. He looked winded, stunned. But then he burst into that stellar grin, holding Gabriel to his chest.

"That's right," he said, voice hoarse with emotion. "I'm your papa."

As Gabriel threw his arms around Lucas's neck, tears began to sting Alicia's eyes.

"And husband," Lucas whispered.

She sobbed once, then went to her new family, holding them against her. Somewhere in the distance, she heard a car drive up, but nothing else mattered right now, and she had no idea how long it was until she heard the slam of doors. Closer, David's voice sounded behind them.

"Showtime," said Lucas's brother. "The big love story that's going to plaster tomorrow's papers. 'Lucas Chandler's whirlwind marriage.' Every woman in the world is going to swoon."

The echo of David's demographic conversation haunted the back of her mind, but she was too busy feeling robbed to care much. Of course they were going to use this wedding as publicity; what concerned her more was the fact that, at David's interruption, her family had separated from one another.

Alicia wanted to ask why pictures were necessary when they already had so many from the wedding. Then she remembered who she was now.

Lucas Chandler's wife.

So she got ready to pose, trying to persuade herself that she really belonged in the same frame with this man.

That he hadn't made a mistake, at all.

* * *

They'd been in the air for two hours when Gabe finally succumbed to the pressure of his new situation.

The boy had been playing with a puzzle at a table. It was one among many amusements Lucas had ordered for the flight, knowing that Gabe's normally scheduled nap would take up only so much time and the child might want to expend some creative energy. David was in a private room at the rear of the plane, knee-deep in business, of course.

As for Alicia, he'd made sure she was comfortably settled on a sofa with a pillow and blanket. She'd hinted at needing her own nap after the excitement of takeoff had subsided and, as a new husband, he probably should've joined her, holding her hand, cuddling with her. But he was too on edge to even be in the same area, too racked with the reality of what he'd done.

To make matters worse, he'd caught the questions in her gaze as he'd left to be with Gabe.

Why aren't you spending time with me?

Little did she know that this was only the beginning. Now that the press had been given their big romance story and the official marriage documents had been signed, he could move on to his other plans to save TCO.

Reluctant to glance back at her—to *go* back to her—Lucas headed for his new son. It was so much easier to be close to Gabe than Alicia. So much simpler to admit that he was allowed to have affection for the boy.

Who the hell knew why?

At the sight of Gabe sticking his tongue out of his mouth as he concentrated on the puzzle, Lucas breathed a sigh of relief. Gabe wouldn't demand anything from him.

But, fifteen minutes later, when the boy used his arm to wipe the pieces off the table in a fit of sudden anger, Lucas rethought his assessment of the situation.

Gabe fisted his hands over the mess, spouting a gush of Spanish words that couldn't have been pretty.

"What is it?" Lucas tried a Spanish phrase Alicia had taught him; he'd already tried to learn some in order to communicate better with the boy. *"Que pasa?"*

Another tangle of Spanish words came out of the kid's mouth, and somewhere in there, Lucas thought he heard him say, "Too hard!"

"Then, you can play something else," Lucas said, thinking he had this all locked up.

But the exhaustion of the day, coupled with all these changes, must've been doing a number on Gabe. He gave a loud cry, then smacked the table.

"Hey, now." Lucas held on to the boy's hands so he wouldn't hurt himself.

The boy was having none of it. He pulled away, eyes getting red and teary as he shook his head, sobbed and jerked away from Lucas.

Okay, he wasn't sure how to handle this, after all. Was it cool to try to hug him? Yeah, right, as if that was going to make everything all better. Should he let Gabe cry himself out? He couldn't imagine just sitting here while the boy carried on.

But he was going to be his *father* now. Shouldn't he know what to do, even instinctively?

What have you gotten yourself into?

Thankfully Alicia had come over and taken a seat next to Gabe. Her bracelet rattled as she reached out to the boy.

"Gabriel." Then she said something in Spanish.

Anxious, Lucas leaned on the table, wanting to help, but feeling that he had nothing to contribute.

But then she glanced up at him, gaze soft, drawing him back into the inner circle linked together by man, woman and child.

Home, he thought. *She's more home than I've ever had.* Why did that scare him so much?

"Your new papa is here, too," she said, clearly translating for Lucas while repeating the words in Spanish for Gabe. "And your papa's not going anywhere, either. He's bringing us to a new home. We're a family now and we won't ever leave you. Do you understand that?"

Gabe's breath stuttered as he sucked it in, his eyes wide and dark, hopeful.

But as much as Alicia's words were comforting the boy, they were bothering Lucas. He found that he wanted so badly to believe in them, wanted to know that Alicia wouldn't leave if she found out what he'd done to her and Gabe, wanted to always be assured that someone in his life stayed, unlike his mother or his serial-husband father or his move-on-to-the-next-adventure friends.

Gabe reached up his arms for Alicia, snuggling into her embrace, and she rocked him while singing a sweet tune.

Note by note, Lucas allowed the song to get to him, too, even if he thought it might be best to keep it out.

Chapter Eight

The first thing Alicia and Lucas did upon arriving at their penthouse was to tuck a completely exhausted Gabriel into bed. The mattress was the biggest she'd ever seen, the guest room already custom outfitted with pictures of *Sesame Street* characters and toys. She was stunned by the efficiency of Lucas's assistants, as well as the decadence of the penthouse…or, rather, her new home.

Yes, she kept telling herself, home, where she belonged.

Afterward, even as Alicia was still reeling from the shock that she, *she* was going to live in this luxurious place, the head of the household, Ms. Boland, gave her a tour. Lucas excused himself to make a phone call while the proper brunette—a young woman who wore a gray business suit, black-rimmed glasses and bunned hair—had gotten her new mistress acclimated. Then, after the personal assistant left, Alicia found herself very alone.

Alienated. Curious. Discombobulated.

Bundled in a new coat that would've been too much for an early winter Mexico night, she wandered onto the terrace, which overlooked Central Park. The cold New York air hit her and she shivered—but not just because of the weather.

I'm really a wife.

Not that Alicia felt like it. During the jet ride, Lucas had almost been a stranger, even if he'd made certain that she was comfortable in every way.

But there'd been something odd about him, as if he were detached. He'd spent most of his time with Gabriel—which she'd loved to watch—or talking in the private back room with David.

It'd seemed as if the only person he hadn't had time for was her—his bride.

Why? Earlier today, during their wedding, he'd kissed Alicia until her legs had just about turned to wet sand. There'd been no lack of passion then, nor a few days ago, when he'd proposed to her so emotionally.

Shouldn't the man who'd talked her into such a headlong move want to cuddle on the plane trip home? Or had he been saving his affection for a time when they could be alone?

She trembled again, her blood tumbling, increasing in temperature. The wedding night. A shared bed.

On a primal level, she was ready for him. But she

was also nervous, fearful of losing control and becoming what she most feared: Her parents. A bad woman who could never wash herself of the past.

She heard a door slide open and shut behind her. Lucas. Every footstep that closed the distance between them thumped inside her chest like cannon shots.

"Beautiful view," he said, voice low. It rode the hairs over her sensitized skin, a verbal stroke, slow and easy.

"The park is much bigger than I ever imagined."

"I'm not talking about the park."

Boom-da-boom went her heart.

He sauntered over, resting his hands on the brick wall while casting her a look brimming with appreciation. She felt like a goddess again, just as she had in her wedding dress, just as she had when he'd proposed to her and she'd believed with every reckless pound of her blood that she'd fallen for him at first sight, and that he'd fallen for her, too.

"You're cold." He shucked off his large tailored wool coat, then slipped it over her own.

The silk lining made his coat slip off her shoulders, the ill fit reminding her that she didn't belong in fine clothing like this at all.

Still, she grabbed at the wool, pulling it around her.

"To the rescue with your coat yet again," she said, referring to their initial meeting, when he'd acted like a gentleman and covered her wet blouse.

"Whatever you need, it's yours." He gestured toward the penthouse. "So what do you think?"

She laughed, indicating that there was no way she couldn't like it. A triplex penthouse at the top of The

Boudin, a historic hotel that attracted the rich and famous. On the limo ride from the airport, Lucas had told her that they would have not only a personal staff but access to a concierge, twenty-four-hour housekeeping, a valet and room service. Its highlights included two terraces, four bedrooms, a library, a media room, a gourmet kitchen, a greenhouse and a small wine cellar. The first floor was an old ballroom, and there were wood-burning fireplaces, crystal chandeliers and marble baths sprinkled amidst the retro-chic furnishings.

He must've translated her pause as polite displeasure. "Maybe it's not to your tastes, huh? I had this decorated when I moved in a few years ago and haven't spent much time here since, with all the traveling I used to do. If you want to redecorate, we'll make arrangements."

His offer pleased her, but she couldn't imagine what in the world she would change about a place like this. "Maybe later. Or..." Absently, she touched the waist-high brick wall, then chanced a peek over it to the long fall below.

A thought shook her. Gabriel. What if he wandered out here?

"Is there a way to childproof the terrace?"

He seemed taken aback, even a little horrified that he hadn't realized this first. "Right. You're right. I'll have it taken care of tomorrow. And we'll get someone to help with Gabe during the day so you can...well, do whatever it is you want to do while I'm at work."

"You're already going back to the office?" They'd agreed to put off a honeymoon until Gabriel knew for certain that this was his real home, but couldn't Lucas at least stick around?

He seemed to catch on to what she was thinking. "Soon we'll take a big trip, okay? You, me and even Gabe."

Her libido didn't love the thought of having to share her husband right now, but every other part of her was content with always keeping Gabriel near. It's what she'd wanted for so long. And, in the end, she would have her husband during the night, anyway, after little boys went off to bed.

She shrugged even farther into the coat. "I wish you could take one day off, Lucas. Just at the beginning…"

His posture straightened. "I really have to go, at least for a few hours. Then…" He paused as if working something out. Seconds later, he offered his killer grin, back to being Mr. Charm. "Then the rest of tomorrow will be yours. I promise. In the meantime, though, there's a stylist who'll be bringing more clothing for your and Gabe's approval in the morning."

He was watching Alicia as if to sift out her reaction to an activity most women loved—shopping. But it'd never been all that enticing to her.

"She'll have some designs for formal wear, too," he added. "You just tell her what you like and it's yours."

"Formal wear?"

"Get ready to be introduced to New York, angel. First up, we're officially meeting my dad at a restaurant the day after tomorrow, when he feels better. He'll meet Gabe this weekend, in a more comfortable setting for the boy, like here at home. Then there's a holiday ball we'll be attending at the end of the week." Lucas seemed to catch her flinch. "TCO is putting it on for the American Red Cross. It's an annual event. Don't worry though, stylists will take care of you. And you won't have to do a thing but what comes naturally—charm every guest there."

Even with her shy sense of reluctance, she couldn't say no to charity.

Would this be her life from now on? Parties, public engagements, marble floors that looked too fancy to actually walk on?

Dear Lord, she wasn't a socialite. She wasn't a billionaire's typical choice in women....

"Alicia," he said, touching her arm.

Her body came alive. But she couldn't allow him to see how afraid she was, how out of her element.

"I'm in an adjustment period." Her smile was shaky.

"Me, too." He took her hand, engulfing her much smaller one in warmth and reassurance. "You're freaked out and I understand that. But I'm convinced that you were meant to be my wife, even if we've got a long way to go before we know each other fully. Having you and Gabe here with me makes this penthouse someplace I want to come home to, Alicia. It was lacking the both of you and I never realized it. If I'd traveled back here without you..."

His grip tightened around her fingers as he glanced away. The slight, chilled wind huffed at his hair, and a muscle in his jaw twitched.

Was he choked up or something? Alicia squeezed his

hand, profoundly touched. So happy to have found what God had always meant for her: People to take care of and treasure. A situation she could depend on to keep her and Gabriel emotionally secure. A predictable pattern to her days that would cover the doubts about her true self.

He cleared his throat but still didn't meet her gaze. "It's been a long day, but there's so much to talk about, like ways to help Gabe adjust, too."

"I know things have gone quickly, but we've got a lot of time to work everything out now."

Married. The reality of that sent a twinge of carnal hunger over her skin.

Instinctively, she slid her thumb over his, an invitation she couldn't take back.

He seemed to stop breathing.

What did she want him to do? Kiss her? Slip his hands under her clothing and coax every piece off her body?

She wanted it and…and she didn't. Lord, help her, she was terrified of what she might find within herself.

When he covered her hand with both of his, she knew he'd seen her panic. Great. Some hot-tamale wife she'd be, he was probably thinking.

"You look nervous enough to jump out of your skin."

He seemed bothered by this, as if something was eating at him from the inside out.

"It's fine, but I… I'm…"

"You're not ready." He laughed, the sound edged with frustration. "I suspected as much—not that I blame you. You're more innocent than ninety-nine percent of the adult population, and I'll bet you're used to more of a courtship than the one you got."

She didn't say anything, even though she should've told him right then and there that she wasn't as pure as he believed.

At her silence, he shook his head. "Listen, how about we…" He laughed again. "I don't know…start our official honeymoon phase in…well, a week?"

A week? Was he serious? He wasn't going to demand anything until then?

He was being more understanding than she could've ever guessed, and, in a way, that unbalanced her. But what had she expected him to be? A caveman or a gentleman?

She thought, once again, of the man who'd offered her his coat to cover up her wet blouse and she knew the answer without a doubt.

She scanned his features, they were shaded with something like guilt. Did he feel badly because she was having such a hard time here?

"You'd put everything off until I…"

"Get used to me? Yeah." He let go of her hands and shrugged, a slant of shadow otherwise hiding his reaction. "This just gives me one more week to romance you, right? A week we need to get everything to normal before we can relax."

"These past few days have been very emotional…" Oh, *Dios,* she felt as if a boulder had been lifted off her chest. She still couldn't believe he was being so giving, but thank goodness for it.

"No apologies. I've told you before and I meant it—I'm just happy you agreed to be with me."

Then, noticing that she was shivering in earnest now, he said, "Come on," leading her back inside, up the spiral staircase and to the third floor, where their grand bedroom awaited. Beyond the thick wooden doors, a canopy hovered over the massive bed, low lights dusking the paneled walls and setting the scene for a wedding-night ritual that would be delayed—just until she got her bearings, she told herself. Just until then.

Softly, he kissed her on top of her head, his breath labored and warm against her hair.

Her pulse felt like taps of rain on a metal roof that was held up by brittle poles. She almost wished there would be a next move, nearly dreading it, wanting it so badly that it was pulling her apart.

When he stepped away from her and headed toward the door, the world seemed to collapse.

"Sleep well," he said softly, his eyes dark and unreadable. He paused, as if wanting to say something else, as if wanting to stay. But he didn't.

No, he just closed the door behind him, leaving her standing there for what seemed like an hour.

It'd been so easy for him to leave her alone on their honeymoon night and, even though it made her feel so much better, it also made things so much worse.

Didn't he want her enough to persuade her?

In the darkness, her confusion raged. One week, she thought.

One week until she had to face her demons all over again.

* * *

"You're going to give me the rundown on our biggest clients then?" Lucas asked an assistant the next day in TCO headquarters.

Barnaby, a slim man with a hundred-dollar haircut and an ambitious suit, made a weary face. During the last hour, Lucas had found that the guy wasn't much for holding back snarky comments, but, somehow, that was kind of refreshing.

Just like Alicia.

"I don't get promotions by filing my nails all day, Mr. Chandler," the assistant answered.

Made sense, Lucas thought. And *he* wouldn't move ahead, either, by staying away from the office. So he'd embarked upon phrase three of the Respect Plan— getting to know his own company.

As both of them strolled through the fortieth-floor lobby, a redheaded receptionist, one he couldn't recall ever meeting whether it was at a social event or just in passing, winked at him. The old Lucas would've veered right over to her, pursuing her sly invitation. But the new one?

He thought of his wife's golden eyes, her beautiful smile.

The new Lucas didn't have any interest in flirting with anyone else. Strange, what a life mission could do to a guy.

And that's all this was, Lucas thought. A crusade to change the playboy reputation, even if it meant running five miles in the gym every day to let off some sexual steam.

He was going to do right by Alicia, even if everything had started off wrong.

As they entered Lucas's pristine office, he lackadaisically clumped his briefcase on the empty desk near a state-of-the-art computer system that he would be using to research TCO.

Barnaby would be key to this. David told him that he'd assigned the assistant to be Lucas's number-one man because, in spite of his pointed wit, he'd proven himself to be a lion tamer who knew how to whip a situation into shape. But Lucas suspected that David had foisted Barnaby on him out of pure competitive spirit, just to make sure his entry into the world of business wasn't too smooth.

Nonetheless, he was here to make sure that his dad noticed his life turnaround, right along with the rest of the planet. It hadn't been easy to ignore the derogatory looks he'd received upon entering the office, the doubtful raised brows and snickers that had trailed him. But he was here. He was ready.

"Anything else you need from me right now?" Barnaby asked.

Yeah, Lucas thought. *Tell my wife that I'm sorry about leaving her alone on our wedding night.*

But he knew delaying the sex was wise—she clearly wasn't ready, yet, and he couldn't stomach the idea of forcing the issue.

So, instead of waking up as a satisfied groom, he'd tumbled out of his own bed, then gone to TCO at the crack of dawn. But, before leaving, he'd made a point to stop by Gabe's room to touch his cheek, to make sure he was really there.

"I think you've got enough to do, for now," Lucas told Barnaby, going to the other side of his desk to sit. As he sank into the leather, he caught a glimpse of the gray, bustling city outside the window, the scatter of a thousand other businesspeople who were doing what they had to do for survival.

"Yes, Mr. Chandler. I'll be chained to my desk until midnight if you need anything else."

"Barnaby."

At the sternness of Lucas's tone, the assistant raised an eyebrow, as if unaccustomed to being challenged. Or maybe everybody at TCO, including Barnaby, didn't think enough of the wild Chandler child to offer any respect.

"We can work one of two ways," Lucas said evenly. "You can launch verbal missiles and I can bat them down every minute of the day until I get tired of it and fire you. Or you can treat me like your boss and eventually end up as a right-hand man to the guy who already owns the majority of this company." He leaned forward, his hands clasped on the desk. "Decide now."

For a long second, Barnaby didn't move. But then, with a small grin, he said, "Welcome to your first day of work, Mr. Chandler. I'll be at my desk."

He turned around and Lucas let out a subtle breath. One down, hundreds to go.

But before the assistant exited, he turned around. "And congratulations on your marriage and the adoption. From the press she's already gotten, Mrs. Chandler seems like a very sweet woman." He raised the eyebrow again. "Just imagine—a new wife who wants to put off her own honeymoon so she can get the household in order. I myself don't know many ladies who would be that giving."

He was referring to the story in today's *Post,* a throwaway line that explained why Lucas hadn't swept Alicia off to somewhere exotic already. But the gleam in Barnaby's eyes said that he wasn't convinced the playboy had been erased, even though none of the TCO employees outside of family were privy to the stunt marriage.

Perceptive, Lucas thought as Barnaby left. He would need people like that on his side if he was going to succeed.

He ran a hand over his empty desktop, realizing again that there wasn't anything pressing for him to work on, that he didn't know what was going on with his company at all.

But, even worse, he had to admit that he didn't know what was happening with the woman he'd left sleeping in a separate bedroom in their home.

His own wife.

The stylist—a woman named Tatiana who wore her hair in a slashing, sophisticated cut—finally left the penthouse, and Alicia sank to the thick carpet.

In front of her, a cinema-sized TV was flashing a Disney movie; it'd been entertaining Gabriel throughout most of the appointment and, during all the fitting and measuring, Alicia had been restless to get back to him.

She didn't like using the tube as a babysitter. She

also didn't like perusing the list of nanny candidates Lucas had faxed over earlier.

The echo of an animated lion cub's roar bounced off the walls, the fancy artwork, the exquisite trim.

Looking at the opulence, Alicia shrank into herself.

This place was so foreign, so unlike her. Did Gabriel feel the same way?

Not judging by the way he was focused on the movie. But maybe that was because he knew she was here and she wasn't ever going to leave him. Maybe that's what made all the difference.

Yet, couldn't she say the same about Lucas? Shouldn't she feel secure because he would always be there, too?

"Ready for a snack, Gabriel?" she asked, trying to get her head back in a more comfortable place.

The child flinched, as if just realizing she was in the same room. Glancing behind him, he smiled. "Hi, Miss Alicia," he said in a chirpy voice, ignoring her question.

Then, turning back to the TV, he reabsorbed himself in the animation. A child's world.

"You can call me Mama now, Gabriel," she said softly, knowing he probably couldn't hear her. But she wanted to voice it, to make it real.

He didn't answer.

Well, perhaps she could talk to him more when she had his full attention. Let him enjoy a cartoon for a while.

Still, she scooted forward, touching Gabriel's back.

He was so tiny, made of skin and bones and the heart of a little boy who needed so much protection and love.

Or maybe she was the one who needed it at the moment. She thought back to the stylist's appointment.

"Now, that's *you*," the stranger named Tatiana had said, pen poised over a clipboard as she adjusted her cat-eye glasses with her free hand.

Alicia still felt uneasy at the memory. Tatiana had dressed her in a tight black sheath by some supposedly hot designer. It clung to the ample curves she'd always tried to hide under loose clothing. The décolletage dipped low, exposing much more cleavage than Alicia had ever dared.

"With the right jewelry and shoes, you'll be acceptable," Tatiana had said, marking her checklist of things to buy.

Smarting from the comment, Alicia had watched herself in the full-length stand-alone mirror they'd set up near the TV and Gabriel. She hadn't been able to move, more aware than ever of how she really didn't fit in, with her toasty skin, her gauche posture.

But none of that seemed to matter to Lucas.

She'd run her hands over her hips. What would he think? Would he be able to resist her now?

But… Absently, she'd touched her bracelet. The silver was cold. Plus, the price tag on this dress probably reflected enough money to pay for the comfort of three orphans for one whole year.

"This just isn't me," she'd told Tatiana, who'd tried to talk her back into buying the dress.

But Alicia had insisted on a more conservative wardrobe, even when it came to the design for the gown that would be tailored for the charity ball.

At that point, she'd felt more isolated than ever. She'd sunk into an invisible hole, hollowed out by the same mortification that had encouraged her abstinence vows.

What would Lucas do if he found out she wasn't what he thought she was—a woman capable of making him a better man? How was she qualified for that when she'd been born at the opposite end of the moral spectrum?

His angel, she thought. If only he knew better.

Then it occurred to her. Was she so much of an angel that he didn't *want* to sleep with her and that's why he hadn't made more of an issue of it? Had she married a man with a Madonna complex in her haste to find her dream?

Unsettled, she gave a final pat to the engrossed Gabriel's back, then stood. She wasn't sure what to do with herself and that threw her off because she'd never felt so at a loss before.

Wanting to remain near her son—her son; how many times would she have to think it to believe it?—she gingerly sat in an overstuffed white leather chair and hoped it wouldn't be ruined by the time she got up. Then, fidgety, she looked around, saw a pile of newspapers that Ms. Boland had dropped off this morning on a nearby table and grabbed one.

As Gabriel's movie played on, she leafed through the *New York Post*.

But a certain large full-color picture made her pause.

In it, she and Lucas were in front of his private jet, arms around each other as he nuzzled her forehead.

Gabriel was looking up at his new father as if Lucas were the end-all-be-all, while the billionaire cupped the child's head in a loving gesture.

She remembered that moment, when a spark of happiness in her chest had met the flash of a reporter's camera.

Then her gaze traveled lower. "The Playboy Takes a Wife!" read the headline.

Tears threatened to bully her, so she held them in. The unread paper crackled as she strangled it.

But she couldn't lose composure. Not in front of Gabriel. Never in front of her son.

In the foyer, she heard a door close and she fought to put herself back together.

At first, Lucas didn't see Alicia sitting near the back of the room. He'd heard the TV even from the foyer and, judging from the bippity-dippity sounds, he'd known it was something Gabe would be watching.

When he saw the kid sitting in front of the home-theater screen, he dive-bombed him, so relieved to finally be out of the office and in a place where he could relax.

"There he is!" he said, scooping up the boy and lifting him.

Gabe squealed, widened his eyes, then spread out his hands as if he were flying. "Man!"

Swinging the kid back down and holding him, Lucas said, "Remember our talks? I'm your daddy now."

Alicia had translated many of those discussions because Gabe couldn't possibly understand the subtleties in English. Lucas even doubted he would understand them in Spanish, but this was something that had to be addressed. Every day, if need be.

Gabe seemed to latch on to the word *daddy*. He brightened up even more, pointing to Lucas's chest. "Daddy?"

"*Sí.* Yes. Daddy."

Those five letters spread through him, warming him through and through. He hugged Gabe, enjoying the feel of how the boy clung to him. He'd never experienced anything like it before, not in a drag race, a free fall or even with his own brother.

"Where's your mom?" When Gabe didn't answer, Lucas tried again, dying to see her. "Mama? Miss Alicia—but we call her Mama now."

"I'm here," said a small voice from behind him.

Blood jerking in his limbs, Lucas turned to her. Her smile was wide yet oddly stiff, and she was back to wearing her shapeless orphanage clothes. They paled next to the white leather and elegant decor. In fact, she looked out of place and tiny, dwarfed by the magnitude of her surroundings.

But to Lucas, she belonged.

She seemed to be the center of everything.

He thrust the rogue notion away. TCO was the axis that held his world together. Alicia and Gabe were business.

Just business.

When Gabe squirmed, Lucas put him down to go back to his movie, then approached Alicia, noticing that the corners of her mouth twitched, as if her smile were about to fail.

"I didn't get the chance to tell you goodbye this morning," he said, unable to voice what was really bugging him.

She nodded, her knuckles going white as she linked her fingers together in her lap.

"Alicia…"

Her smile finally fell. "I'm afraid I'm not handling all these changes very well."

Don't touch her, his callous side said. *Don't get closer than you have to in order to make this work.*

But he couldn't help himself.

He bent down, cupped the back of her neck. "What can I do?"

When she glanced up at him with those beautiful golden eyes, there were questions rather than answers.

What am I doing here?

How do I handle being your wife?

His heart lurched. He couldn't allow things to implode now. Not when he'd already come so far.

He knew what was needed. He just had to win her over again, right? That's all there was to it.

"You know what would be fun?" he asked.

She looked doubtful that anything could be fun. "What?"

He thought of their picnic under the oak tree, their Wiffle-ball game, and hoped she was remembering those days, too.

With a playful smile he didn't even have to summon, he gently nicked her under the chin. "How about I surprise you?"

And, when her own smile emerged—a real yet tentative one this time—he drew her out of the chair.

Determined to make this work.

Chapter Nine

With all the personal upheaval, Alicia had almost forgotten it was December, a time of year she normally loved, with all the carols on the radio, the fun of buying presents and the anticipation of a Christmas feast.

How had Lucas known that he could cheer her up just by reminding her of the holidays? she wondered while her little family, dressed in heavy coats, gloves and knit hats, stood in front of the Christmas tree at Rockefeller Center. It rested in grandeur over a rink of colorfully garbed skaters, as well as a lighted angel that was shining in the early evening's darkness.

Being here made Alicia want to sing and thank God for this wonderful opportunity she'd been given. Today, she'd just forgotten how lucky she was, that's all.

Lucas provided a reminder when he'd first taken her and Gabriel to Toys "R" Us, where their son had tirelessly explored the wonderland of toys and, at the same time, given her ideas for his gifts. Then Lucas had ushered them to the breathtaking holiday windows of Saks Fifth Avenue. After they'd gawked at the intricate tableau, he'd urged them inside the store, telling them to pick out whatever they wished. Money was no object.

Alicia couldn't quite get used to that philosophy as she helped Gabriel choose his own clothing. The salespeople had been patient as the child had flitted from one rack to another, too active to try anything on. Ultimately, while Lucas had entertained Gabriel by going up and down the crowded escalators with him, she'd selected a few winter outfits, even though the price tags had floored her.

Afterward, they'd come to the Christmas tree, and both Gabriel and Alicia had been swept up in the spectacle.

Amidst the spirited throng in the plaza, Lucas—the only one hardy enough to brave the chill without a hat—was holding Gabriel so he could get a better view of the skaters.

"Flying!" the little boy said, pointing a mittened hand at a young girl as she whizzed by, her scarf floating behind her.

"You want to skate, too?" Lucas asked the child. Then he turned to Alicia. "I can arrange admission."

Just then, a big man in a red jacket crashed to the ice in an amazing spill. The onlookers collectively recoiled and went, "Ooh."

Gabriel emphatically shook his head. "No want to skate."

When Alicia reached out and patted the child in sympathy, she laughed, her breath coming out in a plume of smoke. Gabriel was instantly amused. He giggled and imitated her, creating his own puckered clouds.

"Blowing smoke sure beats entertaining the masses with *my* skating skills," Lucas said drily.

As Gabriel kept huffing, Alicia said, "You sound relieved that the activity was ixnayed."

"I am." He chuckled, squeezing Gabriel, who laughed. "Believe me, I'd rather take part in sports that don't highlight sequins and spandex during competition."

"That's right, we don't want to chip away at your machismo." She'd heard about his racing cars and foolhardy derring-do. "Unless you could get killed before you cross a finish line, you're not into it."

At first, he seemed surprised at her lighthearted teasing. Heck, she was a little taken aback by it, too, but Christmas in the air had made her feel free, happy.

Then he nodded, his grin wry. "I won't ever be into that sort of thing again, Alicia. Those days are long gone."

Good. She didn't relish the idea of a husband who took part in freewheeling activities that could easily kill him. "Long gone?"

"Yeah." Lucas smiled at Gabriel as the child clapped his hands at a woman who was spinning on the ice like a graceful toy top. "After my father's health scare, I realized that I hadn't lived up to any of his expectations, and that didn't sit right with me. So one of the first things I did in my effort to change was cut out the daredevil stuff."

With a start, it hit her—she really knew so little about this man. She'd been so busy focusing on the benefits for Gabriel and her own craving for family that this small detail had been swept under the carpet.

Impetuousness, her cautious side said. *See? You're paying a price for it now.*

Apparently sensing a change in her, Lucas turned from the ice rink, leading them away as he threaded a path through the thick crowd and got out his cell phone to call their driver.

She took the opportunity to piece together everything she did know about her husband. In the days before the wedding, during the few short conversations they'd had, he'd mentioned a few more details about his relationship with David, as well as his dad's close call with death. But it was only now that she was even beginning to comprehend what sort of effect Ford Chandler's near demise had really visited on Lucas.

At the thought of meeting her father-in-law tomorrow at dinner, she blew out a breath. It iced the air like a ghost.

They ambled back toward Saks, where they would be picked up. In one arm, Lucas held Gabriel and, with the other, he reached back for Alicia so they could link hands and dodge all the other people on the sidewalk together.

Even through her glove she felt his skin blaze against hers.

When they were ensconced in the limo and Gabriel

was busy looking at a new cloth picture book about tug-boats, Alicia glanced at Lucas sitting opposite her.

"Your father," she said. "You must care about him a lot if he got you to change your lifestyle."

A muscle ticked in his jaw as he nodded.

His dad was obviously a touchy subject, so she tread lightly. "Since he was too sick to come to our wedding, I wonder what he thinks about us? Is he unhappy that it happened so quickly? I mean, maybe he wanted you to settle down, but will he believe you rushed into it just as you, the daredevil, rushed into a lot of other things?"

He laughed, and it wasn't with any joy.

"Don't worry—he supports the kinder, gentler me. But still…" They were stuck in traffic, so his gaze was trained on the buildings visible through the window. "I think the Chandlers own a quarter of these proper-ties. *That's* what my dad is proud of. That's the bottom line."

The emptiness of his words saddened her. "I'm sorry."

"Don't be. My dad's a first-class ba—" He stopped himself. "Beg your pardon—jerk. But you have to be ruthless in business, I suppose. At least, that's what I'm learning."

"Learning?"

"For the first time today, I spent more than one hour in TCO headquarters."

Oh. Really? "I don't understand. I thought you were an important part of the company."

"Not before my dad's stroke. Along with this whole life makeover, I decided to actually get my hands dirty doing something other than playing in the sandbox.

The odd thing is, I'm pretty sure I fit into TCO about as well as I do with my dad and mom."

"Which isn't much?"

He finally faced her head-on. "Which isn't much."

Leaning forward, she wrapped her fingers around his. Words weren't needed, not when she understood the canyon between child and parents so keenly, herself.

Gabriel chose that moment to bolt up in his seat, tossing the book away. "Toooooot, toooooot!" he said, imitating the tugboats in the pictures.

As if thankful for the reprieve, Lucas held her hand tighter, then grinned, pulling his son to his side. The child laughed, always up for having a good time with his adored idol.

All through the rest of the ride, through the trip in the elevator up to their penthouse, through a catered dinner from a restaurant down the street that Alicia honestly wished to have cooked herself, instead, she felt it—a strengthened connection with her husband. A ferocity to make him happy because that's what he'd done for her today just when she'd been at her lowest.

But after they tucked in Gabriel and it was bedtime for them, too, Lucas settled at the dining table to look over some paperwork he'd brought home.

Today, she'd realized how much of a stranger he really was.

Less than one week until I become a real wife to a man I barely know, she thought. *Just a matter of days.*

She retreated into herself, once again the woman

who had avoided sex for years—the woman who was perhaps even afraid of having it.

Quietly she went to her cold bed, listening for the sounds of her husband retiring to his own room a half hour later.

Wishing, in spite of everything, that he would've come to her, instead.

After another day at work—one filled with so much research about TCO that Lucas's head was set to explode—he found himself rushing home. Alicia met him in the foyer, already dressed for dinner with his father.

The oxygen gushed out of him.

She wore just slightly more makeup than usual, with pink lipstick and a bit of blush. Her dark curls were pinned up and, in cameo softness, tendrils brushed the rose-and-black lace shawl that covered her shoulders. A black dress floated down to her suede pumps, the sleeves long, yet sheer.

Damn, she was a woman who seemed to have no idea just how gorgeous she was in her classy ensemble.

"Wow," was all he could say.

"I…" She shrugged, then tugged at her skirt as if it were too tight. "Tatiana, the stylist, picked it out. Someone also came in to do my makeup, even though I'm perfectly capable."

Unable to help himself, he sauntered toward her. Slowly, he kissed her hello, wishing again that she would've forgotten all about the postponed honeymoon and invited him into her room last night.

He sipped at her, tasting lipstick and sweetness. Not caring that he was ruining the makeup job.

Leaning into him, she seemed to both perk up and relax.

"You look like a million bucks," he said against her mouth.

She pulled away slightly, her breath warm on his lips even at this tentative distance. "I do?"

"Hell, yeah. I mean, *heck,* yeah." He rested his fingers at her neck, stroking his thumb there, trying to keep her from backing away even more. "My father's probably going to wonder why he didn't find you first, the old goat."

She made a surprised face and he laughed. "It's a joke. You know—serial husband? Remember?"

"I remember." After a pause, she seemed to gather her wits, then started to help him off with his long coat. "So how was work, *honey?*"

He chuckled at the abrupt teasing, trying to keep his frustrations in check. "Well, my assistant, Barnaby, could enter the Snippy Race in the Olympics and take home the gold, but…" He shrugged. "Other than that? Still not great."

"Why?"

He hesitated, weighing the idea of keeping her in the dark about everything, not just this relationship. It'd be so much easier never to tell her what he'd done, but more and more, he kept thinking he needed to do it.

Yeah, right. That'd be perfect, he thought. *Alienate your wife and ruin the good thing you have going. Just shut up and she'll never know the difference, okay? Shut up and just make her happy.*

But she was his *wife* now. He liked the thought of her being interested enough to want to ask about the reasons work could've gone better today. Liked the thought of being honest with her.

So he went halfway, at least, telling her about how the junior executives smirked whenever he asked them questions about their projects. He told her how, today, David had "forgotten" to give him the time of a meeting with the top-rank players in the company. His truthfulness felt good, but he knew this was as far as he dared go with it.

"David can't do that." Alicia looked pissed enough for both of them. It lifted him up knowing that someone was on his side.

She continued, walking with him through the foyer and toward the common area. "You've told me before that you're the majority stockholder."

"Right."

"So why does David feel justified in walking all over you?"

Because I'm the face. I've never been anything even remotely resembling the brains of TCO.

It was too sad—too embarrassing—to admit.

As they entered the common area, Gabe saved him by popping up from behind a couch and yelling, "Man!"

Okay, he wasn't always saying "Daddy," but that would come someday, Lucas supposed.

"Get over here!" He held out his arms, latching on

to the flying boy and swishing him into the air as the kid squealed.

In the background, one of their housekeepers, Mrs. Carillo, stood, her hands filled with plastic toys. She'd obviously been keeping Gabe occupied while Alicia got ready.

"Hi, Mrs. Carillo," he said while Gabe pulled at his ear.

"Mr. Chandler." She nodded to Alicia, then disappeared.

"Magdelena loves playing with Gabriel," Alicia said. "I even talked her into babysitting him tonight since I don't want to leave him with some random stranger."

"Who would?" Lucas dipped his son, increasing the volume of Gabe's gaiety. He lifted him again, succumbing to laughter, too. "Maybe we should hire *her* to help you with Gabe all day."

Uh-huh, he thought. That would go over real well with the social set. Nannies were trophies and the more credentials they came with, the better. He could imagine the raised eyebrows a housekeeper-turned-nanny would inspire.

But he kind of liked the thought of tweaking everyone's noses like that.

"Hire Mrs. Carillo?" Alicia said. "I actually like to spend all day with Gabriel."

Lucas thought of all the plans he'd had for his wife: Hostessing charity benefits, showing her off to the press as the woman who'd turned the playboy around. When would she find time to do that if she didn't get some help with Gabe?

But, as much as it pained him to admit it, he didn't want his new son to ever think he was being shuffled off for an extended amount of time. He would have to be an ogre to do that to the boy.

Lowering Gabe so he could take off for the toys Mrs. Carillo hadn't cleaned up yet, Lucas fixed his gaze on Alicia.

"You'll need a rest every once in a while because Gabe could tire out an army. Why not let him have two people to play with—you and Mrs. Carillo?"

"Three," she added. "You seem to be doing pretty well in the play department when you get home from work."

Really? Lucas had never expected to be decent at it. Maybe Alicia had been right when she'd told him he was meant to be a father. Or maybe she just had no idea what he had up his sleeve.

Stricken with remorse, he clammed up, loosening his tie and walking away so he wouldn't have to face the woman he was betraying.

"I'll be ready to go in fifteen minutes," he said, leaving his family behind without a second glance.

Even though he was dying to look back at them.

Alicia knew that arrangements had been made to buy out the city's trendiest new restaurant for this first meeting with Ford Chandler.

Betheney, which Lucas told her had been named for the wife of the celebrity chef and owner, was decorated with Spanish flair: dusky red-and-beige paintings of flamenco dancers, a mahogany bar and candlelit tables, filigreed screens separating the limited tables. It would hold only twenty-six diners and promised a magnificent experience.

As Alicia walked into the establishment on her husband's arm, she was once again overwhelmed—and it wasn't just because of the riches. There were about ten people here, and she'd only been expecting David and Mr. Chandler. Interestingly, Lucas seemed surprised to see some of them, too, and she wondered why.

She was also worried about Gabriel. Before leaving the penthouse, both she and her husband had sat him down to tell him where they were going for the next few hours. She hadn't known what to expect, predicting that perhaps the child she knew so well would feel abandoned and throw a tantrum. But Gabriel had already taken to Mrs. Carillo and he'd transitioned into the babysitting part of the night without a fuss.

Still, Alicia had her cell phone on just in case.

In the meantime, she was determined to make a positive impression on her father-in-law, a man who'd taken on gargantuan proportions in Alicia's mind.

Ford Chandler greeted her right away, using the aid of a cane. When he took her hand and kissed the back of it, she could see a little bit of Lucas in him. It wasn't his height or the way his silver hair didn't want to go with the flow of how it'd been combed, it was more in the gaze—a predator's violet shine.

"My son told me you were beautiful," he said, his speech slightly slurred by the aftermath of his stroke, "but you surpass that, Alicia." He was still holding her hand.

Lucas nimbly removed it from his father's grasp. "Yeah, she's a keeper. That's why I married her."

Mr. Chandler gave his son a veiled look that Alicia couldn't begin to translate, then turned back to her. "We're overjoyed to have you in our family, and I regret I couldn't make it to the wedding." Something in his eyes went hazy, as if that sentiment had been genuine. "But I am looking forward to talking with you more."

"Gabriel's looking forward to meeting you this weekend, too," she added, even though her son had expressed no such thing. It sounded like something a new wife should say, though.

"And I'm excited about that, as well." Her father-in-law smiled, but she wasn't sure what he was actually feeling. "I can't quite believe I've got a grandson now."

David, who was in the corner chatting with the other guests over drinks, waved at Lucas. Alicia felt him stiffen.

Why did this seem more like a business meeting than a family dinner?

Or was this how all the Chandler gatherings went?

Based on Lucas's feelings about his brood, Alicia thought she knew the answer.

"Dad," he said, "why don't we take a seat."

The older man gritted his teeth, glanced at Alicia, then covered with another smile. "I'm out of the sick bed and hardly an invalid. I can tolerate a little standing."

"Then, I guess you won't mind if I introduce my wife to David's friends." Lucas took her elbow and, even though his touch was gentle, there was a grip to it. "Whoever they are."

"We thought we'd invite the Tadmere group."

Tadmere? Sounded like business to her, all right.

A tight laugh escaped her husband, and he started to lead her away. But not before Mr. Chandler got in one last comment.

"Just look at you, Lucas," he said, his smile wobbling a little.

When his eyes went a softer shade of blue, she realized that this man was surrendering to his son in a very subtle way. A father who was trying to reach out, whether Lucas knew it or not.

From the way her husband remained stiff, she wasn't sure.

Ford sighed, as if acknowledging he wasn't getting anywhere. "I suppose my congratulations wouldn't mean much."

"They might," Lucas said, "if you meant it."

Why wouldn't he? Was there something going on she wasn't aware of?

Without another word, Lucas guided her away, leaving Mr. Chandler to make his slow way back to the table, his hors d'oeuvres and beverage. There wasn't much distance from one end of the room to the other, and Lucas seemed intent on taking his time to get her to the other guests.

"Sorry about this," he said between clenched teeth.

"The lack of intimate family time?"

"That, plus all my dad's 'beautiful' talk. Not that he wasn't right—" here Lucas slid his arm around her waist, making her skin flush "—but I don't want to hear my dad saying stuff like that."

Is this what had been bothering Lucas back there? That's all? "No harm done."

"So you say." He stopped her about fifteen feet away from David and his crowd, turning to her and clasping her elbows so their arms connected like two fortified bridges. "Listen, you need to know what's going on— as far I can tell, anyway. Tadmere is a media-savvy company TCO is trying to acquire, but there are some… difficulties."

Lucas took a deep breath, then paused. What was wrong?

"Like what?" she asked.

"You don't want to know the details." His grip on her grew a little tighter. "Just be your charming self, okay? The hostess who spun me for a loop the first time I saw her."

Lucas warmed inside. He wasn't lying. Alicia had turned his world upside down immediately, and he'd never gotten over it. In fact, if he admitted it, he was still reeling, especially right now, with his arms pressed to hers.

She blushed at the compliment, even if he hadn't come right out and told her he loved her. And he wouldn't. That was one lie he couldn't bear.

"I'm ready when you are," she said, lifting her chin and smiling at him in confederacy.

Alicia, the perfect wife. The smartest choice he'd ever made. His father seemed to agree with that, and it had confused Lucas even more.

Had the old man been coming around back there or

was he just playing with Lucas? He'd seemed sincere when he'd complimented Alicia and maybe he'd even held out a white flag, but their history was too full of hard feelings for Lucas to give in that easily.

Alicia had taken his hand, nudging him toward David and their guests. From Lucas's research, he was familiar with a couple of faces—the owners, a brother and sister who were resisting the sale of Tadmere to TCO because of Lucas's reputation. But the others, all men who seemed to be of Latin persuasion from the gist of their conversation, were a mystery to him.

Why had David invited them?

During a discussion in which Alicia requested a club soda from the waiter and proceeded to charm everyone with her answers to their questions regarding Refugio Salvo, Lucas noticed how the crowd warmed up to her. She had social talent, and David had been right on target when he'd noticed her potential.

Potential that went so much deeper than being a fake wife, Lucas thought, his gut twisting.

As Alicia encouraged the others to talk about their families, David drew Lucas aside, gesturing to the bar and pretending they were going to refresh the nonalcoholic champagne that the Tadmere siblings approved of.

"Da-amn," David said as they set their glasses on the mahogany bar and allowed the waiter to serve them. "How did we get so lucky with her?"

"How did *I* get so lucky?" Lucas grasped his champagne flute's stem so hard that he was shocked it didn't shatter.

"She's incredible. You've got yourself a real—"

"Why are the Tadmeres here? And who is everyone else?"

His brother shrugged. "Second question first—those are Tadmere associates. First question next—Tadmere needs to see up close that you're not the terror they thought you were. And from the way they're enjoying Alicia, you've done good."

He hadn't done any good at all. "Associates of Tadmere? What does that mean, David?"

"Just let me handle everything, Luke. Okay?" With one of those smirks Lucas had seen so much around the office, David said, "Stop with your TCO research and stay home with your family. I've got all this under control."

"Got what under control?" said Alicia's voice.

Both David and Lucas whipped around to find her behind them, frowning. In the background, the guests were being led to the joined tables by the waitstaff, and clearly, Alicia had come over to summon them, too.

"Hi, sis," David said, saluting her with his drink.

Lucas could see some temper in her gaze and he remembered how ticked off she'd been earlier when he'd mentioned how much things sucked at the office. Had she heard David brush him off?

More importantly, just how *much* had she heard?

Panic separated his veins, but when she directed her next comment at David, Lucas calmed down.

"I'm sure you'd find that, if you gave Lucas some respect, he'd be your greatest asset."

Respect. The concept echoed, pierced, shredded.

But he still wanted it. God, did he ever.

David looked amused at her polite feistiness. "Really."

"Oh, yes." Alicia didn't know exactly what they'd been talking about, because she'd only heard David's demeaning tone. But she remembered how angry Lucas had been just about an hour ago when he'd come home from the office and she suspected this conversation had to do with that. "I get the feeling Lucas could do a lot more than anyone gives him credit for."

Out of the corner of her eye, she caught Lucas's smile and she thought that maybe someday he could believe in himself as much as she did.

"Well," David said, straightening up from the bar and smoothing his fancy suit. "This is a perfect match— two people who need to mind their own business."

Taking a sip from his drink, he shot Alicia a meaningful look, then tried to leave.

But not before Lucas grabbed his brother's arm in a gesture that would've looked friendly to a casual observer. Yet to Alicia it was a threat.

"You don't talk to her like that," he said, voice low and dangerous.

David began to laugh, and Lucas gave his arm a tiny shake.

A long beat passed between the brothers before David casually liberated himself and donned a civil grin as he moved toward their guests.

That left them alone. So alone in this room full of strangers.

"What was that…" she began.

Gaze going soft, Lucas smoothed the hair back from her face. "Politics, Alicia. He's sore because I'm infringing on his territory."

"But it's also *your* territory."

"That's right," he said, bending toward her to kiss her forehead. His kisses formed words. *My territory.*

The significance wasn't lost on her as he claimed her with his touch.

A touch that told her just how much he was looking forward to their upcoming honeymoon.

Chapter Ten

Work was a bitch the next day.

David was obviously sore because of how Alicia had stood up to him the night before, so he'd seemed to take great pleasure in diverting Lucas to oversee the charity ball, which was already being handled by a party planner. The message was clear: he was emphasizing Lucas's PR responsibilities instead of inviting him to become a more significant part of running the company.

Yet Lucas was sticking to his guns, bringing home a briefcase full of files that Barnaby had pulled for him: memos and clippings regarding Tadmere.

When he entered the penthouse, the first thing he heard was a Christmas carol coming from the common room. Laughter threaded through the crystalline notes.

Lucas abandoned his briefcase and coat to Ms. Boland, whose brunette hair had mistletoe tucked into its bun.

After he greeted her, he said, "Sounds like there's a party going on."

"You'll see, Mr. Chandler." She smiled, and he realized, maybe for the first time, that this stoic woman who'd always tried so hard to fade into the woodwork—perhaps to avoid his reputed wolfishness and keep her job—was capable of being merry.

Drawn by the warm, festive sounds, Lucas made his way to the common room, lingering in the entrance when he saw what his family was up to.

Next to a bare Christmas tree that waited in the corner, Alicia and Gabe were constructing something of an art project. They'd draped wrinkled earth-toned paper over tables to create rocks and hills, then used simple plastic kitchen wrap to shape a waterfall that tumbled down over some of the "terrain" and into a pool of "water." Fake construction-paper palm trees hovered over that pool.

At the moment, they were working on what looked to be a structure, using bamboo as wood.

Contentment overwhelmed him. Maybe it was the music. Or maybe it was the beginnings of a Christmas tree in a playboy's penthouse—a place that he'd never bothered to decorate in past years. Or maybe it was...

He swallowed, not daring to even think it, because it would go against everything he'd been telling himself about this marriage.

Still, he couldn't stop the longing as he watched his

new family. Gabe looked so comfortable in his new wardrobe, even though his Ralph Lauren pants were missing and he was just running around in his underwear. And Alicia…

She was dressed simply in a white blouse that was untucked, velvet sweat pants and bare feet. Her hair was tied back, curls tumbling past her shoulders.

Once again his hormones revved, spinning in the sand of his frustration. What the hell had he been thinking when he'd put off sex?

Pressure built inside of him, and he almost walked away to remove himself from temptation before it was too late.

But Gabe spotted him, dropping a piece of bamboo and rushing him. "*Es* him!" he said in a hybrid of Spanish and English.

As was their standard greeting, Lucas hefted the boy high above, making him giggle, then held him to his chest, planting a kiss on top of his dark head.

As Lucas's eyes met Alicia's, her face went red, as if a thousand secret fantasies had flooded her at once. He was reminded of the first time they'd met, how she'd seemed bowled over then, too.

Controlling himself, he nodded at the project. "Busy day?"

"Slightly." She brushed her hands together to wipe them off, smiling at him in pure joy. "First, Magdelena said yes to taking care of Gabriel. She'll switch over as soon as Sarah—*Ms. Boland*—hires another personal housekeeper."

First-name basis with all the help? Lucas had always

been cordial with his staff, but now it seemed ridiculous that he'd never called Ms. Boland anything other than that.

"Oh," Alicia added, "and Sarah said something about providing her with a Christmas shopping list?"

"Yeah." Gabe experimentally touched Lucas's nose, and Lucas scrunched it, teasing him. "That'll be taken care of."

"Choosing gifts? Isn't that something we'd like to do?"

He absorbed her confused tilt of the head. Never in his life had he bothered with shopping. Well, there'd been one year, when he'd gotten old enough to believe that Christmas was about giving and all that. But then he'd presented his handpicked gift—a tie clip that he'd purchased from a street cart during a walk with his nanny—to his dad. It hadn't been pretty. In Lucas's little-boy heart, he'd really thought Ford Chandler would love the funky Martian on the cheap metal. But his dad had kind of just flicked it away like a gnat, and that had been the last Lucas had seen of it.

Afterward, he'd gone with the family's personal shopper, too, not having the courage to try again, himself.

But now maybe he did have the guts to buy for his family, especially after the way Alicia had defended him to David last night. He suspected his opinion and effort might just matter to her and Gabe, after all.

"We'll take care of the shopping ourselves, then," he said.

"Excellent." She went up and down on her toes,

hands clasped behind her back. "So…what do you think of the decorations so far?"

He nodded toward the art project, then set Gabe down so the boy could run back to it. "I know what the tree is, but I'm not so sure what's going on in that corner."

She held out her hands in a ta-da motion. "The tree is for you, since you're probably used to one, but I thought we'd bring some Mexico into the place. It's a *Nacimiento*. A Nativity scene."

"Ah." Suddenly the bamboo did seem to be taking the shape of a manger, and he noticed a tiny straw-filled crate by her feet that could double as a baby's bed.

Gabe rattled off some Spanish, then got a baffled look on his face as he glanced at Lucas.

Alicia laughed and answered her son, then spoke to Lucas. "He doesn't know the English for what he said, so I'll translate. He told you that we'll put Baby Jesus in the bed late on *Noche Buena,* Christmas Eve. We normally celebrate on that day and go to mass that night, then eat leftovers on the twenty-fifth. Does that sound good?"

He could only nod, touched that someone would want him to be a part of this.

"And the sixteenth is coming up. It's the beginning of *Las Posadas,* which is traditionally nine days of candlelight processions and festivities. But we'll give it our own personal touch."

Gabe held up a stick of bamboo. *"Feliz Navidad!"*

Lucas smiled. *Feliz Navidad,* indeed. His first happy Christmas. His first inkling of what his life could be like every year if things were different. If he could only open his heart as easily as he'd opened his home.

Ms. Boland appeared from the other room, a camera in hand. "Mr. Chandler, I wondered if you'd like to record this?"

"Photo!" Gabe said, hopping up and down.

Lucas was sick of pictures, flashes that normally captured him for newspapers and magazines, but he wouldn't say no to his son. Besides, this wasn't the press. This was real.

Too real.

He walked past Ms. Boland—Sarah. "Thanks for thinking of it," he said.

"You're welcome, Mr. Ch—"

"It's about time you called me Lucas, all right? Just…Lucas."

As he gathered his family in his arms, pressing his cheek against the softness of his wife's hair and churning with hunger for her, the camera flashed.

And in the viewer that Sarah Boland showed them, Lucas saw a happy family that ripped at his heart.

During Gabe's bedtime, Lucas reclined on the boy's lowered mattress, reading the blanket-bundled child a selection of his favorite books.

Yet after the third Big Bird story, when Gabe tumbled out of bed and picked out a Cookie Monster adventure, Lucas offered another option.

"How about I tell you about the three bears?"

Gabe seemed excited about that, so Lucas shut off the lights, nestled the covers around the kid again and attempted to piece together what he remembered about a plot. It had something to do with a little blond trespasser who pigged out on bear porridge, fell asleep and then…Lucas wasn't sure, but he made it so that the bears adopted Goldilocks just as he and Alicia had adopted Gabe, and that seemed like the best ending anyone could've dreamed up.

He wasn't sure how much the boy liked it, because by the time he was done, Gabe was asleep, his breathing deep and even.

Poor guy, Lucas thought, smoothing back the kid's hair. Worn out from decorating both the Nativity scene, as well as the tree. Lucas had helped, too, and all *he* wanted to do was go to bed. But not alone. Hell, no, not alone.

As if summoned by the beacon of his sexual yearning, Alicia appeared in the doorway, her curvy figure silhouetted by the hall light. Lucas imagined his hands on her hips, her waist, running upward and pressing her into the heat of his body.

Inspired, he crept out of Gabe's toy-strewn room and shut the door. His wife's perfume wafted over him, heady and all-powerful.

Silently, she linked her arm with his, leaning into him as they walked aimlessly. He didn't know where she was leading him, but he could wish it was someplace with a mattress and her body stretched out next to him.

All he knew for sure was that her breast kept brushing against his bicep, and it was driving him crazy.

A few more days, buddy, he thought. *That's all.*

"I've been trying to put together a schedule," she said when they were far enough from Gabe's room so they could talk.

"I've been meaning to get together with you on that." And so much else. God.

They ended up in the common room, where the lights were out and the Christmas tree was shining with the blue bulbs they'd strung around the branches. The azure glow permeated the area, making it surreal and peaceful.

She sat down on the floor in front of a couch, her back against it, and picked up a gingerbread man that Gabe had been eating earlier. He settled next to her, legs bent, arms resting on his knees.

"The holidays are going to be busy," she said, "so I figured I'd wait to think about another church wedding until afterward."

He remembered how, back in Mexico, he'd promised her a bigger ceremony to make up for the speedy circumstances.

"You just tell me what you need and you've got it," he said. "Speaking of scheduling, you've got your dress and all the trimmings for the charity ball this Friday?"

She sighed a little nervously. "I suppose I'm ready."

"You're going to shine, just like you always do. Don't worry about it."

"Even if the spotlight will be on us? I've seen the tabloids, Lucas. I…"

He touched her hair, and she dropped the gingerbread, then smiled at him in apology. Skittish, he thought. Was she as lit up with desire as he was? Was she wondering if he'd forgotten about his promise to postpone the big night?

"I know—you weren't prepared for everything that came with this marriage. Not yet, anyway." He traced his thumb down her cheek, mesmerized. Soft, so soft. "But, in spite of everything, you're doing a great job."

Business. His tone rang of it. Yeah, she was being the perfect pillar of decency for him. But what was *he* to *her?*

He wasn't sure he wanted to know.

Her breath seemed labored as the quiet enveloped them. When she finally spoke, her voice was croaky.

"How did your day go?"

The change of subject made him drop his hand to the couch.

"All the decorating made me forget to ask," she added.

"I'd rather not have to think about the office when I'm with family, anyway." Not when Gabe and Alicia were turning out to be the only release he had from the stress of TCO. "Work was work, in more ways than one. David was taking petty revenge out on me for my upstart demands to know more about the company. And I think he's still smarting from the way you backed me up."

His heart lifted as he recalled how she'd defended him at Betheney. How it'd seemed so natural for her to do so.

Alicia leaned back against the couch again. The shift in position brought her lips that much closer to his.

"If David doesn't appreciate you," she said, "he needs to know what he's missing."

Lucas tried to laugh, but it was bothering him that

he was keeping her at arm's distance when she was so invested in him. It wasn't right.

His next words slipped out before he could think about what he was doing. "Those unknown guests at dinner last night? I asked David who they were and he told me not to concern myself."

"But you will concern yourself, right?" Even though Alicia knew that Lucas had been more into his daredeviling than TCO in the past, she believed with all her heart that he would be successful at whatever he put his mind to now. He'd done too much for the orphanage for her to doubt his effectiveness. "You're going to look into what's going on around TCO?"

"I guess I was planning on it." Lucas smiled, almost to himself, as if he were treasuring her faith in him. "I brought home more paperwork, thinking I'd get down to the nitty-gritty of something or another."

"Good. That's great, Lucas."

He gave off an aw-shucks aura that captured her. Tremors shivered down her chest, through her belly, humming in a place that she'd been denying for too long.

Suddenly, she was aware of just how close they were sitting, how his skin seemed to vibrate against hers, even if he was inches away. As he turned to her again, his gaze focused on her lips, causing them to tingle.

Ready, she thought. *Maybe I am ready....*

But when he laughed tightly, then turned back toward the tree, she lost any confidence she might have had.

Three more days, thought the side of her that had avoided physical contact for so many years. *The pressure's off for a little while longer.*

Because sex would change everything, especially *her*. It would bring her repressed dark side screaming to life and, now that it was so close, she was less sure than ever that she could handle what would come to the surface. Her father's daughter.

As almost an apology, she leaned her head on Lucas's shoulder, and they both watched the tree. It was such a sweet moment that she wished it would last forever, with no worries, no expectation, no fear that everything wonderful would soon come to an end.

He rested his head against hers. "This is nice," he said softly, voice strangled by something that was part frustration and part…what? An emotion she couldn't identify.

"Nice," she repeated, staring at the lights of their tree.

As he held her hand, she closed her eyes, thinking how much she didn't deserve this husband.

A man who understood her probably even more than she understood herself.

Two shocks awaited Lucas the next morning.

First, it'd been waking up in front of the Christmas tree embracing Alicia, then it'd been temptation at work.

But, at the end of the day, as he rode up in the elevator to the penthouse, he dwelled on the first one more than the other, because his wife had been consuming him for hours.

They'd somehow fallen asleep, silent, wrapped in each other's arms. Upon waking, he hadn't so much as breathed because he hadn't wanted to disturb the adorable pattern of her sleep. She'd felt so good, so innocent against him, and he'd realized that maybe he'd been doing things wrong his whole life.

Holding her made him feel closer than he'd ever been to a woman, and he hadn't even needed sex. Whoa.

But it was true, and that scared the tar out of him because the last thing he needed was to get this close.

Without waking Alicia, he'd carried her to her bed, then tenderly tucked her in and kissed her. It'd taken all his willpower to leave the room, but when he'd done it, he'd felt like a bigger person in some weird way.

He'd gone into work early, before the scent of coffee filled the halls and the click of keyboards interrupted the silence. At quarter after ten—he knew the time because he'd marked it as the moment he'd officially lost his wits—a mergers-and-acquisitions executive he'd previously "dated" had entered his office, congratulated him on his marriage with a disbelieving grin, shut the door and offered him the chance to have his way with her that night.

He'd said no. *No.*

It's not that his body wasn't scrapping for some activity, but he didn't want it from anyone but his wife.

Lucas had no idea how that'd happened. Where was his need to cling to the lifestyle that'd kept him sane for so many years? Wasn't he making himself vulnerable, just as his father had been so many times?

What had happened to his business marriage, for God's sake?

Yet, now, as he entered his home and saw Alicia, everything seemed to coalesce. Nothing mattered but her—not his sanity, the office or even his thwarted libido.

And, when he saw Gabe showing him how he'd learned to somersault at the park today, life seemed complete.

After a home-cooked dinner featuring *chimichangas,* Lucas helped Alicia give Gabe a bath. The boy was in one of his moods, but Lucas and Alicia worked together to calm and discipline him. In between building Nativity scenes and getting the household in order, she'd been interviewing and checking into therapists for their son and, after Gabe retired, they sat at the dining-room table and settled on one.

But now, as darkness peered in the windows, Lucas decided to focus on his research, just to distract himself. Next to him, Alicia created a scrapbook boasting pictures of Gabe.

Still, every few seconds, it seemed, Lucas would look up and take her in, bolstered by the sight of her, knowing that she was there to support him in anything. The notion built him up so high that it felt as if nothing could tear him down.

Funny, he thought, how the last person in the world who should be respecting him actually did.

A confession about how this marriage had come about bucked against his teeth, but he knew everything would crash down around them if he said something. Yet, dammit, he had to tell her. He couldn't live with himself if he didn't.

But…no. Not if he wanted things to stay as they were.

With a start, he realized that he'd become too attached to let her and Gabe go.

Off balance, he went back to a Tadmere global asset

report that Barnaby had put together, attempting to re-cover. And when he came across something that disturbed him even more only fifteen minutes later, Alicia noticed.

"What is it?" she asked.

After only a slight hesitation, he decided to tell her. It was a consolation prize taking the place of everything else.

At the same time… He glanced at the report again, knowing he couldn't tell her every detail about the hor-rific suspicions that were forming in his head.

"Tadmere," he said, throat scratched.

She put down a picture she'd been trimming, as well as the scissors. "What about it?"

He had to be careful. "Well, first off, I've told you that they own a lot of American TV and radio stations. I didn't realize they had some in Mexico. David never told me."

She blinked. "Mexico."

"I can't shake the feeling that David was hiding this information from me, even when he invited those extra guests to dinner the other night." Latin Tadmere execu-tives who, he suspected, had been summoned to see just what a change Lucas had made from playboy to de-voted husband.

With a Latina wife.

He didn't reveal that part because he wasn't sure if he was right about David's intentions. After all, Lucas wasn't a real businessman. And what if he was wrong? That would make him an even bigger joke than he already was.

Besides, how could he explain the doubts that were forming? Doubts that David might have steered Lucas into a relationship with a Latina so TCO could get friendly press in key demographic communities that tuned in to Tadmere stations.

It would devastate her, and that's the last thing Lucas wanted, even if he'd set her up for it in so many ways.

Good God…it would devastate *him*.

"You know," she said, forehead furrowed, "I heard David on the phone once, back in Mexico. He was saying something about a demographic…." She picked up the picture again, avoiding his gaze.

He was about to pursue that comment, but he was afraid to. Yup, the guy who went extreme bungee jumping in New Zealand and drove Formula 1 cars was just plain chicken.

Had David been referring to how Alicia might help with customers from across the border? Had her ethnicity been some sort of selling point with Tadmere?

Or was Lucas just jumping to cynical conclusions because he was paranoid?

For the first time in his life, he wanted to rip David's head off. Not for how he might've manipulated Lucas but for how Alicia had been reduced to a statistic. He wanted to do some damage to himself, too, for getting her into this.

Most of all, he wished he had the courage to tell Alicia everything right now. But he couldn't.

And it wasn't just because he was afraid that the truth might tear this business deal apart.

Chapter Eleven

Finally, Friday, the charity ball arrived.

After kissing Gabriel good-night and letting Magdelena know that they might be back late, Alicia took one of the limos by herself to the Waldorf-Astoria, where she was meeting her husband.

He'd been forced to stay late at work—something to do with David taking a sudden trip to Los Angeles—so she'd messengered one of his tuxes to TCO headquarters. But, before sending it, she'd given in to a whim, pressing her face against the material, smelling it, taking the imagined essence of him into her.

Nighttime fantasies of Lucas were dogging her, as was the niggling feeling that she was missing something important about Tadmere and "demographics."

Worst of all, clock stroke by clock stroke, she was coming to realize that this fear of sex was ruining her more than the act itself ever could. Lucas had never, ever made her feel cheap, so why did she believe making love with him would ruin her?

Alicia was still grappling with her doubts as the limo drew up to the prestigious hotel. While tamping down her nerves, she smoothed her dress, a blush-satin concoction with extended, fashionably buttoned sleeves, an Empire waistline and a chiffon-paneled skirt that flowed down to the pearl-strapped low-heeled slippers she wore. She'd refused the help of the makeup or hair people, whom Sarah Boland had suggested, instead, electing to do everything herself. This, of course, meant that she wasn't wearing much besides blusher, a bit of lipstick, mascara and a simple hairstyle that swept the curls off her neck. Lastly, she wore her charm bracelet, having entwined it with a long strand of pearls around her wrist. It reminded her of who she really was, who she needed to leave behind if she was going to make her marriage work.

All in all, she felt like a girl playing dress-up in Cinderella's ball gown, but she attempted to put that out of her mind. Tonight wasn't about how she looked, it was about TCO raising money for the American Red Cross. She wondered if, someday, she could do the same for orphanages, especially Refugio Salvo. Lucas had been encouraging her to take up philanthropic activities, and, as soon as she arranged their formal wedding, Gabriel's comfort and the household, she would make a great effort to organize her plans.

Before she knew it, her door opened and flashes from the waiting cameras greeted her. For a thin-blooded second she didn't know how to react. Hide because she didn't belong in this dress, in this limo? Or smile because she was now the wife of a man who'd been born into such fame and fortune?

Putting on a false sense of belonging, she stepped onto the red carpet. But then, out of nowhere, a strong hand enveloped hers. She knew the feel of that grip. Lucas.

His warm skin sent a hush of comfort into her, calming her and allowing her to be Alicia Sanchez Chandler, a woman who had every reason to smile.

And she did, beaming, glancing up at him through the flashes. Out of the corner of her eye she caught a peek of the reporters, but when she saw how her husband was gazing at her, she lost all focus except for him.

He looked bowled over at the sight of her, as if he'd never seen a female before. He clasped his free hand lightly over his heart as if to keep it inside his chest.

"Alicia," she heard him say over the camera clicks and the calls from the photographers to look their way for a picture.

At the gritty tenor of his voice, sexual heat rose up from her center and through her body, dabbing her with longing. The sound of him owning her name made her feel innocent and craved all at once, and there was no shame in it at all.

How could she doubt that he valued her, wanted her, celebrated her with every heartbeat that pulsed between them?

I love him, she thought. *I have from the first minute I saw him. He deserves to know exactly who he married, deserves to have me tell him that I'll always be his angel, no matter what he finds out about me.*

No one else on that red carpet seemed to exist as he carefully tucked her hand into the crook of his arm and escorted her into the hotel. She was faintly aware of Art Deco grandeur, marble and flowers suffusing the lobby and halls as they made their way to the gala.

"How was Gabe before you left?" he asked.

She loved that he was thinking of their son instead of the party. "He and Magdelena were playing dress-up, so he was occupied enough to not concentrate on the fact that we won't be there tonight. By the way, he really liked how you called from work to let him know you'd be home later with me." In fact, Lucas made a daily habit of calling from the office, just to tell Gabriel he was on his mind.

Just to tell Alicia he couldn't stop thinking about her, either.

Lucas adjusted his bow tie with his other hand. "He feels comfortable with Mrs. Carillo. Magdelena."

"Very. She's a godsend." Alicia squeezed his arm. "And how about you? Did you get your work done?"

His bicep tensed. "Not quite. I've got something to discuss with David about this Tadmere business, but he took that trip to L.A. and won't return my calls. I stayed a little longer in the office because I was having some meetings with key personnel in order to get even more caught up."

Strange, she thought. Why was David being so cagey?

"Do you trust your brother?" she asked.

Lucas's lips drew into a thin line before he answered. "I used to. Implicitly. But…"

Not anymore. It was easy to supply that answer.

"Hey," he said, lightly nicking her under the chin and shooting her that killer smile. "Why're we talking about TCO when I've got a fairy princess on my arm?"

She melted right then and there.

At that, he got a very translatable look: intense, hungry, his glance brushing her mouth. He started bending toward her, and the music from the ballroom swelled.

"I won't be able to focus in there," he said, his breath whispering over her lips. "I won't be able to think about anything except you."

And as his mouth covered hers, her brain went dark, blanked by everything but the sensation of a moist, warm kiss.

Why wait until tomorrow night? she thought. *I want my husband. I'll have my husband.*

Her lips sent that message and, when he disengaged and cupped her face in his hands to gaze at her, she knew he understood.

They'd finally made it into the ballroom after a rush of guests interrupted their kiss outside. But, now, as Lucas absently listened to a Chandler executive teasing him about how the company playboy had been invaded by a hardworking clone, he couldn't feel any pride at this evidence of the respect he'd been striving for.

No, he couldn't think beyond Alicia.

Had she wordlessly invited him into her bedroom tonight?

Unable to stop himself, he looked around for her again. She'd already done him proud, fitting in with this do-gooder crowd and talking charity with several younger prominent, liberal socialites in the room. With the snootier WASPs, it would take longer for her to be accepted, if ever. He hated to subject her to their type of behavior, but if anyone could handle their bitchery gracefully, it was Alicia. She might even end up changing their outdated attitudes, too.

He scanned the crisp white sculptures of the charitable winter wonderland. It was decorated so that icicles seemed to drift from the ceiling. Fake downy snow dusted the corners, and white lights frosted angels and snowflake tunnels.

When he found her, he was almost brought to his knees by so many things: her earthy, shining beauty; her pure seductiveness; the guilt.

He'd spent more time at work today because, after David's convenient trip, Lucas had decided to approach some of the top executives and tell them straight out that he was going to be a more important part of TCO from now on. Since they knew he owned the majority of the stock, they heard him out. Lucas hadn't been asking for a rebellion against David or anything, but he had been laying groundwork in case the crap ever hit the fan.

As it just might if David decided to acknowledge Lucas's questions about what was happening with Tadmere.

He must've been staring at Alicia with such intensity that she felt it, because she met his gaze, matching it with the same heat.

His belly flip-flopped, arousing him.

As a notorious, very young heiress who was just coming of party age intercepted Alicia, his wife seemed to startle back to the moment. But after only a few minutes, she excused herself, leaving the room.

Gradually, the big-band music and the conversation filtered back to him. He laughed when he was supposed to laugh at his crowd's jokes, reacted when he was supposed to react, all while remaining on the fringes.

Where had she gone? And why did he miss her so much?

A short time later, he felt a pull on the back of his tux jacket. He turned around to find Alicia, who was smiling at the rest of the group. When Lucas saw the locker-room admiration in the other men's eyes, he bristled, slipping an arm around her waist.

"Mind if I borrow my husband?" she asked, all charm. A return to the hostess who'd enchanted him back at Refugio Salvo.

Before the group could answer, she'd pulled Lucas away, guiding him toward the door. "I checked in, and Gabriel is sound asleep. Magdelena's staying in the guest room tonight."

"How much longer do you want to hang out here?"

As she slipped her hand into his while they exited the ballroom, the hairs on his skin stood on end. God, one touch and he was a goner.

"I already thanked everyone who set up the event for

TCO," she said. "I told them you were coming down with something."

Well, since he hadn't been able to say much more than "boo" tonight during most conversations, he thought that might work. Going home sounded great to him. He'd been too consumed with his wife, because being away from her was a poison in his blood, killing him from the inside out.

She led him toward the lobby, and his body started echoing the distant rumba from the ballroom, deep and low.

One more day, one more day…

But when she pulled him into an elevator, suspicious hope clouded his vision. The car was thankfully empty, and, when she pressed a floor button, then wandered over to the opposite side to give him a shy glance, he began to give in to hope….

Her soft dress flowed around her, spotlighting the blush creeping up her face, emphasizing the sexy angel he'd come to need way too much.

"I couldn't stop watching you in there," she said, her blush deepening.

"Admiration from afar." Lucas tried to ignore the throb that was starting to beat in his groin. "Story of my life lately."

"I imagine you're not used to waiting for a woman. Especially your wife."

An inadvertent lump weighed in his throat, making his voice ragged. "Are you taking me to a room, Alicia?"

She touched that ever-present bracelet around

her wrist. Tonight, the charms were poking out of the pearls.

Slowly, she began to take both the pearls and the silver off, then secured them in her purse. Lifting her head, she looked him straight in the eye. There was a fire in her gaze, and it screwed into him like a column of heat.

"I didn't want to wait anymore," she said. "I mean—"

He was across the elevator in a flash, not caring if there were security cameras. Voraciously, he locked his mouth to hers, his fingers burying themselves in her hair with such tender roughness that pins hit the floor.

As her curls fell down to her shoulders, she answered him with such urgency that she seemed to blur into him, flame melding with flame. Before he knew it, his tux jacket was ripped open, his shirt jerked out of his pants.

The elevator doors parted, but it took him a moment to realize it. Still, Alicia must've been attuned to what was happening, because she dragged him into the hall, fumbling in her tiny evening bag.

"Key," she murmured.

Impatiently, he helped her find it and, between more kisses, they stumbled to a room she'd obviously booked when she'd disappeared from the event.

After the key had worked its magic, he pushed open the door, and it crashed against the wall. Lucas barely registered that it was a room, not a suite, but he didn't care. Hell, no. Alicia was all that mattered. His fantasies were coming true, his wife pulling him down to her for another long kiss as she dropped her bag to the floor.

He sipped at her, and she opened her mouth to him, allowing him to slip his tongue in. She was so warm, moist, tasting of a fruit cider they'd been serving downstairs.

His groin clutched, pounding with the blood roaring between his legs. He was getting so hard it pained him.

Slowing things down, he ran his tongue against hers, exploring in languorous time. It was seductive, delicious, but hardly appeasing his appetite.

It's actually happening, he thought, the realization knocking into him. He never thought he could feel this strongly about someone, but it wasn't as scary right now as he'd imagined. Not even close.

His arousal nudged against his fly, pushing him onward.

With a groan, he went deeper with his tongue, engaging hers in one long, sinuous stroke, then another. At the same time, he pressed into her, allowing her to feel his excitement. Her breasts were full, stimulating him to even greater heights as he imagined them bare in his palms.

Unable to hold back, he coaxed his hands around her, trying to locate a zipper. He didn't find one, discovering, instead, that there were intricate buttons down the front of the dress. He undid the first, then the next.

He heard her gasp, then pause, breathing against his mouth.

"Alicia?" he said, asking, needing.

After a pulse beat, he felt her nodding. "Yes. Yes."

He continued, heart in his throat. When he had the modest décolletage loosened, he saw that there was a bra built into it. With great care, he peeled the two sides back, revealing her full, naked breasts.

An emotion he couldn't name split him like a tree that'd been standing solid for years, only to be hit by lightning and transformed into new shapes that had opened themselves to the sky.

Her dusky nipples were tightened into buds, and greedily he ran a thumb over one, as if he'd discovered some rare gem.

"Why did you hide under so much clothing?" he asked.

"I…"

Wincing, she swallowed hard, leaning back her head.

He flowed with her momentum, guiding her toward the bed, laying her on it.

"You what, Alicia?"

She sighed, resting her head against a hand, glancing sidelong at him as he rubbed her nipple. She bucked slightly, then moved with his motions.

"Long story," she whispered tightly, closing her eyes. "But I…well, you know, I'm modest."

"Raised in a pious house. I know that. Are you afraid of making love with me?"

She bit her lip, and he had his answer…or, at least, part of it. He knew women who came from strict homes, but they'd gone against the grain, especially with him. In fact, it'd been as if a few of them had used Lucas Chandler to prove just how naughty they could be.

"It's not just sex," he said. "It won't be just sex with us, Alicia."

As the words echoed in his head, he wondered where the hell they'd come from. Even so, he knew with all his soul they were true. Lord, help him, they were true.

She opened her eyes, dark pools of mystery. "Lucas…"

"Yeah, angel?"

Almost sadly, she smiled at that. "Before we… I'm…" She blew out a breath, then watched him anxiously. "I'm not the angel you think I am. At least, not in that way."

Her meaning sank into him, and he stopped rubbing her breast for a second. "You're not a virgin."

"No." She said it as if she were crushed. "There was one time—"

He just about laughed, but that would've been a mistake. She was taking this seriously. Did she think he had some good girl/bad girl complex that would destroy him if he found out she wasn't pure? Well, he had called her his angel, but…he hadn't meant it that way. She was his angel because she'd saved him in so many ways.

"You really think that matters to me—a guy who's hardly pristine?"

She nodded, still gauging him.

Shaking his head, he stroked the underside of her breast. "You're twenty-three, and there aren't many women your age who haven't been with a man."

"So you don't care?"

"I care. I care about all your experiences and everything that's built you into the amazing woman you are. It wasn't your reputation that made me value you, Alicia, it's your…your soul, I suppose. Your actions. I'll take you any way you come."

Had he just said that? The playboy?

Yeah, he had, and he'd brought the smile of smiles to her. Now her eyes weren't dark with reluctance, they were beginning to shine with something else altogether. Invitation. Trust.

Leaving any guilt behind him—because how could he feel guilty about falling for her?—he cupped his hand under a breast, reveling in its curved weight. Primitive appreciation curdled in his belly, and he used his other hand to begin working her clothing off her, little by little.

As he bared her to him, he whispered gentle endearments, everything but the three words that really mattered. He couldn't love her, but he could honor and respect her in other ways. He could make this marriage a strong one, even if it'd started out for the wrong reasons.

He removed her shoes, then allowed the dress to fall to the carpet in a rustle of satin and chiffon, then tugged off her white cotton panties with both hands. Short of breath, he contained his crazed urges and sat back to worship her.

She was more beautiful than he could say, with her ample hips and curves, her smooth rosy-brown skin. He bent down to kiss her again, then used his lips to tattoo her from neck to collarbone.

Grasping his hair, she led him to her breasts, where he nipped and laved, taking her nipples into his mouth. He swirled his tongue over them, slow and deliberate, drawing them into even stiffer peaks.

"Oh…" she murmured, shifting beneath him.

By this time, his erection was howling for release, but he restrained himself. Alicia needed honey-slow seduction, and he was all for lingering inside of her when the time was right.

As she shifted in fevered demand, he took the next step, coasting a hand down, over her ribs, her stomach, to the thatch of dark hair between her legs. He eased a finger between her folds, hearing her moan.

"Are you happy, Alicia?" he asked.

"Almost," she ground out.

He laughed, feeling her getting primed for him. Pressing her nub, he drove her to squirm and cover her face with an arm.

Damn, he loved watching her like this, loved watching her in more sedate times when she was being a mother, too.

He loved…

Pushing the word away, he slipped a finger inside of her. She gasped loudly, lifting her hips, and he swirled, inside, out.

He was set to explode, but he'd wait. Dammit, he'd wait….

"Lucas…"

There it was, the final summons. Fumbling with his clothing, he nonetheless managed to get out of it and secure a condom from his wallet.

Soon, he was sheathed, poised over her to enter. "Ready…"

"Yes."

Alicia wrapped a leg around him, pulling him down

to her. When he entered, there was momentary discomfort, but she set her teeth against it, grinding her hips against him with panting insistence. The bad girl was back, she thought, and Alicia had missed her. Heaven help her, she'd been so wrong about holding that girl back.

All but burning with a passion so frantic that she could barely restrain it, she welcomed her husband— her husband, not a disposable lover but a man who truly mattered—inside. She knew the difference only now, as he filled her with something more than the physical.

She was tight from her abstinence, but as she shifted back and forth, urging him to fit into her, the pain turned to pleasure, the shame blasted away by the good of what a married couple were meant to do.

While they moved together, her body riding the waves of his thrusts, every motion soothed her and stoked her.

Just the way...I am...

Values me... Wants me...

So right... So right...

The thoughts piled on one another until they seemed to reach the sky, trembling in a haphazard tower.

I love him, I love him....

The building blocks of her emotion quaked, rattling her bones, jittering against her skin, as Lucas drove harder into her, their bodies sticking together and sliding in exertion.

I love—

Without warning, a shot out of the darkness crashed

the tower. At the climax, she crumbled, tumbled, hit the ground with such force that she broke apart.

But she was so put together. So complete.

Soon he came to his own peak, and they held each other in their marriage bed.

In the quiet scatter of emotion, Alicia even thought she heard him say "I love you," but she was too over-wrought to know for sure.

"I love you, too," she whispered without restraint, the sentiment disappearing into the comforting black-ness she saw when she closed her eyes. She nestled against him, flesh against flesh, her heart against his chest. "I love you, too."

Chapter Twelve

He'd told her he loved her.

Lucas sat in his office, his chair facing the window while he stared at a jagged skyline. It was Saturday, and TCO headquarters was subdued, populated by die-hard workaholics who didn't know the definition of what a weekend was.

Or by people who needed a place to sort things out.

His body still felt as alive as it had last night, fired with memories of caresses and sweat-slicked passion. After pressing against each other in the afterglow, he and Alicia had rested, stroking each other with quiet wonder, then gotten dressed in the midst of a new awareness.

Afterward, during the limo ride home, he'd found

himself unable to think of any light quips to chase away the silence. That's how he'd always handled sex in the past—a good time followed by the playboy's escape route: flattery that eased any disappointment his partner might have at his lack of commitment.

But he'd found himself much too committed last night, not wanting to let her go. Ever.

His confession—and hers—had reverberated around his skull.

Love. But how could he love a woman he was lying to?

When they'd gotten home, crossing the threshold hand in hand, their son had been asleep. As Lucas had kissed him in the night-light-dimmed room, it'd struck him: They were a real family. This wasn't an act, anymore, and he couldn't function under the weight of secrets, not if he really loved his wife and son, as he'd murmured in that one unguarded moment.

For the rest of the night, he'd tried to convince himself that his feelings were false, that they'd only been the product of finally getting what he wanted from Alicia's body. They made love once more, then again, but nothing changed.

Yet…he *couldn't* fall for her, he told himself over and over. He couldn't allow himself the luxury of it.

With the break of morning, when everything was more vulnerable in the light, Lucas panicked, cornered by his mistakes. Not knowing how to handle a kiss good-morning or even a breakfast with Gabe, he'd told his family that he needed to go into the office for a short time.

Now, at his desk, he held a hand to a pounding temple. How was he going to tell his wife what he'd done? Because, if he wanted to live with her, touch her, ever feel that he'd *earned* her, he needed to come clean.

But he knew exactly what the consequences would be—he'd *always* known. She would hate him and make his nightmares about becoming his own emotionally downtrodden father come true.

Dammit, he had no idea how to protect himself from what would inevitably happen. And to make things worse, there was a child's happiness and well-being at stake....

Behind Lucas's chair, someone cleared his throat. Lucas had forgotten Barnaby had come in, too, and they'd been having a conversation before Lucas's mind and body had collapsed into one big heap of muddled idiocy.

"Sorry about that," he said, swiveling back around until the view of his spartan office met him.

Barnaby sat in the middle of it all, a man dressed to the nines in a natty button-down shirt, tie and slacks. Surrounding him were Lucas's fledgling attempts at making his office more of a place he wanted to be: framed pictures of Alicia and Gabe by the Nativity scene, by the Christmas tree, on the couch lightly roughhousing one night before bedtime.

The photos both calmed Lucas and sent him into a mental upheaval once again.

"Glad I gave up Saturday morning to be here," Barnaby said, but he had a faintly ambitious glint in his eyes that told Lucas he was halfway kidding.

"Trying to sort a lot out." Lucas sighed, laying a hand on the reports Barnaby had set in front of him about an hour ago, memos that his assistant had some-how intercepted. They confirmed that David had been setting up meetings behind Lucas's back. "I hate to think that my own brother would want to keep me in the dark about a company I own, too, but…"

"But what more evidence do you need?"

"I'd like to hear him tell me to my face."

That's right—he wanted David to admit that he'd had his eye on a woman like Alicia for Lucas all along. And now Lucas wanted him to confess that he might even be concerned about Lucas overstepping his Face duties and stepping on David's Brain ones, too.

"What you need to do," Barnaby said, "is continue impressing the other executives. The more you prove that you're serious about this company, the more re-ceptive they'll be. It's going to take a long time to erase your reputation, but you should keep at it. Your work with Refugio Salvo was an excellent start."

Lucas narrowed his gaze. Was Barnaby truly on his side? Dumb question. Of course he was. If Lucas gained power, he would be the assistant's golden ticket. But he sensed something else—could it really be respect?—as the other man picked up Lucas's favorite picture from the desk, the one in front of the Christmas tree.

"My family," Lucas said, pride flooding him, sur-prising him with its strength.

Barnaby grinned at the photo. "In all honesty, I thought you were a real fool before you got married, Lucas. But you've turned it around. You really have."

He knew it was true. Alicia and Gabe had invaded

his soul. Maybe it was because he'd opened himself to changing after his father's stroke. Or maybe it was just because there was some kind of magic that one person saved for another one, and Alicia had been the woman to put a spell on him. Gabe, too.

But even in the light of this epiphany, a tug of fear still worked at Lucas.

What happens when the truth comes out? How will I cope if I don't protect myself?

From the doorway, a calm, low voice intruded.

"You're right, Barnaby," David said. "Lucas has really changed a lot."

He found his brother practically holding Ford Chandler up on one side as the older man used his silver-tipped cane to balance on the other. Their similarities wormed into Lucas: their dignified postures, their height and build. It occurred to him that David was on the fast track to becoming Ford Chandler, except, like the old Lucas, he'd taken care to avoid any emotional attachment to women. David Chandler would never emulate their dad in that respect.

"In the office on a weekend?" Ford asked, his eyes losing a little of their light. "This is serious."

At the veiled reference to Project Turning Over a New Leaf, Lucas's heart lurched—and not just because he was remembering Alicia. Clearly, Barnaby had known about this charade, but that didn't mean Lucas wanted him to hear this private talk.

David was giving Lucas's picture-riddled desk a measuring scan. His expression said what he was clearly thinking: *Yes. He's very serious.*

Setting down the Christmas-tree photo, Barnaby nodded at David and Ford. "I've got a lot of work waiting for me."

"And I've got a lot to talk about with my family," Lucas added. "Thank you, Barnaby. I really appreciate everything."

The assistant nodded again and headed for the exit as David led his dad farther inside. After the younger Chandler helped Ford to a couch, he closed the office door and made his way over to Lucas's desk, then picked up the photo Barnaby had deserted. After a second, he took it over to their dad, who smiled.

Lucas could hardly believe his father's receptiveness. Was Ford in the mood to put together another family, with a new wife? Or...

God, it was rough to consider that maybe, just maybe, the old man had changed after the stroke, too. That he'd started to make amends with his good-for-nothing son.

As if to prove it, his dad gave the picture back to David, his gaze misty. "I get to meet him tomorrow. My grandson."

Lucas could only nod, swamped by emotions he couldn't hold back. Respect. Here it was. So why didn't it feel better?

"You're really getting into the role," David said.

Heat crept up Lucas's skin, from his neck to his face. Part remembrance of last night, part anger at his brother. "We need to talk."

But David spoke up first. "Luke, here's a word of advice. Don't be carrying photos of that woman or the boy in your wallet or keeping them on your desk. All business. Just remember they're all business."

Are they? Lucas thought. *Have they ever been?*

On the couch, Ford didn't say anything. He just stared at the floor, leaning on his cane.

David was watching Lucas closely—too closely, as if he knew exactly what had happened at the ball last night. And maybe he did, with all the executives who were around to see how Lucas had lavished attention on his wife.

"Not that real emotion and passion for your charade is a bad thing," David said lightly even though his eyes were like granite. "The more genuine the act, the better. But I'd hate to see you break her heart with the truth."

"Bull." Lucas stood with such force that his chair hit the wall in back of him. "David, we've got something to hammer out here, so don't stir things up around Dad so you can avoid it. You flew out to L.A. on some useless trip just to make me stew. And did you bring Dad here to witness everything, hoping he'd see that I'm actually not fit to run the company, even in spite of all your 'support'?"

His brother didn't even try to deny it. He tapped the photo frame against his leg, the only sign of agitation. "You're *not* fit, Luke. Sure, you're great at a party and your marriage has done us a lot of good, so far, especially with Tadmere. But you're not executive material. Admit it."

From the couch, his father was watching with interest, as if seeing how Lucas would hold up under this onslaught. Lucas even thought he saw his dad urging him on with a subtle gaze, as if he didn't want to be disappointed by a human being, yet again, in the remaining time he had on earth.

Yet, how could Lucas not disappoint him? He'd already let *himself* down, and God knew how Alicia and Gabe would feel after they found out the truth. He hated who he was, hated the weakness in character that had allowed him to fall prey to David's orchestrations.

Protect yourself, his instincts yelled.

"I'm not the one who needs to do some admitting, David. Why didn't you tell me that Tadmere has television and radio stations across the border?"

David sent his dad a cocky glance. "Luke, if you'd possessed any interest in TCO, whatsoever, you'd have known. All of a sudden you're not trusting my business sense?"

"Not since I put two and two together. Tadmere and their Mexican interests. Our need to get in good with their customers. Your proposal to have me court not just a good woman but one whose ethnicity could be used to sway the demographics."

"Come on, Luke, would you have said no to a relationship with her even if you'd known what all of the plan entailed? I just didn't involve you in the more unsavory details because I didn't think you needed them to function as the Face. Besides—" he raised an eyebrow "—you're the one who went and put a family together."

Stung, Lucas thought about how much he'd just wanted to please his father with this new reputation. How he would've done anything—*had* done anything.

Knowing that David had planned to exploit Alicia's ethnicity wouldn't have held him back because he'd wanted to be a "better man" too damned badly.

He'd just gone about it all wrong.

He glanced at his dad, finding that the old man looked more exhausted than ever. Was he hoping Lucas had some kind of heart, after all?

How could Lucas finally please him, once and for all?

Anger riding his words, he decided that maybe the truth should start here, in front of his father. "There's a difference in what we perceived a relationship with Alicia to be, David. She was…" His heart swelled. "I really wanted to be with her, just because of who she was, not because she was a statistic or political ploy. I needed her and Gabe's goodness in my life. Marriage was the excuse that finally allowed me to admit that I was missing something only she and my son could give me."

Sapped by the admission, Lucas planted his hands on the desk, almost afraid to look at his father. But he did. Dammit, if he was any kind of man, he could face the most influential person in his life—the dad who'd been such a cold role model, the paternal figure who held such inexplicable power over Lucas.

He found the old man's eyes watery with a pain he seemed to be reliving before Lucas's very gaze. His wives. Maybe he was recalling each one of his own heartbreaks, each vow he'd made to never fall into a woman's trap again.

Maybe he didn't want Lucas to fall into it, either. Or was there more to it? Was this a test?

Probably. Lucas was too used to the father who'd been so stony to him while growing up. Maybe Ford Chandler wanted to see if his son was tough enough to run a corporation and that's why he wasn't explaining anything.

Did he want to discover if Lucas would be destroyed by a woman, too? Or did he just want his son to be happy now?

"Luke," David said, looking as if he felt sorry for his brother. "Think about what you're saying. Do you really believe you're the type of man who can make Alicia happy beyond money? Seriously?"

It was as if all his doubts had been given a voice.

His defense mechanisms revved up again, because when Alicia found out what he'd done, he would end up just like the old man. Crushed and wounded, sidelined by a frail body and heart.

Maybe you just need to tell her everything before you fall even further for her, his defenses screamed. *Maybe David's right, and you should just push her away before she finds out herself how useless you are.*

"Anyway," David added, looking at the Christmas-tree picture once more, then discarding it on the desk, facing it away from him, "you'll be happy to know that our plan at least worked. Tadmere's executives loved Alicia and they had a lot to do with persuading the big bosses to trust us. It seems that they think you chose well when it came to a wife and that all the rumors about you might've been…inflated. So early this morning, over breakfast, the Tadmere siblings signed the company over to us."

David seemed to want to high-five him or something, but there was no celebration in Lucas. Just a dull, empty space that had opened up, swallowing all the hope and love he thought he'd had for Alicia and Gabe.

It wasn't real. It was all just a plan that had worked out for the betterment of TCO.

Over on the couch, Ford Chandler sighed, speechless.

And, behind the barricade of his desk, Lucas glanced at the Christmas-tree picture of him, Alicia and Gabe, all huddled in a laughing group and smiling at the camera without any show or pretense.

She was going to turn him away when she found out about this marriage.

She was going to surprise him.

Alicia couldn't just sit at home, waiting for her husband to get back. Not when she was obsessed with replaying every single touch and kiss, her body urging her to be with him again, to seek out more, more, more.

So she'd put together a basic snack in a wicker basket: sliced smoked Gouda cheese with dainty crackers, apples and oranges, sparkling mineral water, freshly baked chocolate-chip cookies. Though she knew that he would, no doubt, attend some expense-account, high-class restaurant for a noontime meal, her efforts were an excuse to go to him, to extend their afterglow.

So this was what love felt like, she thought, kissing Gabriel goodbye as he built a skyscraper out of lettered wooden blocks with Magdelena's help. She promised she would be home in a couple of hours—and she meant it, knowing she would miss Gabriel after a short time.

But this was her honeymoon, and she needed to be alone with her husband.

She also needed to finally tell him everything that had been haunting her. The truth about who she really was, the ugliness about how she'd been conceived. Now, more than any other time, she knew Lucas would accept her, warts and all. Hadn't he said as much last night?

I'll take you any way you come, he'd told her, and she'd believed it. The soulful way he'd made love to her had only confirmed that, too, creating a confidence she'd never possessed before meeting him. She had nothing to be afraid of.

On the way over in the town car, she called ahead. He wasn't answering his cell, so she tried his work number. She was forwarded to his assistant, Barnaby, who was also working on a Saturday. Smiling at Lucas's ambition to be a bigger part of the company, she thought that, as long as he still spent all that time with her and Gabriel, she wouldn't complain.

Barnaby arranged for her to be let in, and a fawning security guard escorted her to the fortieth floor. The assistant greeted her at the elevators.

"Mrs. Chandler, it's wonderful to finally meet you."

She was so anxious to get to Lucas that she probably sounded rude when she refused his escort and asked how to get to her husband's office by herself, instead.

But Barnaby seemed to understand as he gave her directions.

"Thank you so much." She reached into the basket, gave him some cookies. "Hope you get to go home soon."

She waved farewell as she walked toward her husband's office.

It wasn't hard to find, with his name embossed in gold plating on the door. She knew Barnaby had told him to expect her, so she wasn't surprised to discover him alone at his desk.

What she hadn't expected was his dark gaze.

"Hi," she said hesitantly, wondering if she'd interrupted something important with her snacktime whim.

Yet, when he smiled at her, his eyes lighting up just an instant before the joy switched off again, she wasn't so sure that he hadn't been waiting just for this moment, when he could talk to her.

Was something wrong?

He helped her put the basket on the desk, their fingers brushing and sending flares up her skin. He grinned again, flashing dimples, and she thought maybe she'd been imagining everything.

"I've missed you," he said, leaning over and kissing her.

As their lips fused, she sank into the searing delights of last night's lovemaking, her body reliving the ecstasy.

"Me, too," she said against his lips. "I couldn't stay away."

Kissing her again, he gathered her against him, holding her so tightly she thought she might break apart if he hadn't been the glue that held her together.

He pulled her onto the desk until she was sitting.

Files shifted over the top of the wood, but he didn't mind. She was the most important thing on his to-do list, obviously, and that brought back her self-esteem, full-roar.

Releasing him, she reached into the basket and began to parcel out the food. "Getting lots done?"

He paused, turned away from her to snatch an apple. He stared at it, his gaze going hard again. "Too much. I'd love to forget about all of it."

With force, he bit into the fruit. Heart aching for him to touch her again, she caressed his arm. She could make him forget anything, could make him think that she was the only person who existed. She was positive of that.

"I want to tell you something that's been bugging me," she blurted, a little shocked that it'd just come out like this. But she'd been talking herself into spilling everything all the way over here and she didn't want to wait, anymore.

For a second, he seemed reluctant to hear what she had to say, so she rushed to explain. "It's not about you, believe me. In fact, last night, everything you said, what you made me feel… I want you to know who I am before we go on. You deserve to know, wife to husband. I don't want there to be anything between us, anymore."

Slowly, he set down the apple.

She had to get it all out before he looked any more worried. She hated making him uncomfortable like this.

Taking a breath, a twinge of panic almost made her stop before she'd started. This private knowledge had marked her so deeply, so awfully, that letting it out was almost like opening a Pandora's box.

But it was the right thing to do. No secrets. Lucas was going to love her any way she came.

Going for it, she forced the story into the open, telling him about her grandfather's deathbed confession—her papa's prostitution, the one-night stand that had turned into a pregnancy, the abandonment.

All the while, Lucas never seemed judgmental. In fact, he seemed shattered in some heartbreakingly silent way. Still, he kept his distance while she spoke.

Heart racing, she ended the story. "I tried to find them, both my mom and dad, but I kept running into dead ends."

"That's why you sold your home and went to Mexico."

"Yes." She plucked at the skirt of her suit. "It's almost like I was led down there, to find Gabriel. To find you."

He fixed his gaze on the floor.

A snap of doubt nagged at her. "I didn't want you to regret having a marriage that turned out to be a lot different than what you first thought it would be."

It was as if she'd slapped him with that last statement.

In a terrible instant, her fears crashed over her. Had she been wrong? Was he disgusted by her now that he realized he was committed to someone with a background that would dirty his new lease on life? Was he afraid of the bad press she'd bring now?

The returning shame throttled her even before she could shield herself with the reminder of everything he'd told her about accepting her, valuing her.

"Marriage," he repeated, closing his eyes and running a hand through his hair. "Alicia, I…" He shook his head. "Dammit, you don't have anything to be ashamed of. Not at all."

Of course Lucas didn't think any less of her because of this story. Alicia wasn't responsible for the sins of her father, even if she'd been raised to believe the opposite. But that wasn't the reason he was ripped up.

No, his self-disgust had hit him with a vengeance, barring him from even glancing at her. Lies, all his lies, when she was so intent on the truth… He didn't deserve even a look, a touch—nothing from this woman. And, just as David had said, Lucas knew he would never deserve her.

He hadn't even earned the privilege of being a father to Gabe, who needed to grow up knowing the value of truth.

God, his son. Lucas's heart cracked.

Instinct urged him to protect himself. To keep his world together before she exercised her power to tear it apart by rejecting *him*.

Before he could even think, he moved to the other side of the desk, removing himself from the temptation of her skin, her perfume, memories of the beautiful life they could've had. "I've done something that…"

This was it, but he couldn't go on, not when he wanted to hold on to what he'd found in Alicia and Gabe so damn badly.

At first, she just smiled at him, so innocently that it slayed him. "What have you done besides make me and Gabriel happy, Lucas?"

But as he stood in silence, she seemed to catch on

to the seriousness of what he was about to tell her. One of her hands grabbed at the edge of his desk.

"Lucas, what're you talking about?"

You don't deserve her, instinct screamed. *You never will, so let her go before this goes any further.*

"Our marriage—" his voice was tight in his throat "—it's a sham."

Chapter Thirteen

Lucas's announcement still bounced off the walls, punching Alicia with hollow ripples of sound that invaded her but didn't hurt. No, they didn't hurt just yet, even though they should have.

He was saying he really *didn't* love her, right? That he wasn't accepting her, after all?

As she endured the mental pummeling, her gaze locked onto the pictures on his desk, as if she needed to cling to some kind of friendly anchor.

Christmas trees, Nativity scenes, Gabriel clowning in front of the camera, Alicia and Lucas with their arms around each other, their skin touching and nearly fusing with the warmth that always connected them…

Jokes, Alicia thought, as the pictures warped in the hot tears flooding her eyes. *Tragic jokes caught on film.*

Across the desk, she was aware of how Lucas was waiting for her to react, his body taut.

The body she'd rubbed up against last night, the body that had joined hers in a reverent, personal matrimony.

Sham... It didn't make any sense. He'd said he loved her. He'd even shown her that. And she'd welcomed the love as if it'd been a part of her that had finally come home.

"I—" she shook her head "—I don't understand."

"You should know the truth." He'd become so cold, so unlike the man she'd come to cherish.

As her gaze locked back onto him, the room blurred even more, and not only because of the tears. Nothing was clear.

But then a teardrop fell from one eye and she caught a bleary half view of him. Unlike the normally light-hearted man who operated under such charm and stature, Lucas looked beaten, his shoulders hunched, his face mapped with devastation. He was a mirror of the pain that was just beginning to scald her as the truth of his statement seeped into her.

"I married you specifically to clean up my public image and to help TCO acquire Tadmere," he said, voice rigid, agonized.

Hadn't he already decided to redo his life when he'd met her? And hadn't their marriage just happened, without any plans, whatsoever? It almost sounded as if she'd been part of some clinical scheme....

He was watching Alicia as if asking for her to yell at him, to wound him. But she was too numb.

It must've been the shock that made her say, "Are you telling me this because you think I'm not good enough for you now?"

"No. That's…God, that's not it, at all, Alicia."

Nonetheless, the deeply engraved fear ached. Shrinking into herself, she instinctively buried her face in her hands. Suddenly, her fancy new clothing felt like a hard shell that hung off her with an alien weight; she longed for her old clothes, her old life.

Maybe the agony would disappear if she went far enough into that shell.

"Alicia."

She heard him move toward her, but she angled her body away, the motion edged with an anger she was only now admitting.

"I don't blame you for hating me." His voice was ravaged. "I'm sorry. I did it because Tadmere wouldn't sell unless I polished up my act."

He'd done it for his dad, too, she thought. For his dad, not for her or Gabriel.

Ire was eating her up, gnawing its way through her uncomfortable designer suit. She raised her face from her hands, realizing her fingers were damp.

"So there it is," she said, her stomach quivering from repressed rage. But if there was one thing she'd learned from loving this man it was that holding back was ridiculous. She'd done it too long because of her parents and she'd realized last night that it'd been a mistake.

Now she wasn't going to restrain anything.

"Your poor inner playboy made you do it?" she said, facing him.

He was obviously struggling for control. "I won't make excuses."

"Then what other reason could there be, Lucas?"

Before the question was even out of her mouth, it all hit her, each piece clicking into place. How he'd seduced her with promises of family when he knew damn well she wanted it more than anything. How he'd accelerated their courtship by telling her he wouldn't be around for long and that they should live for the moment. How she'd heard David mention demographics on the phone. How Lucas had been concerned by Tadmere's ownership of Mexican companies. How Lucas had taken a Latina wife just as TCO was getting more desperate to buy Tadmere, which owned Mexican outlets.

"There's more to it, too," he said as she slipped off the desk and almost stumbled toward the windows, away from him. "Besides polishing my life for public consumption with a storybook relationship, it was only later I found out that Tadmere had holdings across the border. Getting together with you was a good way to court Tadmere's executives, as well as the people who'd be listening to and watching the stations down there."

"I was good PR. You chose me because of my ethnicity."

"No."

She heard the rustle of his clothing as he came nearer, but the sound only ratcheted up her anger.

"Stay—" she turned to him and held up a hand; it trembled "—away." Shaking her head, she held back a new attack of tears.

For a fleeting moment, he went from ice-cold to thawed, one hand stretched out to her in supplication. Even so, she couldn't reconcile what she was hearing with the family they'd become, the love they'd just started to share.

With his betrayal.

It occurred to her that this arrangement was the reason he hadn't forced the honeymoon issue, but she was hardly grateful. Allowing her to decide when the time was right was the least he should have done.

Even if the part of her that still loved him gave him credit for it.

"So you didn't choose me because of my background when that's what TCO needed to secure Tadmere?" she asked.

"I didn't deceive you about that part, Alicia. I really didn't know about the Mexican businesses." That muscle in his jaw flinched and he fisted his hands by his sides, as if arming himself. "David's the one who suggested a relationship, but I wanted the marriage and adoption. *I* did. He only planted the idea in my head after he saw the obvious attraction between us."

"Attraction." Such a casual way to describe what she thought they'd had.

But there was something much more important at stake here. Gabriel. Oh, Gabriel.

"The worst thing about this," she said, on the cusp of tears again, "is Gabriel. That child loves you, Lucas, and you've set him up to be abandoned again. Didn't you think about that?"

"I did, over and over again." Unclenching his fists

at the mention of Gabriel, Lucas seemed to succumb to the self-loathing she'd seen so many times, the destructive pattern she'd wanted to save him from. "I thought about what I was doing to the both of you every day. But in that moment I proposed to you, I knew I could give him a good home. And I thought I could make you happy. Believe that, at least. I really thought I could."

At his forced tone, something yanked at the core of her, yet she ignored it. She had to or else she'd be twice the idiot she was now. Lord, help her, she wasn't about to suffer because of someone else's sins again.

She wouldn't waste one more precious second doing that.

"So what do you want?" she asked. "Am I supposed to pretend this is okay? That a trip to Rockefeller Center or a shopping spree will get things back to normal?" Back to the happiness she'd experienced for such a short, wonderful time?

"I don't expect you to forget. But..." He stiffened again, then turned around, revealing an icy gaze that was much too close to David's. Yet, there was something below that frosty glance...almost as if there was a plea in the depths of color, a cry to make him stop. "I can make this marriage worth your while, Alicia. Gabe has a home and we can keep it that way. And you've got the money for your charities, you've got a family. Maybe I can't give you more than that—"

It was as if she'd been slammed off the edge of the earth.

Cheap. *Dios,* was she so cheap that he thought she could be bought off?

He really didn't value her. She'd been wrong. So, so wrong.

"You're making me feel like I'm my father," she said, hardly able to talk with the emotional grit in her throat. "You make me feel as if I can be had for money. I never thought you'd be the one to do that to me."

At her pain, he seemed to crumble, his gaze turning sorrowful, his hand rising again as if begging her.

Seeing this strong man completely defeated almost undid her. Her impulsive, love-stricken side wanted to run to him, to find a way to work this out. Because, in a way, he was right—why throw away what they had? Why take away Gabriel's family? The family she'd been praying for?

Yet, she couldn't forget this. He'd taken advantage of the poor little girl he thought she was, exploited her need for acceptance.

"I won't be your pawn," she whispered.

He jerked as if impaled, just as she'd been earlier, but she took no satisfaction from it. Yet, she wouldn't allow herself to sympathize with him.

Not anymore, she thought. Not after this.

Dear God, why couldn't she just find someone to love her? Her parents, now Lucas... What was wrong with her that they all treated her so badly?

And to think she'd almost had her family. So close. So, so close.

She grabbed at her jacket, pulled at it to keep her emotions in check, to keep herself in that shell, secure.

"Odd," she said softly, "I almost believed that there's dignity in love, but I can't imagine there is now." Her chest pulled itself apart with sadness as she prepared to go. "I almost left the shame behind, but this brings it to a new level."

As Lucas watched her leave, a tortured groan escaped him. He moved toward her retreating form but held himself back, just as he'd been holding back all the real truths in an attempt to defend himself from the rejection he knew was coming.

He did love her, so much. And now that she was turning her back on him, he couldn't control it anymore.

But hadn't he been right about the outcome? All his worst fears had come true because now she was abandoning him. But he deserved her scorn, deserved every harsh truth she could dish out.

"I'd give anything for you to forgive me," he said as he went to the door, his shields wearing down. "I don't want you to hurt, Alicia. I'd take all your pain on me if I could."

In the hallway, when she glanced back at him with those watery eyes, he thought that maybe, just maybe, she believed him. But then her doubt returned, barring her from his best intentions.

Couldn't she believe in him enough to think that maybe he could change someday if she stayed?

No, God no, he thought. He'd destroyed her ability to trust him, and that left him with next to nothing.

In fact, he *was* nothing because, without her, he was just a tycoon playboy who had no emotions or heart. An empty good-time guy who wasn't capable of anything more.

It was true. Now that she was leaving him, he realized that living with her and taking the risk of getting decimated by love was so much better than coming home to an empty place.

He needed her forgiveness. Needed her and Gabe. He didn't want to live without them, even if it meant he would be as ruined as his father was now.

She was shaking her head, fending off his plea for a second chance. "Maybe I can forgive you, but I can't forget, Lucas. I can't forget how I was just a thing to you."

"You aren't. Listen to me, Alicia, you're…" *Say it.* "You're my world." His ears rang with the emotional outburst, but he meant it. Meant it with all of his soul. "You and Gabe."

With a stifled sob, she rushed down the hall.

"Alicia, don't go! Don't hide. Don't run away from this like you did when you sheltered yourself in Mexico, in the orphanage, under those strict clothes and vows."

Whipping around, she revealed a face streaked with the red trails of tears. "I'm still that woman, plain and simple! And thinking I'm anything that'll fit into this fake life of yours is just another lie!"

She shot him a look that he interpreted as, *And thinking* you're *anything more than a playboy is a lie, too.*

Or maybe that was his conscience giving him that final kick in the gut.

Whatever it was, he watched her run down the rest of the hallway, then disappear around the corner, out of his sight.

Losing the last of his hope and strength, he slumped against the wall, allowing it to hold him up.

Gone, he thought. *The best thing that's ever happened to you is gone, and you're the reason she left.*

But that was no huge surprise, because wasn't that the way of things? His father had always reminded him that women leave. He'd seen it with stepmother after stepmother.

And Lucas's woman—the wife he'd fallen head over heels for—was leaving, too, because he was too weak to hold on to her.

But, God, he loved her more than anything, loved Gabe more than he could've ever imagined.

The thought held him up, even without the wall, as he trained his gaze down the hallway, his mind furiously scrambling for ways to keep his family from falling apart.

At first, Alicia had cried so much that the tears had become meaningless. On the way back to the penthouse in the town car, on the trip up in the elevator, in the taxi she had summoned once she had quickly packed enough clothing and toys to comfort Gabriel as she blindly searched for direction…

Now, two weeks later, as she watched her son playing with a Slinky on the withered carpet of the motel room she could barely afford with her own money, Alicia was done with tears. They hadn't helped her to decide where to go from here or how to drive the love she had for Lucas out of her heart.

He had called on her cell phone over and over again, asking her to meet with him. But she hadn't returned any of his messages, even if his voice was ragged with remorse.

"I'll do anything to make this up to you, Alicia," he'd said from the first phone call on. "Please, just believe that."

Every day, every hour, every *minute,* Lucas's heartfelt confession at the office played over and over in her head, as if it'd been recorded on a loop and she'd been strapped to a chair and sentenced to listen to it for hours on end.

You're my world. You and Gabe…

But what about love? Had she just imagined hearing it that night at the Christmas fund-raiser? Why wasn't he mentioning the one thing that just might make her reconsider?

He'd proposed that they keep their business marriage together, but he hadn't said he loved her. That told her everything.

On the floor, Gabriel dropped the Slinky, his lower lip wobbling as he turned to her.

He didn't need to say anything, because Alicia knew that face. The big, sad brown eyes filled with questions she hadn't been able to answer.

Why aren't we living with Daddy? You let me see him every night, Mama, but you never stay for dinner with us. Why, why, WHY?

"Are you ready to go to Daddy's now?" she asked, throat raw. It'd be cruel to keep her son away from Lucas, so she'd worked out temporary visitation via Magdelena. The boy loved his adopted dad beyond measure, and she knew Lucas felt the same way about his new son. But that didn't make coming to any decisions easier.

Gabriel brightened up for a moment, clearly joyful at the prospect of visiting with Lucas. Alicia had offered up the lame excuse that Daddy and Mama were on a "vacation" from each other, because it was the only thing she could think to tell him. The truth would hurt Gabriel beyond imagination.

Sheltering him from the truth was the only option she could come up with right now.

As she led her son to a waiting taxi she'd reserved for every night at this hour—dinnertime with Daddy— she once again tried to think of a better story for Gabriel, something with a happier ending. She was always going to be his mother, no matter how much she had to scrimp and save to stay in New York so he could keep visiting Lucas. But how would her so-called husband fit into their future? She had no idea, but it was obvious *she* wouldn't be able to live with him anymore.

Right? Wasn't it obvious?

You're my world. You and Gabe...

Alicia's chest caved into itself while the taxi traveled from Jamaica and into Manhattan. Soon they were inching along Fifth Avenue, the sidewalk traffic visible from the tinted windows. Gabriel merely stared outside from the height of his car seat, face devoid of its usual glow.

Not for the first time, guilt hit her full force. How could she deprive her child of Lucas's genuine affection? Of the privilege Gabriel would enjoy if she could only allow herself to take the first step and give Lucas the chance to make it up to her as he wished to?

And how can you deprive yourself of the man you love?

Gripping the material of her modest skirt, Alicia

pushed away her fear and watched the view, too. All those people buzzing around, shopping for gifts three days before Christmas, enjoying the sights of the city, bundled against the twilight chill. She wished she could be one of them, with Christmas on her mind and "Jingle Bells" playing through her head instead of all her regrets and doubts.

Two weeks ago, before she'd known the truth, everything had seemed so beautiful. She'd been so ecstatic, just like life with her grandparents before her *abuelo* had told her about the taint of her birth. Ignorance had, indeed, been bliss.

But then the poison apple of wisdom had fallen into her hands and Eden had been taken away from her.

Anger reemerged, but it wasn't necessarily at Lucas now—it was at circumstance.

Why was she allowing something other than herself to control what she really wanted? A family. A life full of nights with the Lucas she'd fallen in love with.

Why was she bowing to outside forces and surrendering her happiness to them again? *Why?*

The more she dwelled on it, the more rebellious she became. Oddly enough, she knew that Lucas still valued her. His courtship had proven that over and over; either that or he'd been a very good actor. But she didn't buy that at all—she knew deep down he had felt something for her.

Love?

She recalled that day in the office, when he'd finally laid his emotions at her feet before she'd run away from him. Would a man like him—one who feared abandonment himself—have continued calling her, begging her to listen to him unless he really did love her? Why wasn't he repeating it again and again on the phone then?

That was the only thing holding her back. If she could just hear him say it…

Twenty minutes later, Alicia and Gabriel stepped into the penthouse elevator at the Boudin, a familiar, painful experience. The marbled elegance that had once felt so alien now seemed like an abandoned part of home, because that's where it had once led.

Home, with the man she still loved, even after everything.

At the end of the ride—Gabriel hadn't even enjoyed it as he usually did, she noted with sinking disappointment—they came to the lobby.

"Daddy's not home yet," Alicia said. She'd been careful in arranging to drop her son off with Magdelena before Lucas was scheduled to leave the office in a half hour. "But he'll be here soon."

"Mama come for food?" Gabriel said as Alicia rang the doorbell. Hope kindled in his dark gaze.

"Not tonight." She smoothed back the hair from his face.

"Why no?"

Again blank spaces served as answers.

Why? Why won't you give Lucas a chance to redeem himself? Didn't you once believe he was capable of becoming that good person he wished to be?

As she flailed for a decent response, the door eased open.

Revealing the one person she'd been trying so hard to avoid.

At the sight of him, she couldn't take in oxygen. Dizziness swept over her, her belly clenching with such force that she almost weakened, throwing herself into his arms. She'd been so afraid this would happen if they came face-to-face.

Yet, all she wanted to do was be near him, against him.

His lips parted as if to say something, but he didn't speak. No, his reddened, desperate gaze said it all.

His devastation, still fresh after all these days, hammered at her. So did his appearance. It looked as if every hour had taken a swing at him, connecting with bruising mental force that had beaten the life out of him.

Sorrow tightened the area behind her eyes. *Lucas.*

"Daddy!" Gabriel yipped, throwing himself into Lucas's arms.

Tearing his gaze away from Alicia, her husband broke into an anguished smile, grabbed on to his son as if his life depended on it.

"It's been just one day and I missed you," he said into the boy's hair. "I've missed you so much."

"Me, too!" Gabriel had latched his arms around Lucas's neck and wasn't letting go.

Before Alicia could break down, she took a step backward. "I'll see you in a few hours, Gab—"

"No, wait, Alicia," Lucas said. "Wait?"

Whispering into his son's ear, Lucas let the child go. Gabriel yelped, taking off into the penthouse. As if not wanting to break the connection, Lucas watched the boy disappear.

"I've been waiting to see you, too," he said softly. "Come in?"

She caught a whiff of Italian food. The scent broke one of the threads holding her together, leaving her dangling. But she didn't look at him. She couldn't, not if she wanted to keep herself from getting her heart thrashed to pieces again....

"I have to go."

"Don't." He stepped over the threshold. "I made sure I'd be here to see you tonight. Enough is enough. Please stay here, listen to me." His shoulders lost some of their heft. "I want you to see that I really have changed because of you and Gabe, even though I know you won't forgive me. I can't blame you for that, but I want to try."

As Lucas waited for her answer, he swallowed hard. Honoring her requests for maintaining distance had gotten to him. He hadn't wanted to disrespect her by hunting her down at her motel room, didn't want to force her to take money to maintain her separate residence, either. He'd known she wouldn't accept anything from him, but he'd done everything he could, anyway— except tell her that he loved her over the phone. It wasn't something to be said over an impersonal distance. He'd been waiting weeks to do it in person, knowing the words would sound cheap unless she could *see* just how much he meant it.

Only problem was, she'd be able to see how much of a disaster he'd become since she'd left him.

Alicia was eyeing him as if he were going to reach into her chest and yank out her heart—but he'd already accomplished that. Now all that was left to do was return it and hope that she would give it to him again with as much love as he felt for her.

"Stay," he said, the word raspy.

She looked like she wanted to enter so badly, yet she waited a beat, as if expecting him to say more.

And he would, if she would just come into their home.

Inside, he'd set up an I-love-you dinner that would show her just how much he meant it—everything from hundreds of roses to a recreation of their first meal together from Bella Sofia. But he'd made *this* meal himself, with a little help from Magdelena. He wanted everything to come from his heart, his soul.

He wanted her to know, without a doubt, that she meant everything to him.

He hesitated, suddenly unsure of himself, even though he saw how she felt clearly, agonizingly.

What if she's just not going to give you another chance? he thought, chest constricting. *What if she's beyond grand gestures—*

But then Gabriel ran into the foyer, and Lucas tore his gaze away from Alicia's for only a moment. How could he resist with his son?

"Rose!" the little boy said, holding up a thornless flower to his daddy, as if in sweet offering.

But all he saw were the elevator doors smacking closed.

She was gone.

Then realization crashed in on him. *You should've told her how much you love her right away, dammit. You didn't need fireworks to give her what she wanted.*

He bent down to give Gabriel a fierce hug, then whispered a promise in the boy's ear.

"I'll be right back, okay?" He strode out the door to go after Gabriel's mommy.

The wife he wasn't going to lose again.

Alicia leaned her forehead against the wall of the elevator car, eyes closed.

She'd given Lucas the chance to tell her, but he hadn't said it. The only words she'd wanted to hear, and he hadn't been able to come out with them.

I. Love. You.

That was it. Simple and pure. And she'd thought she'd read the sentiment in his eyes, but…

She opened her eyes as the doors opened, allowing her to walk into the Boudin's lobby and straight to the waiting taxi that would take her back to the motel.

She entered the taxi, ensconced in its heat, but the warmth didn't go any deeper as the car pulled into the street. No, all that remained within her was a stillness, the feeling of a house that'd been emptied of its furniture and life.

She'd only wanted to hear an *I Love You.*…

The taxi driver's low voice startled her.

"New York idiots," he said, glancing at his side-view mirror. "A moron is running up through the traffic, ma'am. But do not worry—our doors are locked, so you are safe from him, okay?"

Before she could react, there was a pounding at her window. She jerked away from it, hand to her throat.

As her eyesight adjusted, she saw Lucas, face flushed, eyes wild as he held up his hands in a plea.

"I love you, Alicia!" he yelled.

Her body flamed. *I love you,* he'd said, truth in his steady gaze. His admission bounced through her mind like the echoes of a triumphant chorus.

And he'd come after her. *Her.* His wife.

Something like a laugh—or maybe a sob of relief—shook her. "I…" The words had caught in her throat, so she cleared it, digging into her coat pocket and offering a fistful of money—how much, she didn't know—to the driver.

"Please unlock the door. My ride's done."

"Ma'am?" the cabbie asked.

"Please."

She heard the driver do as she asked. Right away, Lucas pulled it open, and a blast of cold air enveloped her.

"I saw you take off in this cab and ran you down," he said, grabbing her hands and taking her out of the taxi. "I'm not letting you get away this time. I love you. I mean that and I'll say it a million times to get you to believe it."

Horns blared at them, imitating the volume of her growing joy as it consumed her. While she caught her breath, Lucas held up a hand at the waiting vehicles, then pulled her to the sidewalk, where people dodged them.

Alicia barely felt the brush of their coats against her body. All she knew was that Lucas really wasn't going to surrender her without a fight.

That he *loved* her.

Holding her hands tightly, Lucas was dressed only in his cotton shirt, his cheeks flushed with cold.

But he didn't seem to mind that. "I fell for you the instant I saw you. And Gabe…I saw myself in him and I knew right away I couldn't live without him, either. But I wasn't honest with you about why I asked you to be my family. I couldn't be."

"Lucas—"

"Please just hear me out, because I'm never holding anything back again. It took me a long time to come to terms with how I felt because I thought opening myself up to you would make me weaker, just like my dad." He raised her hands to his chest, where she could feel his heart pounding. "But, all along, something was telling me it would be okay and I gave in, convincing myself that I was marrying you for business and never realizing the truth—that I wanted you more than any woman I've ever met. That I wanted to protect Gabe and keep him from all the disappointments I saw in his future."

Tears had started to slip from her eyes, coating her face. He reached out dry them.

"I'm willing to endure whatever punishment you have in store for me," he said. "I just want to go home with you. I want to hold on to all the good that came out of a bad situation. Please, Alicia."

Her breath hitched on a sob and she couldn't say anything.

"Okay. You still think our marriage can't be real." His tone was jagged, desperate. "Then I'm going to take care of that."

Right in the middle of the sidewalk he fell to his

knees, holding her hand between his again, almost as if he were in prayer. His violet eyes locked onto hers and in them Alicia could see a universe of love. It rocked her until her knees shook, threatening to take her down.

Voice raised, he said, "Alicia Sanchez Chandler, marry me again. I love you more than any man could ever love a woman. I'll love you until we're both old and our children need to wheel us around. I love you with all my heart."

Some people on the sidewalk had stopped to stare. There were even some mutters of "Lucas Chandler?"

Yet, he was oblivious, watching her with unadulterated hope, his emotions bare.

He loved her. He'd said it, not in the dark of night but in broad daylight in front of everyone. It was real. Pure and real, no matter what her worst fears told her.

How could she live without this man? How could she not give him another chance?

At her hesitation, a woman from the crowd said, "Girl, you'd better say yes before *I* do."

"Aren't they already married?" said another.

Alicia ignored them. Lucas Chandler was hers. She'd known it right from the start. She couldn't let him get away, couldn't miss this opportunity for happiness, even if they would both have to work for it.

Emotion overrode fear, her answer bursting out from the bottom of her soul.

"Yes," she whispered. "Yes, I'll be your wife."

As the growing crowd broke into "aws" and applause, Lucas jumped up and scooped her into his arms, hugging her to him until she almost lost her breath.

Amidst the clapping, he whispered in her ear, "I

know we have a lot to talk about, but I wanted to make you see that I'm serious. That this isn't any secret plan. Not anymore."

"I know. I love you, too. I always have."

She kissed him, the people around them whooping and cheering them on. Their voices merged into a chorus, a holiday carol of celebration and togetherness, a hymn of perpetual love.

When he set her on her feet, looking into her eyes and cupping her face in his hands, she eased off her coat, shedding at least part of her shell. She slipped it around him, just as he'd done for her that first day they'd met, then again on the penthouse terrace when she'd felt so out of sorts and he'd known just what she needed.

Comfort.

He pulled her into his embrace, warming her, too.

Yes, they had a long way to go in coming to terms with what he'd done, but she knew he was sincere in wanting her to be his wife. She knew that more than anything else now.

Soon, after arriving home, they gathered Gabriel into their circle also, sitting with him in front of the Nativity scene as they turned on a string of lights that represented the stars.

And, as Lucas held Alicia and their son to him, telling her everything she wanted to know about him, her eyes fixed on the bracelet she'd just laid to rest at the head of the bed where Baby Jesus would sleep on Christmas Eve.

A gift, she thought.

Because, in return, she'd found the best gift *she* could've ever hoped for.

Another chance at forever.

Epilogue

One year later

The family was preparing to attend late-night mass after a light meal that Alicia had cooked. The feast would come later, after the candlelight service, and Lucas's stomach was already growling at the thought of what his wife would conjure.

Last Christmas, it'd been a banquet of American and Mexican foods—everything from corn-husked tamales to enchiladas to miniburgers that Gabe had practically inhaled.

The penthouse was already redolent with the flavors of this year's offering and, as they all stood in front of the Christmas tree, guessing at what was in certain gift-wrapped presents, Lucas could tell he wasn't the only one starving.

"There's no smell like the aroma of your wife's cooking," David said, his blue eyes gleaming.

From the couch, their father chimed in. "Lucas managed to buck the Chandler trend and pick the right one the first time, didn't he?"

Gabe, dressed in church finery, giggled as his grandpa tickled him. Ever since meeting last year, the two had gotten along famously. Ford Chandler, of course, had no skill for handling difficult behavior, and Gabe seemed to sense this because he never got into one of his moods around Grandpa. True, the four-year-old had improved over the past months with the aid of his therapist and a stable home, so maybe that also had something to do with it. Still, he did have his moments, and it was always a trial for Alicia and Lucas, even if they loved Gabe to death.

When Alicia came from the direction of the kitchen, smoothing down her simple yet elegant white-velvet dress over her slightly rounded stomach, the oxygen went heavy in Lucas's lungs. He hadn't seen her wear the pristine color since their private church ceremony months ago, but he lost his ability to breathe every time he caught sight of her, anyway. A year hadn't mellowed the charged attraction between them at all.

She caught his hungry gaze, and a slow smile spread over her mouth. It was almost as if they were the only two in the room.

But leave it to David to remind him that this wasn't true.

"How'd the angel get from the top of the tree to the ground?"

As everyone laughed, Lucas caught David's gaze wandering to Alicia's growing belly. Sometimes Lucas wondered if his brother longed for love, also, but was too broken to come to terms with it. At any rate, the brothers had reached a tenuous understanding about business, David finally realizing that Lucas was at TCO to stay. The Brain had even developed a grudging respect for the way Lucas had actually turned out to be a natural at negotiating and running mergers and acquisitions—not that he would advertise that or anything.

David had also done his share of apologizing to Alicia for his part in the relationship plan, especially after he'd realized what a commodity she really was to TCO. Thanks to her, the company had introduced a prestigious charity foundation that focused on funding and building orphanages. Gradually, she'd forgiven David, just as she'd come to forgive Lucas. Lord knows he'd worked his rear end off to earn it, too. Among other things, he'd never lied to her again.

"Ready to go?" Lucas asked his wife as she stood next to him, raising her face for a kiss.

He obliged her, soft and slow, relishing every moment.

"Always ready," she said.

He rested his hand on her belly. Five months and counting. Alicia hadn't wanted to know the sex yet, so there was a lot of expectancy in the air.

"Meet you in the lobby?" David said, nudging Lucas as he left.

Lucas grunted, never taking his eyes off his wife.

"Daddy," Gabe said, running over and inserting himself between Lucas and Alicia. "Are you and Mama and baby coming?"

With a smile that he couldn't hold back, Lucas ruffled Gabe's hair as his son kissed his mom's belly.

"We're all going together."

"Yessssss," he said, doing a *Home Alone* imitation. He'd just watched the movie yesterday.

Gabe followed Uncle David and Grandpa to the foyer. But, before they left, Ford Chandler glanced back, caught his son's eye and gave him an approving smile.

Lucas had done good by falling in love. His dad had made that clear many times since last year.

He'd earned respect, all right—and it'd all come about because of Alicia. Just not the way he'd thought it would happen.

"Doing okay?" Lucas asked her as he smoothed back a curl from her brow.

She huffed out a breath, nodding. "All is well. Magdelena is seeing to the final touches of our feast."

"I'm talking about your parents." When Alicia's past would come full circle.

At the end of last year, they'd decided to hire a P.I. to track down her parents, just so she could really find closure. The crack investigator had been successful, and Alicia had made arrangements to contact each of her parents after the holidays.

"You're finally going to meet your family," he said,

drawing her against him, showing his support, his un-flagging love for this woman.

"I've already met them," she said, holding him close. "I've had a true family for a while now."

As he felt her belly pressing into his hip, he reached down, resting his hand on the child they were going to cherish.

A family that had grown out of what was supposed to have been only a fake marriage.

A union that couldn't be more blessed and real.

* * * * *